Gordon, Mildred
Night after the wedding

DATE DUE			
NOV 23 79	MAY 12 '80		
NOV 23 79	MAY 28 '80		
DEC 5 79	JUN 6 '80		
JAN 9 '80	MAY 1 '81		
JAN 9 '80	DEC 28 '81		
JAN 30 '80	AUG 3 '83		
FEB 6 '80	NOV 17 '84		
FEB 20 '80	AP 7'89		
MAR 7 '80	MY 16 '90		
MAR 19 '80	JY 24 '90		
MAR 26 '80	JY 22 '91		
APR 4 '80			PRINTED IN U.S.A.
APR 21 '80			

GAYLORD 234

NIGHT
AFTER THE
WEDDING

By THE GORDONS

NIGHT
AFTER THE
WEDDING

❖❖❖❖❖❖❖❖❖❖❖❖❖❖❖❖

The Gordons

DOUBLEDAY & COMPANY, INC.
GARDEN CITY, NEW YORK
1979

All of the characters in this book are fictitious, and any resemblance to actual persons, living or dead, is purely coincidental.

Library of Congress Cataloging in Publication Data

Gordon, Mildred.
Night after the wedding.

I. Gordon, Gordon, joint author. II. Title.
PZ3.G6567Nh [PS3557.O67] 813'.5'4
ISBN: 0-385-14012-6
Library of Congress Catalog Card Number 78-20073

Acknowledgments

Our gratitude to the American Humane Association's Hearing-Dog Program, 5351 South Roslyn Street, Englewood, Colorado 80110, and especially to its master trainer, Agnes McGrath. This program operates solely through contributions, and the personnel were generous with their time while we were doing research. We would also like to gratefully acknowledge the information we culled from the following sources: *From the Lands of the Scythians,* The Metropolitan Museum of Art; *Center on Deafness Publication's Series No. 1,* a publication of California State University at Northridge, California; *An Introduction to American Sign Language* by L. J. Fant, Jr., published by the National Association of the Deaf; Dr. J. H. Schultz's *Das Autogene Training,* published by George Thieme Verlag; and *90 Days to Self Health* by Dr. C. Norman Shealy and published by Dial Press.

". . . around the body of the king they bury one of his concubines, first killing her by strangling . . . and some golden cups . . . and raise a vast mound above the grave . . . seeking to make it as tall as possible . . . fifty young men are killed along with fifty horses, and the dead horses and riders are mounted around the royal tomb . . ."

> —Source unknown at beginning of investigation entitled: "Subject, John Doe; Victim, Catherine Doyle, aka Cathy Doyle."

NIGHT
AFTER THE
WEDDING

1

Cathy Doyle lifted the heavy, old, wooden garage door, putting her tennis muscles to practical use. She drove in, and turning off the lights, realized how dark the night was. In a quick move, she swung the car door out, banging it on a rubbish can. Frozen immobile, her tall, slender frame sat half in, half out of the car.

Any little thing shattered her nerves. Up until today, there had been too many weeks of job hunting, and nights wondering what would happen to her.

What would the welfare people say if a college graduate of twenty-two with long blond hair walked in looking as if she belonged in a Porsche advertisement? Get lost, sister, they would say, and make room for the hungry. Hungry? She could look well fed on a leaf of lettuce—and add a pound.

It was hot. So hot.

Hurriedly she left the garage. Outside she stopped suddenly. The overhead floodlights were out. Usually they beamed down from near the red tile roof line of this sprawling two-story Spanish house. Had she accidentally switched them off when she left that morning? An electronic device turned them on at dark and off at daybreak. There was a switch, however, inside the kitchen door that controlled them.

Quickly she walked toward a mailbox a few feet away. In the far distance an ambulance raced with siren screaming. Not so far away a police helicopter circled, its rotor blades thrashing, its beam scouting the ground below for criminal activity.

She expected a big black cat called Pancho to materialize. Usually he greeted her on arrival, a lonesome soul needing affection now that his people, the Hoovers, were on vacation. She was house- and cat-sitting for them. Fifty dollars a week, a real break.

Unexpectedly she felt very much alone, though she never had up here before. The house sat in Encino on an isolated hilltop, with no neighbors nearby. Once this had been a lemon orchard. Above rose a long straight line of eucalyptus trees, planted in the time of the orchard to protect it from winds. Below stretched the myriad, twitching lights of San Fernando Valley, a million people claimed as taxpayers by the octopus that was Los Angeles. An octopus that was eating them out of their homes. The furious onslaught of traffic on two nearby freeways was a steady, blurred roar. But up here there was a strange kind of quiet, an otherworldness in contrast to the frenzy below. There were great pines with tired boughs sagging from a long drought that had turned the needles brown before their time. Still, with it all, the hoot owls kept their amorous dialogue going on an intermittent basis, as if they had to think out each hoot.

The Hoovers had been concerned about her spending a month alone. "Don't you want a girl friend to stay with you?" Mrs. Hoover had asked.

"I'm not afraid," Cathy answered. She would have had to split the fifty dollars with another girl. "I've spent most of my life alone." The last four winters, attending college, she had lived in a small room over a garage, and the summers, here and there, getting a job wherever she could. Years ago her parents had divorced. Three years ago her mother had died. Her father lived in Clinton, North Carolina.

She continued, "Of course, if you'd feel better—"

"No, no. We've lived here fourteen years and never had an incident of any kind."

Cathy whistled now for Pancho. She did wish he would come. He talked little but was good company.

Entering the kitchen, she left the door open to make certain the overhead lights came on outside at her touch to the switch. They did.

The cuckoo emerged from the Swiss clock above her to sound the time. She jumped a little. Nervously she fingered the costly ruby ring her father had given her on her eighteenth birthday.

She switched off the kitchen lights and passed through a dark dining room, heading for the long curved stairs with their black wrought-iron railing. As she started up, she brought herself to an abrupt halt. In a niche halfway up, a candle burned before a fire-blackened wood statue of the Virgin Mary. Mrs. Hoover said they had found it in Guatemala, a survivor of an earthquake and fire that in 1773 had destroyed the ancient city of Antigua.

She stood in shock. The candle. She had never lighted it.

Then she remembered and proceeded up the stairs, blowing it out as she passed. The night before she had had a few friends in. Probably one had put a match to it. Still, she had passed it this morning coming down the stairs. But in the daylight, would she have noticed?

At the top of the stairs, she smelled a distinct cigarette odor, and she did not smoke. She had noticed that kitchen smells gathered on the upper landing. She shrugged. The cigarette odor was a leftover from the party.

She entered a den with a window ajar. A sign was pasted on the window: "Leave open a few inches. Cat entrance." An aging walnut tree stood a foot or so beyond a little balcony. Pancho would climb the tree, jump to the balcony, and enter by the window, then head downstairs to the furnace room which doubled as his dining area.

She called and whistled. He would be out gopher watching, his favorite pastime. Not that he caught many or even tried very hard.

She left the door to the master bedroom slightly ajar so he could join her when he decided to retire. She undressed in the dark and felt better. It was so hot and still.

Two months ago she had been graduated from Pitzer, one of

the Claremont complex of colleges fifty miles east of Los Angeles. Graduated with honors. With banners flying, she had ridden forth in her Pinto to conquer a world that promised excitement, adventure, and romance. A glamor job, a husband who would take pride in her career, whatever it was, and in time maybe a baby or two. Maybe. She wasn't sure about that yet.

At first she had been selective and bid for only the high-paying, interesting jobs. Then as her savings disappeared, she grew desperate.

All that, though, was in the past. Today a women's wear chain had hired her as an assistant buyer, to start work Monday. This was her second interview for the job. On the first, the personnel manager had offered her little hope. He was in his sixties, his face pinched by too much studying of figures, his mouth a faded line, his lifeless eyes rude in open appraisal. Did she drink? Use marijuana? Expect to marry? Would she promise not to become pregnant? Did she go to parties? How often?

Today he said, "I called up Pitzer. They wanted to tell me about your grades. I told them to hell with that. Is she emotionally stable? I asked. Does she have problems? They told me you didn't, far as they knew. That's important to me. The last four women on this job—they all knew this business which you don't, but we'll train you—they had problems. One fought with her husband, another was a hypochondriac with a damn alarm watch that kept going off to tell her it was time to take her medicine, and another was going to sex therapy classes, which with her spread wasn't going to do her any good, and the fourth was a plain drunk."

He rose by way of dismissal. "If you get problems, don't bother coming in. Don't phone. Just disappear. Commit suicide. Quietly."

She took a cold shower, luxuriating in the sunken tile tub with tropical plants bunched on one side. Her shower cubicle in her small one-bedroom apartment two miles away in Sherman Oaks could barely accommodate her. She had an unexplainable prejudice about sunken baths. They were so ostentatious. She hated status symbols. But then, the Hoovers had started with no more than she had. So what was wrong with the American dream materializing?

She slipped into a short gown with roses embroidered across the top and a broad band of lace running around the bottom. Her father had sent it two Christmases ago.

In bed she turned on a table lamp and picked up *The Complete Works of Saki*. She was halfway through. She whistled again for Pancho. If he were in the house, he should have finished his dinner.

About a half hour after she dropped off to sleep, she was awakened by soft footsteps on the stairs. That would be Pancho. Coming up the stairs, he sounded like a person.

A few seconds later, the form of a man, merely a moving figure blurred by the dark, stole through the door. Her first instant thought was that the Hoovers had returned ahead of schedule. She was still drugged by sleep. "Mr. Hoover?"

Then as the man moved swiftly toward her, she was clubbed by shock. She scrambled for the sheet she had pushed to the foot of the bed, thinking to cover herself, then countermanded the ridiculous decision. There was an alarm button low on the wall nearby that alerted a private security agency, and a telephone secreted under the bed.

The man grabbed her arms and held them in such a vise that only her body flailed about. She never knew why she didn't scream. Not that it mattered. There was no one within hearing distance. He appeared to be not more than forty, and of medium height with a little pot stomach. He smelled of cigarettes, cologne, and mouthwash. Even at close range, there was not sufficient light to make out his features.

"Hold it, Cathy. Nobody's going to hurt you." He had a low, pleasant voice. "I just want to talk with you. Just dropped in for a little visit, you might say." He laughed softly.

She quieted. A long time ago she had considered what she would do if she were ever attacked. She had programmed herself. Don't struggle. Not at first. If you do, he may beat you, half kill you. A police officer, talking before a college group, had said, "If you can, play along quietly and try to talk him out of it. Play for time. Someone may come along or there may be a noise that will scare him off. Don't resist until you have no other alternative."

If she could get to the bathroom a few feet away and lock herself in . . . her mind was overcoming the shock and fear. In sports she had disciplined herself to shut out emotion and concentrate on the game.

He released her hands. "Stay where you are. Don't move—and keep your hands where I can see them. All right?"

She was conscious the gown exposed her legs almost to the thighs. She started to pull the sheet up.

"I told you, stay put!" He shoved her back down. His rough hands sandpapered her tender skin. They tarried a second, then withdrawing, brushed her breasts.

She fought to still the tremble. He was taking his time, building the terror. Well, she'd show him. He's got a victim this time who's not going to fall apart. But she had to play it intelligently. If she were too aggressive or belligerent . . . the newspapers said a woman had died from a beating a few days ago.

He continued, "I know there's an alarm down back of you and a phone under the bed—and if they're cut the signal gets through that something's up. I know all about this old house."

He glanced out the big picture window that looked down on a patio and pool. "Nice setup for a murder. Do you like murder stories, Cathy?"

He didn't wait for an answer. "I doubt if anyone would know you had been bumped off until the newspaper boy got to wondering about the papers piling up."

He turned back. "Isn't the Virgin Mary something with the candle lit? Did you see how her eyes shone? My wife would love to have her. Collects all kinds of old things."

She sagged with relief. If he had a wife . . . "I like old things, too." She had waited to talk until she had her voice under control. He obviously was a psycho. "What do you want to talk about?"

Casually he sat in a chair near the bed, in the manner of an old friend come by to visit a sick relative. "I've been sent for the money, Cathy. They sent me since I'm not like the others. I do things quietly and They wanted me to get the money without doing anything to you, like raping you or beating you up."

Her throat was dry. "What money? What're you talking about?" She moved her body imperceptibly toward the bed's edge.

"Don't you hassle me! You're too smart to play dumb and I'm too smart to let you."

He hesitated, then added, "They don't figure to get it tonight. Not likely you'd have it on you." He laughed. "I'm just here to make the setup. They don't figure you for a thief. So They haven't put out a contract on you. They figure you think it's your money. You don't know it belongs to Them. Do you, Cathy?"

His badgering, intimate tone angered her. "How can I answer that? If I say I don't know what you're talking about, which I don't . . ."

"They want to be fair. They'll pay you a hundred thousand bucks although They don't have to. It'd be an easy hundred thou. And you need it. I've done my homework. You're behind with the rent money and you've got a car payment . . ."

His voice dropped to a whisper. "It would be laundered money. You could spend it without worrying but if you tried anything with the million two—"

"Million!" She came bolt upright.

His eyes bored into her. "I try to be a good guy and you act like a hooker playing the Virgin at Mass. . . . I've got this ulcer. It's a bad one. Should have an operation. I didn't used to get upset so fast. If I weren't a good guy . . . some of the others if they were here with a naked girl in bed . . . do I make myself clear?"

She nodded. Her mind was in a whirl. God, what do I do?

"All right. Guess we understand each other. I hope so for your sake. Bring the money to the Forum tomorrow night. There's a circus playing there. I bought you a seat."

Tossing a ticket on the bed, he rose. "You're thinking you'll call the police soon as I leave. But what will it get you? The cops won't buy a cock-and-bull story about you having a million two and if they do, so what? They pick me up and I'm clean and they have to let me go. So you'd never see me again which would be too bad because I'm with you. I like you. I don't want to see you hurt. The more I checked you out, the more I liked you. You're like my wife. Beautiful in every way. I'd feel bad if anything happened to that face and body."

His voice took on a sad note. "If I don't get the money, Cathy, if I don't get it, I hate to think of what will happen to you. They'll send in a gorilla who knows how to make little girls produce."

2

At 1:33 A.M. Gail took a call from a woman who identified herself as Cathy Doyle.

Gail shook her husband of a day awake. "Mitch," she said, "it's for you."

He roused slowly, floundering about like a fish, then reached across Gail for the phone. His body grazing hers brought her hand up to tousle his thick, dark hair. God, how she loved him. He was outspoken, honest, always himself, never any pretenses, never any big guy stuff. With her he was gentle and thoughtful. But with the cheap burglars, hoods, con men, and prostitutes who passed through his floor-creaking, dark, musty law office he was cynical and cryptic, doubting their stories, seeking to rasp the truth out of them.

She caught snatches of the girl's conversation coming out of the phone. The girl was by herself, house-sitting . . . a man broke in . . . no, he didn't harm her . . . had to be a psycho . . . he had left and she had locked herself in the bath and was talking from a phone in the john . . . a million dollars . . . deliver at a circus . . .

The girl talked rapidly, and most of the time, calmly and sensibly. She had to see Mitch right away.

"Not tonight," he said. "I'm on my honeymoon."

What a honeymoon. Married the night before, and tomorrow he had a case going to trial at 10 A.M. Little Eddie, who had left a calling card behind during the burglary of a television shop—his driver's license.

Gail whispered, "It's okay, Mitch, to see her." He shrugged.

"Why call me?" he asked the girl. "Why not the police?"

"I'll tell you when I see you."

"Do I know you?"

"No."

"Any of your friends?"

"No."

"Where'd you get my name?"

"I can't talk much more. He said They'd do something awful to me if They caught me going to the police and—"

"Who's *They*?"

"He didn't say. Please, Mr. Mitchell, I've got to see you."

"You're safer where you are. He won't return. If he'd been going to rape or kill you, he'd have done it."

"Please, Mr. Mitchell . . ."

"Make it eight in the morning. My office. Give me your name again—and the address where you are."

He jotted them down. Cathy Doyle. Cathy spelled with a C.

Hanging up, he saw the alarm in Gail's deep green eyes. "Don't let it bother you, Shad." He called her by the nickname (short for Shadrack) he had given her two years before when she had applied for work as his secretary. "You know yourself that in our business somebody's always going to kill someone but they never do."

He kissed her softly, holding her head in his big, weathered hands. "And when they do try, they miss. I represent the poorest marksmen in the world."

She pushed him away and sat up very straight. Her gown had a deep V-cut. Her breasts were as tan as the rest of her. She was a sun worshipper. "But you don't *know*. Nobody knows what goes on in a psycho's mind—and what if he does come back and kill her."

"I've got to get some sleep. You kept me up all last night."

She smiled, then said earnestly, "You could never live with it, Mitch. You talk a good game but I know you."

For a fleeting moment she was caught up in the horror of only three nights ago when she herself had innocently become involved in an extortion case. A car had blown up, and she still suffered from cuts, bruises, sore muscles, and above all, the trauma.

"Good grief," he said, picking up the phone and dragging it over her, "I think I married a conscience—and they're the worst kind."

He dialed. "Who are you calling?" she asked.

"Lefty Morgan."

"That weasel!" Lefty was a shifty, eye-twitching, sniffing runt, a second-story man who ran scared if a Pekinese barked. He wore crepe-soled shoes, a slept-in suit, and shirts that would frighten a savage.

"He owes me a favor," Mitch responded.

"Two hundred dollars—and we need the money."

He let the phone ring. Lefty was a sound sleeper, and then again, he might be out working.

Lefty answered. "Lefty, Mitch here. I got something I want you to do. . . . Yeah, I know what time it is but I've gotten up a few nights for you, remember? Now, listen, I've got a woman sitting all by herself up in a big house in the Encino hills who says a man threatened to knock her off and then took off. I want you to go up there and watch the house in case he returns. You know, keep to the bushes where you won't be seen but don't let anybody get in. . . . No, she's by herself. No one else has any business around there. . . . Yeah, rough 'em up if you have to but no shooting. You got that? No shooting. And don't bother her. I've got a date with her for 8 A.M. and I want you to follow her to my office but don't talk to her. You got that?"

When he hung up, Gail said, "I think I'd rather take my chances on a stranger than have that creep hanging around."

He smiled. "He can't help what he does. It's a compulsion, same as alcoholics can't help drinking.

"Don't forget," he added, "he helps pay the bills for the poor people who need us."

He never turned anyone away, white, black, yellow, or brown. Sometimes Gail would protest. They badly needed paying clients. "Dammit," he'd say, "you can't let a kid go down the drain because he's done something wrong once. He may never again. I siphoned a gas tank when I was fourteen-fifteen —and an old codger caught me. He scared the wits out of me but he didn't call the police. I've never forgotten that. We all make mistakes and need a second chance."

"And a third and a fourth and a fifth," Gail would say.

He would only laugh. Always he had high hopes the repeaters would change. He would lecture them, which was not within the province of an attorney.

He dialed again. Cathy Doyle took a long time answering and when she did, he could scarcely hear her. "I'm sending a man up there to watch the house. So you needn't worry. Go to sleep. . . . No, he's not with the police. He's a friend of mine, a good friend."

Gail groaned.

Hanging up, he sat by her, took her into his arms, and held her tightly. She said, "I didn't know you got calls at night."

"What d'ya think I married you for? I've got to have a secretary nights as well as days."

His hands began to roam. "I thought you were sleepy," she said.

"I like your grammar," he answered. "*Were* is the proper tense."

3

Munching a hamburger he had picked up at Joe's, Lefty Morgan squatted behind an oleander bush that was an enormous bouquet of pink blossoms. From here, high up in a deserted old corral, he could see the layout below. Floodlights bathed the place like a movie set.

He was not as hungry as he had thought. He stuffed half the hamburger in a coat pocket. On a job he always wore a suit complete to vest. He needed pockets for jewelry items. Occasionally in the rush of doing business, he'd had to leave the attaché case, and his gross for those nights had been what he carried on his person.

He fumbled about in his vest for a candy bar. He liked a sweet to end a meal. Finished with it, he took a cigarette butt from another pocket. He bent low to keep the struck match from showing.

A great Dane came sniffing around. He was extremely cautious, not knowing what to make of a human in this strange setting. He approached tentatively. Lefty remembered a magazine article that said a person could stare an animal down. Lefty tried. It didn't work. The dog stared him down. Well, it went to show one couldn't believe everything he read. The dog shrugged and took off.

Lefty felt badly about this situation. Here was a house that was a sitting duck, if a house could be called a sitting duck, deserted except for a frightened girl locked in a bathroom. He could take his time. A spread like this might bring in $5,000 and his fence downtown would give him $750.

However, he would never do that to Mitch. He was a man of honor.

He felt drowsy. The hamburger, the hot night, the quiet, the little sleep he had had recently . . . He yawned and stretched. If he could only move about . . .

In a dressing room off the bath, Cathy found Mrs. Hoover's robe. Her nerves quieted somewhat, as if a robe could offer protection. In a sewing niche, she fumbled in the dark until she discovered a small pair of shears. She dropped them into a pocket.

She glanced out. The floods still burned. Nearby she heard the quick, sharp barks of coyotes. She shuddered. She had never convinced her relatives in Massachusetts that in parts of this city of millions, coyotes, deer, foxes, raccoons, skunks, and other wild life still roamed. Undaunted by civilization, they came down nights from the nearby mountains.

If only she could call Gary . . . if he knew, he would come so fast. She needed his strong arms about her, holding her until it hurt. If she could only get through to him. . . .

She had to regain control of herself. Her thoughts were a phonograph record hopped over by a frantic needle. Over and over she replayed what the psycho had said. The mind could control its thoughts, she kept repeating. The mind could still the tom-tom pounding of her heart, the coursing of blood that threatened a blackout.

She had found little comfort in talking with the lawyer. His skepticism had shocked her, yet she could not fault him. He had reacted the same as she had the time a woman approached her on the street speaking gibberish. She had wanted to run, yet also to help a pathetic soul.

She must sleep. With sleep, she could fight wildcats. Without it, she tended to self-destruct.

Getting clothes at random out of Mrs. Hoover's closet, she fashioned a few into a pillow and spread the rest out. She curled up, with her body in a fetal position.

Then she heard a whisper of movement outside, someone tiptoeing toward the locked door. She rose as if jerked up by a puppet string, one hand going to the scissors. The floor beyond the door creaked, the footsteps no longer were masked. She waited, breath stilled, for the doorknob to turn.

Then there was silence. Nothing. He was standing there listening. The lock would stand little pressure. It was meant only to keep children or other family members out. One hard shoulder thrust would snap it.

A light, soft scratching came over. She sagged against the wall. She was half-laughing, half-crying. Steadying herself, she debated whether she dared to open the door. She wanted the cat badly. If she had him, she could sleep. He was the only contact she could reach out for in her happy, normal world of an hour ago.

She chanced it and he streaked in. She hugged him and he struggled to escape. He was an adult, a man, and no kitten to be smothered with mawkish sentiment. Letting him have his way, she stretched out again. Within minutes, he shaped the contour of his body to fit hers. He, too, needed security. He sensed by her strange behavior that something was awry.

4

Hurrying from the parking lot, Mitch could scarcely keep up with Gail. They had overslept, and getting showered and dressed, bumped into each other repeatedly. They were not yet accustomed to the other's ritualistic movements. They hadn't finished unpacking Mitch's clothes and belongings—he had moved into her place the day of the wedding—and couldn't locate socks that matched. They laughed, shouted, and embraced much too much. "Mitch," she said finally and firmly, "keep your hands off me or I'll never get my make-up and hair-do on."

The street was unkempt with dirty scraps of papers whirling in the slight breeze. It was flanked by two-story, turn-of-the-century buildings. Theirs had a hash house on the ground floor. *Breakfast Special, 66¢.* Windows unwashed, a torn shade hanging limply, and by the ancient cash register a 1950's calendar on the wall. A collector's item. Marilyn Monroe in the nude.

They went up a wide stairway, taking uncovered, splintering stairs that groaned with each step. Their office was the second on the right. The first was a music shop. *Two-thirds Off— Slightly Used.* Pianos, organs, stereo sets, citizens band radios, etc.

The upper part of the door was frosted glass. *Law Office— Frank Mitchell.* Inside, her desk fronted the door, a decrepit, leperous one picked up by Mitch at a garage sale for ten dollars. Wobbly straight-back chairs from the same sale were scattered about the room in such disarrangement they looked artistic. Back of her desk hung a faded picture of Justice Oliver Wendell Holmes.

Mitch nodded toward the portrait. "Good morning, your honor." It was a daily ritual.

The phone was ringing. "I'm not in," he said, going into his office, which was separated from hers by paneling so thin she could hear every word said.

She picked up the receiver. "Mitchell Law Office."

A man's rough voice said demandingly, "Put Mitch on."

"He's got a case going to trial this morning. May I take—"

Slam!

Damn him!

"Who was it?" Mitch called out.

"One of your best clients. No name, no number." She added, "Soon as you get back this afternoon I'm going to run out to see Mamma. Okay?"

Her mother, a heart patient in a convalescent home, adored Mitch. "Don't you dare try changing him," she had counseled. "He's good for you just the way he is."

She watered the philodendron. "Mitch," she called, "it's growing! By the way, don't make any dates for Thursday night. I want to go bowling."

"Okay."

"And Sunday morning. Church."

"Okay." He never went, she always did.

"And tonight. The Dodgers are on television." She was an avid sports fan. A hotheaded one.

The door opened and Cathy Doyle walked in slowly, a furtive animal in alien territory. Gail noted a fist clenched at one side. Her unset hair fell to her shoulders. She wore no make-up, no nail polish. She was in jeans and a tank top.

Her tired eyes moved tediously about the cubicle. "I've an appointment—"

"Go on in," Gail said. "He's waiting for you."

Cathy hesitated, then with effort straightened. Tossing her hair back, she eased into Mitch's office.

Mitch said, "Sit down." He didn't rise. Only last week Gail had told him, "Look, you bum, get up when a lady walks in."

He had given her a twisted smile that could melt any reprimand. "I haven't seen a lady in years." She had whacked him with a newspaper.

"Don't you dare try changing him." Still, if she could smooth off a few rough edges and get him out of his tired, old clothes and into some mod ones, when and if they got the money . . .

Mitch suggested Cathy tell her story chronologically and in detail. She did, haltingly. There were seconds of sheer terror as she recalled incidents. Mitch caught himself staring at her, trying to determine if she were a consummate actress or honestly frightened.

"I've got $97.50 in my checking account and $13.40 here in my purse. That's every cent I've got. But I can take care of your fee if it's not too much. I can borrow a little and I've got a job starting Monday. If I could pay you so much a week . . ."

Mitch nodded. "Any wealthy relatives who might have a million handy?"

"Not even a thousand."

"Boy friends?"

She shook her head and her hair bounced. She sat on the edge of the chair, her spine straight, one leg swinging nervously. Her fingers toyed with the ruby ring.

"Why didn't you call the police?"

She took a deep breath. "I've got this phobia. I panic around the police. It's like some people can't stand high places."

"Where'd you get my name?"

"I don't know. Maybe I saw it in the newspapers."

"Maybe you didn't. I don't handle cases that get in the papers."

Her eyes fell from his. She shrugged slightly.

"What do you want me to do?"

She brightened. "I need advice. Do I go tonight or don't I? And if I do go, would you . . . would someone go with me or follow me?"

"The police could put a man or two on you, tailing you, and pick up this character."

She leaned forward and he caught a pleasant scent. "Couldn't you do the same? What about the man you had watch the house last night?"

"It'll cost you. The police wouldn't."

"Soon as I start work, I can handle it—if it's not too much."

"Why do you think you have to go tonight?"

"Shouldn't I?"

"I don't like people who answer questions by asking questions."

"I'm scared they'll do something to me if I don't. He said They'd kill me if I don't. I'm awfully vulnerable. I park off a dark alley at the apartment house and then walk along a tall hedge—"

"If you show up without the money . . ."

"I know." Her lips trembled. "Maybe I'll find out what's going on . . . or convince Them I don't have it. I'm in limbo until I find out what this is all about. If I don't go, I'm in bad trouble. They'll think . . . but a circus. I keep asking myself, why a circus? Why not a coffee shop or my apartment? Someplace quiet?"

"Too dangerous. A fixed location. Too easy for the police to stake it out. But a crowd scene, with you moving about, They can choose Their own time and spot and have an excellent chance of making a getaway if the police try to apprehend Them."

He toyed with a pencil. "I could hire a photographer. Somebody who looks like an amateur. A girl, perhaps." He was talking more to himself than to her. "With fast film, she wouldn't need a flash, and with the right lens she could stay some distance from you. If we got a picture of the guy making contact, then I've a friend at the Sheriff's who'd run an ID. With luck we might make an identification."

She brightened. "Would you?"

"You're certain you never saw this guy before? Never been threatened before?"

She shook her head.

"He didn't pick your name out of a telephone directory."

She stared at the floor.

"He could have been after the Hoovers but you say—"

"He knew my name, where I lived, that I was house-sitting, all about me."

"Do you know where they are?"

"They left an itinerary, case the cat got sick or something happened to the house. It's there in the kitchen, the itinerary. I—I can't go back. I could give you the key . . ."

For a moment he studied her. He could spot a liar. He had encountered so many. A voice not on pitch, a slight hesitation, an uneasy body movement, a mind hacksawing its way through a knot. She had no such surface indications. Still, there was only a thin line between lying and not telling the whole truth, stretching or shortening it.

She swallowed hard under his gaze.

He rose to look out the window. He turned then. "What are you mixed up in that's given you this phobia about the police and sends you running for a criminal lawyer?"

She bristled. "That's not fair, Mr. Mitchell. I finished at Pitzer a couple months ago. You can call them. They'll tell you I was never in trouble. You can check the Claremont and Pomona police records. It's all so ridiculous. How could I make a million at Pitzer? I live in a tiny apartment in Sherman Oaks. I drive a Pinto."

He sat in the window sill. "What'd it cost you there? At Pitzer? Seven, eight thousand a year?"

"Six."

"Who paid for it?"

"My father. He's not here. He lives in North Carolina."

"Wealthy?"

"I don't think so. I don't know. I haven't seen much of him. He set up a trust fund years ago for college. I haven't taken anything else from him although he's always offering. He's awfully generous. So good to me. But I want to be on my own. I don't think you should become a drain on your parents when you grow up. At Pitzer I was a work-study student in the library. Two-fifty an hour."

Mitch returned to the swivel. He said, not unkindly, "Look, we get hookers in here and shoplifters and con artists, and that's about all the women I see. I tell them they've got to level with me. If they're guilty, they've got to tell me. Not that I won't represent them. But I can't do a job unless I know the facts. Then, too, I've got my pride, believe it or not, and I'm not going to let some smart-ass prosecuting attorney steel-trap me."

He paused, thinking: Something's wrong here. Something's wrong. But something's right, too.

He continued, "You're a nice college kid, a breath of fresh air around here, but the same goes for you. I've got to know what goes on. I don't buy this story he's a psycho or a nut. They don't go to that much trouble. They don't think that far ahead.

"As for the phobia about the police, I buy that but I don't believe it's psychological. You've got reason to be scared. As for just happening to have my name handy, I'll bet somebody I defended gave it to you."

Near tears, she said angrily, "I come to you for help, I'm desperate, I'm in some kind of horrible danger, and you question me like I was a criminal."

He got to his feet. It was going to be a long day and it was just starting. "You must understand that I deal mostly with people who have to be shocked and frightened into telling the truth and my methods are geared according to how they think. I'll be back in a minute."

Outside, Gail was opening the mail. He motioned her to follow him into the hall. "Get anything?" he asked.

"Moose's check bounced. For the third time. And the landlord wants the rent by 5 P.M."

"Tell him we never do business on a religious holiday."

"What holiday?"

"Look it up. Got to be one."

In the corridor outside, Gail said, "You were awfully rough, Mitch."

"She's covering."

"I suppose so."

"She could be big trouble for us."

For a moment, neither spoke. For a year, he had never made a major decision without consulting her. "You're a part of the corporation now, Shad," he had said once. "Some corporation," she had answered.

She said, "I've got a feeling she's what she seems. She needs you, Mitch."

"How do you explain—?"

"I can't."

"Okay."

A friend, Martha, a secretary in the next office, called out in passing. "Hey, no smooching in the hallway. Ordinance Seventy-seven, paragraph double zero."

Mitch waved and went back inside. Martha asked Gail about lunch. "I'd better not today," Gail told her. "I've got to get the name on my driver's license changed—and the credit cards."

Martha smiled. "Guess you should. Once you pick up dogs, cats, men, and parakeets, it's awfully hard to ditch 'em. See you."

Mitch said, "Can you come back at four? We'll see what we can do then."

He thought she was going to cry. But she was made of

sterner material, as he was to discover in the days ahead. "I feel
. . . I feel . . . I guess you know. What about your fee?"

"We'll set a figure—won't be too much—when we see what
we're going to do. You can pay so much a week. Okay?"

"Better than okay."

"Were you followed here?"

"I—I don't think so. I watched in the rearview mirror . . ."

"Doesn't matter—except if he knows you came here, be honest with him. Tell him you had to get legal advice. After all, if
you did have a million stashed away, you'd want to know how
to handle it. Tell him I told you to co-operate. But be vague.
Try to draw him out. See if you can find out where the million
came from, how you got it, what the racket is. Try to get him
to talking about himself. It's fantastic how much people drop."

"I'll try—but I don't know. I get uptight . . ."

"Sure you do. I would, anyone would. But keep in mind
that's his game plan. It's psychological warfare. He figures he
may get the money easy but again maybe not. So he uses all
the standard gimmicks to break you down mentally, physically,
and emotionally. These creeps have worked it so many times
they can break most anyone. Same as a wrangler can a wild
horse."

He got up. "I've got to get moving. I suppose it could be a
case of mistaken identity. Then again, they may know you
don't have the money but figure to use you to get it. So many
angles—but usually the victim has some idea what it's all
about."

"I'm not holding back. Honest, Mr. Mitchell."

"Okay, I'll see you back here at four."

He couldn't pull his gaze away from her retreating figure.
She had everything, good looks, great shape, poise, charm, and
restrained, subtle sex. What in the hell was she doing in his
office?

5

Hawk sat his chair as if he were driving a dumptruck. He was a big, energetic, outgoing man, a onetime New Mexico football player with the facial scars to prove it.

People who scarcely knew him called him Hawk. More properly he was Lieutenant Ralph D. Hawkins, lately head of the police department's Heavy Squad, now of the Special Information Unit. The unit developed and supervised contacts with informants, produced information from other sources, and evaluated evidence before presenting a case to the prosecuting authorities. In addition it was a catchall for matters that the administrative heads had no pigeonholes for.

"Angel!" he yelled. He never used the intercom.

Angela Simmons appeared. She wore mauve hugger pants and a breast-tight sweater. She believed the female body should be delineated as sharply as a Rand-McNally map.

"I tell everyone I've got a hog caller for a boss. I've told you before, I'm only eight feet away."

"I'm going to get a punctured ass." Hawk indicated a broken chair spring.

"Maintenance says you're entitled to only one new spring every six months."

"You're putting me on."

"I wouldn't do that."

"Not much." He saw she meant it. "Crazy world. Everyone's gone bananas. Did you read about the city councilman who had a heart attack? Says it was caused by the nasty things his fellow councilmen said about him and he's going to collect $100,000 from the state for disability brought on while on the job."

Angela's eyes brightened. "Pneumonia."

"What?"

"Pneumonia. I got it last winter because you insisted on keeping your window open. Must be worth $10,000."

"Get out of here and get me Frank Mitchell. Tell Barney to come in. And the General."

He rearranged a picture on the wall. He couldn't stand a picture a speck askew. Angela called that she had Mr. Mitchell on the line.

"Mitch," Hawk said, "we've got an old friend of yours here. Lefty Morgan."

"What!"

"Yeah. The copter detail spotted him shortly after dawn sitting in the brush up in the Encino hills casing a home . . ."

"Had he broken and entered . . . ?"

"Maybe a hamburger stand. They took a half hamburger off him, two candy bars and four cigarette butts. He says he was working for you."

There was a long silence. "Mitch, you still there?"

"That's right. I sent him to watch a house where I've got a client. I thought she might be in some danger."

"You sent Lefty Morgan out to protect a client? Lefty Morgan?"

"Yeah."

"Who's the client?"

"She doesn't want her identity revealed."

"Look, Mitch, if you're covering for him—"

Mitch took the offensive. "I know the law. Don't you tell me what the law is. You'd better get him out of there right away. A citizen out for some fresh air, enjoying the morning, which is the right of everyone under the Constitution and the Bill of Rights. Taking a little exercise for a heart condition—and your men run him in."

Baker, the black newspaper boy, dashed in. Hawk raised a hand Indian-fashion. "How," he said. Baker raised his hand. "How."

"Something on your mind, Baker?"

"When you get time . . ."

Hawk returned to Mitchell. "Hold it, will you? A matter of great urgency has just come up."

He turned back to Baker. "It's only the White House. The President can wait."

It would do Mitch good to stew.

Baker said, "My scout troop . . . well, some of us boys, we're going to this camp—"

"How much."

"Ten bucks."

"Robber! Just because you know I'm wealthy. Is it integrated? I don't want to support a segregated camp and have the Supreme Court on my tail."

Barney Carlson drifted in. He was short, thin, amiable, fiercely loyal to Hawk, a bad credit risk, and possessed of a remarkable talent for becoming involved with women.

Hawk turned to him. "Get Lefty Morgan out of here before he stinks up the place. Tell him we've got sensitive people living in Encino who don't like their fellow man sitting around under bushes munching hamburgers. And, Barney, check out the house he was watching. I want a complete run-down. The neighbors, mailman, newspaper boy, United Parcel . . . and, Barney, I saw that girl waiting for you last night. Where do you find 'em? Can't you ever date some nice kid like Angel?"

Before Barney could answer, he returned to Baker. "Well?"

"Yes, sir, we got three white boys." He grinned. "Window dressing."

"Angel!" Hawk called out. "Give Baker ten bucks."

She appeared in the doorway. "You haven't paid me back that twenty—"

"Don't quibble, Angel, over mere pittances. How!" He raised his hand again in the Indian greeting and Baker, all smiles, responded.

The General had entered. He was only a few months from retirement and felt out of place in this world of younger men. He was uneasy around Hawk and that bothered Hawk. He kept him busy mostly at desk work. The General didn't walk too well.

Hawk handed him a paper. "Good report. Keep after it, will you? See if there's any factual basis or if somebody's dreaming."

An informant, previously trustworthy, had advised that a

well-known figure from a Miami crime syndicate had arrived in Los Angeles and was reported to be negotiating "a big deal."

Hawk turned back to Mitch. "Sorry to keep you waiting, Mitch. On behalf of President Carter and his human rights campaign I want to apologize for detaining a fine, upright citizen like Lefty Morgan. He's being released and his property is being returned to him. Every cigarette butt."

Mitch slammed the receiver down and sat thinking. He had never had a client from Encino. That was not his territory. His was the grubby parts of this big, sprawling monstrosity. Hawk knew that. Hawk would suspect that something important was taking place—which was more than Mitch knew.

Gail called, "Nine-thirty."

He roused himself. "Get me Wilbur Randolph. It's under Williams, Randolph, and Carson."

He would talk with Randolph about the Rick Arness case. Arness, a banker, had been kidnapped and held for $400,000 ransom. Instead of calling the FBI or police, his wife had phoned Randolph, their long-time attorney. The authorities had known nothing about the case until the ransom had been paid and the banker freed. Mitch wanted to learn how Randolph had kept it from the FBI and police and handled the developments. How did a lawyer who had no police powers or authority to use weapons go about dealing with criminals? What precautions had Randolph taken, what were the hazards?

6

Cathy parked before an apartment complex of two hundred rabbit hutches, called units by the realtors, walked her black boots into a morass of mud created by a leaking sprinkler, remembered she had forgotten to put the car into the "Park" position, and hurried back through the same mud.

She called a halt then. She was fast coming apart. She took a swimmer's deep breath, squared her shoulders, and stilled her heartbeat.

Oh, God, how she wanted Gary, needed the crush of his arms about her, the warmth of his body, his rough lips on hers, needed to talk with him. And George, his shepherd, nuzzling her with his cold nose, his tail wagging the body whenever she came around. "We're the Three Musketeers," Gary would say, patting George, then her. He was tall, outgoing, had an instant smile, and enough of a neatly trimmed beard to balance the boyishness in his deep blue eyes. He would be out jogging now. He covered two and three miles a day. Only a week ago they had run together along the sands of Zuma beach. A day chiseled by a gem cutter. A picnic lunch, then they were shouting like kids as they battled the cresting, foaming waves.

Heading for her tiny apartment at the far rear, she passed by sun-seared ivy that looked as if a blow torch had been put to it. It would be another day of over 100. Even the squawking jays and scolding mockingbirds had been stilled.

She had to get someone up to the Hoovers' tonight. She would call a secretary she knew, an older woman who augmented her income by house-sitting. Cathy could ill afford to lose the money. For the new job she needed clothes. She had to change her image. No more jeans, T-shirts, tank tops, and such. No more sloppy college days.

How could any harm come to her at a circus? Of course, none could. She was just building up a bogeyman. That was like her. She worried. Even mornings when she awakened with nothing to concern her, she worried.

Mr. Blanton appeared in her path. He was the manager, a tall skeleton in his late sixties with slimy, alligator eyes that missed little and a smile fixed concrete-hard by time. In talking with a woman, young, old, or in between, he believed in the laying on of hands. Still, he was prized by the tenants the way a watchdog would be. He was an insomniac who walked the grounds restlessly nights.

"Oh, Miss Doyle," he said, "I have something to tell you. I assume you were house-sitting last night."

She nodded.

"I couldn't sleep. I only sleep about three hours a night. I don't know how I keep going but I guess the good Lord intended it that way. Well, I was passing your unit when I heard your radio go off. I know you keep it going when you're gone. Well, naturally I thought you'd come home but when the lights didn't go on in your bedroom . . . they always come on a few minutes after you get in late at night. Not that I keep track, mind you, but I can't help noticing, can I?

"Well, I didn't think too much about it but I did wait because I was concerned about you. I heard movements and then there was something like a low scream. I tell you I was scared. I knocked on your door and knew then it wasn't a scream but something like metal rubbing on metal. When no one answered, I knew you weren't in because you always come, so I used my passkey and went through the apartment, and then I checked the radio and it had been turned off. I thought I should tell you because it was all very mysterious. You may think I'm imagining all this—"

"Nothing was disturbed?"

"Come on, I'll go with you." He slipped his hand about her elbow. As they walked, his body brushed hers. "I thought I'd catch a burglar in the act. Have quite a few, you know. Seven last year. All convictions."

At the door she had to steady the key. Inside she opened the drapes. Suddenly she was very grateful to Mr. Blanton. "Would you come with me . . . ?"

She looked in closets and under the bed. Then she saw the checkbook. She kept it underneath her lingerie in the second dresser drawer. Now it was on top. At that moment the phone rang.

The voice said, "Morning, Cathy darling."

"I can't talk now."

"I'll be going," Mr. Blanton said. "Got to check out a license number. A strange Thunderbird parked last night back in the alley. The police work with me on these matters."

After he was gone, she said, "The manager was here. He said you went through my apartment."

He laughed softly. "You're making that up, Cathy. I was there but he didn't know it. If he'd opened the broom closet I would have had to knock him out. I called to explain and apologize. They ordered me to check out your place and I had no choice. I put everything back the way I found it. I didn't slash up the stuffed animals on the bed. Just squeezed them. My wife's crazy over stuffed animals. Has a whole shelf full. I buy her one every Christmas. I had to file off the padlock on the trunk but I'll buy another and bring it to the circus tonight. You'll be there, of course, Cathy?"

"Do I have a choice?"

"And the money. You'll bring it?"

"What would I do with it if I had it? Walk in with a suitcase? To a circus?"

The pause was frightening, seconds the length of minutes.

His voice squeezed a trigger to the explosion point. "One hundred and twenty ten-thousand-dollar bills should pose no problem. Divide them up and put rubber bands about them and shove them into your purse. You got that, Doyle?"

It was no longer "Cathy."

"One thing more. Don't you get your boy friend in on this. They're awfully good at staging accidents. If you so much as tell him . . ."

He didn't finish the sentence. He didn't need to.

For a second she was rocked back. Then she got a tight grip on herself. She held her voice steady. "So I walk up to the teller and say, 'Give me a hundred and twenty of your ten-thousand-dollar bills'? How many big bills like that do you think banks keep? There's *no* way I could . . . even if I had it. I've told you—"

"Now you listen to me, Doyle. I was hoping you'd be cooperative but if you're not going to be . . . They got a guy with whip and chains. They got an acid thrower . . . I'd try to stop Them but I'm only the front man, the nice guy."

The receiver went down quietly. She sat stunned.

She crossed a postage-stamp yard that matched the doll-size house. It was white stuccoed and partly hidden by a pink hibiscus gone wild. Wide pillars with an ancient Egyptian look rose at each side.

Her knock on a glass-paned door was answered by happy barking inside. George recognized her walk, her knock. He disappeared but was back in a moment bringing Gary, his jaw fastened loosely about the man's hand.

Gary's eyes lit up. He pulled her in and held her so tightly their bodies were one. In vain, George nudged her for attention.

Struggling for breath, she broke loose. "George," he yelled. "Cut it out." He looked down at her. "He's as happy as I am."

He and George were inseparable. The dog slept on an old blanket in a corner of Gary's bedroom and kept a favorite bone buried under the blanket. Now and then, over Gary's protest, Cathy took the blanket to the laundromat. "He just gets it smelled up the way he wants it and you come along and ruin it," Gary said, and added, "That's another demonstration of the kind of plastic culture we're living in."

She bent down to rub George's chin. If Gary had to choose between them, she honestly believed, he would take George. He had a love for the dog that was tenacious and a little frightening.

"I'll get some Cokes," Gary said.

When he brought the glasses, she sat on an ottoman facing him.

A week ago they had sat on the beach in the same position . . .

A smelter-like sun scorched water and earth. Kids screamed, mothers yelled, chunky women in tight bikinis paraded their buttocks, girls dropped their halters to even the tan, and both sexes pushed along truck-like bellies as if they had no muscles for cinching them up.

"I love you," Cathy said. "I want to marry you. I don't have a job to offer. I'm about to lose my car. My prospects don't look good. What about it?"

"Hey," he said, "I'm supposed to do the proposing if any's done."

"I'm perfectly within my rights in accord with the Equal Rights Amendment."

He fell sober. "We've been all over it."

She set her jaw, flounced her blond hair. "We're getting married. There's no reason . . ."

He brushed sand off her legs. "What about mornings when we get up? Other couples are talking to each other, the guy's in the bathroom shaving and his wife's dressing in the bedroom."

"Who wants to yell from room to room?"

They had been over the ground so often. It was the same old record.

"And nights when we go someplace. We drive in silence."

"Oh, for heaven's sake, Gary, be reasonable. What does it matter if we can't talk in the car nights? What's so blasted important about that? People do too much talking anyway."

He raised his voice. "For God's sake, I've got to see your lips, Cathy. I've got to see them! You'd be living in a silent world half the time. I can't have it. I can't do it to you. You've got to understand. If I didn't love you so much . . ."

She put a hand gently on his. "I try imagining I'm deaf. I've stuffed cotton in my ears. But I don't think anyone who isn't . . . deaf, that is . . . can know what it's like. People staring at you or looking away too quickly, like they don't want to see you. Oh, I've seen them, I know . . ."

She took a quick, deep breath. "But what if you'd been born in a ghetto and were spending your life butting your head against a stone wall and never getting a job? Or what if you were one of those poor souls who can't compete in our aggressive society, who barely make a living and often not that? Don't you see, despite your deafness, you've got it made. You're brilliant, and you've got all kinds of charisma . . ."

Now with George between them, eager for a touch of affection from either, she said, "I've got a job. It starts Monday."

She told him about it. She was desperate to tell him, too, about the terror of last night, about the circus tonight. She wanted to talk it all out.

Don't you get your boy friend in on this . . .

For another reason she didn't dare discuss it with Gary. Like Mr. Mitchell, he would want to know why she hadn't gone to the police. She could no more explain it to Gary than she could to the lawyer. She could but she wouldn't. Also, Gary would insist on going with her tonight, and if refused, would follow her. He might accidentally place himself in great danger. She couldn't communicate with him if her back were turned, and no one else could.

"For God's sake, I've got to see your lips, Cathy. I've got to see them."

He had been totally deaf since he was ten. He had been in an automobile accident. One moment he was a part of the wild cacophony that daily hammers the eardrums, and the next he was in a world of total silence. Still, he was far more fortunate than those born deaf. He had heard words spoken, and remembered, and with the help of parents and teachers, maintained a fair speech pattern. At the New York League for the Hard of Hearing, he had added to his vocabulary.

In his pre-teens he had been in the Boy Scouts, asked no special consideration and had been given none. In high school, he had been on the debating team. He would state his side, then sit in the audience and lip-read the opposition. Since he couldn't hear the music, he never went to dances. He had a few dates to daytime affairs but what girl wanted to go out nights with a guy who had to get her in the light to communicate?

That is, until Cathy came along. They met at a football game. She was a sophomore at Pitzer and he a junior at nearby Pomona. She invited him to go horseback riding and after that they dated every weekend. In his junior year his parents died, and then an aunt he loved dearly, who left him the little house. He dropped out of college that same year and took a job as a computer programmer. Then the company failed and for months he had been unemployed.

What would it be like, she wondered, to live in a world without sound? No little night noises, rustle of leaves, or birds singing. No roar of the city, sirens wailing, cars honking. No dogs barking, or meow of a kitten, rustle of clothes, cry of a baby. No running of water, fall of rain, or thunderstorm. No whispering of intimacies, no laughing.

George was his "hearing aid." George nudged him awake when the alarm went off and came and got him when the doorbell rang. George was protective, too, overly so at times. He snarled at strangers and when Gary invited them in, George would sit and stare ferociously, ready to pounce if he thought the invader was a threat to Gary.

George was no ordinary dog. He was a graduate with honors of the American Humane Hearing Dog Program in Denver, the only higher learning institution of its kind. To get his "degree" he had studied for a rigorous four months such courses as routine obedience (learning to heel and sit and come with voice and hand signals), and "auditory awareness," also called speech keying, which included answering the doorbell, waking people up when the alarm went off, letting mothers know their babies were crying, finding someone seconds after a smoke alarm started beeping, and recognizing possible "danger signals" out in public (in a shopping center, for instance) and calling his master's attention to them.

George's training had cost $1,800, borne by the 100-year-old American Humane Association, which had given him to Gary without charge. Gary was one of the lucky ones since the college, as with most small institutions, lacked funds and could take only forty students a year. The demand for graduates was pitifully high. With more than thirteen million people in the United States suffering from serious hearing impairment and one million eight hundred thousand deaf, the college had a waiting list of hundreds.

The school had even flown George out to Los Angeles, accompanied by the noted hearing dog dean Agnes McGrath, who knew the sign language. She spent five days assuring herself that George would have a good home and that he and Gary were compatible. Also, she gave Gary instructions about "reading" George. That is, watching George's reactions when they were on the street. If George turned suddenly, the sound might be only a car backfiring or a garbage can knocked over. It could be, too, the wail of a siren or a car horn sounding a warning of imminent danger.

George's life story itself was as sad as anything Charles Dickens ever wrote. He had been on Death Row in the Denver Animal Shelter, only twenty-four hours away from being put to sleep, when Mrs. McGrath and a veterinarian chanced along looking for potential students. Mrs. McGrath didn't care what breed they were but checked them for temperament, alertness, enthusiasm, and health. She considered only dogs six to eighteen months of age. She quickly passed up the "snappers." Later, the dogs chosen as applicants were given physical and intelligence examinations.

George's class of ten was fully integrated. The students included a hundred-pound Doberman, a nine-pound Yorkshire terrier, a "fourth-generation mutt," a collie, and a mixed breed dachshund. One of George's best friends flunked out. He was not returned to the animal shelter but sent to a less handicapped person as a companion. Some of the dogs took special courses intended to fit them into the homes where they were to live. One had lessons in getting along with cats, another in understanding the vagaries of water beds, a third a course in detecting burglar noises, and a fourth in picking up dropped objects, such as wallets.

At the door, Cathy clung to Gary, not out of longing but rather security.

"Something's wrong, Cathy." He possessed a sixth sense, honed acute by deafness.

"Don't be silly."

He held her away to look into her eyes. She averted his study.

"You're scared," he said.

"I've got an appointment at four." She glanced at the

Mickey Mouse watch he had given her as a gag. She could not have treasured it more if it had been an engagement ring.

"How about tonight?"

"I'm tied up."

"Doing what?"

She hesitated. "Some of us girls, we're going out to dinner." She bent down to say good-by to George.

"Just remember to phone the next-door neighbors if you ever want me. They don't mind coming over."

"The Graysons?" He nodded.

She must remember. The Graysons. Sometime she might need them. Sometime soon.

7

Lefty Morgan drifted in. He had a shifty, shuffling walk. "Hi, kid. How ya doin'?" He was munching peanuts from a jar.

One of these days when he called her kid, Gail was going to sock him. "He's not back yet. Sit down."

"Good peanuts." He poured a mound of them on a transcript she had just finished typing. "Didja hear what happened to me this morning? Wasn't doing nothing and the cops picked me up. Can you imagine? I wasn't even working."

He crossed himself. "Goes to show the breaks you get when you're on the level."

She tightened her fists to control her nerves. The trouble wasn't all Lefty Morgan. At the convalescent home at noon, she had found her mother looking weaker than ever. "I could give you a lot of medical terms," the doctor told Gail in the corridor, "but the heart's tired. It's plain worn out. She could go any day."

Hugging her mother, Gail fought to keep back the tears. Her

mother noticed. "Don't worry about me, hon. I've still got some time left. And I've had some great years with you."

Her mother had asked about Mitch. "Sometimes I think I've got a rival," Gail said, laughing.

Now she took a phone call. "Mitchell Law Office." She had to ask the party to speak louder. Down the hall, the discount music shop had its electronic equipment set at siren pitch. A rock group yelled, screamed, sobbed, cried in terror, and shouted with a madness unknown since the caveman. One of these days the building would disintegrate.

"Oh, hello, Marilyn . . . I've got him booked solid today. Could you come in tomorrow morning . . . What! How do you know? . . . There's nothing Mitch can do until tomorrow. I'll call Suitcase and arrange for him to put up bond . . ."

She hung up and Lefty asked, "Was that the Marilyn with the big boobs?"

"I wouldn't know," she answered icily.

"Fine woman. You don't find many like her. Most of these young prosties . . ."

A woman the personification of the stereotyped grandmother came through the door. She was time-withered and gaunt in face but young in walk. "Hello, Gail dear. How was the wedding?"

"Best I ever had. Mitch'll be in any minute."

A month before, Clara Bitson had been hysterical when she had sought out Mitch. After considerable questioning, Mitch learned that she had been clipping obituary notices out of the newspapers and mailing a Bible C.O.D. to the deceased, whose loved ones usually paid since they thought this was probably the last act of their dear one.

"I was only spreading the word of God," she said. "They got the Bibles, the relatives did, and some of 'em read 'em, I know, and they got the Holy Spirit. I was only aimin' to spread the gospel. Didn't make much on 'em. Took most of the money and sent more Bibles around. Me and the Gideons and the American Bible Society done a lot of good work, and now they want to put me behind bars, and it's like the early martyrs who died for preaching the word of God."

She stared at Lefty working his way through the peanut jar. He offered her some, which she refused with a scornful twist of her mouth.

Mitch entered briskly. He didn't want the clients to trap him. "Be just a moment," he said to Lefty, and to Clara, "I won't be long."

Gail followed him into his inner office. "We won it. The prosecution threw in the towel. Little Eddie was terrific. Said he dropped his wallet the afternoon before when he was in to buy a television set. He identified the set down to the dust on it."

Gail was not amused. "He saw it by flashlight."

"That's an assumption unsubstantiated by evidence."

"Mitch, I don't like seeing you get these scum off scot free."

His smile vanished. "We'll talk about it later."

"Later never comes. Okay, I'm not going to hassle you the second day of our marriage."

He put a hand about her waist and pulled her to him. "You don't have to tell me. It's a lousy, crummy business sometimes, and I hate it, and I love it, but if I were practicing in Beverly Hills, the crumbums would be the same except they'd be wearing Brooks Brothers suits and Gucci shoes and be flanked by business agents, tax men, publicity guys, and gun bearers. But we'll talk. I promise. How's your mother?"

Gail shook her head. "The same. She asked about you."

"I'll get out there first thing tomorrow morning."

She referred to notes. "Marilyn called and said a report was out on the street that the police will arrest her tonight. Not for prostitution. Something else. I set it up with Suitcase to post bond and she'll be in tomorrow to see you. And for heaven's sake, get a hair cut."

He smiled, unperturbed. "Send Lefty in."

Lefty entered, a cat about to spring.

Mitch said, "Sorry to hear the police rousted you."

"I wasn't even working. Peanuts?"

He shook some into Mitch's hand.

"I've got to have your help again tonight." Mitch said.

Lefty was instantly wary. "Doing what? I don't want no cops—"

"I'll see to that. I'll be there. It's the same girl. I want you to follow her at the Forum and sit near her."

"Doing what?"

"Nothing unless someone tries to strong-arm her."

"What's she done?"

"Somebody's after her."

"Why?"

"None of your damn business. You owe me two hundred. I'll knock off a hundred."

"Throw in the Hoover house. Tell me it's okay—"

"Why you rotten little s.o.b.," Mitch yelled. "If you dare touch that house—"

Lefty grinned. "Just kiddin'. I wouldn't think of it. I've got principles." He crossed himself.

"The hell you have."

"I may get shot—and for a measly hundred bucks—"

"If you want to weasel out . . ."

"What do I do?"

"Gail will fill you in. Now get your ass out of here." He raised his voice. "Clara."

Muttering, Lefty shuffled out. "A hundred measly bucks!"

As she sat down by his desk, Clara smiled sweetly. She smoothed out her prim flowered dress and patted her white hair. Her right cheek bulged a little but she never chewed tobacco around Mitch. He was a square.

"I've got good news," he said. "Since it's your first brush with the postal inspectors, they've agreed to dismiss the charges provided you sign a cease-and-desist agreement. That is, you promise not to send any more Bibles out."

She looked crestfallen. "You mean I can't spread the word of God?"

"Sure you can. Go down to the Salvation Army and get a big drum and pound it on a street corner."

Gail interrupted. "Miss Doyle's here."

"Tell her to come on in." He turned back to Clara. "I'll have the papers to sign in a few days. I'll call you. Don't leave town —and don't put anything in the mail."

"It's like I was in Rome. A martyr. Being fed to the lions."

"Yeah. Well, just keep that picture in mind, Clara."

Gail brought Cathy in. It was four sharp. Mitch liked that. Punctuality. Cathy stood very straight, shoulders back.

"I was followed," she said, out of breath. She took the same chair, crossed her slender, Indian-brown legs, and swung them nervously. "A Thunderbird. I stopped at a bank to be sure, and went in, and when I came out and started up again, there was the Thunderbird behind me."

"The same guy as last night?" Mitch asked.

"I don't know. He stayed some distance behind me. But it was a man."

"Can I get you coffee—a Coke?" Gail asked.

Cathy shook her head. "I almost upchucked my lunch."

Mitch pushed the swivel back. "Don't worry about being followed. He just wanted to see if you were going to the police."

"He searched my apartment last night."

"Take anything?"

"No. Looked through my checkbook and broke the lock on my trunk."

Gail said, "You'd hardly keep a million lying around."

"He called me shortly after I got home. To make sure I was bringing the money. He said . . . he said . . ."

Her voice broke. "Take your time," Mitch said.

She sat up straighter. "He threatened my boy friend. Said if I told him—my boy friend, that is—anything about this he might have an accident. He said They were good at setting up accidents."

"Have you told him?"

She shook her head. "He's so vulnerable. He's deaf. He has this dog, George, who warns him when anyone comes around but if They killed George first . . ."

She was breathing hard.

Mitch said, "The guy's using your boy friend to tighten the screw on you."

"He doesn't mean it?"

"I didn't say that. I have to assume that anyone threatening murder means it."

He shuffled some papers. They crackled from the heat. The sun shafting through the window was smelter hot. Down the hall the Grateful Dead added their part in rasping raw nerve ends.

"So here's what we do," Mitch said. "Or rather, what you do. Follow his instructions. Take a big purse."

"I don't have one. I don't carry much gear."

"Gail will loan you one. Now I've arranged with Security at the Forum to rescue you if They try to seize you or force you to do anything."

He referred to notes. "We've worked out the parking arrangement. You drive in the Manchester entrance to the parking lot as close to seven-forty as you can. After the guy at the parking entrance takes your money, there's another young fellow who routes the cars. He's got your license number, and will motion you to the right. You circle around the Forum until you're a little this side of the ticket windows. Drive very slowly as if you're looking for a parking space. By then there'll be none in these sections. But keep on the watch and a red 240-Z Datsun with its tail lights on will pull out ahead of you, and you drive into that spot. This will do two things for us. First, if anyone's following you, he can't park near you, and second, we'll know where you are and can protect you."

"But when I leave my apartment—"

"I'm getting to that. I'll be running a surveillance on you from the time you leave until you park at the Forum. Two Security men will follow you in. Gail will be waiting and will also trail along after you. If she sees anything that looks wrong, she'll signal other Security men."

"I'm so scared."

"Don't be," Gail said quietly. "You've got everything going for you. Mitch and I will be near you at all times—and the gentleman"—she half-gagged at calling Lefty that—"who watched the Hoover house last night will also stay close. What's more, you'll be perfectly safe with a crowd around you."

Gail believed that but Mitch knew better. A gun under a handkerchief pressed into her rib cage with a threat to pull the trigger if she resisted, someone waiting in her car . . . there were so many ways a clever criminal could kidnap her while Mitch, Gail, and the Security people stood by helpless.

Mitch continued, "I don't think you'll get a chance to talk with this creep. He knows if he sits down by you the police may move in the second you hand him your purse. What I think will happen is this: He—or a friend—will grab your purse after the circus ends, since seventeen thousand people spilling out of the Forum is one big mob. He'll move fast to lose himself but while he's moving he'll empty the contents into a popcorn box, or something like that, drop the purse, and probably pass the box to another guy who's waiting. They do it so fast it's like a magic act."

"I'll wrap the strap around my wrist."

"Don't! You could get killed. You never know about these characters. Let him have it. Carry it loosely so he won't hurt you when he grabs it."

"Okay." She was breathing hard. "I've got to know what it's going to cost me."

"Whether you've got a million dollars or not, the fee's going to be something you can afford."

She sagged. "You still don't trust me."

"I'm not in a business where I can trust people."

She was near tears. "I'd like to tell you to go to hell but I need you so."

Gail spoke up. "This isn't Pitzer, hon. You're in another world now. A suspicious, calculating world. We see it all, the good, the bad, and it's often hard to tell one from the other."

Cathy rose unsteadily. "I'll prove to you that I'm what I am. I shouldn't have blown up. I'm grateful for what you're doing."

Mitch smiled. "Forget it. Get some rest if you can—and eat a good dinner. It's important. I've seen people go to pieces because they hadn't eaten."

"And force yourself to think of something else," Gail said. "Give your mind a rest. You must have something planned, something to work out . . ."

"I've got to go tonight," Cathy said, as if talking to herself. "I'll make it. I know I will."

"Of course." Gail put an arm about her. "We'll be there. We'll see that nothing happens."

That nothing happens. So easily said, Mitch thought, so easily said. A crowd of thousands, a lone girl, and the criminals would have their strategy meticulously planned. They would control the time, the exact place, all the factors. All that he and Gail and Lefty and the Security people could do would be to react in seconds, and hope to God their lightning judgment was correct.

After Cathy was gone, Gail said, "I got you into this—and I'm sorry. You shouldn't be following her. It's too dangerous. What if the criminal pulls her over on the way to the Forum, what do you do? You take a chance of getting shot. All because of me."

Mitch rose and stretched. "I would have taken the case even if you'd said no."

"Because she was desperate and you wanted to help her?"

"No."

"Why then?"

"Because I'm so damned curious."

8

By five o'clock Hawk's spirits were withered. "I feel as tired as an old coon dog," he told Angel.

"You look it," she said.

"Get out of here."

His eyes followed her. She was in a blue pastel pantsuit bought in the May Company basement. No matter the price, she could put more feeling into her clothes than any female he knew. Yet she handled the phone calls, paper work, and officers with crisp efficiency. Day after day, she took their razzing, and loved it, and had quick comebacks. She helped relieve the tension and the pressure. She shared a camaraderie that came from working together in a sordid, revolting world that often stank of human depravity. Mostly the people they met had arteries clogged with the cholesterol of hate. And the citizens on the outside watched like hawks ready to pounce if a mistake was incurred under fire in a split-second judgment call.

Angel was good for his men. A couple of months back when there had been talk of transferring her, Hawk had threatened to resign.

All afternoon he had reviewed the department's list of informants and the cases they were working. Once a month, he read summaries to determine whether the informants were to be continued, and if so, whether their compensation was in accord with what they produced. They covered the spectrum of humanity. They were dirty and stank, and smelled of Chanel No. 5. They were winos and drifters, and Rotarians. They slept under newspapers in alleys, and covered themselves with Saks sheets. They suffered from the malnutrition and diseases of the very poor, and ate at Perino's and had private hospital rooms at Cedars-Sinai. They cursed God, and never missed a Sunday Mass. They lied and cheated and killed for a few bucks. Even in poverty, however, some had an integrity and goodness born of who knows what.

They fell into three groups: those who reported the facts accurately, objectively; those who embroidered slightly, often without realizing they were doing so (their imaginations busied themselves with every facet of their lives); and those who spun pure fiction. Sometimes they wove the story so realistically in their own minds they came to believe it. Sometimes, too, they tried to set an enemy up in a police trap, even to getting him killed.

The informants were the beating heart of any law enforcement agency, from the two-man police department to the FBI. They furnished the facts, fiction, gossip, and fantasy that solved cases. Yet even the homicide and other officers who lived by the information they furnished had little respect for them. The best were tainted by the fact that they had turned against their fellow man, no matter how vile that fellow man was. The curse of Judas was on them. They were traitors to causes and betrayers of trusts given them by friends and relatives, sisters and mothers, their own children.

Hawk hated most of the lot. There was nothing that some would not do for money or revenge or fear of being prosecuted themselves for a crime the authorities held over their heads, a Damocles sword that would fall if they ever held back useful information.

Still they were not all of that ilk. Scanning the list, Hawk noted that payments included $20 monthly to a black shoe-shine boy who reported when a certain New York Mafia character arrived in town (he always got his shoes shined the first day he came in), $100 to a middle-aged receptionist for a lending firm that financed rackets as well as legitimate projects, $240 to a small jewelry store owner who was a "retired" fence with friends in that field, $325 to a onetime Mexican Mafia killer now in ill health, and $425 to a computer programmer for an insurance company that was being raided by its own officers.

The list included many who refused payment. Among them were a secretary whose boss was a suspected dealer in narcotics, a prostitute who had a customer bankrolling a car theft ring, a schoolteacher whose brother was wanted for murder, an accountant for a confidence game, and a "runner" of messages for known criminals.

The secretary, the schoolteacher, and the accountant furnished information because they believed it was their duty to do so. The prostitute and the runner because of the Brownie points they might earn. If they themselves fell afoul of the law, they would have a "friend in court."

Hawk constantly campaigned for more money. In his latest bid before the police commission, he had cited the fact the FBI had paid two and a half million dollars in ten years in Chicago alone to 5,145 informants. If he had money like that, he could reduce crime in Los Angeles considerably and immediately.

A few minutes after five Jenny sauntered in. Her full name was Dr. Jenny Barton and she was the department's psychologist. In her late twenties, she had a schoolteacher look, a little severity about her lips but dark, vibrant eyes that held the promise of lighter moments. When she first arrived on the job, Hawk had let her know he would tolerate but never welcome her. He thought psychology a college game invented by far-out professors. She took his attitude with a smile, and in time, convinced him that she was as effective in her field as he was in his. She did such a good job, in fact, that they had been out twice for hamburgers. For Hawk, that was tantamount to an engagement. No one around, however, took it seriously. No one would ever get Hawk to the minister. He was too rigid. He had to have the papers on his desk exactly so, with not a paper clip out of place. If anyone moved a chair, he moved it back.

"How about a quick dinner at Sambo's and afterwards we go shopping?" She sat on a corner of his desk and a stack of papers slid a few inches.

He frowned. "What're you shopping for?"

"I don't know."

"You don't know?"

She laughed and her light brown hair swirled. "Well, how do I know what I'm going to buy until I go shopping?"

He sorted that out, then shook his head. "You need a psychologist. Wish I knew a good one."

He told her not tonight, that he was bushed. She reminded him they had a date for the next night, to go to the Hollywood Bowl to hear the Los Angeles Philharmonic. "They're playing 1812," she said. "You'll like it. It's noisy. They shoot off fireworks and fire some cannons."

"I like Tchaikovsky with or without cannons," he retorted.

She fell sober. "I've had two lengthy sessions with McNair."

His body tightened. "Yes?"

"She's a definite schizophrenic."

His voice had an edge. "You're telling me she didn't know what she was doing?"

Wealthy, glamorous, twenty-three-year-old Suzanne McNair had shot and killed her tennis pro lover. She had phoned the police and confessed. Next week the case would go to trial. Her attorney would base the defense on temporary insanity.

"I'll have to testify to that." Her tone brooked no dissent.

"We arrest them and you people get them off."

She said sharply, "I'm not 'you people,' Hawk."

"Talk to her again."

"I've got to call it the way I see it," she continued stubbornly.

"Umpires, referees, and psychologists!"

She took a deep breath. "Okay, Hawk, I'll see her again."

"Thank you." His tone was cold.

Barney burst in. He had the drive of a five-year-old. He asked if he were interrupting. They said no and Jenny left.

"I've got a run-down on the Doyle woman," Barney said. He looked on Hawk as a father figure. Anything Hawk wanted, Barney did, willingly, happily, and thoroughly. With direction he was a good officer, but his personal life dismayed Hawk. He paid bills only under duress and roamed bars dating heavy-drinking, braless women who ran up exorbitant restaurant and discotheque bills.

"Let's have it," Hawk said.

Barney referred to notes filled with shorthand. Once he had studied to become a court reporter. "First, the Hoovers who own the house. Thomas P. Hoover, wife, Laura. They're in Bavaria on a vacation. He's a broker with E. F. Hutton. She does a lot of charity work. Two sons, not at home. One working with Phillips Petroleum at Bartlesville, Oklahoma. The other, with Chase National in Caracas. No indication of any criminal activities or associations.

"Now for the girl. She's Catherine Doyle, twenty-two, white, single, lives alone, a graduate in June from Pitzer with high scholastic honors. No known contacts with criminals. I checked the Los Angeles, Pomona, and Claremont indices. Nothing there. Pitzer said she had never been in trouble. Taught Sunday school class for a time at the First Methodist Church, Claremont, worked with black students on arrival at college, was active in all kinds of causes on the campus, well liked. She rented an apartment in Sherman Oaks two months ago on leaving Pitzer. Other tenants know little about her. They reported no girl friends in to see her and only one boy friend, identity unknown. Nothing much there. But then things got interesting."

He hesitated, checking his notes. "Go on," Hawk said impatiently. He had only contempt for pauses or clearings of the throat. An officer should have his material well in mind and set it forth with a clip to it.

Barney continued hastily, "I talked with the manager, one Abner Blanton, who roams about nights in the apartment complex. It's big, about two hundred units. Doyle has a very small one at the rear, on the alley, next to the garages. He seems to know everything that goes on—"

"A nosy guy."

Barney nodded. "He's not above looking in windows. Told me about one gal who comes home, gets out of her clothes, never pulls the shades, and parades around in the buff. He's had complaints but says he doesn't know what he can do—"

"Let's get back to Doyle."

"Sorry. She does a lot of house-sitting, he said, and last night, he was wandering around—couldn't sleep, he said—and heard a noise in her apartment. Sounded like a scream at first and then he recognized someone was filing metal. He went in with a master key but the guy had fled. Well, when she returned this morning he told her about it and went into the apartment with her. He saw a padlock filed off a trunk. Noticed metal droppings on the floor. She pretended not to see it, he said, although she did. He didn't mention it. Said, quote, Figured she knew who'd done it or was covering for some reason, unquote."

"Strange."

"I got more. He advised there had been a Thunderbird parked in the alley that night that didn't belong to any of his tenants. He took down the license number and had already reported it to the West Valley Police Division. It proved to be a rental car from a Ventura Boulevard lot. It was checked back in early this morning. The customer paid cash. Name of Ralph Catania. He showed an Arizona driver's license with a Tucson address."

Angel appeared in the doorway. "The General—when you have a few minutes. It's important."

"Send him in." Unlike the other officers, the General never felt free to come in. That annoyed Hawk.

"Barney's finished," Hawk said. "What've you got?" Then to Barney, he added, "Don't go."

The General coughed. He looked even older than he had a week ago. Hawk desperately needed a replacement. But he would never recommend dismissal of the General. In his time he had been an excellent officer. He had earned the right to finish his tenure with grace and dignity.

"I have a good friend," he began slowly. "He is not an informant. A good friend."

"I understand."

"He called me a few minutes ago. I promised I would keep his identity confidential even within the department. He advised that one Frank Mitchell, an attorney, had called Security at the Forum. That's that arena out in Inglewood—"

"I know the Forum," Hawk said.

"Mr. Mitchell said that a client of his, a woman in her early twenties, would be attending a circus playing there tonight. He advised Security that she might be in grave danger and asked if they could post some men around he could signal if an unknown or unknowns threatened harm to the young lady. Security promised they would do this. My friend has no knowledge of the details or the name of the young lady."

"Did he say what kind of danger?"

The General shook his head. "One more point, though, I just remembered. Mr. Mitchell asked that no law enforcement agencies be notified. He said the situation did not warrant it and that if they were informed, that might greatly endanger his client."

Hawk exploded. "Damn that Mitch. Wait till he wants something from us . . ."

He ran a hand through his hair. "Can't be extortion or blackmail. She's got no money. Unless she's a go-between. That could be. Kidnapping for ransom? We haven't a kidnap going.

Could be someone's forcing her to engage in a crime for them. A girl just out of college. No record. She'd be a great front."

He turned to the General. "What about your friend? How close can he cover for us?"

"As close as they know in Security."

That meant he was in Security.

Barney spoke up. "What about running a tail job?"

Hawk nodded. "Get a couple of men on her. You handle it, Barney. Make it a loose tail. First, though, clear it with the department. Ask permission to follow the case later if we're on to something. Notify the Inglewood police we're coming in."

"I'll ask my friend to keep on it," the General said. He stood a little straighter and his eyes were brighter. He was no longer an old man tolerated because of his past. He was back on the line.

"Call me at home," Hawk told both. "I've got a gut feeling about this."

9

Martha drove Gail home. Mitch would follow shortly. The car, out in the sun all day, was a bake oven, and the world about them seared.

"You look like you've been through a wringer," Martha said.

"Does it show that much?"

Martha made a left turn from a right lane. "It takes a lot of getting used to, a man does. Believe me, I know. I've been through three. The male species lusteth after you in the bedroom but in the rest of the house you're on your own."

Gail laughed. "For your information, Mitch and I've been married forty-eight hours and we're still in love. It's a case at the office."

"Oh." Martha didn't believe her. She had never cared for Mitch. He was too roughshod.

On her apartment stoop, Gail found boxes stacked high, more of Mitch's gear that a friend had moved for him. By the door, too, was a new lawn mower that Gail had given him last Christmas when they had expected to buy a small home. Inflation had drowned that dream as it had others.

Their next-door neighbor, a fading redhead in her late thirties who was due a touch-up, stopped by. "I see you got a live-in boy friend."

"He'd better be a live-in one," Gail answered. "He's my husband."

"Oh, shucks," the redhead said, "that takes all the romance out of it. Me, I go for the disposable kind."

You and Martha, Gail thought. Call it marriage or commitment, or whatever, Americans seemed to be on a sex turnstile. If you don't make it this time around, try again. If you can't find what you want on the job, try bar-hopping. Look over the merchandise in the immediate neighborhood, the divorced, the widowed, the young, even the old. A thousand years from now, historians would crack skulls analyzing the whys of a nation's 180-degree turn from Puritan ethics to adultery, rape, molestation, deviation, polygamy, polyandry, and musical chairs.

She pushed the lawn mower in and put it by the fake fireplace. For a few days it would be a conversation piece.

She started picking up Mitch's things. In two nights, he had wrecked her neat, tidy apartment. She had been forewarned, though. For two years she had begged him to organize his desk, which looked like headquarters for a Boy Scout paper drive.

"As you grow older," her mother had said, "you realize how few ever find lasting love. Don't let trivia destroy it. We've all got habits that bother the other one, and eccentricities, and we all blow up now and then. In my time, I've seen a lot of love die under a barrage of darts. Maybe the psychologists are right. Maybe we tend to self-destruct. Don't let it happen to you and Mitch. You've got something wonderful going for you. Hold on to it."

She was drinking a Coke when the phone rang. She spilled some.

"Mr. Mitchell, please." A young man's voice, very pleasant.

"May I have him call you? He should be here soon."

"Would you give him a message, please? Tell him that we do not want him to interfere in any way whatsoever with plans Miss Catherine Doyle may have for tonight. If he does, he would place himself and Miss Doyle in grave danger. I want to repeat that we will not tolerate any interference on his part. Do you have that?"

For a moment she was too shocked to answer. Then she asked softly, "Who is this?"

"Are you Mrs. Mitchell?"

"Yes. He'll want to know who called."

"My name wouldn't mean anything to him. I'm only the advance man. But if things don't go right, Mrs. Mitchell, the execution squad will move in. And they might include you, Mrs. Mitchell. They just might."

When Mitch came in, she was still sitting by the phone, a hand locked about it, her thoughts pounding. She repeated the conversation. "We'd better not go. We don't know anything about the girl except what she's told us. We don't know what we're letting ourselves in for."

She saw the warmth drain from his face, the cold determination in his eyes, the jaw set. Time and again when she had attended court as a spectator, she had seen the same fierce resolution as he tackled an unfriendly witness or offered summation.

"She's a client," he said. "She's counting on us."

He opened three boxes before he found the .45. He had taken it in for an unpaid bill.

She shuddered.

Cathy left the front door open while she searched the apartment. She then locked the door and every window, pulled the drapes and shades, and switched on the air conditioning. She had to be doing something, so she watered the yellowing dieffenbachia, the piggyback a teacher had given her, and a creeping Charlie that refused to die even if forgotten for weeks on end. Life for them was the tropics one month, the desert the next. She never could remember.

She rearranged the dried flowers in the Sunshine Dime Baking Powder can, and blew dust off her grandmother's Bible, which had the date Jan. 12, 1893, inscribed on a fore page. Had it been a special day, a happy one? A gift from a boy friend or husband? The special days were too few and it was good having something to remember them by.

She stood breathless, thinking. She had an hour before she would leave. If she rested, she would conjure up more terror than she could absorb. She had only certain simple, specific instructions to follow. Use the Manchester gate, turn right, park in the space deserted by the red Datsun, walk into the Forum, and take her seat.

She should have no difficulty in doing that. Her ultimate purpose, though, was to talk with the creep who had invaded the bedroom last night. Was it only last night? It seemed a week ago.

Somehow when he asked for the purse or seized it, she had to engage him in conversation. She had definite questions in mind. She had no doubt he would answer them since the answers would mean nothing to him. If he sat down by her, she could easily get him to talking. If he tried to grab the purse, she would resist. Despite the instructions given her by Mr. Mitchell, she would wind the strap around her wrist.

All right, so now I'm organized. I won't think about it. I know what I'll do. I'll whip up a chocolate mousse for Gary. She set out the ingredients—eggs, chocolate bits, sugar, heavy cream—and deftly created a mouth-watering, fluffy cloud.

The recipe was her mother's. Three years ago she had died unexpectedly of pneumonia. Never before had she been ill and yet within two weeks, she was gone. At times Cathy felt an overwhelming need for her, and tonight was one. Her mother would instinctively know what to do in this situation and would act swiftly. Her mother had been an ambitious, driving, frenetic person. Even at home she had seldom enjoyed a quiet moment. She was plagued by a restless compulsion to be doing something. She had reared Cathy with care but not a loving care. She had reveled in meeting Cathy's physical and emotional problems. They were a challenge, the same as selling real estate. One met them, one solved them head-on, and moved to the next.

In the same manner her mother had solved her own problems. When Joe Doyle left home when Cathy was ten, never to return, Cathy remembered her mother had cried briefly but the next day was out looking for a job.

Her father had been a onetime teacher, then a branch bank manager. He was a big, outgoing man, six feet three, with a ruddy face, a lumbering elephant walk, and flapping ears that Cathy played with when quite little. The moment they met him, people loved Joe Doyle. Cathy worshiped him. When he came home, he would stretch out for a half-hour and she would wait patiently. Then he would play games with her, help her with her homework, watch the television shows she liked, and tell her tall stories.

He would take her shopping, and along with clothes and toys, buy her books and records. "Read everything," he would say, "mysteries and the classics, Blondie and the Wizard of Id and Santayana. And listen to everything, rock and opera and country music and jazz. You can learn a lot about people from their music, books, and comics."

He had taught English literature at Torrance High School, then one day quit, saying he could not ask his family to live on his income. "Why, the garbage men in San Francisco earn more money than I do." His sense of humor had prevailed. "They may contribute more to society, of course."

He went into banking and learned fast. His fellow teachers said he was money hungry and he admitted he was. "I'm going to make a million." His friends agreed he would succeed in any field. He had guts, determination, and discipline.

After he left home, he wrote Cathy every week, all through the years. They were long letters that consoled her in times of trouble and advised her during her growing-up period. He had left a trust fund for her education and she started drawing on it when she entered high school. He had worked with a bank in Tulsa, then moved to an insurance company in Birmingham, and afterward to a lending institution in Atlanta. For several years now he had been semi-retired and living in Clinton, North Carolina. She had wanted to visit him summers but her mother said he had remarried and his new wife would not accept her. Her mother had never said a word against him, and for years kept a picture on a bedroom chest. One day when Cathy was a sophomore in high school, the photo disappeared.

In the years since he left, Cathy had seen him but twice, once at her high school graduation and again four weeks ago. The last time he looked ill but denied he was. He tried to revive the old camaraderie but was too weak to bring it off. He had shown up unannounced, talked for a couple of hours, and then left, saying he had to be in San Francisco on a business deal the next morning. He was sorry, he said, that he had been unable to attend her college graduation. He loved her and wished more than anything else he could have been with her through the years. Sometimes, though, he said, one could not control one's life.

She had not heard from him since. She had written but there had been no reply, and this was not like him. She feared he was ill somewhere, maybe dying, or had died. If he were dead, would she ever know? He had never mentioned friends or his wife.

The knock on the door was faint. She called out, "Who is it?"

Mr. Blanton's voice came over, and she opened up. "Can't be too careful," he said, "with all the rapists and muggers around."

He handed her a copy of *Architectural Digest*. She had told him she wanted to become a decorator or fit somewhere into the home field.

"Thank you, Mr. Blanton."

"Nobody's been bothering you again, have they?"

"It must've been some kid last night. Probably looking for money. I feel safe with you around."

"Why, thank you, Miss Doyle. Mighty kind of you to say."

The phone ring paralyzed her.

"Well, I'll be moseying along. If you ever need me, you know where I am."

Before picking up the receiver, she sat down and braced herself.

"Hello." Her voice cracked. Somehow she had to control it. She couldn't let her fear show through.

There was only heavy breathing.

"Hello," she repeated. Then she remembered and calmed herself.

In a matter of seconds, Gary was talking. "I called, Cathy, darling, to tell you I love you and hope you'll have a fun night out with your girl friends."

At first she had had trouble not talking when he phoned. In time, though, she had trained herself to sit quietly. Still, she wished tonight more than ever that she could tell him how much she loved him.

He laughed. "I hope I'm talking to you, Cathy. I'm always afraid it might be someone else. I'm going to watch the news on television."

The same old Gary. He was such a comfort. So outgoing. And brilliant. He had so much to offer, if he could only overcome his fear of rejection because of deafness. If she could only persuade him to enroll for his senior year at California State at Northridge, at the Center on Deafness . . .

She had pleaded repeatedly with him. "Look, Gary, their grads have jobs, good jobs with big industries, hospitals, education, government, you name it.

"And you're not hidden off in a corner. There's none of this 'concept of invisibility' that society has imposed on the handicapped in the past. You're a part of the university the same as all of the twenty-five thousand students. You can take any course you want and there's an interpreter off to one side of the lecturer and . . ."

The interpreter "spoke" Ameslan, an acronym for American Sign Language, used by most of the nation's deaf people, a language not based on English. "If English did not exist," wrote L. J. Fant, Jr., in *An Introduction to American Sign Language*, "Ameslan could still exist, just as French or Spanish exist independently of English." The interpreter also "spoke without voice" (for lip reading).

"One of the hearing students makes a carbon copy of his notes and gives them to you when the class breaks up." She had been excited over the possibilities—and he loved her for her enthusiasm. "There are some two thousand hearing students who know Ameslan. So you've got somebody to talk to just about everywhere on campus. And I'll take a night class in it so I can go around with you.

"And they don't coddle you. You don't get any breaks because you're deaf. The same admission requirements, the same grades in class. They figure you've got to compete successfully on campus if you're going to make it in the outside world—and I like that."

Since its founding in 1972, the Center on Deafness had granted 221 master's degrees, 72 bachelor's, and quite a few doctorates. The students had ranged in age from fifteen to seventy and come from twenty-nine states and three foreign countries. The university itself had several deaf instructors on its faculty, teaching subjects ranging from geology to drama. The center, too, had established a videotape library with an interpreter appearing in one area of the TV screen. The library included entertainment as well as educational films.

"There's no limit to what you can do," she said, "and it's right in our back yard. We don't have to go three thousand miles. No limit, Gary. Why, there was this one man, he was blind as well as deaf, he got a 4.0 grade for his master's, and a good job with the government."

"I don't even have enough money to get you a decent birthday gift."

"Don't be so downbeat. There are scholarships and grants . . ."

Now he was saying over the phone, "God, Cathy, how I'd love to hear your voice. The sound I'd love most in the world to hear."

"I wish you could," she whispered to herself. "I wish you could."

10

The long bank of open-faced garages fronted a broad alley. They ran the length of the block. Mitch drove slowly past the halfway point, then found an empty stall and pulled in. He hoped the rightful tenant would not appear for the next ten minutes.

Three stalls away, the bank broke to permit entrance to the apartment complex grounds. A narrow, badly cracked sidewalk running from the alley to the apartment buildings was closed in by Cathy's ground floor apartment on one side and an oleander hedge on the other.

Before turning off the ignition, he sat immobile a moment. What the hell was he doing here? It was not a new thought. He was forever getting into situations he never knew exactly how he had got into. He made decisions too quickly. He reveled in action. The fact hit him hard that this should be a police operation, not amateur night.

He got out, opened the trunk, and unfastened the big black clamp that held the spare tire. He heaved the threadbare tire out and pretended to inspect it. He was sweating. The sun would not set for more than an hour. The time was six-fifty. She would leave at seven.

In that ten minutes six cars pulled in or out. No one paid the slightest attention to him. That was a big city for you. His one fear was that Abner Blanton would happen along, note a new face, and ask questions.

At home he had grabbed a quick sandwich and a chocolate malt. The phone call Gail had taken from the criminal puzzled him. He wanted to believe the threat was a bluff but that would be a dangerous assumption. "We'll have to operate on the basis he meant it."

Her quick laugh took him by surprise. "Any other husband would have told me to forget it, that there was nothing to it." She kissed him. "That's why I love you, Mitch. You put it right on the line."

He had driven her to the Forum and left her. She would brief Lefty and the Security men. She was so capable, but with it all, feminine. Why did this case have to come up? Why couldn't they have gone home, had a good dinner, skipped television, and gone to bed? Like any other couple on the third night of their marriage?

At exactly seven he heard Cathy close her apartment door. She slammed it hard, a signal that she was leaving. She headed the other way along the stretch of garages. He dropped the tire back into the trunk, and was behind the wheel when he heard her car start. She backed out and headed west. Only seconds later he backed out and headed east.

He drove around the block to a through street. She had driven slowly and he caught up with her. He passed her, then after the next stop sign dropped back. The dinner-time traffic was still running heavy. He kept three cars behind her.

A short distance beyond the Ventura-Sepulveda intersection, she took the San Diego freeway on-ramp south. It was a long, circulating approach and he lost sight of her. Even though it was only a minute or so, he found his heart pounding. He had no knowledge of how to run a surveillance. He was frightened he would lose her, yet he dared not keep too close. The criminal, too, might be following her. Discovery could prove disastrous.

As instructed, she kept in the slow lane. He passed her on the fast one, cut to the middle, then slowed and fell in two cars behind her. Every few miles he repeated the pattern. It was not easy. Although the speed limit was fifty-five miles an hour, only a few drivers adhered to it. Most were pushing sixty-five or seventy. The fact that the California Highway Patrol wrote thousands of tickets daily failed to deter them.

We're like the wildebeests, Mitch thought, those strangely gaited antelope with long forelegs and short rear ones he had seen one summer on Tanzania's Serengeti Plain. The great migration was taking place. Tens of thousands blackened the countryside. The lions followed, and occasionally one would cut a wildebeest out of the herd. The herd would only shift direction a little and continue. We're like that in the big cities, Mitch thought. Each day a few of us are cut out of the herd here and there, and slain. But the great daily migration to jobs and return continues amid muggings, rapings, strangulations, knifings, and other violence. Like the wildebeest, we don't know what to do to protect ourselves.

Had the girl he was following already been cut out? Was she about to become a statistic on a crime sheet somewhere?

A Porsche shot past and moved in front of Cathy. The Porsche set its speed in accord with hers. Mitch tightened his grip on the steering wheel. In the near distance a police helicopter circled lazily. Its metal flashed in the sun. Behind him a trucker revved his motor up to a roar, wanting him to move over. Stubbornly Mitch kept to his lane.

The next time he looked the Porsche was gone. The copter still soared aimlessly. If the officers had been scouting the ground, they would have brought the craft considerably lower. Mitch was bothered.

A line of cars on Manchester crept along in the slow lane, waiting to turn right into the Forum's parking area. Overhead, 747s and other craft roared low on the air lanes leading to the nearby Los Angeles International Airport. By contrast, across the street, stretched the green undulating grounds of a cemetery.

Cathy held herself in tight control. She remembered a psychology class. Fear engendered by anticipation destroyed one physically and mentally and impaired judgment. She would take tonight step by step.

"My heartbeat is calm and regular," she murmured to herself. "My heartbeat is calm and regular. My forehead is cool, my forehead is cool."

She believed in autogenics, that the mind could manipulate the body. It could slow the pulse beat, steady the nerves, relax the muscles, quiet the emotions, even order certain organs how to behave. All one had to do was to sit quietly and repeat the necessary instructions.

"My heartbeat is calm and regular, my forehead is cool."

In minutes her heartbeat slowed and the heat of the night ebbed from her forehead.

She braked the car suddenly. She had come close to tailgating the one ahead. A couple in their thirties were in the front seat, three pre-teens in the rear, laughing, shoving, yelling. By tradition, the circus was theirs and adults were only a necessary appendage, a pocketbook to dip into.

She paid the parking fee. Fifty feet beyond was a young man in a red blazer directing traffic. He motioned the cars ahead in a straight line, then recognizing her license plate, waved her to the right. The Forum rose nearby, an imposing circular building done in the fashion of ancient Rome. She rolled along very slowly, on the watch for a red 240-Z Datsun. A hundred yards away, she spotted it, and when she was only a few feet away, it pulled out. The driver, a young man, gave no indication he saw her. He turned to the right, away from her, and paused only long enough to assure himself that she had seen him and was backing into the space.

She fluffed up her hair, glanced by habit at herself in the rearview mirror, and taking a deep breath, stepped out. No one was about. She proceeded directly to one of the circular ramps that led to the colonnade, and hence to the entrance.

The ticket taker said, "Aisle Twenty-seven," returned a stub, and she entered a carpeted, well-lighted corridor that circled the amphitheater. Hawkers were shouting their wares. Programs and mechanical monkeys on a string and balloons and whirling lights and all kinds of glitter. If she had been with Gary, the occasion would have been a merry one, taking her back to childhood. Once when she was eleven, her father had sent her money for ten tickets, so she could take all of her little friends.

A tall, lanky girl ushered her to a loge seat six rows above the floor level. Cathy's control began to slip. She had thought she would spot the attorney or his wife. Suddenly she had the strangest feeling that she was on her own. So what? If she were, she told herself, she could handle it.

Her father once had written, "We depend upon friends and loved ones for comfort and support in times of trouble, and that means a great deal. But when you get down to the bedrock, Cathy, when you're caught up in a violent storm, or have to make a decision that will affect the rest of your life, or in the end when you're dying, you have to meet the situation alone. You set your jaw and tighten your fists and meet it head on. Your mother had this kind of guts and I think I have and I know you will. You take life as it comes, you roll with it, you adapt to it, you slug your way out of bad times, and you come up surviving, and sometimes I think that's the greatest triumph of all, just surviving."

Sitting next to her was a boy of four bouncing on his seat. "Hello," he said. He knew the world was his friend.

"Hi, there," she answered back, the tension snapping.

"Don't you have any children?" he asked.

"Not yet." He was puzzled. All adults had children.

She and Gary. She wanted a boy exactly like Gary. He wanted no children. Deep down, she knew, he thought no son or daughter could ever love him fully and completely.

The clowns got busy, the same old painted faces, big noses, bald pates, and bizarre clothes. The kids screamed and roared. The band blared forth. That was one thing about circus bands. They didn't ease into numbers. The parade began and past her unseeing eyes streamed elephants with ears and trappings flapping, highly bred horses ridden by bored girls in tights, aerialists walking proudly, a clown on stilts, and midgets running and tumbling. On and on they came but her vision was blurred. *God, how long will he make me wait? Until the show was over? She could never sit here two hours. Never.* She had an overwhelming compulsion to run, to escape this building, get back in the Pinto, and drive like fury for home.

Her hands tightened about the purse. She was a puppet master drawing the strings ever tighter. Now she had control but any second the strings would snap . . .

Three rows behind her, also on the aisle, Mitch sat. He never took his eyes from a small area about her. It was as if he had drawn a circle. He watched the hawkers. It would be easy for someone to masquerade as one.

He noted her alertness, the straight back, the quick shifting of her head at any movement about her, the little startle at unusual sounds. Light flecks danced across her blonde hair. She was thin but her face held a sturdy Scandinavian look. There was none of the fragile, helpless female about her. He sensed she had coped before with a bruising world and had come out unhurt.

He was still burning from a discovery he had made before entering the Forum. After parking he had drifted past her car. There, pasted on top, was an iridescent red circle that from the air would mark the Pinto day or night. The police needed no cruise car tailing her. The helicopter had done that. But why? Did the police know something he did not about Cathy Doyle? Had Hawk somehow learned she had a rendezvous this night? Had Lefty spilled?

In that traditional circus voice, as if heralding the Second Coming of Christ, the announcer called attention to the center ring. In a never-before-seen, death-defying act, an aerialist would attempt four somersaults in the air. The drummer began the long roll, the spotlight caught the aerialist in dead center as he left the launching pad and swung into space. The crowd was hushed, every eye on him. Mitch kept Cathy Doyle riveted in his circle of attention. Now would be an ideal time for the contact man to make his play.

Wandering along the first row a photographer was casually taking section pictures of the crowd.

From the top row, far to Cathy's left, Gail had an unobstructed view of the girl. With a Minolta, Gail had snapped several practice pictures in that direction, pretending to focus on the act in the center ring.

She felt for Cathy Doyle, felt deeply. She realized she should not take the problems of Mitch's clients to heart, any more than a physician should a patient's. In time that would destroy you. Yet she knew what fear was doing to the girl. It paralyzed thought and muscles. Sometimes you wanted to scream and other times to hide.

Perhaps she had steered Mitch wrong. Maybe Doyle was not what she seemed. An attractive person could simulate honesty so easily. One wanted to believe, to help. But regardless of whether she was play-acting, she was in some kind of serious trouble. And Mitch and Gail needed the fee, no matter how small. They had to buy another car. At 140,000 miles, Mitch's five-year-old Ford was constantly at the mechanic's. The car would come first, then some inexpensive clothes, and in time, a honeymoon. Perhaps to Hawaii. A home was out. They never could afford one. She thought it a tragedy that most young couples starting out could not buy a home.

Occasionally she sneaked a look at Lefty, who was directly above Mitch, on the top row. He needed a shave and a hair cut.

His lips were moving. He was talking to himself.

Lefty finished the hot dog, rubbed his hands together to wipe them. He was hurt because Mitch had not told him what this was all about. Mitch should trust him. Mitch knew he had never lied to him, not even when it was painful to tell the truth. Lefty was a man of honor. His word was his word.

The dame was in a jam. That was obvious. And a high-class dame she was, too. No hooker or shoplifter. Probably some mobster's girl friend on the run from him. Frankly, though, Lefty would never go for her. She was not his type, too lean, no boobs to speak of, and her backside was merely so much structural engineering. But the Mafia bosses liked them that way. They thought class was a hungry-looking broad. He would take Marilyn. Now there was a female with boobs you could . . . well, he had better get his mind off Marilyn. He crossed himself.

He remembered other circuses. They had been a good source of income. One afternoon he had lifted fourteen wallets. That had been in the distant past. Then he had read an article that said one should think big and he realized he was wasting his talents.

Near Cathy he spotted a woman with a diamond ring worth at least two thousand dollars. He hungered to follow her home, case the layout, and return another night. He sighed audibly, a man who recognizes an opportunity lost.

He sighted a photographer down there at ground level, just beyond the first row, taking a picture of the crowd. By rote Lefty covered his face.

The photographer moved on to another section. Lefty wondered about him. He couldn't figure out why he would be taking pictures. Probably a new racket. That was the trouble with the world today. Everybody had a racket. No wonder kids grew up the way they did.

Cathy caught herself letting down her guard, sat up straighter, and finished the Pepsi. According to the program, the performance was only three acts from finishing. Even without a program she would have known the long night was coming to an end. The four-year-old beside her no longer bounced. The spring had run down.

Suddenly without warning a black vendor of popcorn was at her side. She had not felt his presence coming down the steps. He shouted, "Popcorn, anybody for popcorn?" and dropped an eight-by-ten yellow envelope into her lap. He was instantly gone. Swinging sharply about, she saw his back disappearing into a corridor high up.

Gail snapped a picture. Mitch rose to follow him, indicating to Lefty to stay. A Security man moved swiftly into Mitch's seat to keep watch over her. Another, for the same reason, walked down the aisle past her, pretended to look for something, then retraced his steps, keeping her in his line of vision.

The envelope was not sealed. Cathy took out a photograph, a crowd shot. It had been taken during the aerialist's "death-defying" feat. Everyone was looking up. Everyone except Gail, Mitch, Lefty, and four men. Circles, in heavy black ink, had been drawn around their faces. At the bottom was a notation, OVER.

On the back side was a note printed in capital letters: YOU BETRAYED ME, CATHY. I WAS NICE TO YOU AND YOU BETRAYED ME. I WILL SAY A PRAYER THAT YOU WON'T SUFFER MUCH BE-FORE YOU DIE. I'LL PUT FLOWERS ON YOUR GRAVE, CATHY. RED CARNATIONS.

She sat stunned but there was no outcry. For minutes, it seemed, she stared at the photo. Calmly she returned it to the yellow envelope. Slowly she rose and started up the steps. There was no power within her that could have forced her to sit out the performance. She walked steadily, the purse dan-gling loosely from one hand. "Don't panic," a voice inside her shouted. "Don't panic."

11

Cathy pulled up before the hospital's emergency entrance. A nurse hurried out with a wheel chair.

"Miss Doyle?" she asked.

Cathy nodded. "What shall I do with the car?"

"Leave the keys and I'll have someone park it."

The nurse wheeled her past the examination room and into an office. "The other parties will be here soon?" the nurse asked.

"I think so." She was answering by rote. She was too numb to understand what was being said.

After the nurse left, closing the door gently behind her, Cathy looked about. An enormous desk, files in a corner, white walls that bounced the light off, and open drapes. Closing them, she surprised a man glancing in. A foot path ran outside and there was the occasional fall of feet. She made sure the windows were closed and locked. For air conditioning purposes, they were. The door, however, to the corridor had no lock. She dropped into the big, plush swivel behind the desk, leaned back, and broke into a sweat. The ordeal over, she let go and a heavy trembling coursed through her, so pronounced it shook her entire body. She took a slow, deep breath. "My heart . . ." she began.

Lefty arrived next and told the dark-haired Filipino receptionist he was there to see his wife. "Cathy—Cathy . . ." He couldn't remember her last name.

"You'll have to wait. Over there. The doctor's with her now."

Lefty bristled. "I'm Frank Mitchell's chief investigator."

She looked him over and his face reddened. He hated authority of any kind. "Damn foreigners," he muttered, taking a chair.

Gail and Mitch came in the back entrance. At their conference that afternoon Mitch had set up the meeting at the hospital. "If they're running a tail on you, you can tell them you thought you were having a heart attack. It wouldn't look right if you went to our office or we went to your apartment. Too, the heart business could come in handy later. If you were always about to have an attack, it would throw them off balance."

When Gail and Mitch entered, Cathy rose but Mitch indicated she was to stay put. The first thing he noted were her eyes. Seemingly, they held no comprehension. He shoved straight-backed office chairs up to the desk for Gail and himself. He was breathing hard. He had chased the vendor and lost him. Without comment Cathy handed him the envelope. He held the picture so Gail could see and together they read the note on the back.

"Oh, God," Gail whispered to herself.

"Who are all those men?" Cathy asked.

"That's our man, Lefty, covering his face," Mitch said. "The others are Security men from the Forum. I don't know them."

They were not all from Security. He recognized one. Barney Carlson, Hawk's man.

"What'll I do? Do I go back to my apartment—and wait . . . wait . . . ? I don't think I can. I don't know what's going on. I don't know how I got into all this. You're my lawyer. You've got to tell me what to do."

Mitch said quietly, "We've got to get the police in on this, Miss Doyle. I haven't the know-how, and a private detective would bankrupt you. Two, three hundred dollars a day. Maybe more."

"No!" The word "police" had shocked her back into normal awareness.

Gail said, "Your life may be at stake. We can't take the responsibility—and you mustn't."

"I don't want to hear any more about it. I'm staying with you, Mr. Mitchell."

"We've got something tangible to go on now," Mitch continued. "He hired a photographer, paid a vendor who saw him, and we've got a hand-printed specimen, and maybe fingerprints. I might track down the photographer and the vendor but there's not much I could do with the hand printing or fingerprints. But the police could. They might wrap this up within a day or two."

She sagged back in the chair, closed her eyes.

Gail reached over to touch her. "We know how you feel but the time's come . . ."

Mitch said softly, firmly, "If you're sitting on a million dollars, you should tell me. With that kind of money we could get a detective agency. If you've done something wrong, you must tell me that, too. I'd hold it in strictest confidence. I'm bound by my oath as an attorney to do that. It's like I was a priest. I have to know, so I can figure out which way we go. Maybe I wouldn't want to call in the police—but the judgment should be mine since I'm your attorney and know the law."

"Look," Gail said, "we're dealing with one or more persons who have imagination and daring as well as ruthlessness."

Cathy sat up slowly, her body stiffening. She toyed with the ruby ring. "I guess I'd be suspicious of me, too, if I were you.

But you've got to take me at my word. Before God, I don't know of any reason why this guy comes around and thinks I've got a million dollars. I'll take an oath on the Bible. And the worst thing I ever did, some of us girls smoked a little pot once, to see what it was like, and I got scared of what it did to me, and I've never had any since."

Mitch switched tactics. "Maybe you ought to talk to someone else about this. What about your father?" The ring had reminded him.

"He's—he's—I don't know where he is right now. We're close, very close. He's the greatest, and I love him dearly. You see—well, he was through here a few weeks ago, and he was going up to San Francisco, and said he was returning to North Carolina but had moved and would let me know where he was."

"What about men friends? Have you lived with anyone in the recent past?"

"I don't sleep around, if that's what you mean!"

She was furious. Mitch had the response he wanted. He had to eliminate the possibility she might be protecting a man.

He persisted. "What about your boy friend?"

She stared at him coldly. "I know what you're driving at. That he's involved. Well, he isn't. And no one else I know is."

"Why don't you sleep on it?" Gail asked. "Everything looks better in the daylight."

Cathy failed to hear. "They're not going to kill me, are They, long as They think I've got the money—but They may torture me, mightn't They?"

She was brutally honest and he liked that. "Don't dwell on it, Miss Doyle. That's what They want. To reduce you to a shambles. As I told you, it's psychological warfare. The note mentions suffering and dying and putting flowers on your grave. Emotion-packed words. They'll break you slowly until you say to yourself that nothing in the world is worth all the anguish and terror, and you'll give in to Their demands. Everyone's got a breaking point."

"They'll never break me," she said. "Nobody ever will."

"I'm not sure They're after money at this point," Mitch continued. "They must know you don't have it. When They think They have you within Their power, when you'll do anything They say, They may use you as a front to get a million dollars from a source we don't know about."

He rose and walked about. "We'll get you a room here tonight and request Admittance not to register you. Only the nurses on your floor will know you are there. Stay until noon tomorrow. I'll call you in the morning and we'll work something out. Okay?"

He would buy a few hours' time.

12

At 2 A.M. Mitch still sat at the small breakfast table in their apartment scribbling on a big, yellow legal pad. He would jot something down, then mark out a few words, erase, tear the sheet off, and start over again.

This was the quiet time of night when he worked best. Gail was asleep, no muffled voices came over from adjoining apartments, no dogs barked or horns honked or kids shouted. The heat had barely ebbed. He had the window open and sat in his boxer shorts. His skin, white as a bed sheet, had seldom known sunlight. The most exercise he got was lifting lawbooks. There was a bicycle path nearby and Gail proposed they rent bikes. But he had a one-track mind. He loved law as some men do golf.

They had returned home from the hospital exhausted. Sandy, the redhead next door, had come running. United Parcel had left a package with her for Gail.

Gail introduced them. "Sandy Staver, Mitch. She thought you were my live-in boy friend."

"Hi, Mitch."

"Hello, Miss Staver."

"Sandy."

"Okay, Sandy it is."

Gail said, "Sandy's been awfully good to me since Herman died."

Herman had been Gail's cat and confidant. When troubled she would talk with him and he would cock his head up at her, puzzled by the unusual tone but looking as if he understood and sympathized.

"I'm really a washed-out blonde," Sandy said, apropos of nothing. "But no one ever paid any attention to me until I dyed it red. Now when I walk into a bar, you wouldn't believe what happens."

"I would," Mitch said.

"Gotta run. Gosh, I wish I'd seen you first, Mitch. I'd sure like to take you home with me."

She was gone then. Nervously, Mitch fumbled with the key. "Some friend you've got," he said.

"It's all talk."

"Not what I saw."

She gave him a playful push into the apartment. "And that's all you're going to see."

Now Gail appeared sleepy-eyed in the doorway. She was in a shimmering, thin, low-cut gown. As for the rest, Mitch had the impression he was seeing her through milky glass.

"Darling, please, we've got another rough day coming up. You've got to get some sleep."

"I've eliminated several points." He took a second glance her way. "You look good even when you first wake up."

She sat by him. "Don't be silly. What've you cut out?"

"The phobia business. After what happened tonight, it's more than a phobia. Most people would be so frightened they'd break a leg getting to the police. She's hiding something and she's terrified the police will find out about it."

"I can't argue with you on that," she said, "but she seems,

well, I've just got this feeling about her that I can't put down. I know it isn't logical—but a lot of things aren't logical."

He sighed audibly. He was so damn tired. "Granted. But my point is that it's not a phobia. Well, now for the next point. I put forth the hypothesis that They—whoever They are—might be planning to use her as a front for a scheme that hasn't become apparent. But I've struck that one. It's obvious that They are convinced she has the money, and are definitely working toward a pay-off by her of the million plus."

"But the bank corroborated the amount she said she had in her checking account," Gail said. "She has no safety deposit box. Pitzer said—"

"I'll get to the money in a second. I put down another possibility, mistaken identity. They have the wrong girl. This does happen and I don't think we should eliminate it completely. But it doesn't happen very often. So I've put it out here to one side, just to keep it in mind.

"About the money, checking the bank doesn't mean much. At first thought it looks like it would be difficult to hide a million dollars. But think about it. You could scatter it over several safety deposit boxes, bury it under the floor of a house or apartment, all kinds of places where you could hide it."

Gail said, "I don't even know where to put the twenty dollars emergency money. I keep switching it around. In the hamper, under my lingerie, under the mattress . . . Mitch, when are we going to have a baby?"

She could come up with the most irrelevant questions at the most inauspicious times. "Soon as we get a little money."

"Would two thousand dollars be enough?" Her aunt Grace had promised to will them her A.T. & T. stock.

"I don't know. It's not the down payment but the upkeep. For heaven's sake, Shad, can we have the baby some other night? I'm trying—"

"Okay, okay."

He hurried on. "Let's assume she doesn't have the money. She was very convincing when she swore before God she didn't. But she didn't swear she didn't know where it was. I should've asked her. I slipped up there. Maybe it's not her money but someone else's. She's protecting someone. However, she has no family except a father she's seen only twice since she was a child, and a boy friend she says wouldn't be of any help. She has friends, of course. Could be one of them. But I don't think so. She's got guts and intelligence and wouldn't go along with an illegal scheme no matter how much there was in it for her."

"Wouldn't she?" Gail asked.

"What d'ya mean?"

"Isn't there a point at which we would all do it—if we were desperate enough, if we had hungry children, if we were starving?"

"Jean Valjean and the loaf of bread."

"We all rationalize about everything we do. If the scheme wasn't too far out, she could tell herself that there was nothing too wrong about it."

"She's not starving—and she's not money hungry. Remember, she said she wasn't taking anything more from her father. Something about once kids were grown they shouldn't become a drain on their parents."

"Maybe she did something when she was younger. Got pregnant, shoplifted, embezzled, and she's scared it will come out if she goes to the police."

"Maybe *you* should be the attorney of record. I hadn't thought about that. I'll ask her tomorrow."

"Let me, when you're not around. She might respond better to a woman if it's something quite personal."

"I'm not splitting my fee with you."

"A Mexican dinner out."

"Okay."

"So where are we there on paper?"

"Not very far. But I've eliminated some possibilities."

Tomorrow he would track down the photographer and the black vendor who had handed Catherine Doyle the envelope. Earlier, Security at the Forum had called. They had tried to talk with the "popcorn man" but frightened, he had taken off. They had no legal reason to detain him. They gave Mitch his address.

"I'll get us some hot chocolate." She busied herself about the stove.

He got up. His shorts, plastered to the chair by the heat, sounded as if they were ripping.

She laughed. "Don't you have any pajamas, Mitch?" When he grinned, she continued, "I thought we weren't going to have any secrets from each other. You never told me you slept in the buff."

"You never brought it up. You know what I tell clients when I put them on the witness stand. Answer the questions concisely and briefly. Don't volunteer information the questions don't call for."

"I should've known when I married a lawyer . . . And I went out and paid ten dollars for this gown."

"You mean—"

"Saves money. Oh, well, I'll give it to the Salvation Army. Someone will get some good out of it. Mitch! No, Mitch! Not in the kitchen! I always wear something in the kitchen. It's just when I sleep."

13

At 7 A.M. the heat rose smelter-hot from the asphalt. In slow motion, Hawk dragged himself out of the car, remembered the keys, and reached back in for them. Wearily he trudged toward a building mostly of glass.

As he neared his office he struggled to put a little spring into his step. He had been up most of the night. About 1 A.M. he had received a call reporting that a key informant inside a truck hijacking ring had suddenly gone cold. His memory about past hijackings had failed him and he had given two false tips. It was an old story. Someone had got to him, threatened him or paid him off. For two hours Hawk had talked without shaking him.

Angel followed Hawk into his office for the customary morning briefing. She reported on night developments she considered he should know about. In a few words she summarized the results in numerous investigations that involved informants.

As he listened he shaved with an electric razor, then slapped his cheeks with lotion. "Barnyard 5," Jenny called it.

"I want some respect today," he told Angel. "I'm beat."

"I'll show it when you pay me back that 'pittance' you owe me."

Hawk looked aghast. "I'm shocked you'd bring up such a small matter." He dug three ten-dollar bills out of his pocket. "Here, take this, you money grubber, and let's hear no more about it."

She left with a swirl of a miniskirt. He felt better. There was nothing like a miniskirt to start the adrenalin flowing. What was wrong with designers, to kill off the best-looking style to come on the American scene? Congress should make it mandatory that all women under thirty be required to wear them. And those over thirty who weighed more than 150 should be required to wear that great Hawaiian cover-up, the muumuu.

He called to Jenny, who was standing in the doorway, to come in. She looked sober. "I saw McNair again. My first conclusion stands. Schizophrenic. Definitely."

He shrugged. "Forget it."

For a moment she studied him. "I thought you'd be put out with me."

"All we can ask of friends is to be honest."

She glanced away. "I was hoping we were more than friends."

"What's more than friends? Sweethearts, lovers—they change with the years. But friends in my book are for life."

The tension broke. She could feel the old camaraderie settling, the warmth and glow of a log fire on a chilly night.

"Hi, friend." She dropped with relief into the nearest chair. "Why don't we have a quiet evening, go to dinner somewhere and talk? I don't think you need the War of 1812 tonight."

His eyes brightened. She was extremely sensitive to his feelings.

"Jenny," he said, "you're better than Tschaikovsky any night. You know—" he hesitated, then plunged ahead—"I'm getting old and need someone to care for me—and I've got a whole drawer full of socks that need darning."

"When?"

"When what?"

"When do I start darning socks?"

He looked away. "Soon as I get a few things out of the way."

Angela put a report on his desk. "He wants to wait until he can collect your Social Security check."

She was gone before he could threaten to fire her.

Jenny smiled. "About tonight—I know just the place. Out on Pico. The food's excellent and it's quiet."

At the door she turned. "I must tell you I've never darned a sock in my life. But I have other talents."

That you have, Jenny. That you have.

He watched her as she left. What a woman.

Barney came in. "I tried half the night to reach you . . ."

"I was out boozing around as usual."

After the helicopter had reported by radio the location of Catherine Doyle's car, Barney and a fellow officer, Ryan, had followed her into the Forum. Barney reported in detail exactly where everyone had sat and the delivery by the popcorn man of a "rather large" envelope to Doyle.

"I thought I should watch her for possible further developments and followed her out to her car."

"Both of you? What about the vendor?"

"We slipped up there, Hawk. I thought we should tail Doyle."

"Why didn't Ryan get the man's identity? You could've split up."

"We can still get it. The concession manager will know who was in that particular section."

"It's not like you Barney."

"I'll tighten up."

"See that you do. Go on."

"She checked into a hospital and pretended she had a heart attack. Frank Mitchell and his wife used a back entrance. They talked in an office for about forty-five minutes, then she was admitted as a patient. She's in Room 414, will leave at noon today. Lefty Morgan followed her into Emergency, tried to talk with her, but got turned back at the desk. He sat waiting for an hour, then left, but returned about midnight and spent the night sitting outside her door."

Hawk looked out the window at the ant people scrabbling about below. "I don't know how I can justify spending more money. We don't have a case. She went there obviously to make a contact or get a message—and she got a message. And that's all we know."

"Why don't we bring Lefty Morgan in? With the kind of record he's got—"

Hawk was curt. "I don't go on fishing expeditions. You know that, Barney. Besides we might scare someone off if there is anything going on."

"Let me have today on it. Just today. See where she goes from the hospital. I'll find the popcorn guy. Could be he read the note."

"If it was a note."

"Right."

"Come on in," Hawk called to the General, who hovered in the doorway, like a nervous schoolboy outside the principal's office.

"What's on your mind?" Hawk asked, wanting to be rid of him. To Barney, Hawk said, "Sit down. We'd better talk it over."

"You'll remember," the General began, casting a sideways glance at Barney, "that we have an informant in the organized crime section by the name of Marissa Dubrovnik." He talked slowly. The wheels these days didn't turn as fast as they once had.

"What about her?"

Hawk remembered meeting her at the time the General had enlisted her. She was as hard and tough a woman as Hawk could remember, a dark-haired Slav in her early forties with only a few vestiges of the beauty she once had had. A perfumed letter browning at the edges. In her late teens and twenties, she had worked as a nude model for *Playboy, Penthouse,* and similar magazines, then had married a wealthy Chicago mobster by the name of George Batton. He looked the part of a shrewd financier, which he was. Always impeccably groomed, he wore the latest in men's fashions, read the best books and magazines, attended the opera, and could converse on virtually any subject.

For years they loved and fought. She had diamonds and furs and used them sparingly. She never looked the part of a mobster's wife. He saw to that. Then in the fifteenth year of their marriage, she was in an automobile accident. She suffered a seriously damaged hip and extensive neck scars. He sent her to the best surgeons but when it became evident that she would limp badly the rest of her life, he divorced her for a younger woman. Her investments went bad, she pawned and lost her jewels, and when the General came across her she was living in a dark, dungeon-like rooming house not far from the Bunker Hill area. During her marriage she had made many friends, and done favors for many. Whenever they were in Los Angeles, they dropped by to see her. For old times' sake, they gave her money and expensive gifts. They talked about the "business projects" the various syndicates, including the Mafia, had underway.

As an informant, she had produced. In the past year, the authorities had solved five cases from the "bits and pieces" she gave them.

At the time of his talk with her, Hawk had noted her ex-husband's photograph on her dresser. She was not bitter. "He married me for sex and as a pretty bauble to show off. The bauble tarnished. He was good to me. I'd never rat on him to you studs. Not if you offered me ten thou. The others, who cares?"

Now Hawk repeated, "What about her?"

"Didn't I hear you talking about a party by the name of Catherine Doyle when I was here yesterday?"

Hawk came upright in the swivel and nodded.

The General continued, "Dubrovnik says she has some 'hot

dope,' to use her words, about a woman named Catherine Doyle. It has something to do with the Carney outfit in Miami, and with a pay-off of better than a million dollars that's going to take place in Los Angeles within the next forty-eight to seventy-two hours."

"Go on."

"That's all she'll tell me. Wants five hundred dollars to spill the whole story."

"In addition to the three hundred a month we're paying her?"

The General nodded. "Cash before she talks."

"What about her?"

"She's never stuck us. But I wouldn't want to handle it without you along. She wants us to come by at four."

Hawk turned to Barney. "Tell Ryan to keep a tight tail on Doyle. Tell him to get another partner. Then report back here."

He swung back to the General. "I think we'll play a few hands of stud poker with Marissa Dubrovnik."

14

A little before sunrise Gail awakened, sleepily stretched her long frame, and realized Mitch was alongside her. A happy feeling swept her. They should have married a year ago. Mitch, though, had wanted to save up a nest egg, a thousand dollars. He had a nightmarish fear of going broke and having to borrow from friends.

She cared little about money. "What will money get us, Mitch, that we don't have already? We've got each other, and we're in good health, and have a place to live, and all we should eat, and clothes. Well, I guess we do need clothes. You especially. But we've got it made—and I hope we never become a couple of work horses plodding along day and night so we can give the bankers some money to play with."

At the office, the morning was a routine one. Marilyn was waiting when they arrived. She had been arrested on a charge of "rolling" a wealthy Texan, taking his wallet, which he said contained eight hundred dollars. "I've never rolled a sucker in my life. Never stole a buck from any of the bums. We got into one hell of a fight and he got mad and made the story up."

She was a product of the streets, ran with a pack of young male animals on New York's East Side, hitchhiked to Los Angeles to break into the movies, and drifted into prostitution. She loved it, liked the money, excitement, and competition. She was still a street animal, tough and ruthless but kind to those who didn't compete with her or bother her. She was big-breasted and big-hipped, had a man's muscles, and an aging prizefighter's tired, battered face. Gail could never understand why men patronized her. If they had to have a woman, why didn't they go down to the nearest bar and pick up some attractive girl who was out for a night's adventure?

Mitch put in a call to Cathy. She had slept little but sounded calm. He arranged for Lefty to bring her to the office at one-thirty. Earlier he had left instructions with the hospital switchboard to hold all calls to her room.

About ten he left to track down the vendor and the photographer. Afterward he would visit Gail's mother in the convalescent home. He took with him a ham-on-rye sandwich Gail had fixed.

The house was doll size on a twenty-five-foot lot. The paint was scaling and torn shades hung at the windows. The yard was edged and mowed. Paint and window shades cost money, a yard, mostly labor.

Mitch rapped gently on the screen door. A tall, thin, good-looking black in his early twenties appeared.

"Bo Hawthorne?" Mitch asked.

"You a cop?" he countered, his face a mask.

"A lawyer. I want to talk to Bo Hawthorne about something

that doesn't concern him—something he may have seen when he was working last night at the Forum."

"What'd this Bo Hawthorne see, man?"

"I've got a client who's in grave danger. A girl, her life's been threatened. Bo Hawthorne handed her an envelope last night. We think the man who gave him the envelope to deliver may be the guy we're looking for."

The man's eyes grew large. "So this Bo Hawthorne's in big trouble just 'cause he gave the girl a—a letter?"

Mitch shook his head. "If he was, the police'd be here, not me. Fact is, the Forum gave me this address." Still the other hesitated and Mitch added, "If I could talk to Bo Hawthorne and he'd tell me about the man, he might save a girl's life."

The man studied Mitch for a long moment, then came to a decision. "You're lookin' at 'im, man. I'd ask you in but there ain't no place to sit. I'm sorry about the girl, honest. I had no idea—"

"Of course you didn't. Now tell me everything you can remember—what the guy looked like, how come he picked you, everything."

Bo Hawthorne frowned as though to recall the scene. "The circus was windin' down, you know—and he stops me in the aisle and says would I give this envelope to this girl and he hands me a bill. Honest to God, man, I didn't know it was a fiver when I took it—but any kind of foldin' money is an awful lot to me. I got two kids and this job selling stuff at the Forum don't pay nothin' much and I can't get no other. But my wife can stretch a buck from here to 'Frisco and we get by. We ain't never goin' on welfare."

Mitch looked at him with new respect. "Did he say why he didn't give her the envelope himself?"

"Said they'd had a fallin' out and she wouldn't take it from him."

"Did you open it?"

Bo looked uncomfortable. "Wouldn't a been a crime, would it?"

"Oh no. It hadn't been mailed. I was hoping you did—open it, I mean."

"Matter of fact," he said with relief, "I did peek in. Got to

thinkin' what if—if it wasn't like he said. Like it was something might get me in bad trouble. I got trouble enough, man."

"So you looked inside," Mitch prompted.

"It wasn't sealed good, peeled back real easy. But there
wasn't nothin' in it but a picture."

"No writing?" Bo Hawthorne shook his head.

"Nothing written on the back?"

"Didn't see nothin'—then can't say's I looked."

"Ever see this man around before?"

"Nope. You know, you see so many people you don't see no
particular one."

Mitch prodded. "Can't you remember whether he was short
or tall, black or white, about how old he was?"

"Well, they wasn't much light and, you know, I wasn't 'spe-
cially payin' attention. But he was white. He was real dark but
he was white, you know what I mean?"

"Dark complected?"

"Right. That's it. Looked like a foreigner but he talked
American. Talked real nice. And he smelled good, too. After
shavin' stuff, now that I think of it."

"Good! That's what I want. About how old would you
guess?"

Bo shook his head. "I'm no good at guessin' ages. Forty,
maybe. And again might've been forty-five. Middlin' build,
middlin' tall—I'm sorry—"

"You've been a big help, Bo." Mitch assured him, and
offered his hand. "I hope you find a good job."

"I will, man. I will. Just have to keep lookin' and prayin'.
Something's got to turn up. Just got to."

As Mitch got back into his car, he felt good. True, he had
learned little as far as a positive identification went, but he was
beginning to get a feel for the criminal, for the intangibles
which set one apart as definitely as physical characteristics. But
mostly he felt good because for a few minutes he had been in
close encounter with courage and hope and determination.

The circus press agent gave Mitch the photographer's card.
Big Ed Somerset, Big Ed's Studio.

"He said he wanted to take some crowd pictures for *Los Angeles* magazine," said the press agent. "I told him okay as long as he stayed inside the rope around the arena. What do you want with him?"

"Got a client who would like to buy one of the pictures. The one she's in."

Big Ed's Studio was in a run-down area of Inglewood. It was on the second floor of a deteriorating building that was like a human of that age, beginning to totter.

Mitch pushed through a warped door into a huge studio area that looked as if a ten-year-old had blitzed it. In the years Big Ed had been there, it was obvious he had never straightened it up. Gingerly Mitch stepped over camera equipment and boxes. He took his time casing the place. He saw Big Ed sitting in a far corner at a battered, paper-littered desk. He was a massive man with an expansive, untrimmed beard and uncontrollable long hair. Out of squinty eyes, he watched Mitch approach, said nothing.

"I don't need to ask if you're Big Ed," Mitch said pleasantly.

"What can I do for you?"

Mitch explained.

"Get the hell out of here!" He pushed the swivel back sharply.

Mitch stood his ground. For a moment, they stared eyeball to eyeball, two moose squaring away.

Mitch said quietly, "A girl may be killed today, tomorrow. An innocent girl just out of college. The guy who's going to kill her hired you. You're not in trouble now but if you cover up for the killer—"

Big Ed pulled open a screeching desk drawer. "I've got a .45 here that says get the hell out of here."

Mitch raised his voice to match Big Ed's. "You're aiding and abetting. You're headed for prison."

The .45 in one hand, Big Ed moved his massive frame with unbelievable agility around the desk. "I'll help you get to the door," he roared. He raised the .45 to bring the butt down in a slamming blow on Mitch's skull. Mitch sidestepped and tripped him. The room shook as Big Ed hit the floor.

Mitch picked up the weapon that had fallen free. He aimed

dead-on for Big Ed but as he squeezed the trigger, he raised the barrel and the shot tore into the wall. Big Ed doubled up, thinking he had been hit, and moaned.

Mitch tossed the .45 into the corner where the desk sat. He walked slowly out of the office with Big Ed screaming oaths at him.

Shortly after one, Mitch returned, sad. He had been to see Gail's mother. "It's hard to watch her go slowly down hill. She talked to me about her exit, as she called it. She felt good, I know, that everything was arranged." He handed her a key. "She wants you to bring everything from her safety deposit box the next time you go out to see her."

Gail, near tears, followed him into his office. He wasn't good with words and gave her a tight little hug instead. He reported briefly on his talk with the popcorn man and his encounter with the photographer.

At one-thirty Lefty accompanied Cathy in. "I would have married Gail here if Mitch hadn't beaten me to it." He crossed himself. Gail shuddered. He took off then on "some important business." He would return within the hour.

Gail said Mitch had a matter of urgency to finish and took Cathy down to the coffee shop. They sat in a booth by a street window, and after they ordered, Gail tried to initiate a "woman-to-woman" talk. She was getting nowhere when she noted a man out on the sidewalk who would walk a short distance, then reverse himself and pass them again.

A few minutes later he entered the coffee shop, took an end counter seat, and ordered a tuna sandwich and coffee. He was within hearing distance. He unfolded a crumpled *Herald-Examiner* and pretended to read. Pretended, Gail thought, because his gaze shifted repeatedly in their direction. He was short and squat with a head shaped like a bowling ball and about as devoid of hair. When her eyes caught his, he stirred the coffee vigorously. Gail became increasingly nervous, and even before they finished, suggested they leave.

Back in the office, they found Mitch's door open. Giving

him a warm smile, Cathy took the initiative. "Your wife asked me some personal questions and I want to repeat that I have nothing in my past that would interest you. I never went in for sex, drugs, or liquor. I would never do anything to hurt my father."

Mitch said, "But you saw him only—"

"You don't have to see someone every day to love them. There were letters and phone calls. Lots of them. Almost every week. I can't say I ever loved my mother. She wasn't the kind you loved. I admired her, yes, and respected her, and I wish she were here with me today. You see, Mr. Mitchell, she was a very strong woman. She would know what to do. I don't think there ever was a problem she couldn't solve or a situation she couldn't control. She solved all my problems. She never let me tackle anything. Perhaps if she hadn't been so strong, I'd be stronger. Excuse me. I'm talking too much. I'm nervous."

"There are times when we all need to talk," Mitch said.

"Mr. Morgan was awfully good to me." After sitting outside her door all night, he had spent a good part of the morning with her. "I think he's cute. He told me he was just doing it to help you. Said he was in the jewelry business."

"He was what!" Gail exclaimed.

Mitch grinned. "Yes, well, I guess you could call it that."

"He offered to get me anything I wanted wholesale. He's a dear."

Mitch got quickly to his feet. He had to get the situation in hand. "I've asked him to stay with you the rest of the day. Gail will spend the night with you. We'll tell the manager—what's his name?"

"Blanton. Abner Blanton."

"Gail will ask him to be on the *qui vive*—"

"He's like an old watchdog."

"I'm sure the criminal will contact you soon and I want you to tell him that I will handle all negotiations, that I'm your lawyer and I insist—"

She broke in. "Negotiations? Isn't that the same as saying I have the money?"

"They're convinced you do. So it won't alter their thinking.

And with this amount of money, it isn't unusual to have a go-between. It's often set up that way in cases of kidnapping for ransom, blackmail, extortion, that type of crime. Don't use the word, go-between, of course. And don't engage in needless conversation. Tell him you can't, on the advice of your attorney, that I'm handling everything. It makes sense. It's a whale of a lot of money. For all he knows I may have it, or access to it."

"May I ask what you're going to do when he calls you? If he does."

"Right. He may not. But They're so hot to get the money, I think They will. I'll have to ad lib it. I'll try to find out who gave you the money, what kind of crime it came out of, who had the money, and where it was before it was turned over to you. I hope we can get a few leads that we can follow up and use to convince Them you couldn't possibly have it."

She sagged. "It's like I've been watching a television show, and a girl was about to be beaten up, and later she would be killed, but now it's toward the end, and I think, I hope she'll be all right." She laughed nervously. "I knew you'd come up with something, Mr. Mitchell. The police never would have."

When she was gone, Gail drifted back in. "We've got to do something about Lefty. He's trying to sell her a hot diamond ring."

By five-thirty, the old creaking building was beginning to settle down for the night. The Grateful Dead and the others had been silenced, and gone, too, was the hustle along the corridor. Now there were only occasional footsteps pounding or tapping their way over the bare, splintering floor. In the quiet, also, could be heard the groaning of the building's arthritic joints.

Gail was uneasy. Mitch was gone and she was alone. All day she had been growing more apprehensive, and without reason. No one was about to burst through the door to harm her. No one had reason. Yet every footstep outside prompted her to stop typing and wait until the step had passed. Recently Mitch had grown more and more concerned about her. Muggings, rapes, and robberies were on the increase in the neighborhood.

"I think you'd better lock the door when I'm not here and ask people knocking to identify themselves." She refused to do that. They would lose business.

An hour ago he had left for the city attorney's office. Before that she had heard him on the phone. He had tracked down the Texan who had signed the complaint charging Marilyn with theft.

"I hate to see you flying out here from Houston off and on for a year or so," she heard him saying. "You know how these cases drag on. . . . Yes, well, I'm also thinking of your wife. I don't see how we can keep this out of the papers. . . . Now hold on, I'm not going to give anything out. But all of this will be a matter of public record and I know it will get a big play in Houston. I don't like it but that's the way it is. . . . Now, look, I'm not trying to frighten you. I only want to be helpful. I've never met you but I know most Texans are gentlemen. It's part of your great heritage. You never take advantage of a woman. Now if you sit down and think about this, I know you wouldn't want to ruin a girl's future. . . . All right, so she's thirty and not a girl but she's still a lady. What people do in private is none of my business but when she comes into my office she acts like a lady and I treat her like a lady. . . . I'm not concerned about the nature of her business. I know, though, from dealing with her for years that she's a person of integrity. Isn't it possible that you lost your wallet somewhere? She swore to me she didn't take it. . . . I don't think she would swear before God she didn't if she didn't."

He crossed his fingers. "She goes to Mass every Sunday. . . . Well, all I ask is that you think it over—the trips you'll have to make out here, the stories in the Houston papers and on television, and most important, how you'll ruin a girl's life for a paltry eight hundred dollars."

He had barely hung up when Gail stormed in. "How could you! You talk about lawyers playing games, so what are *you* doing? And wipe that smirk off your face."

Mitch shifted uneasily. "Now, Shad, calm down. If he drops the action, I save the taxpayers money as well as clearing my client. Anything wrong with that?"

"I mean it, Mitch. You threatened him—"

He restrained a flash of anger. "I did not threaten him. I stated the facts. He'll have to return here for the trial and there may be postponements—"

"If you can arrange them."

"Right! I'm not going to see a wealthy guy shove a poor, defenseless woman around."

"Defenseless! She could take on a Tasmanian tiger."

He managed a smile. "Let's talk about it later, huh?"

She sat on his lap. "I didn't mean to get so wrought up but I don't like to see you . . ." His kisses stopped further comment. For a long moment he held her tightly, then threatened to dump her.

"Now get back to work before someone barges in and thinks I'm having an affair with my secretary."

The phone rang. The Texan promised he would refuse to press charges. He would inform the police he was mistaken. Still, there remained the city attorney who had the final decision, and Mitch had to talk with him. Without a complaining witness, the city attorney would have no case. He could, of course, force the Texan to testify but that was highly unlikely.

It was some moments before Gail recognized the distraught voice over the phone as Lefty's. He had lost Cathy. He had stepped outside the apartment to smoke, and when he returned she was gone. Gail told him to stay at Cathy's place until she reached Mitch, who would call with instructions.

For a long moment she sat in thought. Obviously, Cathy had a mission to run she did not want Lefty or Mitch to know about. Slowly Gail was beginning to have the same nagging doubts Mitch had had all along. When she was away from Cathy the doubts would burgeon but with her they vanished. She seemed forthright, honest, sensitive, utterly feminine and lovable. Yet it was evident that she was guilty of concealment. It could be a small matter, mostly an imaginary one. Or it could be of serious proportions, something illegal she had drifted into. One she thought she could handle and control, and no longer could.

Gail was pulled out of her speculation by the jerking, groaning halt of the ancient elevator at the far end of the corridor. A pair of footsteps approached, making their way slowly, deliberately. An older person, perhaps, or a young man taking his time, reconnoitering. Definitely they were a man's.

The doorknob turned, and Old Charlie, the night watchman, ambled in. "Evening, Miss Gail." He always called her "Miss Gail" and she liked it.

"For me?" she said, taking a long, narrow box he offered.

"Flowers, I suspect. Fellow drove up and gave them to me for you. How is Mr. Mitchell?"

"Fine. We missed you last week."

"Had a touch of Anno Domini. Grabs me and can't get out of bed. Be seeing you, Miss Gail. Sure happy you and Mr. Mitchell got hitched."

He shuffled out the door and she tore into the box. A dozen long-stemmed, dark roses. A note fluttered away. She grabbed for it but missed, and fumbled under the desk to rescue it.

The note was typed: GAIL, DARLING. I WON'T BE ABLE TO STAY FOR THE BURIAL. WOULD YOU BE A DARLING AND PUT THESE ROSES ON CATHY'S GRAVE?

There was no signature, written or typed.

15

Barney breezed into Hawk's office. He always gave the impression he was a time bomb about to explode. He was sweating but no matter how hot the sun, he had the energy to defy it when everyone about him was in slow motion.

He gave his report. Frank Mitchell, the attorney, had talked with the popcorn vendor before Barney reached him. Hawk's eyes took on the angry glint that came into them when a person or situation got in his way. "Damn that Mitch!"

Barney nodded. For a fiver a stranger had handed him, the vendor had delivered a large envelope to Catherine Doyle. First, he had opened it to find it contained a photograph of a section of the circus audience.

Next Barney had contacted the circus office and learned about the photographer, one Big Ed of Inglewood. "I had a little trouble there. I thought he was going to pull a rod on me. I threatened to take him in for resisting an officer. He said Mitchell knocked him down and tried to kill him. Fired a shot point blank but missed."

"Mitch did that? I don't believe it."

"I'm just repeating what he told me. He said a woman came in late yesterday afternoon, said she was from *Los Angeles* magazine, and they wanted several crowd shots. She gave him the sections she wanted."

"A woman?"

"That's what I couldn't figure, either. He could've been lying, to throw us off. Said she was about sixty, average height, not slim, not heavy . . . you know, the kind of description that could fit half the female population of that age. I'll type up a report."

"A woman," Hawk repeated, thinking. "About sixty. Doesn't fit, does it? You know I'm coming around to your idea of pulling Lefty Morgan in. Make an informant out of him. Give him some hamburger money."

"He may blow us."

"I don't think so. He runs scared all the time. A rabbit."

Barney was on his way out when Hawk called him back. "Barney," he said quietly. Barney tensed, knowing that tone presaged trouble.

"Barney, what's wrong with your Porsche?"

Barney looked away. "It's—it's getting along in years. Sort of beaten up."

"Exactly how old?"

"Three. Why do you ask?"

"The Mercedes people called. About that $24,000 model.

They wanted a credit reference. I couldn't give it to them. I'm sorry, Barney, but you're going to have to get along with that old, beaten-up Porsche. I know what a traumatic shock this is but people somehow do get along with old Porsches, you know, and manage to eke out some happiness."

Hawk got his coat from a rack, preparatory to leaving. "You've got to shape up on two points. One, live within your salary and give the collection agencies a rest. And two, women. For heaven's sake, Barney, at least pick your girls as carefully as you would a horse at Santa Anita. That old bag I saw you with at the coffee shop the other morning, she's old enough to be your mother."

Barney swallowed. "She *is* my mother."

Hawk stopped deadstill. "Oh, what the hell," he said, blustering out the door.

Hawk and the General made their way slowly and with care down a long, dark, rambling corridor that dipped and rose. They passed the dim outlines of doors that seemed sealed by time. They heard only low murmurs and the gurgling of water to indicate that somewhere behind those doors might be life of some kind.

"Can't she afford a better dump?" Hawk asked.

"She gets a thousand a month from her ex," the General said softly, "but she starts drinking when she gets up and doesn't quit until she goes to bed. Not that she's ever drunk. To talk with her you'd never know she had a drink. Doesn't seem to hurt her brain. She's never muddled. It's the liquor bill that keeps her down here."

The General had a spring to his step that Hawk didn't know he still had. He talked livelier. He was no longer a pensioner to be tolerated. He was handling an important lead, dealing with an important informant. Once again he felt the equal of the younger officers.

In semi-darkness, the General knocked on a door in the far recesses of this aging rabbit warren. He called out softly, "It's me. Ed."

Marissa Dubrovnik swung the door wide open. She was more handsome than Hawk remembered. She was in a pink negligee that revealed little but suggested a figure trim for her forty-odd years. Her raven hair fell loose about her shoulders, giving her a seductive look. She had the neck scar fairly well concealed with heavy make-up.

She gave the General an affectionate kiss on the cheek which embarrassed him. Hawk wondered about their relationship. One of the cardinal rules of dealing with an informant was never to become emotionally involved.

"You remember Lieutenant Hawkins," the General said.

She led them inside, walking with a decided limp. "So good of you to come, Lieutenant." She took the General's arm to balance herself. "It's getting worse." She indicated her right leg. "The doctor says I'll be on crutches soon."

Although the room was quite large, actually expansive, it looked crowded. A single bed took care of one corner with an expensive velvet spread pulled neatly over it. By its side was an Italian, gold-leafed stand with several books stacked on top, a clock, a few pill containers, a diary, pens and pencils, and a picture. In another corner was a tiny open kitchen with a midget refrigerator and a hot plate. To Hawk's right, she had arranged chairs to suggest a sitting room. The chairs faced a television set that sat on a low Italian table, done also in gold leaf.

Hawk noted all this quickly, then his gaze went to the wall over the sitting area. Across the entire area were blown-up pictures in color of Marissa Dubrovnik in the nude, shots from the years when she had posed for all those magazines.

"Not bad, huh?" she said teasingly. "Puddie—that's my husband or was—Puddie used to say I had the best body he'd ever seen. It's pretty much gone now, the body is, but I plastered these up to remind myself that I was once something. An ego trip, I guess you'd call it. Sit down over here. How about a drink?"

Hawk shook his head. Without asking, she brought a Bourbon for the General, and Hawk took note. The rule was: never drink while on duty.

She broke up their idle chatter. "Let's get down to business.

First, I want you to know, Lieutenant, that I don't like being an informant. I don't like ratting on people. I would never do it to Puddie because he's a great guy. To me he is, maybe not to you, but I don't give a damn what others think. Sure, he kicked me out after the accident but I knew the score. I knew when I got older there'd be another. A young one. That's how men are made. I've figured it out that a man needs a young woman every decade of his life to keep him running strong. So I had a decade and a half. I was lucky."

She took a cigarette from a gold-plated case and the General was quick to light it. "Thank you, Ed."

She continued, "But the others, well, I've a daughter in a private school. She's seventeen and beautiful and smart. I never thought much about how this world was run until she got into her teens and then I got to thinking, what a lousy place it is, and why don't I do something to try to clean it up for her and all the other kids coming along. So, I rat on the bastards. I don't like it but I do it. For her and for the money. Yes, the money. I need it. Five hundred bucks today, Lieutenant. And what I've got to tell you, it's a bargain. I ought to ask a thousand."

Hawk produced five hundred-dollar bills. He put one bill on the glass cocktail table, but kept the other four in his hand. He smoothed the one bill out.

He leaned back, molding his body comfortably to the easy chair. "For a hundred, what do I get?"

She stared at him out of hard, calculating eyes. "You don't trust me?"

"I don't buy a pig in a poke."

"He means . . ." the General began.

"I don't buy a suit without trying it on."

"You're a damn arrogant bastard."

"Maybe a bastard but not arrogant."

"It's my neck if they catch me talking to you."

"It's your decision, talk or not."

She got to her feet. "To hell with you." She limped about.

Hawk picked up the hundred-dollar bill. He was sweating. The General sat immobile. He could never handle a female informant in this manner. He guessed he was old-fashioned. With Hawk, his approach was the same, man or woman. "You've got to watch out for the seductive ones," Hawk had said. "They'll put you to the gun quicker than any man."

She eased herself back down. In doing so she arranged the peignoir so that it partly revealed her breasts. What an old trick, to soften up a man.

"It's the Carney outfit." The words came out businesslike. She had made her pitch, put on an act, and took rejection the way a good salesman would.

Hawk put the bill back on the table. He took a deep breath. He had bluffed and won. Now he would get more of the story, more details for his money. She would be less tempted to hold back, to tell the General tomorrow that she had come across additional information and milk them for another few hundred.

She continued, "They operate out of Miami under the name of the Hong Kong Finance Company. Don't ask me why Hong Kong because they have no association with Hong Kong in any way. I guess it's good psychology. Does sound important, like a big English banking conglomerate. They're into stolen securities and treasury notes and bonds. Anything that's negotiable and not registered. Do you know that there are about a hundred million dollars' worth of stolen securities floating around? And more coming on the market every day? It's so easy for a clerk or someone in a brokerage house to pick up a few and walk out and nobody knows they're even gone until months later, sometimes years."

Hawk interrupted. "Give me the setup. I want specifics. Names."

"You'll get one name. Only one. He's the only one out here."

Hawk put another hundred-dollar bill on the table and leaned back. He noted the General still hadn't touched his Bourbon. She was on her third straight scotch.

She leaned over to pick up the two bills. "His name's Sammy Porter. He's known as Soft Shoe, and also Sammy Oscar and Ralph Catania. I don't know him, never met him, but I've heard a lot about him. He lives in Tucson, has a wife and two children. Lives quietly in a wealthy area up in the Catalina foothills, near the Skyline Country Club, on a street off Camino Arenosa. Now and then he gets a call from the Mafia or one of the other mobs when they want a job done quietly. He's very smooth and gets results. His reputation is that he's an expert in terror. He killed an old man once that way. Never touched him. Simply frightened him to death. He calls it the Chinese water torture."

She poured herself another drink and deftly pushed the General's full glass out of sight under a floral arrangement. "He started out in New York as a limousine driver, got to chauffering one of Anastasia's old mob around and he offered him a job. He's been moving up fast. He doesn't have a reputation as a killer but my friend says he is. He applies the terror technique first since the authorities don't get too stirred up over threats. But he'll kill, my friend says."

Hawk sat up straighter. He had a name. So often informants never came up with one. They couldn't nail a friend and live with themselves. "Where do we find this guy?"

"He's around."

"You don't know?"

"I know."

Hawk put another bill on the table.

"He's at a Beverly Hills hotel. One of the big ones. I don't know which one."

"What name is he registered under?"

"Samuel J. Oscar."

"What about a woman? About sixty."

"A woman? I didn't hear anything about a woman. Sammy usually works by himself."

"What's he out here for?"

"To collect a million dollars."

"From whom?"

"Don't push me. I'm trying to think."

He put the fourth hundred-dollar bill down.

She smiled. "He's been sent here to talk with someone by

the name of Catherine Doyle, who lives in Sherman Oaks. I don't have the street address."

"She has the money? A million dollars?"

"More than that."

"Cash or securities."

"I don't know. I imagine, negotiable securities."

"Where'd they come from?"

"I don't know. You have a record on her?"

"Let's say, she came to our attention recently. A college kid. Graduated in June."

"They like them young. Especially the Carney outfit. You're more daring when you're twenty-two."

"What else about the deal?"

She shrugged and Hawk tossed the last bill with the others. She scooped them up and pulled her peignoir about her throat. She no longer had reason to stir up the male libido.

"I don't have the details but apparently she defected. They sent Soft Shoe out to reason with her, if he can, and if not, to get the money any way he can."

"To kill her?"

"They don't play games very long. You know that, Lieutenant."

Hawk nodded. "I can't quite picture her . . . She was at Pitzer all last year but I suppose she could have been a mail drop for them. Holding hot money until it cooled. A nice college kid in a small prestigious college."

"I came to the same conclusion."

"Will you be getting more information?"

"What more do you want? You've got the girl's name, and Soft Shoe's, and where he's staying, and a general outline of what the operation is. You got yourself a good five hundred dollars' worth. The next time around don't treat me like some cheap con woman."

"And don't you call me an arrogant bastard, you hear?"

After they were gone, she sat a long time in the dark, drinking. Then she hobbled over to the television, switched on the light in the two porcelain cats, and from underneath the set took out a picture of a young girl, a carbon copy of herself at seventeen. She never displayed it where friends from the old days might see it. They might insist on meeting her, and offering her a "job."

She remembered herself at seventeen. Papa was a barber and every morning at seven, he trudged off with his lunch in a brown paper bag. Soon afterward, her mother, a salesgirl at J. C. Penney, would leave. Marissa could see them still. There had been happy weekends at the beach in the summer, movies, bowling, neighbors in for parties, dates, and vacations to Wisconsin's lakes. A happy time.

Seventeen. Almost all A's in school. A chance to model. Her first check a fortune, three hundred dollars. An older man, a brilliant talker, attentive, gentle, generous. Her first modeling in the nude. The human body was beautiful, he said. Her parents pleading with her to return to school and to her high school sweetheart.

She put the photograph on top of the television. Cheri, Cheri, she whispered, finish school, and please to God, marry some nice ordinary guy. A barber, a shoe clerk, a truck driver, a bank teller.

She finished off the bottle and was dozing when the knock came. Gently, at first, and not sharp enough to stir her. Then, quite hard, and she got to her feet with effort. Slowly, she returned the photo to its hiding place. The knocking grew more persistent and the doorknob was turning, rattling.

16

From Mitch's office, Cathy drove straight home with Lefty sitting alongside her. His slow, easy talk calmed her.

"Use to wanta be a mouthpiece like Mitch. Studied it a little. Did ya know it's a crime in Los Angeles to shoot a jack rabbit from a moving street car?"

He had a nice, low laugh. "They never take the old laws off the books. Just keep piling 'em up year after year."

Constantly she watched the rearview mirror but saw no one following her. Once in the apartment, she told Lefty to make himself at home. She headed straight for the phone and with nervous fingers, dialed her father in North Carolina. "That number's not in service any longer," an operator with a southern accent informed her.

She didn't understand. He would have no reason to discontinue phone service. He had described his home and the town so graphically that she had a vivid mental picture. He lived in a great, old white mansion with pre-Civil War pillars. The street was called Butler, named after a distinguished family, some of whom still resided along it. It was a wide, winding street through a thin forest and the homes were set far back in rolling expanses of green. His had several wings and cathedral ceilings. What fascinated her the most was his description of the atrium: apples strung on a dogwood tree. Downtown there was a Confederate soldier turned green by the years, and a plaque that said a Provincial Council officer had founded the town in 1775.

She dialed the information number for North Carolina.

"What city?" the operator asked.

"Clinton. The name's Joseph Y. Doyle."

After a few seconds, the operator said, "I have no number for Joseph Y. Doyle. Could it be listed under another name?"

"Would you try Fayetteville?" Her father had occasionally mentioned trips to nearby Fayetteville.

"Sorry, no Joseph Y. Doyle."

In the kitchen she found Lefty washing dishes and remonstrated with him. "Worked one time in a hash house. Can't get your daddy, huh?"

She walked about thinking. "I've got to reach him. I've just got to." He had promised to call her immediately on returning to Clinton and never before had he failed to follow through. Something had happened.

"Mitch never told me what this was all about," Lefty was saying.

Absently she said, "I'll ask him to tell you. I can't myself without talking to him first. You understand?"

"Sure, ma'am. I don't pry. Never have. Mind my own business. Always have. You got any other kinfolks, ma'am? Living?"

She shook her head. "I was an only child."

"Me, too. Never knew my father, and mother was an old sot. Beg pardon, miss, didn't mean to—"

"I understand. No reason to glorify a woman just because she's a mother. Doesn't automatically nominate her for sainthood. I bet you had a rough childhood."

Doglike he lapped up the sympathy. "Yeah, I got kicked around a lot and was in trouble most of the time. Did some things I oughten a done."

She recognized the knock at the door. Mr. Blanton. He had a book he thought she would like to read. All the time he was craning his neck. *The old goat. He thinks I'm having an affair.*

She introduced Lefty and added, "He's a friend of my father."

Mr. Blanton had something to say but strangely held back. He coughed a few times, remarked about the heat, then backed to the door. "Miss Cathy . . ."

"What is it, Mr. Blanton?"

"Your birthday, it is the sixteenth, isn't it?"

She showed her surprise. "How did you know?"

He relaxed. "I got spies everywhere. You wouldn't believe it."

After he was gone, Lefty lit a cigarette. "Do you mind, ma'am?" He saw she did. "I'll just step outside."

She moved about absently tidying up. She was deeply puzzled. She had not mentioned her birthday to anyone in the complex, and except for Gary no friends had been around. Gary would not have brought up the subject. How could Mr. Blanton have found out and why was he interested?

She laid her clothes out for the next day, then on the first ring, grabbed the phone. It was a woman's voice, deep-throated.

"Miss Doyle?"

"Yes."

"I'm a neighbor of Gary's—"

"Mrs. Grayson?"

"Yes. He's been hurt badly. He was in an accident out in front of the house. The paramedics are on their way. He keeps asking for you. Can you come at once? He may be dying. I don't know. He's bad hurt."

"Oh, my God! Tell him I'm coming. I'm coming right away. Tell him to hold on, hold on."

She slammed the receiver down and ran for the door. *The car keys. Where are the car keys? In my purse. But where's my purse?*

Frantically she checked all the likely places and found the purse in the kitchen. She was barely out the door when she began shouting for Lefty. She never broke her run for the carport, but all the time was screaming his name.

The car wouldn't start. She hadn't turned the key in the ignition slot. It roared under the hard press of her foot and shot back recklessly. A horn sounded loudly behind her and she braked to let another car pass. The driver shouted something. Once more she cried, "Mr. Morgan!"

In her rearview mirror she saw the figure of a man dwindling ever smaller. It could have been Mr. Morgan. She couldn't go back, she simply couldn't.

Oh, God, be with Gary. Please, God.

Traffic ahead grew misty. She was crying. She saw through the windshield as if in a rain and there were no wipers. Once she swerved in time to avoid hitting a Volkswagen. Once she ran a red sign and heard the shrieking brakes of a car on her right.

Briefly she thought, it's a hoax, a trick. But Mrs. Grayson had called, and she had been beside herself.

Don't get your boy friend in on this. They're awfully good at staging accidents.

Awfully good at staging accidents.

Stop signals tore her insides apart. By only a minute or two, they delayed her. At those times, however, she saw Gary bleeding and suffering. A minute could set her imagination off on a wild spree. A minute might mean the difference between seeing him, kissing him, holding him, and being told he was gone.

Gone? No one used words such as that. Not gone, or passed away. In school we were taught to say "she died" and "death was near." One faced up to death. One didn't clothe it in euphemisms. But what did it matter what phraseology one used? If "gone" was gentler, she thought, why not use "gone"?

She whispered prayers. She believed in prayer, believed that prayers were answered. Her father always ended his letters, "God be with you," and when she was a little girl, he had admonished her to attend Sunday school and church. Her mother was too busy, but Cathy had gone because he wanted her to, and anything he wanted she would do happily.

Bringing the car to a rocking stop before the house, she noted no one was about, and the panic burgeoned. They had taken him away. She went running, sobbing, up to the door, pounded on it, heard George barking. Turning the knob she found the door unlocked and pushed in past George, who jumped all over her, barking with joy. She screamed, "Gary! Gary!" knowing if he were there he could not hear his name, yet having to scream it. His bedroom was empty, the bed made, everything in order—he was a neat person—and there was no one in the tiny guest room. She glanced in the bathroom and then in desperation, knowing she was too late, went to the kitchen.

There he stood by the stove, his back to her, putting on a casserole. Her touch frightened him. He whirled about as if set upon. She was crying and hugging him. He tried to lift her face so he could see her lips but couldn't. He gathered her up in his arms and carried her to the living room where, still holding her, he sat on the sofa.

She felt the trembling in his arms and knew he was terrified. Something awful had happened and he couldn't hear. George, sensing tragedy, snuggled up to them, whining low. He, too, couldn't fathom what the crying was about.

She fought down the tears and gained control of herself. Leaning away from Gary, so he could see her lips, she told him Mrs. Grayson had called and said he had been badly hurt in an automobile accident.

"She said she thought you were dying." Once again she couldn't hold back the sobs. "Oh, Gary, I love you, I love you."

His comprehension was slow in coming. "Mrs. Grayson? It couldn't have been Mrs. Grayson. She's working at the bank."

He held her a moment tightly in his arms. She heard his heart and it was beating as hard as hers. "It was a hoax, Cathy, one of those terrible telephone calls people get now and then from someone who's sick, terribly sick."

"Gary, let's get married. Tonight. I need you, Gary. I love you. There's this church out near where I live that I go to and we can phone the pastor and maybe have it at his home."

"I haven't any money. I can't support you. And it wouldn't work out. God, Cathy, don't think I don't want to. I love you so bad it hurts. I want you day and night. I keep trying to figure it out, how maybe we could, but I always come up with the same old answers."

"Tonight, Gary. It's got to be tonight."

"California requires a three-day waiting period."

She didn't hear. "I've got a little money in the bank and a job coming up Monday. And you'll get a job. You'll make it big. I know you will."

"Maybe a caretaker somewhere."

"Don't talk that way!"

He kissed her until it hurt.

She broke away. "I've got it all worked out. We'll get married, I've got this job, and we'll get by, and you'll go to California State at Northridge this fall and get your BA and maybe a master's."

Talking was helping her forget the phone call and the resultant terror.

"And let you support me? No way!"

"Other guys do—and you're no different from other guys."

"Now wait a minute—"

"If it would make you feel better, I won't give you a nickel.

I'll support myself and you can make it on your own. I'll have steaks nights and you potato chips."

He smiled, "You're something, Cathy."

"You'll think about it?"

"Yeah."

"Seriously?"

"Yeah."

She reeled about at the ringing of the phone. She said, "The phone," so he would know, and went into the dining room to answer it.

She collapsed in a chair at the sound of the voice. The criminal. She turned so Gary could not read her lips. George quietly nuzzled her legs.

"Cathy dear, I've been wanting to talk with you—"

Before she realized it, she was screaming. "What a horrible, horrible thing to do to anybody. You're sick, sick, sick . . ."

His voice rose. "Listen, Cathy, it wasn't my idea. . . . Shut up, will you, and listen. . . . I said it wasn't my idea. But I'm not getting anywhere with you—and I've been nice to you but you brought the police last night and the Security officers and your lawyer. I feel sorry for you but I told you, I warned you—"

"You're cruel, cruel!"

"Please, Cathy, I'm doing what I can but you've got to come through. Do you know what They are talking about. They're proposing that there be a double funeral and burial. You and your boy friend."

"Oh, God!"

"They were going to kill you today but I pleaded with Them and They said if I could get the money tonight . . ."

She tightened her fist, lowered her voice, and managed to speak as if she were handling a business transaction. "I've instructed my attorney, Frank Mitchell, to handle all negotiations with you. You talk with him."

There was a pause. He had not anticipated this development. "Does he have the money?"

"I've promised him that I will not discuss the matter. He will handle it."

"If this is a trick . . ."

"He tells me it is not without precedent. He says lawyers often negotiate in the case of ransom and other payoffs."

"This is *not* a ransom! It's *our* money. All right, I'll call your lawyer but if he doesn't come across with the money, there's nothing in the world I can do to stop Them. Just remember, a double funeral, a double burial."

With a "Good night, Cathy," he hung up.

She sat in shock. Gary asked, "Who was that? What was that all about?"

It took a second to corral her scattered-shot thoughts. "A man. He's been bothering me. He seems to think I owe him money. He had a woman call and tell me you'd been injured. He's threatening to do something to me."

She looked away. Her hands moved nervously. *Don't get your boy friend in on this.* . . . Now she had to, so he could be on the lookout, take precautions.

She continued, "He says if I don't pay up, he'll do something to you. I don't know what he's talking about."

Gary dropped into a chair across from her. "Where does he get the idea you owe him something?"

"I don't know. I honestly don't. Oh, Gary, if he hurts you because of me, if he does anything . . ."

"I can handle him."

"He talks wild. He might try anything. He says it'd be easy to set up an accident."

"Rubbish!"

"I don't think so. He'd do anything to get the money."

"How much?"

"A lot. A million dollars."

"A million dollars!"

"Crazy, isn't it?"

"What do the police say? Why haven't you told me before?"

"It just happened. I didn't want to alarm you. I've got an attorney. He's handling it for me."

"You didn't call the police?"

"He said They'd kill me if I went to the police. And you, Gary, you . . . Please don't press me. I don't know what it's all about. Honest."

He was puzzled. He couldn't assimilate it all. "You'd better bunk down here tonight."

"I've got a girl friend coming over."

"I didn't mean—"

"I know you didn't."

She got up. "I've got to be going."

"I'll follow you in my car."

"I was hoping you would. Oh, Gary." She went into his arms. He pressed her against the wall until their bodies melded.

"I've got to be going," she repeated. "I love you. Oh, God, how I love you."

He had questions, lots of them, but she was leaving. He had the strangest feeling she was running from his questions. Of course, that was in his imagination.

As he followed her home, he found himself with a stranglehold on the wheel. *Cathy, what are you into that a stranger threatens you? And to add to the torture, threatens me after perpetrating a cruel hoax? Cathy, what is going on? I want to help you, Cathy. You've got to let me help you.*

17

Although there was nothing to forewarn him, Lefty Morgan was destined to have a busy evening. After he left Cathy, upon Gail's arrival to spend the night with her, he headed for McDonald's where he had three hamburgers and two Cokes. He fished out an old toothpick from a vest pocket and was working with it when a man who identified himself as Officer Barney Carlson stepped up. He said that Lieutenant Hawkins had long wanted to meet Lefty and would Lefty accompany him to Hawk's office.

Lefty's toothpick started quivering. "What you booking me on?"

"You're being invited, sir, not booked."

The "sir" bothered Lefty. "Do I have any choice?"

"Of course. However, if you don't accept the invitation, the lieutenant might suspect your motives."

"I don't know what you're talking about."

Barney smiled. "I don't, either. Come on, Lefty, let's go."

By the time they reached Hawk's office, Lefty was a basket case. Hawk rose quickly, offered his hand, asked him to sit down, and suggested Barney shake out a cigarette for Lefty.

"You may not know this, Mr. Morgan," Hawk began, "but we have any number of fine, upstanding citizens who co-operate with us. That is, help us. Naturally, when they give up their valuable time, they should be compensated. To get down to brass tacks, we would like to enlist your assistance on a case from time to time. We know it would be a sacrifice for you and we could only offer you two hundred dollars a month—for car expenses."

"A stool pigeon."

Hawk was shocked. "We quit using stool pigeons years ago, Mr. Morgan. But we do have aides the same as the President of the United States has."

What a con man, Barney thought, watching Hawk with unabashed admiration.

"What you want me to do?" Lefty's eyes swiveled nervously.

"We ask our good citizens who help us to hold everything in confidence, and we know you would. We have to explain to some that there are laws about obstructing justice by talking too much and rather severe fines and sentences but with you, of course, we would never mention such a thing. We know you would never divulge a word of what is being said here to, well, say Frank Mitchell. Are we in accord on that?"

"Are we what?"

"Do you agree?"

Lefty shrugged. "If you say so. I've got principles."

"That's why we invited you to come here tonight."

"What do I do first? As a good citizen?"

The irony was not lost on Hawk. "Well, to get on with it, we happened to see you at the circus last night, and we saw

Frank Mitchell and his wife and a girl named Catherine Doyle. As a good citizen, can you tell me what they were all doing there?"

"I dunno."

"Why were you there?"

"Mitch asked me."

"What for?"

"To help the Doyle girl if anybody tried to hurt her."

"Who would hurt her?"

"Mitch didn't say."

"We have information she has a lot of money, maybe as much as a million dollars, and someone's trying to get it from her."

"How much?"

"Maybe a million."

"Somebody's handing you a lot of crap."

"How much has she got then?"

"Nobody said anything to me about money. Just that she might get hurt."

"Didn't Mitch say who was going to hurt her or why?"

"He didn't tell me nothing."

"Now look, Mr. Morgan, all of our good citizens are very frank with us. They don't hide the facts. You sat in the bushes out in Encino watching a residence where Miss Doyle was house-sitting, and you sat behind her at the circus, and you sat outside her room at the hospital all night, and you were with her all day. Are you telling us that you don't know why you did all of this, a man of your stature?"

"A man of what?"

"A busy man like you."

"I did it because Mitch asked me to. He's my friend. I do things for him, he does things for me."

"You mean to tell me he never told you anything at all about Miss Doyle, and she didn't either, even if you were with her all day."

"I didn't ask."

Hawk slumped back in exasperation. "Get him out of here," he said to Barney.

"When do I get my two hundred dollars?" Lefty asked.

"Get the hell out of here," Hawk shouted.

Lefty shuffled out, mumbling, "A fine way to treat a good citizen."

Lefty talked to himself all the way home. That Hawk had a nerve asking him to turn stool pigeon. He wouldn't rat on his worst enemy, if he had one, which he didn't. Most everyone liked him. That was because he had principles. A time or two he chuckled to himself. He had told the absolute truth. He had no idea what was happening, and he was glad he didn't know. Not if Hawk was interested.

The girl was in trouble, and he felt badly about that. He had grown to like her immensely. He wished he had a daughter like her. She treated him with respect, and seemed fond of him. She was thoughtful, like asking him if he wanted coffee, if he didn't want to rest after such a long night, if he wished to phone anyone and tell them where he was. She was appreciative and few people were these days. Several times she had thanked him for watching over her last night and staying with her all day.

He parked before a small, respectable apartment building, a rabbit warren near Pico and Overland. The cops might give him a ticket for leaving his car there all night but he was weary and anxious to be inside his own hutch.

As he stepped out of the car, the figure of a man—it was so dark he couldn't see his features—approached him. A stick-up, he thought. He wasn't particularly alarmed because as soon as he identified himself, the man would move on. It was a little courtesy between members of the same fraternity.

"May I stop you for just a moment, sir?"

There was that "sir" again. Two con men the same night.

The man continued, "I'm one of the Carney boys and since you're working either for Frank Mitchell or Catherine Doyle—"

"Mitch."

"Thank you. We're in a bad situation and thought you could help us. The Doyle girl has a million two hundred thousand dollars of ours and refuses to turn it over."

"A million . . ." There was that figure again. He couldn't believe it.

"A million two—and we're offering her a hundred thousand . . ."

"A million!"

"You didn't know?"

"Somebody's on angel dust."

"It's our money and she's got it hidden somewhere. We thought you might know where and for a price, something like twenty thousand dollars, you might tell us and help us recover what is ours from this little sneak thief."

"Twenty thousand?" His heart pounded. He had to watch it. He had angina.

"What about thirty thousand?"

"Thirty thousand?"

"Fifty—and that's it. Plus we might do you a favor sometime."

"I don't know where it is."

"Has Mr. Mitchell got it?"

"He didn't say nothing about it."

"The girl—did you look around? Did she go poking around somewhere, like checking a hiding place?"

"She ran out on me this afternoon."

"Yes, yes, we know about that. Would you like to get her to talking, and also Mr. Mitchell, see what you can learn?"

"I got to think about it."

"I'll check with you tomorrow. Remember, fifty thousand dollars in cash. Bills that can't be traced. You don't have to pay any income tax."

Lefty leaned against the car. He'd be glad when he got back into his old routine. No one putting the pressure on him.

A million dollars and then some. And that penny-pinching Mitch, working him all night and all day, and all he was getting was a hundred bucks. Mitch, his friend. No wonder he refused to tell him about the case.

And the girl. It hurt him deeply to know she was in a racket. He had thought she was a fine, sweet girl. Well, it just went to show you never could tell.

Fifty thousand. A laundered fifty thousand. He would keep on the lookout. Shouldn't be too difficult, if he kept his eyes peeled, to spot a likely hiding place. He would teach that Mitch a lesson that Mitch would never forget.

18

Mitch was about to leave the office when Hawk strode in. He never knocked. He just appeared. It was a little after nine and Mitch was not in the mood to welcome anyone, least of all Hawk.

"Hello, Mitch," Hawk said. "Thought I'd drop by to see how you're doing."

Mitch gathered up some papers. "I was just leaving."

"Where's Gail?"

Mitch frowned. "Home."

"It's a hell of a way to get a free secretary."

"What about the free psychologist you're getting?"

"Not yet."

"That's right. Think it over carefully. Take ten years or so."

Hawk put his big frame down carefully into a chair that was losing its stuffing. "I want some information."

"About Catherine Doyle?"

Hawk's right leg, crossing over his left, stopped in mid-air. He recovered quickly. "I'll put it right out in the open. We've come into information that she is involved in a crime that is either in progress or about to be committed."

"I have no knowledge of that."

"You mean to tell me you don't know anything at all—"

Mitch bristled. "You've no right to approach an attorney about a client."

Hawk slapped the chair arm and dust rose. "I do if that attorney might be involved—"

"She's not involved in any crime, past or present, and neither am I. Now . . . I've already told you more than I should have."

"I don't know why we are always locking horns," Hawk said resignedly. "You're not a bad guy. Just stubborn, devious, evasive, uncompromising . . ."

"Thank you."

"If you're covering up a crime—"

"Since when are you a prosecuting attorney?"

"I don't want to see you disbarred."

"I appreciate your concern."

Hawk used the straight-into-the-eye technique. "Something was going on out at the Forum and you were a part of it."

"Yes, we went out to see the circus. Gail and I."

"You didn't sit together. And this Doyle woman just happened to be there? And that little bit of slime, Lefty Morgan? And every Security man on the Forum's payroll?"

"It was quite a gathering, wasn't it? These coincidences always amaze me."

Hawk persisted. "I'll give you the benefit of the doubt. Maybe she isn't being honest with you."

"About what?"

Hawk gave up the eyeball-to-eyeball strategy. This Mitch was one tough guy. "I'm sure you told her that if she knows anything about a crime she should report the facts to us—or she'll be guilty of obstructing justice, maybe being an accessory before or after the crime. Does she know that?"

"I'll give her your message."

"For the record, you know nothing about a crime in progress or committed?"

"I said and I repeat that my client is not involved in any manner whatsoever in a crime, to the best of my knowledge."

Hawk got to his feet. He would try the towering-over-them technique. "What do you mean, to the best of my knowledge? Why do you lawyers hide behind phrases like that . . . to the best of my knowledge. Do you have doubts?"

Mitch was enjoying himself. He had Hawk off balance. "Most people," he said casually, "cannot state flatly something they do not know fully or remember exactly."

"I repeat, do you have doubts?"

"You haven't any business coming here, trying to break down an attorney-client relationship that the law considers as holy as that between a priest and a communicant at the confessional."

"Don't go dragging religion into this. As I said, you're devious, evasive—"

"Don't keep flattering me. It's embarrassing."

Hawk backed toward the door. "One thing we agree on, we hate each other's guts."

"Let's leave it at that," Mitch said pleasantly. "I like to know where I stand with a man."

"Okay. See you again sometime, Mitch, I hope not. Give Gail my sympathy. I don't know what gets into a fine woman like Gail . . ."

Mitch tilted back in the swivel. He had bested Hawk and that didn't always happen. Hawk was a shrewd interrogator who thought exceedingly fast. He would move down one corridor of a maze and if blocked, swiftly explore another.

Mitch's euphoria soon faded. What was it Hawk said? . . . "We've come into information that she is involved in a crime that is either in progress or about to be committed."

What did Hawk know that he, Mitch, did not?

19

Shortly after seven, Gail had arrived at Cathy's apartment. Lefty was waiting impatiently to be off for McDonald's. He had raided Cathy's refrigerator twice without satisfying his hunger. We can't afford him, Gail thought. He's worse than a teen-ager.

When Gail approached him about returning the next morning, he hesitated. Cathy said, "Would you, please? It would mean so much to me." He capitulated and Gail was amused. Older men were invariably susceptible to a girl's attentions.

When he was gone, Cathy burst out with an account of the phone call telling her Gary was injured and perhaps dying, and all that happened thereafter. She was shaken in reliving the episode but managed to keep a tight rein over her emotions. Occasionally she stopped when that control seemed about to slip away. Gail was to learn later that Cathy believed in talking to herself, admonishing her nerves to be still, her heart to slow down. "It's autogenics," she said. "I can tell any part of my body what to do."

Now she said, "Poor Mr. Morgan. He was terribly upset. But I didn't run out on him. I kept calling for him all the way to the car. He says he got to talking with Mr. Blanton and they drifted off. He should've heard me. I think I was screaming. Can I get you something? Coffee? Tea? I've got some little cakes."

"I'd like tea."

She put the kettle on. "It just isn't me any longer. It's Gary, too. A double burial, a double funeral, he said. I know They're doing everything They can to break me. I'm sure They mean it, too, if They don't get the money. I can't take a chance. You and Mr. Mitchell were right. I should've gone to the police. I never dreamed They'd bring Gary into it and threaten to kill him along with me."

She reached a conclusion. "I'll call the police but give me a few hours. Just a few hours. I've got to talk with my father. This girl, I was in a sociology class with her, she lives in Raleigh, and I called her, and she said she had friends in Clinton, and she'd phone them, and try to locate my father."

The teapot whistled. Gail asked quietly, "Is he involved—in some way?"

Cathy whirled about. "Why do you keep asking me such horrible questions?"

"I'm sorry. But it was only a natural reaction to your waiting to call the police until . . ."

Cathy poured the tea. "I'm not involved—and he isn't. They

are here, aren't They? After me, not in North Carolina after him."

They took the tea into the living room. Cathy turned up the air conditioning. The heat still persisted in the nineties. They sat about a low cocktail table which consisted of a sheet of stained plywood, cut artistically, set on a piece of old stump. ("The whole thing cost me six-fifty.") The table was cluttered with books. A large sculptured head of an African native girl served as centerpiece. ("A girl friend sculpted it for me.")

She said softly, "I always talk with him when I'm in trouble. Like when I was only fifteen, and this boy held up a service station, and wanted me to testify he was with me at my home that night. I was paralyzed until I talked with my father."

"And not your mother?"

Idly Cathy thumbed through a paperback copy of Tolkien's *The Silmarillion*. "She was too busy. I want to tell Mr. Morgan what this is all about. He doesn't know and if he's going to stay days with me, I think he should. Is there any reason—"

"Let's wait and see Mitch about that."

Cathy picked up a large envelope. "Take a look at this. I found it on my doorstep. I didn't say anything to Mr. Morgan about it."

She took out a three-by-five white file card. Gail read: ". . . around the body of the king they bury one of his concubines, first killing her by strangling . . . and some golden cups . . . and raise a vast mound above the grave . . . seeking to make it as tall as possible . . . fifty young men are killed along with fifty horses, and the dead horses and riders are mounted around the royal tomb . . ."

Gail was bewildered. "What does it mean? I don't get it."

Cathy shrugged. "Something to frighten me. Rather awful. Fifty dead men on fifty dead horses. Must be from one of the ancient writers. I had a course once in Ancient Literature. Homer and the *Iliad*, that kind of thing. That's nothing, though. Look at this."

She handed Gail a newspaper clipping, neatly trimmed. Gail's face turned dark on looking at the gruesome picture of a girl dead in a clump of shrubs. Her body was twisted about like an old gunny sack heaved out of a passing car. The headline read: GIRL STRANGLED IN NORTH WOODS. The story gave details but Gail's eyes went to the notation along one edge, carefully printed: "One of the Gorilla's jobs."

"Oh, God," Gail whispered to herself. There was nothing to indicate where North Woods was. The date and newspaper's name had been clipped off.

Cathy was saying, "I guess I'm supposed to come apart. Go into hysterics. But I'm all right. That is, I'm all right now but suddenly I'll collapse. I have in the past, under pressure. It wears on me and I don't know it. Then, wham, it's like someone knocks my legs out from under me."

After a moment, Gail said, "I've got something to tell you. Mitch and I talked about it and we couldn't make up our minds. But you've got to know."

Cathy straightened. She set her jaw to take another blow.

Gail told her about the roses that Old Charlie had delivered. "There was this note attached," Gail continued, "that I should put them on your grave. It said that he—the sender—wouldn't be here at the time. Mitch thinks They've got a plan, all written out. 'Send roses tonight.' They check it off hour by hour."

Cathy finished her tea in one swallow. "Roses. How long do they stay fresh? Two days, three?" She tried laughing. "They wouldn't expect you to put faded flowers on my grave."

At the ring of the phone, she dropped the cup, which shattered on the floor.

Gail said, "I'll get it." But Cathy already had seized the receiver.

"What?" she said, not comprehending. "No, I did not call you. . . . No, I did not leave a number. . . . No one's died here—and no one's going to. . . . I understand. . . . A hoax, yes . . . yes."

Hanging up, she turned to Gail. "Some mortuary. Said I'd called in and wanted information about a package deal. A *package deal!* Everything's a package deal today. Said they understood someone in the family was terminally ill. I wish I could call Gary. I can't call him and I want to so often. . . .

We've got to get married. . . . I shouldn't be bothering you with this. . . ."

Cathy picked up the pieces of the shattered cup. "It was my grandmother's. How strange it is that we respect age in china but so often we don't in people."

She settled back. "We love each other so much but we've got a problem. He doesn't think he should ever marry, because he's deaf. He's sensitive about it and I suppose I would be, too. That's why he came out here from Chicago, to get away from relatives who were always saying, 'Poor Gary.' He hates sympathy. He wants to be looked on as just anyone else his age. I think it's the same as with some of the black girls at Pitzer. We wanted to make them feel at home when they first arrived and we did too much. We went far out of our way to help them and some didn't like it. They just wanted to be one of the girls. That's the way it is with Gary. People want to protect him, to help him, like he was retarded. He keeps saying, 'I can talk. I speak English.' I think if he got a job, he would get over it and we could get married."

Gail nodded. "A job helps. Talk about being depressed. Once I beat the bushes for six months looking for work."

Cathy continued, "We need each other so badly, to work together, to plan, to talk things over, to give each other confidence. . . . I mentioned a job but I really don't want him to get a full-time one. I'd rather he went to CSUN and got his BA and then a master's. First, we'd get married . . ."

As if spurred by mental telepathy, Gary called then. Again Cathy was the first to the phone. Waiting for him to begin talking, she gave Gail a smile. "It's Gary. He waits to give me time to get to the phone."

"What if the line's busy?" Gail asked.

Cathy turned sad. "He just talks then to a busy line, and I don't even know he's called. But it doesn't happen very often."

He began slowly, "Cathy, I'm worried about you. So I had to call to tell you that I love you and want to help if I can. I'm here if you need me. George and I'll be over in the morning about eight. Why don't we go up to Zuma beach and talk about it? Well, I'll see you soon. Have a good night. I love you until it hurts."

Cathy whispered to herself. "I love you, too, Gary. I love you . . . need you."

Gail awakened out of a deep sleep and saw the time was two-thirty-four. In the adjoining twin bed Cathy slept soundly, exhausted physically, emotionally, and mentally. They had turned in a little after ten. Talking had calmed both.

Gail was unable to peg why she had come awake. She was about to drop off when she heard a sound she found impossible to identify. It came from outside the kitchen door. It could have been someone working on the lock. But when it came again, it seemed more like the forcing of a door or window.

Slipping out of bed, she trudged in her bare feet toward the kitchen. In the living room she rummaged in her purse and came up with the Mace. Thus armed, she stealthily approached the back entrance. She stood quietly by the door, keeping her breathing as low as possible. She heard only faint, normal night noises.

She debated whether she should pull aside a drape and peek out the window. To do so, she might make herself vulnerable. She could not call the police since that would be betraying Cathy's trust in her.

Then she heard a faint shuffling and something like burrowing. She pulled the drape a little aside. Only a couple of feet away, in a rose garden, a man was bent over doing something. He stiffened up a little on his haunches and lit a flare. He proceeded to put it down a gopher hole, which he then covered with dirt.

Gail collapsed into the nearest chair. The next day she was to learn that Abner Blanton roamed the apartment complex most of the night. He used flares to fight the gophers. He was afraid that if he put out poison, he might kill a cat or dog. He never seemed to achieve any decisive defeat of the enemy. In time the residents came to call it the Great Gopher War and predicted it might last longer than the Thirty Years' War.

Abner Blanton never knew what happened. The blow to the back of the skull, a few inches above the first vertebra, came so suddenly that there was no limbo of consciousness. One moment he was bent over, perfectly all right, and the next completely blacked out. Since he was near the ground, he crumpled rather than fell. The weapon was a dull instrument powered by hardened muscles. The aim was to the mark, as precise as if fired at close range from a revolver. He had had no warning by sound, smell, or other sense.

20

Mitch returned home beat. The heat, the long hours, but even more than those factors, the abrasive characters he mostly dealt with had taken a toll. Where were all the pleasant folks of his childhood and college days? Where had they all gone? He had come to believe that one of life's greatest virtues was in people being considerate of one another, and kind, even in the heat of argument or in the jostling of bodies in a great city. Somehow the Japanese had it, and even if it was mostly on the surface, it was a gesture that eased the going on rough days.

The apartment seemed strange without Gail. He dropped his jacket on a chair and tossed his tie toward a table but missed. From the refrigerator he got a Coke. The shelves were dotted with little plastic containers holding dabs of food. ("I can't bear to throw anything away with all the hunger there is in the world," Gail had said.) There was a small basket of mushrooms. He had been with her when she bought them. She had spent minutes picking out stemless ones. ("Why pay for the

stems?") On the same trip she had weighed herself and panicked. She was two pounds overweight. She weighed on every
scale she passed, the same way as she set her watch by every
clock she saw. She accepted as the absolute truth what every
scale and clock recorded.

Closing the door, he shuddered. Greater love hath no man,
he thought, than to go marketing with a woman.

He telephoned Gail and learned about the file card with the
strange quotation, the newspaper clipping, and the call from
the mortuary. Just talking with her revived him. He thought he
loved her most because she was comfortable to be around. She
had kidded him about that. "Like an old shoe, you mean."
Well, it was like that. An old shoe should never be demeaned.
He remembered dates he had had in high school and college:
vivacious girls, aggressive ones, a few so made-up they looked
plastic, and one or two who were openly seductive. They scared
him and he had avoided women until he met Gail. At first he
admired her efficiency as a secretary, then grew fond of her because of her compassion toward the timid and the weary and
the beaten souls who shuttled through the office, and then
loved her for her innate goodness, the ease and adaptability
with which she moved through each day no matter how tough
the struggle. She had no idea, he was certain, that she was what
she was. Do we ever? he wondered. Good or bad.

A light tapping took him to the door. Sandy stood there, the
redhead from next door. "Hi, Mitch." She had run out of vine-
gar. Could she borrow some? He led her to the kitchen and let
her scout the cupboards. Finding the bottle, she asked where
Gail was and he said she was spending the night with a girl
friend.

"Oh, goodie," Sandy said at the door, "I'll go home and get
my toothbrush and come right back."

"You'll get your fanny out of here and keep it out."

She thought that was funny. "If I were Gail, I'd keep you on
a leash."

After she was gone, he turned off the lights in the living
room and sat down to finish the Coke. He could think better
in the dark. He had barely started when there was more light

tapping. Sandy. She could become a problem. No matter what excuse she had, he would block her from coming in.

Switching the light back on, he opened the door. A man burst in, shoving him roughly to one side. The man half shouted, "Get back! Don't say anything. I'm not going to hurt you."

Before Mitch could react, he had been pushed back into the room, the door had closed, and the man stood with feet planted solidly. He was about five-nine, not overly heavy but with a potbelly, and had a nice though anonymous face. He was dark-complexioned and smelled loudly of English tweed.

"You're Frank Mitchell?"

Mitch quickly recovered. "What the hell do you think you're doing? I'm calling the police if you don't get out of here." Mitch figured he could best the man in a struggle. Too, if he yelled, Sandy would hear. The porous walls absorbed only whispers.

"You've got a client, Catherine Doyle." The man spilled the words out fast. "She said I should talk with you."

Mitch shrugged and moved toward a chair. "I don't usually do business at home."

He noticed the man's hands, a crooked little finger on the left, a prominent white scar across the right, nails manicured. His dark hair had no part and obviously had been fashioned in an expensive salon.

The man calmed. "I apologize but since I've such little time . . . only until midnight . . . maybe tomorrow morning . . . I don't know . . . to wrap this up."

"Sit down."

"When you do."

Mitch continued standing. If this crumb-bum wanted to play it that way, okay. He backed slowly toward the phone, which sat on a small home-painted stand by a scarred straight chair. "You want a million dollars."

"A million two."

"What's your name?"

"What's that got to do with this?"

"A matter of courtesy—but you wouldn't know about that,

anyone who would come crashing in . . ." Mitch was taunting him deliberately. Get a hostile witness off balance.

The man kept wetting his lips. "I said I apologize. I was afraid you wouldn't see me."

"You got credentials on you?"

"I've got credentials." He patted his upper left coat pocket, which bulged.

"Whom do you represent?"

"Myself."

"Interesting. I had the impression I would be dealing with an organization."

The man took his time, lit a cigarette. "They want it tonight."

"Who's They?"

"What does it matter?"

"As Miss Doyle's attorney, I have a right to know."

"She knows. Let her tell you."

"She says she doesn't."

"We're wasting time and I haven't got much of it. Where and when do I get the money? I'm here to talk about that and nothing else. You hear that, Mitchell, nothing else."

Mitch continued to needle him. "What kind of a racket is it?"

"It's strictly a legitimate deal—and she's got our money."

"Cash? Securities? Gold? Stocks?"

"Don't play games. She knows and you know."

Mitch shrugged. "If it's so legal, why don't you file a grand larceny complaint with the authorities?"

"And have her skip out on us?"

"How did she get the money, if she has it? I have no knowledge she has it."

The man leaned back against the door. His eyes were bloodshot. He's had it, Mitch thought. He's about to come apart. He may break before Cathy Doyle does. We always think of the victims and speculate about how long they will hold up. We seldom consider the mental and emotional condition of the criminals. They suffer from the very suspense of the plot they have spun. How long will it take to reduce another human being to a shambles? Will they be caught before the victim bows to their will? Like the victims, they spend sleepless nights. In the dark they survey the steps taken to date and scout their minds for more ways to turn the screw, to strangle the victims to that fine point where they will capitulate but not die in the process.

"Look, my friend," the man began.

"I'm not your friend," Mitch said evenly. "I'm your adversary, personally and legally."

The man stubbed out the half-smoked cigarette. "How about representing us out here? I can get you a retainer of twenty-five thousand dollars a year. With more to come."

Mitch forced a smile. "I've had offers before."

"Twenty-five thousand. More money than you've ever dreamed of."

Mitch said slowly, "I've dreamed of it. Back when I was a law student at USC. A big fine office, a stunning secretary, fees from big corporations. But by the time I got out I knew there was more to living than big fees—or the stunning secretary."

The man stared at him. He shook his head in a daze. "I'm here to pick up the money—and if I don't get it . . ."

"I can have you arrested."

"What for?"

"Threats of bodily harm—to maim—to murder . . ."

The man took a step toward him. "You may think I'm putting on an act but if anything happens to this girl it'd be like someone stabbed me. I'm trying to help her." He raised his voice. "You wouldn't understand how a guy like me meets a girl and wants to save her from getting raped or tortured or strangled."

Mitch kept his voice down. "No, you're not threatening bodily harm yourself but you're telling her about what someone else will do to her if she doesn't comply with your demands. You're working on a technicality—and it won't hold up in a court of law."

He has this act he stages, Mitch thought, but along the way does he talk himself into believing it? Possibly. Later, when someone is maimed or killed by other parties, he can rationalize that he did his best to prevent it. He had no part in injuring or murdering the victim. He had warned her and she had not listened. The criminal mind was a puzzle, a vast maze of meandering channels that defied the analysis of a logical, sane person. That was what made the practice of criminal law challenging, foreboding, frightening, frustrating, and at times when the illogic had been successfully diagrammed, highly satisfying.

Mitch said, "You walk in and expect me to hand over a million dollars to a perfect stranger who offers no personal identification and who doesn't identify the party or parties he represents. What kind of an attorney do you think I would be if I did what you propose?"

"A lousy one—but that's what you're going to do if you don't want to get your head blown off."

"You can skip the threats. They don't work on me."

"I'm stating objectively exactly what I know will happen. You should thank me."

"You sent her a newspaper clipping showing the body of a girl who had been strangled. You had a mortuary phone her. And the file card with the quote about some barbaric people. What was that all about?"

"Ask her. She's the concubine. She knows."

"Concubine?"

The man turned bitter. "You mouthpieces are all the same. Out chasing ambulances for the dough. Okay, I offered her a hundred thousand to turn over the money. They have authorized me to go higher—"

"She's not interested. She doesn't have the money. It's a figment of your imagination."

"You're required by law to submit any offer made. Two hundred thousand if we wind it up tonight. Two hundred thousand."

Mitch turned persuasive. "Be reasonable. My client does not know what you are talking about. I repeat, she doesn't have the million two. Never has. But if you could give me some details —about where the money came from, who had it last, all of that, then perhaps she might help you. She might have some contact—"

"Shut up! You're a con man, not a lawyer. But don't try conning me. I'll tell you this much, I don't have the answers you want. They didn't tell me much. They told me to get my ass out here and do a job. They told me the million two is Theirs, that it belongs legally to Them—and They have never lied to me. I trust Them. If They say the money is Theirs, it's Theirs. Two hundred thousand. If you and the girl try for more, you're dead, dead, dead . . ."

Mitch was quiet a moment, then decided to play for time. "I'll talk with my client and get back to you. Where do I reach you?"

"When will you see her?"

"Tomorrow morning."

"Before noon?"

Mitch nodded.

"You'll put the offer up to her? Two hundred thousand."

Again Mitch nodded.

"I hope to God she comes through. They are cruel, ruthless, and impatient. I'll have to talk my head off to get Them to wait until noon. They know you have a new bride. I don't know what They will do to her, or to Cathy if They don't get the money. Burn their breasts, break their bones, throw acid on their faces. And if that fails, strangle them. And you . . . your car blows up when you turn on the ignition or a shotgun blast blows your face to pieces. They make a clean sweep of the enemy. I've seen it over and over."

"You've made your point," Mitch said quietly. "Now will you kindly get out?"

In his shorts, Mitch sat in the dark in the living room. He should reach for the phone. He should report to Hawk the conversation he had just had. By not doing so he might be withholding information pertinent to the investigation of a crime. If he did, however, he would betray the trust of a client.

In his mind he drew a resumé. (1) They were convinced Catherine Doyle had the million two; (2) he, Mitch, was not certain but what she did; (3) she had been branded a concubine, which translated could mean a girl friend or mistress, and hence there was introduced a new, unknown party, her paramour, who could be called a boy friend; (4) They would not hesitate to torture her physically; (5) if They still did not get the money, They would murder her; (6) Gail was in great jeopardy since They believed that he, Mitch, knew the whereabouts of the fortune or could find out; (7) he had until noon tomorrow to decide on the next step. At that time a new "team" would move in.

He made his decision. There could be no other. Tomorrow morning, he would notify Cathy Doyle, victim, client, and possibly involved herself in a criminal act or acts, that he was informing Lieutenant Hawkins of all developments.

He had no choice but to breach the client-attorney relationship. Already he had delayed too long. Time had run out.

21

A little before dawn—that time of day when the shadowy, mysterious shapes of night begin to reveal themselves for what they are—Cathy stirred. Since childhood she had awakened about sunrise. Her pajamas were knotted and twisted. She had slept soundly but had turned and tossed through several frightening dreams.

Her first thoughts were of her father. In a throwback to childhood, she longed for him. He had looked so ill that night he had come. In words spoken awkwardly, they had stressed their love for one another. It was as if each had a premonition that this would be their last meeting.

That was ridiculous. She believed no more in premonitions than did her father.

She rose up on one elbow. Gail was sleeping quietly, her back to her. Although they had known each other so briefly,

Cathy felt close to her. In many ways, they were alike. It was a wondrous happening to meet a stranger and within the hour to experience the feeling she was an old friend. There were not too many people you could kick off your shoes around, and talk, and know they listened and cared.

Her father. There had been the time when she had been tail-gated by another car. She had phoned him in a hysterical state but as they talked, his deep, easy voice had calmed her. "Don't ever let fear get you down," he had said. "If you're scared, sit down and think it all out. Take it step by step. Most things can be worked out. Decide what your alternatives are and choose the best one and stick with it."

Gary. She wanted his arms about her, his lips on hers, the press of his body against hers. He was kind and gentle and thoughtful. Was there a place in this busy, crazy, rough-dealing city for such men? In time she and Gary would find a small community where perhaps people cared more, where there were not so many bodies jostling each other, and such frenetic rush. It wasn't that the people were different. But in a big city there was only so much time and space.

She was trembling. Little fears that she had subconsciously subdued were again running wild.

She slipped quietly out of bed, took a few steps, and sat in a straight chair. She put her feet squarely on the floor, straightened her back, and placed her hands, palms up, on each knee, careful that the hands did not touch. Taking a deep breath, she closed her eyes.

Her lips moved without sound. "My legs will stop trembling . . . my legs will quit trembling . . . my legs will be quiet . . . my heart will slow down . . . my heart will slow down . . . my heart will slow down . . . my mind will reject all fear . . . my mind will reject all fear . . . my mind will wipe out fear entirely . . ."

She was nearing what she thought of as an "autogenic state," the mind in control, the body totally subservient. Her body was nearing a "weightless state."

For a year she had studied autogenics. Stress induced tensions which could destroy the nervous system and certain other bodily mechanisms and functions. Persons trained in autogenics—which was a must for Russian astronauts—could dissipate such stress in a matter of minutes, could lower the pulse rate.

For a short time she continued instructing her mind and body. Afterward she padded barefoot to the kitchen, where she reheated the leftover coffee. She resisted the temptation to use cream and sugar. She had to hold her weight steady for the job starting Monday.

Sipping the coffee, she groped her way through the shadowy living room to the front door. She opened it to a burst of early sunlight. She stood reveling in it. It was a good feeling to know that she had no fear.

Stepping outside, she picked up the Los Angeles *Times*. She usually stood a moment scanning the headlines but this morning she took a few steps to a point where she could see about the complex. She was surprised to spot a raccoon drinking from the pool. He was a brazen character. He was in alien territory, yet appeared totally unconcerned. Nearby an orange cat, ready for quick take-off, watched him, and overhead a mockingbird hurled obscenities at the cat.

Her gaze went eventually to the rose garden, which was in full bloom. Later she would pick a bouquet for Gary. All of a sudden she had an overwhelming urge to get in the car and drive to see him.

Back in the apartment she was about to close the door behind her when her attention shot to the sofa. With the door open, it was flooded with sunlight. There on the sofa, stretched out on her back, was a strange woman. She didn't move.

The police were persistent. She or Gail had to know who the woman was. When had she arrived? Who else had been in the apartment? What was her name? Was she a friend, a relative, a casual visitor?

She was about forty, with long dark hair, fairly attractive. She was in a pink negligee and matching slippers. She had no purse and no identification on her. She had been strangled.

Throughout the questioning, officers came and went, a photographer took pictures, someone sketched the room, a crime search team scoured the apartment inch by inch, a mortuary ambulance stood by outside waiting for clearance to remove the body.

Shortly after an officer by the name of Barney Carlson arrived, the interrogation ceased. There was a huddle and much whispering. From bits of conversation Cathy picked up, it was evident they had made "an ident." By then they seemed certain, too, that the woman had been strangled elsewhere. Now the primary question appeared to be: how had the killer or killers transported the body into the apartment without making a forcible entry? Who besides Cathy had a key to the apartment? No one, Cathy said, except the manager.

Later, there was more talk. Mr. Blanton reported he had been knocked unconscious. By habit he kept a key chain with the master key on it in his right pants pocket. When he came to, he found it in his left. He had thought that odd but figured he had probably put it there thoughtlessly. He had reported the assault to the West Valley Police Division but no one had yet noticed that the attack and the finding of the slain woman had taken place at the same address.

Through it all, Cathy remained fairly calm. Fearful that she might panic, Gail had been overly solicitous. She had fended off the rougher questions, angrily assailed the officers asking them, brought coffee and a roll, and occasionally put an arm about her.

Though in control of herself, Cathy knew what the message was. They would eventually strangle her the same as They had this strange woman on the couch. This, the placing of the body on her sofa, was the final, grisly step in the terror campaign. The psychological warfare was over.

I may have one more chance, she thought, one more meeting with the criminal.

22

Gail was shaken, and so was Mitch, for the first time since she had known him. She had returned home shortly after Lefty arrived to stay with Cathy. Two police officers also had remained behind, presumably to look for further evidence. Gail doubted that. They had placed Cathy under open surveillance. Where she went, they would go.

Mitch leaned against the shower door, coffee cup in hand, watching her make up. She was in bra and briefs. "Darn!" she said as the lipstick went slightly askew.

He told her about the night visitor. "He said, 'Ask her. She's the concubine. She knows.'"

"Concubine?"

"That's what I said but he didn't elaborate and we were swinging pretty heavy on a lot of things."

"The card said they strangled and buried her with the king."

"Yeah, the king. Who's the king?"

"It's such a forgotten word, concubine."

"It could be translated girl friend."

"No, it has more implications than girl friend. It refers to a woman who is there primarily for sexual purposes. I can't imagine Cathy on a retainer from some stud."

"I think we're reading something into it that isn't there. They saw the paragraph somewhere and tossed it in to build up the terror."

"I wanted so badly to believe her."

"She had to know who the woman was or might be or something about why she was there. You don't have a body dumped on you without knowing something about it. Didn't she scream or anything?"

Gail ran a comb through her hair. "She came into the bedroom and woke me up and said, 'Gail, there's someone dead in the living room. On the couch. A woman. I don't know who she is.' The officers were suspicious because she didn't seem upset. She said it was autogenics."

"Auto-what?"

"She tells the different parts of her body to do as she instructs. She'd had a session with herself when she woke up and told her mind to reject fear. A lot of people believe in it. But it didn't work when it came to her boy friend. She was frantic. She phoned a neighbor—woke her up—and asked her to check on him. She could scarcely contain herself until the neighbor called back. Did you ever set a fee?"

"Not yet. I thought—"

"Five hundred as a retainer. We've got to pay Lefty and you're putting in lots of hours. It's one thing to help a kid just out of college—if you don't mention it to her, I will."

"What about twenty-five thousand dollars?"

She turned quickly, the oddest expression on her face.

He continued, "That's what the scum will pay us to sell out—and that's only a first offer. Aren't you ever going to finish? I've got to brush my teeth."

She stepped back from the basin. "Whyn't you say so? And for heaven's sake, get a hair cut—and Mitch! The pink brush is mine, the blue one's yours."

He continued using the pink one. "You squeeze the tube at the top. I never squeeze it at the top. Little things like that can lead to divorce."

She should have laughed but she was too edgy.

Soon afterward, he left to talk with Cathy. Any minute, he knew, Hawk would arrive to cross-examine her. Mitch would brief her about what to expect. With a murder to solve, Hawk would come with bare-fisted questions. He would bore and bore. Mitch doubted if she could withstand such an assault.

Before he went, he grabbed Gail roughly about the waist and gave her a bear hug. His hands slid over her bare flesh. Why did man ever have to go to work? Omar Khayyam had the right idea. What was it? A jug of wine and thou? He could forego the jug but the thou part . . .

Gail's hand trembled opening the office door. She stepped in warily as if fearing a prowler might be waiting, hastily raised the shades, opened the windows, and adjusted the slightly askew picture of Justice Holmes. She noticed mice droppings on her desk and brushed them off. From down the corridor came the hard beat of a rock band.

"Mitchell's Law Office," she said into the phone.

"Put Mitch on."

"He's out. May I have him call you?"

Down went the receiver. Slam bang.

The day had started normally.

Hawk was the next phone caller. "What'd you marry that bum for when I was around and available? All you had to do was ask."

She laughed. "Guess I got carried away."

"Tell Mitch I'm seeing his client, Catherine Doyle, at ten o'clock. I don't usually call the attorney of record but because of my great affection for him . . . you got that, Gail, you tell him, my great affection . . ."

"I got it."

"They tell me you spent the night with her."

"You want to question me?"

"Should I?"

"You know perfectly well you will."

"How about dinner tonight?"

"I'm booked for the next 365 nights."

"I'll get around to you."

"I'm sure you will, Hawk."

"One question. Just one. Why'd you spend the night with her?"

"I'd rather you asked Mitch."

"Did she talk any about the murder victim?"

"She didn't know her, so how could she? Have you made an ident yet? Know anything about her?"

"We'd know more if your client talked more."

"Don't be too rough on her. She's a nice kid."

"We'll see."

When she hung up and turned about, Marilyn stood there.

"Morning, dear."

"What're you doing up so early?" Gail asked.

"Haven't been to bed yet. Convention in town. I hate the lot of 'em. They get all tanked up and don't appreciate a beautiful lady."

She took two wrinkled hundred dollar bills from her purse and put them on the desk. "Came by to pay my bill."

"It's a hundred." Gail pushed one back toward her.

"Mitch deserves it. He's the best. Two hundred for Mitch and six hundred for me."

Gail shoved the swivel back with a screech. "You told us—"

"That bastard! He wanted me to do things no nice girl would do. Well, be seeing you but not soon, I hope."

Gail was seething as she dialed Cathy Doyle's number. When she reached Mitch, she delivered Hawk's message and then let go. "Marilyn did roll the Texan. She had the nerve to come in here and say two hundred dollars was your share. Don't you see, Mitch, she's splitting with you. You're an accomplice. An accessory after the fact. You've got to make her pay that man back every dollar she stole from him."

"He probably deserved to be taken."

"Mitch!"

He recognized the tone. "Shad, we're in big trouble here. Let's concentrate on this case and then we'll take up Marilyn and see what we can do."

"You'd better!" She hung up without saying good-by.

Suddenly she was conscious of two children standing just inside the door. The boy was about thirteen, the girl a few years younger. The boy was wearing jeans out at the knees and a shirt more frayed than whole. They looked as if they needed a meal.

"Come on in," Gail said.

They entered slowly, timidly. "We need a lawyer, ma'am," the boy said.

"He isn't in now and he's awfully busy today."

The girl, about to cry, said, "We're in bad trouble."

"Don't you go crying, Maria," the boy told the girl. "Nothing's going to happen."

"What's the matter?" Gail asked.

"They're going to put us in jail."

The boy took over. "You know that old junky yard down near the warehouse?"

Gail didn't but nodded.

"We cleaned it up and planted flowers."

"I cut my hand." The girl showed a small scar on her right hand.

"It was legal," the boy continued. "We got permission from the owner, who's a neat guy. He didn't charge us anything and bought a bunch of flowers every week."

"Two last week," the girl said. "He's awfully nice."

"So what's the problem?" Gail asked.

The boy said, "We sold the flowers to restaurants and on street corners. Then yesterday a man comes around and says we've got to have a business license, and another man, he's from the state of California, he says we've got to pay 6 per cent sales tax and he's going to send us to prison if we don't pay for all the flowers we've sold this summer, and we don't have it."

"Would they put a little girl in jail? I'm only eight."

"I'm thirteen. Will the lawyer take our case?" the boy asked.

"I'm sure he will," Gail told them. "Can you come back at nine tomorrow morning?"

"Yes, ma'am! We only got two dollars. Will that be enough?"

Gail smiled. "Maybe a dollar too much."

23

As with the death of any informant, that of Marissa Dubrovnik shocked and saddened alike those who had known her and those who had only heard of her. In a sense she had given her life for the community. While some might find offensive the manner in which she served her fellow man, still she had bettered a little the microcosm in which she lived.

Hawk felt her death deeply. He held himself responsible. It was highly likely that he and the General had been under surveillance when they had visited her and their conversation overheard or taped. One could never be too careful about setting up a rendezvous with an informant. He knew that, and had erred. He could not blame the General. As head of the squad, Hawk was the one who should have checked out the scene. If he had been more observant, if they had gone in the dark of night, if they had met her at another location . . . these were the "ifs" that would haunt him for months to come, even for years, whenever he thought back to this day.

Still, no matter what happened, he maintained by dint of some inner strength the Hawk that he usually was, the extrovert quick with a remark or a decision.

He sat now with Barney and the General. Within thirty minutes of the discovery of the body in Catherine Doyle's apartment, Barney's men had begun their work. They had started with Dubrovnik's place, to try to re-create her life, discover who her friends were, her acquaintances, her daily routine, what the people who knew her could tell them about suspects, and especially to refilm, so to speak, her last day and night.

Hawk said, "We'll decide later, after I talk with the Doyle woman, whether we bring her in. Mitch thinks she's innocent. He could be bluffing. I don't know. We'll have to see."

He turned to Barney. "Tell Jenny I want her in on the cross-examination. She might notice something we wouldn't. Another woman. Get after the Miami authorities and the FBI. Tell them to get off the dime."

They had asked the FBI and Miami the night before for any pertinent data about the Carney organization and the Hong Kong Finance Company. Also, who else besides Samuel Porter alias Samuel J. Oscar, Ralph Catania, and Soft Shoe might be on the scene.

Barney's men had located the hotel where he had been registered. Only a couple of hours before, he had checked out. Surveillances on Catherine Doyle and Lefty Morgan, begun shortly after the interview with Marissa Dubrovnik, had proven negative.

When the meeting broke up, the General stayed behind. He had difficulty talking.

"I know how you feel," Hawk said. "Same here."

The General cleared his throat noisily. "Her daughter's flying in. I'd like to take the pictures down off the wall."

Hawk was cryptic. "It's none of our business."

"She's only seventeen—and when you're seventeen . . ."

"I know how you feel at seventeen!" Hawk quieted. "It's been a long time. Maybe I've forgotten."

But you remember, don't you, General? You're far older than I am but you remember. Behind that vague expression, those feet that move with effort, there's a sensitivity no one around here would ever guess.

Hawk said, "Marissa was proud of those pictures."

The General rubbed his eyes. "I never understood that. Never did. But when you're seventeen . . . your own mother . . . to see her in the nude . . . to know she posed for those magazines . . . a mother you loved, worshiped. You'd never get over it."

He hesitated, fearful of what he was about to say. "Barney's men finished going over it an hour ago and locked up the place. I've got a key."

Hawk came out of his chair. "You've got a key!" He fell back into the swivel. "If the police commission ever hears about this, God help us all."

"She wasn't as bad a woman as she seemed to some."

Nobody was ever as bad as he appeared—or as good. Hawk had learned that early.

The General continued, "We were both lost souls. Time had done us in, I guess. The years had beaten us down. We brought each other a little happiness. Not much but a little. I have never understood why people think it is sordid when you are old and get together but it is all right when you are young."

He added belligerently, "It wasn't sordid. It was beautiful."

He started for the door. "Where you going?" Hawk shouted.

"Back to my desk to clean out the papers and leave. You will have to put me on report."

"I haven't heard a word you said. I've got too many problems to listen to somebody ramble on and on. Do you think I've been listening to all the chatter? Hell, no."

The General turned about, bewildered.

Hawk said, "I want you to meet the kid at the airport and go along with her to pick up her mother's things."

The General stood dumbfounded.

"Come on," Hawk said, rising, "if we're going to get the pictures down, let's do it."

As they passed Angel's desk, she looked up. "Where're you going? You're supposed to let me know where you'll be and you never do."

"To burglarize an apartment. And I'm not giving you the address, nosy."

24

Outside the apartment door, two officers politely asked Mitch to identify himself.

"Is she under house arrest?" Mitch asked curtly.

"No, nothing like that. The lieutenant asked us to stick around to make sure she's okay."

Abner Blanton emerged from nowhere. "Mr. Mitchell," he called. "You *are* Mr. Mitchell?"

Mitch nodded, and Mr. Blanton continued, "Miss Doyle told me you would be along shortly. I have a problem, Mr. Mitchell. Well, I have a lot of problems. I've got a head about to burst. They almost killed me last night, you know. Right over there in the rose garden. Between Helen Traubel and Peace. Look at my arms and me without tetanus shots.

"Excuse me, I shouldn't be holding you up. It's this way. It was on the early morning news and the owner got me on the phone. He said it would ruin the reputation of our fine apartment complex if people heard we had muggings and dead bodies around. He ordered me to evict Miss Doyle. I told him she was a fine young woman—I'm very fond of her—and that it could happen to anybody. Well, I guess it couldn't. Not everyone finds a body in their living room. But—"

"Does she have a lease?"

He nodded. "Ten months to go."

"You tell the owner that if he wants to evict her, I'll meet him in court."

Mr. Blanton appeared genuinely relieved. "I'll take great pleasure in relaying that information. I think a lot of Miss Doyle . . ."

Cathy pulled the door back a few inches, then released the guard chain. She looked sober, bewildered, and haggard. The events of the last days had left their imprint as sharply as does a foot in the sand. She was in the familiar jeans and had on a crisp blue print blouse. She tossed her blond hair back as if preparing for one more joust.

Once inside, his eyes went to the sofa, which was sturdy and dark brown, especially manufactured for tenants who considered other people's property fair game. It had been cordoned off and the impression was that of a museum piece on display.

With purpose she headed for the kitchen. He could imagine the fright that stabbed her each time she walked through the dark living room. Even with hardened detectives, the sight of death's work shocked and repelled. It was the final Wagnerian tragedy.

"Where's Lefty?" Mitch asked.

"Asleep in the bedroom. Said he had a rough night. I told him it was all right, with the police out there. Have you had breakfast?"

He nodded. "Coffee if it's not too much trouble."

She poured from the percolator. "My fifth cup. Usually one's my limit. I don't know who the woman is. Before God, I don't. But they think I must."

Mitch said softly, "Lieutenant Hawkins will be here soon to ask some questions. They sent Their guy in last night to see me. He had no identification. Refused to give me his name or the name of the people he represents or any proof he was entitled to the money. I stalled him to get rid of him and play for time. I told him I'd talk with you this morning."

"You still don't believe me?"

"I'm trying . . . I want to, desperately."

She sat on a kitchen stool. In the soft light and the patched jeans she had a little-girl look. "You've been very kind to me," she said wistfully, "and I've worried you. I'm sorry but one of these days . . ."

"He said the concubine mention on the card referred to you."

She looked up startled. "I don't understand."

"Have you been living with someone—?"

"No!" She half-shouted the word, then subsided. "Gary—I told you about him—we're in love."

"How about last year or the year before?"

"Never! I had a few dates but concubine . . ." She shuddered.

"Did you date any Arab or Iranian students? The quotation on the card sounds like something from the days of Saladin."

"I know a few. But I never dated any. I wasn't asked."

"Did you get through to your father?" He was thinking that if she talked with him, and was honest, he might counsel her to open up.

"I don't know what to do. Nobody's seen him around Clinton and I'm terribly worried. Those officers out there . . . I've got a date this afternoon with personnel to fill out some job papers. And Gary's coming by soon. We were going up to Zuma beach . . . I've got to talk with my father . . . I've just got to . . ."

The conversation invariably veered to her father. Was the fact she had seen him so seldom part of the reason she idolized him? He had not been at home to scold her or lay down rules. He was not irritable when he was tired or when the day had gone badly. He had written letters of praise and adoration and handed out nice, little lectures that had no bite. He was a father of her own imaginative creation who through the years had accrued virtues no one parent could possibly have.

"I've got to talk to you about some things before the lieutenant gets here. First, let me say that Hawkins is a new breed of officer. He never arrests anyone unless he has evidence or witnesses to prove their guilt.

"Now I've got to ask questions, and you may think I'm being cruel, but I ask them because Gail and I care about you, and not just as a client but as a person."

She took a deep breath, to gird herself. "I understand."

Mitch put the cup in the sink, ran water into it, then turned to her. "To begin with, up until now you've been the victim of threats but with the development this morning the situation has changed. You're the epicenter of a homicide investigation. At least for the time being. Everything you say is important. Very important. If you've ever seen this woman, met her even for a few minutes, you must tell me . . . if you've heard anyone talking about her, mention her, by name or otherwise, through hearsay or directly."

She straightened. "I've never seen her in my life. Never."

"Did the guy who's been threatening you ever mention her?"

"Never."

"If you had knowledge of her, and fail to say so, it could be incriminating. Very incriminating. On the other hand, if you do have knowledge and you know it is incriminating—that is, if it is the kind of knowledge that involves you in something illegal, or appears to be illegal—then you must tell me. In that case, I would intervene during the questioning with objections. I would block certain questions so that you would neither perjure yourself nor admit guilt."

"Guilt! I'm not guilty of anything. I can't incriminate myself."

"Let's forget the woman for the time being. Is there anything else that would tend to incriminate you—something to do with your refusal to talk with the police?"

"I've told you over and over . . ."

He put his hand on hers. "Look, Cathy, I deal with the

worst of human nature. Someone said to me once that the world is nothing but a low grade reform school. I don't believe that, although there are times when I wonder. What I'm getting at is this: my experience tells me the criminal believes you do know the answers to some questions. Now that doesn't mean you do. But he thinks you do. Is there any reason he should think that?"

She was half-crying. "I've tried to tell you . . . I don't know how to say it any harder than I have. I don't know what's going on. I don't know. I've got to sit down and have a talk with myself. I'm going to come apart."

An inner alarm nudged Mitch. He turned quickly. Lefty stood there, fumbling with his hands. "You got a pizza, Cathy?"

She was too lost in thought to hear. "Oh, well," he continued, "most anything will do. Haven't had much to eat today."

He opened the big white box to case it. "A man—never put eyes on him before—offered me a lot of money last night. Fifty thousand bucks. All I had to do was tell him where the loot was. Course I didn't know, seeing as how no one tells me anything, which makes me feel like I wasn't trusted, when I got more principles than you can shake a stick at. Wouldn't've told him if I had known. Not old Lefty. I don't sell out my best friends. Course, if my best friends don't tell me nothing and sell me out, when they ought to be coming up with the same kind of money, seeing as how—"

"We won't need you any more today," Mitch said sharply.

Lefty spread peanut butter over a slice of cracked wheat bread. "Same brand as I use. My mother, bless her soul, gone to her Maker five years now, always used it. Guess I'll stick around awhile. Haven't much anything else to do."

"Didn't you hear? Get out!" Mitch was burning. The scoundrel! For a sizable reward he would turn himself in.

"You're welcome to stay," Cathy put in, by way of informing Mitch she would choose her own friends.

Lefty ate like a chipmunk, little, short strokes. "Thank you, ma'am. I'm much obliged. I haven't forgotten the diamond I promised you."

No, you haven't forgotten, Mitch thought. You just haven't picked one up yet.

George hit the door with a bang, shot through the apartment, and skidded over the kitchen vinyl in his exuberance to greet Cathy. She dropped to the floor to hug him. She thought, wouldn't it be a wondrous world if people had George's love and enthusiasm. "Good old George. Good old George."

The tension broke. She was back among the living again.

She rose, and with Gary's arm about her, introduced Mitch, who appraised Gary as if checking out a race horse. Instinctively, Mitch found him to his liking. Gary had a look of stability and character, and a strong masculine charisma. He had, too, a hurt, pensive look. The world would never be his oyster and he knew it.

She and Gary slipped out the back door into a tiny patio overgrown with exotic plants that shaded them from the harsh sun. Holding him tightly, as though he were all she had in this world, she bowed her head on his chest.

She loosened her hold and looked up at him with tears showing but also unexpectedly a smile.

"What's happening?" His rough hand, calloused from gardening, lifted her chin.

She told him about the woman on the sofa. She didn't want to, not in this magic moment, but he would learn about it from the news. "Nobody believes me—but before God I don't know what it's all about."

"I believe you, Cathy."

"Marry me, Gary. Oh, Gary, I want you so. I can't wait. Tonight, Gary, tonight marry me."

His lips enclosed hers. And the world blacked out. There was no patio, no woman on the sofa, no police coming, not today or tomorrow, no need for jobs, no sunshine even.

The world had blacked out and stopped and for a few minutes of sublimity, only two bodies pressed as one. A silent world for her as it ever was for him. Only two hearts beating strong, and his exciting hers until it pounded in her hearing with the roar of surf.

25

Hawk and Jenny entered a brilliantly lit cavernous room spotted with desks. To their left a bank of teletypes chattered incessantly like a bunch of back-fence gossips. Along one wall was a massive electronic board posted with New York Stock Exchange quotations. Customers lounged about or slouched in a covey of theater seats watching the daily drama spread out before them.

Hawk indicated a door to the far right. "I'd rather lose my shirt watching the horses run. If I'm going to gamble, I want some action to go with it."

They stepped into a small board meeting room with a long, highly polished oak table, chairs padded with red velvet, and oil paintings of pastoral scenes on the red velvet wall. The room had the imprint of wealth.

Cathy and Mitch sat on the far side. Hawk nodded to Mitch, who rose. "I'm Hawkins," he said to Cathy, "and this is Dr. Jenny Barton." He added to Jenny, "You've met Mitch."

She offered her hand, then to Cathy said pleasantly, "Hello, Miss Doyle."

She and Hawk sat opposite them. Mitch asked, "What's the idea of meeting in a brokerage house?"

Jenny answered. "I didn't think it fair to Miss Doyle to talk in her apartment in view of what happened, and in looking around for a convenient place close by . . ."

Hawk interrupted. On a case he had a one-track, narrow-gauge mind. "I have here the statements from the officers who talked with you earlier this morning, Miss Doyle. We have your name, address, all the usual statistics, so we'll skip that."

He leaned back to study her, seeking a quick visual appraisal. He had an uncanny instinct—a feeling rather than any logical, reasoning process—for sizing up a person. Her blue eyes stayed with his, as if daring him, refusing to be averted even by the pressure of long seconds passing. She was careful, however, not to appear brazen about it. She sat with her back ramrod straight. Her mouth curving upward gave her a pleasant look. Only a quivering lower lip revealed her apprehensions. She looked so damn young, yet there was nothing vulnerable or naïve about her.

He waited purposely. A fly seeking escape at a window sounded preposterously noisy in the tomblike room. No one moved. They sat rigid in the tension of the moment. Hawk liked this. The party or parties undergoing interrogation had time to think, and if guilty, the inevitable erosion process would begin. The disparities in their stories would loom large in their minds, and they would debate what to say and not to say. The seeds of panic would expand and burst. For some would come a growing compulsion to confess, to find absolution and peace in the knowledge they no longer had to cover up.

He spread a few papers before him. "You have denied any knowledge about the woman whose body you found in your living room."

Mitch broke in. "I don't like the word *deny*. It has the wrong connotation."

Hawk stiffened. "Don't start that, Mitch. You lawyers are always quibbling. I'll put it this way. Did you recognize the woman? Had you ever seen her before?"

"No, never." Her voice was positive, clear, forceful.

"Her name was Marissa Dubrovnik. Does that name mean anything to you?"

"No."

He pushed a photograph across the table. "This picture may help you remember her."

Mitch glanced at a photo of a nude woman in a suggestive pose. "I object to your showing my client a picture of high sexual content."

"I didn't ask *you* to look at it. So shut up!" He fixed on Cathy. "Do you know her? Did you ever meet her?"

"Never. Absolutely not."

"Who put the body in your living room?"

The question stunned her. Her voice quavered. "I haven't the slightest idea. Why would I . . . how would I—"

Mitch hit the table with a palm. "Your question assumes a knowledge she doesn't have."

Hawk continued, "You must have some idea. She was murdered last evening, possibly around seven o'clock, and transported to your apartment. Someone took a big risk in moving her. You must suspect somebody."

"How could I when I don't know the woman?"

Jenny said softly, "We're looking for a reason, Miss Doyle, for the body being placed in your apartment. If we can find the reason—"

Mitch interrupted. "My client has a statement to make which may help. Go ahead, Cathy. Tell it chronologically."

She moistened her lips, took a deep breath. "Yes, I'll start at the beginning. Well, I often house-sit to earn extra money, and a few nights ago at the home of the Hoovers in Encino . . . I'd just gone to bed when this man . . ."

She chose her words carefully and omitted no detail. She moved from the first frightening night to the circus and thence to the discovery of the body. Hawk let her take her time, and not once did he break in.

When she finished, he ran a hand through his thick, dark hair, and shook his head. "I can't believe it. You mean to tell me that all of this was going on and you didn't inform the police. A crime in progress, your life in jeopardy, maybe the lives of others, and you never even picked up the phone—"

"My client didn't want the police in on it." Mitch was brusque.

Hawk appeared appalled. Jenny smiled to herself. She had witnessed his act before. "Here we have a big crime breaking," he was saying, "threats to life, a woman strangled . . ."

Mitch talked above him. "I've gone to the police before with threats and been brushed off. You just don't have the manpower to run down every character who says he's going to kill someone."

Hawk was enraged. "Don't give me that bull! This was no ordinary threat."

Mitch handed Hawk the photograph delivered to Cathy at the circus by the popcorn vendor. "There's a note on the back." He pushed across the table the file card, the newspaper clipping, and his own memo about the call from the mortuary.

Hawk kicked back his chair and stood. "You withheld evidence. Physical evidence. I ought to get you disbarred for this." He glanced hastily at the evidence, handling it by the edges to avoid leaving fingerprints. "What's all this about a king and a concubine being buried?"

"I haven't the slightest idea," Mitch said.

"What about you?" He directed the question to Cathy, who shook her head.

"Must be symbolism," Jenny said.

"That's your department." He handed her the card.

He turned to Cathy. "Why didn't you want us in on this—these threats to your very life? This talk about a fabulous sum of money."

Cathy was properly contrite. "I'm sorry, Lieutenant. I really am. But you see, I've got a phobia about the police. It's like . . . well, my mother couldn't stand tight places, narrow stairs . . . it's something like that. And besides, besides . . ."

"Go on."

"I've got a job starting Monday, and I knew I would lose it if I went to the police and it got in the papers. I need the money. I need it so bad it hurts."

Hawk stared at her. "Have you got a record? Been in prison?"

Mitch came to his feet shouting. "You've already run her name through the indices and you damn well know she hasn't got a record. I object to this line of questioning."

"Shut up!" Hawk yelled back. "This isn't a court of law."

Jenny spoke up in that quiet but firm way she had. "Have you had some horrendous experience with the police, Miss Doyle?"

Cathy shook her head in the negative. "I can't explain it. I know it doesn't sound right . . ."

Jenny continued, "You must be honest with us. You need us, Miss Doyle. I have a feeling you need us badly."

"You sure do." Hawk sat back down. "Don't you know you could be the next one, stretched out on a sofa somewhere this time tomorrow."

Mitch was furious. "You're trying to panic her. You're as bad as the criminal. What're you trying to do? Terrorize her? Break her down? Get a confession any way you can?"

Hawk pretended astonishment. "I'm trying to get a little information and having one damned hard time." He turned to Cathy. "How long have you been working with the Carney people?"

"Carney?" She hesitated, appearing to run the name through her memory. "I don't think I've ever worked for anyone by that name. I do a lot of house- and baby-sitting and work for so many . . ."

Mitch said quietly to Hawk, "Would you like to identify the 'Carney people'?"

"She knows," Hawk retorted. "Don't you, Miss Doyle?"

"You're badgering her," Mitch said.

Hawk hit the table with a fist. "I'm going to boot you right out of here if you keep breaking in."

Mitch said testily, "Just try to. As her attorney, I have every right to sit in on this."

Hawk shrugged. "How about the Hong Kong Finance Company, Miss Doyle. I suppose you never heard of it, either."

Cathy had her hands clenched. "You suppose right."

"Samuel Porter? Samuel Oscar? Sometimes known as Soft Shoe?"

"No."

He showed her a picture. "Yes," she said quickly, "that's the man who's been threatening me. Is that his name? Samuel Porter?"

Hawk shuffled several note sheets. "I see you have no relatives except a father, Joseph Y. Doyle, who lives in Clinton, North Carolina. Is that correct?"

She nodded. "I've been trying to reach him."

He studied another note. "You've a friend, Gary Edison. How good a friend? Are you engaged?"

"Not yet."

"Living together?"

Mitch interrupted. "You don't need to answer that. The question is completely irrelevant."

Hawk glared at him. "Now, Miss Doyle, we'll get down to the nitty gritty. You've got a million dollars. I want to know where you got it, where you've hidden it, and whether it does belong to the Carney people, or if They're trying to hijack it."

She flounced her hair in defiance. "I've told Mr. Mitchell over and over, I don't have a million dollars and I don't know anything about a million dollars."

"I'll be frank, Miss Doyle," Hawk continued, "Marissa Dubrovnik told us shortly before she was strangled that you had absconded with a million dollars that legally belonged to the Carney organization, a mobster outfit with headquarters in Miami that operates out of a front called the Hong Kong Finance Company. Now in view of this, do you mean to sit there and tell me you know nothing about it? You never heard of the Carney people or the Hong Kong Finance Company?"

She was starting to wither. Mitch noticed and was worried. "No," she whispered, "I have never heard of anyone named Carney or the Hong Kong Finance Company."

Hawk dropped his voice. "I must warn you that while you are not under oath, I have reputable witnesses here who would testify to your answers in court, if it should come to that. If you commit perjury—"

"She knows that," Mitch said. "I told her."

Jenny broke in quickly. "Perhaps you'd like to talk with your lawyer in private before you answer?"

Cathy shook her head. "No, I know nothing."

Hawk raised his voice. "You're hiding something from us. You didn't call us. You took a chance of being murdered rather than ask for our help."

"I didn't realize the danger when this all started," Cathy said. "And it snowballed, but last night I realized . . . I told

Mr. Mitchell's wife, who was staying with me, that I would talk with the police the first thing in the morning . . . and then I found this woman." She broke, sobbing. "It wasn't my fault, was it, that she was strangled? It couldn't have been. It just couldn't."

"Of course not." Mitch put his arm about her. "She was an informant and was murdered for talking with the police."

Hawk ignored him and threw her one of his curve balls. "How come you chose Mr. Mitchell as your attorney?"

Mitch exploded. "What's that got to do with the investigation?"

"Answer the question, Miss Doyle."

Cathy said slowly, "He has a reputation for taking on little people's troubles and not charging more than they can afford."

Hawk said, "You learned that from going to Pitzer, living in Sherman Oaks, and house-sitting in Encino? The name of a criminal attorney for hookers, bagmen, and horrible, little hoods? I want to know who recommended him."

Mitch refused to be baited. "I spoke at Pitzer once. It's the kind of school that likes to hear about the little people. I've got more of a reputation than you think."

"Did you hear him talk there?"

"No, I didn't—but I could've heard about it, couldn't I?"

"But you didn't—"

Mitch broke in. "She has the right to any counsel she wishes and her reasons for choosing counsel are strictly between her and counsel."

Hawk shrugged. "Forget it."

"I don't think," Cathy said, "I can stay in my apartment tonight after what's happened."

"You've got to. You may get a phone call. We've got to keep the line of communication open." Hawk turned to Mitch. "What about Gail?"

Mitch nodded and Hawk continued, "It'd be only natural you'd want a girl friend in, and Gail's sharp and smart. But don't tell anybody anything except Gail."

"I'll have to tell Gary."

"You tell him and he tells someone else, and we might as well call a press conference. If They know everything that's going on, you could be pulling the trigger on yourself."

Hawk took a deep breath. "I could pull you in for interfering with an investigation."

Jenny said, "Your boy friend might accidentally give something away. We all do at times, even when we try not to."

Hawk rose. "Well, that's it. Let's wrap it up."

As they started to break up, Jenny said to Cathy, "I've been sitting here admiring your gold pin."

Cathy unfastened it and handed it to her. "It's just costume jewelry. A replica of a Scythian piece. Do you know the Scythians?"

"It's beautiful," Jenny said. The pin showed a small animal curled up as if asleep or dead. "Seems to me a long time ago in school I heard of them."

"They were nomads before Christ's time who roamed the plains between the Danube and the Volga. I wouldn't have known myself except I read up on them after I got the pin one Christmas. It's a snow leopard."

Mitch said to Hawk, "Are the police going to give my client any protection?"

Hawk grinned. "What's wrong with Lefty Morgan?"

He sobered and said to Cathy, "I'm pulling off the officers outside your apartment—they're too obvious—but we're going to keep you under surveillance. Go about doing whatever you want to do, and above all, don't try to spot my men, and if you do accidentally, don't give them away because these other people may be running a tail job, too. Just act natural, follow your usual routine."

He paused deliberately for effect. "I don't need to tell you, Miss Doyle, that if They, as you call Them, don't get Their money quick, They're going to finish you off. So it's the old pattern, we get Them first or They get you. It's a quiet war until the final, ultimate shot. We fight it on a hundred fronts every day—and nobody except us and Them knows it until it's over and the media report it. So if you know something or learn anything, for God's sake, give us a break. If you're not interested in your own skin, you should be in others."

Hawk was an erratic driver. Jenny would cringe, then he would slam the brakes on in time. At the noon hour, Ventura Boulevard was almost bumper to bumper.

"What do you think?" he asked. He had the wheel in hand as though wrestling a bear.

"She's got a quick, perceptive mind and unusual poise for her age. She appears forthright but there's something . . . I can't quite put my finger on it."

"I thought that, too."

"She had a ready, frank answer for all of your questions until you asked her why she went to Mr. Mitchell, and that's such a simple question. But for the first time during the interrogation, she was hesitant and seemed to be in trouble. I think if we knew why she chose Mr. Mitchell, it might open up the case a little . . . Why don't we try the fast lane? There's a truck parked up there."

Hawk pulled into the fast lane. A horn denounced him for cutting in without looking.

"Another thing," Jenny continued, "the Scythian pin was gold. Exquisitely done by a master goldsmith. She said it was costume jewelry and she may think it is."

"Expensive?"

"Very. A beautiful piece."

"I can't press her too hard on why she went to Mitch. A judge would think I was interfering with a party's right to employ counsel of their own choosing."

Hawk pulled the car into McDonald's and parked facing the blank wall of an adjoining building. "Why don't we park over there," she said. "It's shadier."

"I like the scenic view while dining. Damn, it's hot." He loosened his tie, unbuttoned his collar.

She checked her face and hair in the mirror. "She may have a simple explanation for retaining Mitchell. Anyway, I think we should look on her as a victim until we can prove otherwise."

"She's guilty of something."

"You're jumping to a conclusion that has no basis in fact."

"The Carney mob wouldn't send someone out unless she'd had dealings with them."

"She'd never heard of the Carney mob. I'd stake my reputation on that."

"She's an actress."

"Not that experienced."

"I can't look on her as both a possible subject and possible victim. I'd lose all sense of direction."

"Then make it victim. Until we know otherwise."

"You and Mitch—you've been taken in by all that sweet innocence. When you've been in this racket as long as I have—"

"Are you going to feed me or are we going to sit here enjoying the scenery?"

He went for two quarter-pounders, a root beer for her, and a Pepsi for him. They rolled down the windows and suffered. "The General's broken up. He had a thing going with Dubrovnik."

"The General did? I thought he was a loner."

"Even a loner needs someone. A dog, a cat, a woman."

"In that order? I need someone, too, and I'm not a loner."

"You've got me."

"Sometimes I wonder."

"What're you talking about?"

"I'm going to be thirty next month."

Hawk tore into the quarter-pounder. "Thirty's a good age. Old enough not to be embarrassed by mistakes and young enough to take a few chances and make some."

"For a woman, it's frightening. Maybe not for a man."

"It's not the end of the world."

She sipped her drink, then said slowly, "I want a career, which I've got and am going to keep—but I want a home also, one boy and one girl, and that calls for a husband, and at thirty if you don't have one, you grow concerned. Very concerned."

"I offered to let you darn my socks."

"How romantic."

He quit eating and his hand fumbled for hers. "At Christmas, maybe. A Christmas wedding."

"Sometimes I get to thinking . . . well, I don't know whether you love me or love being around me."

With great deliberation, he put his food and drink on the dashboard, then to her amazement took hers and placed it alongside his. He grabbed her, pulled her to him, and kissed her furiously. His hands worked their way over her.

"Not here, Hawk!" she screamed. "Not here!"

Laughing, he let her go. She straightened her clothes and finger-combed her hair. She could scarcely talk, she was so winded.

"You're not in shape," he said. "We've got to get in some practice."

She smiled. "At McDonald's, of all places. With all the kids around."

"The kids? Where've you been? We can't teach them anything they don't know."

26

Back in her living room, Cathy stood transfixed. Her heart pounded. Her old furniture had been moved out, a new set brought in. Two easy chairs with a lamp table between them stood where the sofa had been. A stranger stood before her. When Mitch had dropped her off, this man had ushered her quickly inside. Politely he had asked Lefty and Gary to remain outside. He was most solicitous. Would she care for coffee, tea? He hoped she liked the new furniture. He looked more like a college guy than a police officer, yet he identified himself as one. He said his name was Barney Carlson and that Lieutenant

Hawkins had asked him to change the room around and to brief her. He had a nice smile and a low-pitched voice.

"Don't hesitate to rearrange the furniture," he was saying. "The manager and I just shoved it in from another apartment. Men aren't too good about these things."

"May I sit down?" She had the strangest sensation her legs were about to crumple.

"Sure. I'll get out in a minute. Three things I want to talk to you about. The most important is your safety. We're going to look after you day and night. We'll have officers watching this apartment around the clock and running a surveillance on you everywhere you go."

She sat a little straighter. "That Italian statesman—what was his name?—he had five bodyguards. They killed them all when they kidnapped him. And in Germany—"

"I'll level with you. Even if we had a thousand men on you, somebody might get to you. It's like birth control. Nothing's 100 per cent sure. But the odds are about the same—and that's not bad."

He held out a two-by-two-inch radio device. "Carry this on you at all times. It's the same as the ones executives and sales people use. Except smaller. Keep it set 'on' to broadcast and we'll monitor you. It's mostly for use as a one-way deal since it could be dangerous to talk with us. But if you're sure you're by yourself, and no one can overhear, and you have to talk to us, go ahead. Remember, though, that when we talk back keep the volume down. And don't carry it in your purse. Put it under your clothes somewhere."

"What about my bra?"

"That's the first place They'd look if They searched you. What about putting it inside the top of your jeans. You may look a little pregnant . . ."

She smiled. She felt so much better. She hadn't liked Lieutenant Hawkins but this Barney Carlson . . . well, to use one of her favorite Mexican phrases, he was *muy simpático.*

"I want to show you something else." He led the way into her bedroom. "I dated a girl at Pitzer once. She liked to talk about how brilliant she was."

"We've got some like that. I guess every campus has."

He opened a closet door. "I didn't snoop around but I had to get back in here." He pushed her clothes aside. On the floor, with shoes stacked on top, was a small, rectangular, box-type device. "We call this our 410. It's a telecopier transceiver made by Xerox. It's magic. Lots of businesses use them. They can put seventy-five letters, memos, documents, what have you in this automatic feeder here, dial a number, and three thousand miles away another transceiver duplicates it in a matter of minutes. Since we've got this on a direct line, you won't need to dial. If you've got something to tell us, write it out and put it on the feeder and push this button. That way, you don't have to use the phone or the radio. I've checked the apartment for a hidden mike and the phone company checked for a tap. But that doesn't mean anything. Somebody sitting in a room three hundred yards from here could bring in your voice. And even the experts can't be sure about hidden mikes and taps. Want to make a trial run? Here's a note pad."

She wrote, "I am testing . . . testing." She put it in the feeder, pushed the button.

"Good," he said. "That's all there is to it. One thing more. Only you and we know about this. Don't tell anyone. Lefty, your boy friend, Mitch's wife. I must have your promise on that. It's important. It could be your life line."

She promised. "Did Lieutenant Hawkins brief you about me?"

He nodded. "You're probably burned at him. I know he can be awfully tough—but he's one hell of a guy, fair and honest. He gave me only one instruction—to protect you."

He stood very close to her and a good feeling rose in her.

She stood straight-backed and tense, a fist clenched at one side. He never looked up. He was busy scratching his name to a sheaf of letters. In Personnel, when she had reported in to sign the routine new employee forms, the woman had said brusquely, "The Man wants to see you," and indicated his office across the corridor.

"I don't know who the woman was, where she came from, anything about her. When I got up this morning, there she was stretched out on the sofa. Please hear me out. I know you said if I had a problem . . . but it isn't *my* problem."

His hand stopped in mid-flight. His beady little eyes, hardened by the years, possessed her. "No problem?" he said sarcastically, pressing a button. "I have had drunks and hypochondriacs and oversexed bitches but never, never . . . this . . ."

A secretary looked in. He said, "Show the young lady out and don't ever let her back in. Notify security."

Leaving, Cathy muttered, "To hell with you, mister. There are other jobs."

Going down in the elevator, she leaned in one corner, crying. The other passengers glanced her way, then averted their eyes. All except a white-haired woman who put a hand briefly on Cathy's arm. There were still kind people in this world.

She was breaking and knew it. That was what They wanted. That was why the woman's body had been dumped in her living room. Fiercely, in her thoughts, she swore at Them. They would never break her. Never. No matter what They did, she had the guts to defy Them.

From deep down, though, came a weak whisper. She was a child lost with others in a snowy forest, mustering a show of braggadocio to impress and reassure them—and herself.

At three-sixteen the first message came over Old 410, as the transceiver was called. It read: LEAVING IN FEW MINUTES FOR ZUMA BEACH WITH GARY EDISON AND MR. MORGAN. TAKING GARY'S CAR. BLUE 1977 CHEVROLET. LICENSE PLATES UQS 793. CATHY DOYLE.

Moving rapidly, Barney rounded up another officer and quickly obtained Hawk's permission to take Angela. The plan was: They would rent a motorboat at Paradise Cove and cruise off the Zuma beach but close to shore. They needed a girl to sun-bathe to give the craft a pleasure-boat look. Two other officers would be available on land, the two who would follow Cathy as a part of the normal surveillance.

"I haven't anything to wear," Angela complained before leaving.

"Barney will loan you his shorts," Hawk said. "Won't you Barney?"

Gary had been adamant. He had refused to drive her to Zuma beach.

"What could possibly happen on a beach with people about and all kinds of open space? I need to escape, Gary. I need to get away from it all for a couple of hours."

He yielded eventually to her entreaties. He was frightened for her, and she was touched. He was such a gentle guy, always so concerned.

Lefty sat in the back seat and George was instructed to sit alongside him. Only minutes after they took off, George was on her lap, all seventy pounds, with most of his body leaning out of the window, defying gravity. His tail wagged faster than a baton finishing Khachaturian's "Sabre Dance."

She had worn a bikini under her dress, and when she stepped out of the dress at Zuma beach, she liked the way Gary looked at her. A warmth surged through her, dispersing the day's fears. He fumbled, struggling to unzip her tight, black boots. She leaned down to help and was crushed by his long, muscular arms. She thought he would crack her ribs, and didn't care. George, on a leash, broke them up. He demanded action of a different kind.

Striking across the beach barefoot, she bent a little to offset the strong, persistent blow of the wind. It was unvarying, a nagging kind that scraped the nerves of the hardiest. It tempered the heat but still the sun drained all life. The churning surf cracked and thundered. Not many were about on the long, blinding strand.

Gary went ahead while she lingered with Lefty, who wanted to speak with her alone. "I heard 'em talking—Mitch and that copper." His voice had a whine. "They're treating you like you was dirt. They wouldn't believe Mary mother of Jesus."

He crossed himself. "If I can be of help, ma'am . . . You treated me good. I know what it's like to be kicked around. All my life they been doing it to me. If I can do anything . . ."

She kissed him on the cheek. "I feel good just knowing you're here. I may need you . . ."

"Run along now with your young man. I'll sit here where I can see you. Raise a hand if you want me."

He watched her go, tall and shapely, with blond hair blowing in the wind. He touched his cheek. It had been ages since a girl had kissed him. He wished he were in a different business. Even though she was twenty years younger, still many girls preferred older men.

Man, what a body.

He wiped the thought away.

The woman was about sixty, sick-looking, her angular face gray and shattered into a hundred tiny lines, like plexiglass that had been hit with a hammer. She sat alone in the back seat of a Le Baron parked on Pacific Coast Highway. Her farsighted vision brought Cathy and Lefty up sharp, then followed Cathy across the sucking sand to Gary and the dog.

In the front seat, hunched baboon-like over the steering wheel, sat a man thirty years her junior. He chewed gum as if beating it to death. His big, egg-shaped eyes missed nothing of the action ahead, behind or alongside. A .30-.30 rifle with telescopic sight lay on his lap and extended over the adjoining seat. He fingered it impatiently. Traffic kept up a low, persistent roar.

"Good scene, Billie." His tone was that of a blackjack dealer. "A perfect view. The traffic will cover the shot—and nothing to block a fast take-off."

"We'll see." Her long fingers, with nails manicured but unpainted, expertly adjusted a small sound cone. The cone, which resembled a cheerleader's megaphone, could be aimed like a rifle and register a cough three hundred yards distant. The woman had listened with it to the conversation between Cathy and Lefty. She had set the volume so low, however, that their voices came through as static threaded with whispers.

"Never have a better chance," the man said.

"We'll see."

George had gone wild. He raced to the water's edge, then tore back. He streaked along the beach, as if it were paved, and circling, rushed up to her. He bounded about like a dervish. She bent down to rough up his fur and he gave her a couple of hasty swipes.

"Why don't you kiss him back," Gary called out. "He's getting a complex. Give him a couple of licks."

Laughing, she sat on her heels facing Gary, her back to the ocean. Taking his face in her hands, she kissed him hard. Their lips melded until she had to break to breathe.

He turned deadly earnest. "The police think you know—"

"You'll have to talk louder." She indicated the surf. He deliberately kept his voice low, fearing he would speak too loudly, the fear of every deaf person. She had worked hours with him on the volume level and had set up a signal system. In company, she would move a hand slightly up from the wrist to indicate he should raise his voice. She would drop her hand to suggest he lower it.

"The police think you know more than you're telling. They got pretty rough with me—thought you must've told me."

Her body tensed. "Not you, Gary. Not you, too. Everybody's on me—and I'm so confused and scared. Nothing makes sense."

"But you know something?"

Her hesitation betrayed her. "I don't know who this man is. I don't know what he's talking about. Before God, I don't."

"You're not going to tell me?"

She shut her eyes, fighting back tears. If she told him everything and They found out . . .

He continued, "If I were a hearing person—"

"No, no! It's not that. You've got to believe me, it isn't that. Give me time. A day or two. I wouldn't keep anything from you. I think if you love someone . . ."

He held her hand in a tight grip. "But you did—and you are."

"Please don't hassle me. I haven't done anything, you know that."

"I know you haven't, but . . ."

"You don't trust me."

"Isn't it the other way around?"

"You're being cruel!" George licked her and she buried her head in his fur.

Gary said, "You would've come running if I could hear . . . if you could talk to me without this stupid business of having to face me."

She fought back a sudden burst of anger. She was too exhausted, too near tears, and too close to the breaking point to continue. "If you think that, Gary . . ." She got up. "I'm not going to say something I'll regret because I'm upset. I wish you loved me enough to overlook it and forgive me. I wish you did."

Sobbing, she trudged off down the beach. George was at her heels. He sensed something wrong through the tone of the people he loved. His tail no longer wagged.

With her vision blurred by tears and her senses bludgeoned, she was not conscious of a fully dressed man wearing dark glasses approaching on the run.

The driver looked expectantly at the woman in the back seat. He had told her, "Only eleven seconds." Two seconds to raise the rifle, five to sight and fire, and four to put it down and start the car. He realized he might have figured the time a little too closely. But even with another five seconds, the job would be done so fast that no one around them would likely spot him. Not unless someone was watching him, and he was constantly on the prowl for that.

The woman was having difficulty with the sound cone. The girl was about to pass out of range. She had strayed farther down the beach than the woman had anticipated.

"Not yet," she told the driver.

Higher up on the beach, Lefty followed Cathy. He was never more than a hundred feet from her. He wished he had brought his old Luger. He had expected Gary to be with her at all times, and was puzzled that she would wander away by herself. If he had imagined that would happen, he would have cautioned her. It was not like her to separate herself from Gary and him, to put herself in a hazardous position. Maybe she thought the dog was sufficient protection. But in a showdown, the dog—he hated the breed, smelly, always sniffing around, all over you, noisy nuisances—would be of scant help. True, the hound would attack if she was mugged or beaten up, which was unlikely, but the dog would never suspect a stranger carrying a knife or gun or intent on kidnapping.

He had a feeling about this, a cold, clammy feeling.

Barney was surprised, too, that she would take off alone. He started the engine.

"Come in, Unit Ten. Come in Ten."

Ten signed in.

"Leave car and run tight tail on victim now walking north along water's edge, nearing lifeguard platform. Repeat, tight tail. Man approaching her, about forty, dark-haired, medium height, potbellied, in light summer trousers, blue sport shirt open at neck, dark glasses. Could be suspect."

He slowed the engine and passed within thirty feet. He stopped a short distance ahead and let the motor idle. Angela sat beside him, dressed as she had been at the office.

With relief, Barney spotted Lefty following Cathy, and the other two officers on Lefty's heels. If anything did happen, either he, Lefty, or the officers could reach her within seconds.

He drew himself up rigid. Hawk would never approve such thinking. Seconds were all that a killer might need.

Gary rose to follow her. He was confused and contrite. Had he been cruel? It didn't matter whether he had . . . if she thought he had, that was all that mattered. He had been hurt and when he was hurt, he became the aggressor. He felt guilt and sadness in the pit of his being. She was in trouble and he should have been understanding. She needed laughter and escape and love, and instead he had given her one more problem.

The man was striding along beside her. With street shoes on, he was having difficulty walking in the sand. He was talking. He was Soft Shoe. Never, not even years later, could she mistake that voice.

"Don't stop walking!" he shouted over the thunder of a crashing wave.

She hesitated, more bewildered than frightened.

He repeated, "Don't stop walking! Look straight ahead."

Blindly she followed his orders. Her eyes, sharp now, took in the scene. People were about her, they were close. She could cry out for help and be heard.

"I've got news for you. Are you hearing me?"

She nodded. Deliberately she slowed her walk. He didn't notice.

"I'm quitting Them. I wouldn't go along with Them killing you and we had a row. I couldn't live with my wife if I let Them murder you. They're going to strangle you slowly, give you a chance to tell Them where the money is, tighten the cord until you're near death, let you breathe, do it over and over, and They've been given orders if you don't spill after six tries to finish you off."

Don't panic, she warned herself. Don't lose control of your thinking. He's using emotional words. That's what Mr. Mitchell had called them and with them, he can destroy you.

Soft Shoe continued, "I've figured out how you can get out of this—turn the tables on Them—but I can't talk here. They're watching us from that new Le Baron parked up there. Don't look now but when I leave you . . ."

"They've got a .30-.30 rifle. Don't worry. They won't use it now. They've got some plan, I don't know what it is, to show up with it and frighten the wits out of you.

"Here's what you do, Cathy. Meet me at 4 A.M. at the produce market downtown. The City Market. The Number 14 loading dock. Off San Julian and Eleventh. You got that? Number 14. San Julian and Eleventh. Ask anybody—4 A.M. Come by yourself. If anybody's with you, you won't see me. If you tell the police and they pick me up, you're dead. I'm the only guy who can get you off death row and I've got a plan that's sure-fire. It can't miss and this time tomorrow you're free of Them."

He halted abruptly. "See you at 4 A.M. Number 14 dock."

He headed the other way, climbing toward the highway. She looked about frantically. Then Gary had her in his arms, and Lefty was asking who it was, and George was once again bounding about.

She scarcely was conscious of all of this. She was in shock. All that hammered in her thoughts was 4 A.M. and the Number 14 dock. The City Market. Off San Julian and Eleventh.

27

Entering his office building, Mitch nodded to Old Charlie without seeing him and answered a hello tossed out by someone without knowing who it was. His mind was on the confrontation at the brokerage house between Hawk and Cathy. Over and over he analyzed what each had said.

Only the Drop Dead group bellowing in the record shop jarred him back to reality. They sounded, he thought, like a bunch of trapped wildcats.

"Hi," Gail said. "I missed you."

She went into his arms. She was the one bright thing in his life. With a kiss, a touch on the cheek, a word, she turned on the sun.

"How'd it go?"

"A draw. She matched Hawk point by point. They both used some histrionics. She's a sharp gal with a quick mind. Any messages?"

"A couple. Doc Anderson. He's in trouble again. And Little Augie. He wouldn't tell me what's bothering him."

Talking, they drifted into his office. "Lefty," she said. "I think he's sold us out, and if he has, and he's with Cathy all the time, he could be tipping Them off, setting her up for something."

Mitch glanced over several notes she had placed on his desk. "I'll get rid of him."

"I'm not sure you can. Cathy likes him."

"Let me handle him. These kids"—he had a memo in hand about the thirteen-year-old and his sister—"I know them. Their father's dead and the mother's sleeping around, full of booze. The boy's looking out for himself and the girl. I don't know how they do it but he's keeping both of them in school."

His voice rose. "I don't understand some of these bastards. Here are a couple of kids making it on their own when they could be on welfare costing the taxpayers a bundle, and these guys sit on their fat butts with the heart of a dingo dog . . ."

"I've already set the fee. One dollar."

He grinned. He was going into a scrap he loved. "Get me the Franchise Tax Board in Sacramento."

"God, I love you," she said.

When he got through to Sacramento, he was switched to a half-dozen offices before he found someone who would talk with him. "I'm an attorney representing Frank Gonzales, age thirteen, and his sister, age eight. They sell flowers on street corners and to restaurants. They have no other income and only a mother who's seldom around and when she is she's drunk. I don't know how the hell they manage but they're staying in school. And one of your men comes around and wants to collect six per cent sales tax from them—for all summer. The great state of California hounding a couple of little kids for a measly few bucks. . . . I know what the law is. You don't have to tell me. But you don't collect from garage sales or church bazaars and a lot of other affairs where it might be political dynamite. Well, I'm going to light a few fuses myself. I'll see that it gets a big splash in every newspaper in the country and on television. A couple of Mexican-American kids making it on their own, staying off welfare. . . . Okay, I'll hold off for forty-eight hours while you look into it, but if I don't hear from you by day after tomorrow, I'm going to let go—and there won't be a woman in this country with a dry eye after she sees a picture of those kids."

He hung up with a slam. He felt good. The old juices were circulating with the pound of surf.

"In this corner," Gail said, "Frank Mitchell, the challenger, and in this corner, the state of California . . .

"Now that you're going so good," she continued, "how about taking on Marilyn and getting the Texan his money back?"

"That's a different horse."

"Horse is right. She rolled him, Mitch, and she's cutting you in."

Mitch shook his head. "It's over. Case closed."

He caught the fiery look in her eyes. She was a fighter herself. If she considered something wrong, she hung on like a terrier. "With you around," he had said once, "I've got even higher principles than Lefty."

"Oh, all right," he conceded. "I don't believe in it, I'm dead set against it but you'll hound me . . ."

A sleepy Marilyn answered. "It's the dead of night for me," she complained.

"Look," he said, "you lied to me. You said you didn't roll the guy. You swore it by the Virgin Mary—and I believed you. . . . I know you're a lady and won't do certain things but that hasn't anything to do with the fact you stole his money. So get over here with the seven hundred dollars—I'll keep a hundred for a fee of the two hundred you paid Gail—that makes eight hundred. . . . You either get your ass over here with the money or I'll never handle another case for you. I worked my heart out a couple of years ago, remember?—and if I hadn't, you'd be in prison. . . . No, next week isn't all right." After hanging up, he sat in thought.

"I'm sorry," she said. "I shouldn't've asked you—"

"It's not you or Marilyn. It's Lefty."

28

At five-thirty that afternoon, Jenny, Barney, and the General gathered in Hawk's office. Each felt the tension and apprehension that come when a case breaks too fast, and detectives must outline strategy, draw plans, and investigate leads without giving them sufficient thought.

Hawk rubbed his knotted neck cords. "He used all the old threats—They are going to half-strangle her, six times, he said, before They finish her off—but he made one very interesting change in tactics. He didn't ask her to bring the million. He didn't even mention it. What do you make of that?"

He looked at Jenny. More and more he was coming to respect her analysis and judgment. She said slowly, thinking her way through the enigma, "Several possibilities. He will propose a different arrangement than before for the delivery of the money. One They think is a foolproof scheme. Throwing the money from a moving train. Something like that. Or he may be setting her up for a kidnapping so They can work her over at close quarters. I think we ought to listen to the tape a few times more. His voice has a different quality. The same old urgency and hard sell but . . . a little frightened, like something's about to happen that scares him."

Technical had recorded the conversation as it was being broadcast by the radio Cathy had placed in her tote bag. Within minutes after Soft Shoe mentioned the parked Le

Baron, a cruise car had been dispatched to begin a surveillance. By then, however, the Le Baron was gone and though scores had passed it on their way to the beach, none remembered it. Sometimes Hawk thought the breaks decided more cases than all the detective work. A little kid hop-skipping along sees and remembers a license plate number, and a rapist or murderer is caught. A truck pulls up in daylight to a house and empties it, and not a neighbor is curious.

Jenny continued, "The City Market—4 A.M. It's all a part of the breaking-down process. It's a frightening hour for someone who's already been terrorized for so long. The site itself is nerve-wracking with the rumble and roar of the trucks, men shouting, and what looks and sounds like pandemonium. He'll talk to her under what are the worst possible conditions for her. They've thought this through very carefully."

Hawk spread out two sectional maps. One was of the City Market, spread over ten acres just a few steps from the downtown business district, fifty houses receiving, selling, and loading produce. The other was of the Terminal Market, which covered twelve acres with four hundred and thirty-five stalls. The two markets combined were among the largest in the world, handling the equivalent of ninety-five thousand carloads of produce a year, shipped in from thirty-two states and twenty-six countries. California alone grew more than 40 per cent of the nation's fruits and vegetables.

"He may switch from the City to the Terminal Market at the last minute," Hawk said.

"Will she go?" Jenny asked.

"She's got to," Hawk said.

"Why should she? She's intelligent. She knows we can set up only limited protection with hundreds of big rigs and people moving about, drivers, loaders, dispatchers, and in the dark."

Hawk tightened his lips. "She has to. We can't apprehend the subject with what we have. Only his word against hers, and only threats. No overt action, no provable intent to inflict bodily harm. Even if we could, we want the rest of Them and he's our only line to Them."

"Want me to talk with her?" Barney asked.

"He's more her age," Jenny put in.

Hawk glared. "At thirty-one I'm not exactly over the hill."

"You've been rough with her," she continued. "Barney hasn't. It'd be good psychology . . ."

She bit her lip. She shouldn't have used the word psychology.

Hawk said evenly, restraining obvious anger, "I don't base decisions on books. Never have. Never will. What've you got there?"

He asked the question of Barney. Jenny settled back, hurt. She chided herself. She was being childish. Hawk had the responsibility. He made the decisions. With any crime in progress, one person had to.

Barney ran down the reports his officers had submitted about the investigation to date:

Clinton, North Carolina, had reported that Cathy Doyle's father, Joseph Doyle, age fifty, an investment banker who lived in an exclusive district, had not been seen for the last three weeks. His caretaker advised that he had not been paid for a month, and had no idea of Doyle's whereabouts. Doyle lived alone. His second wife, Sarah Elisa, had died the previous January 20. Doyle's investment interests extended to Atlanta, Birmingham, and Charleston. He was frequently on business trips for long periods, and hence, friends thought nothing of his current absence.

A check of the indices on Gary Edison, Cathy's boy friend, proved negative. In other words, he had no record, not even a moving car violation. He was twenty-four, lived with a dog named George, no known relatives, had worked for eighteen months as a computer programmer but presently was unemployed. He was liked by his neighbors, who reported he was a quiet but friendly person. They said he was in financial straits.

The investigation into the murder of Marissa Dubrovnik had developed no worth-while leads. A policewoman had been stationed in the apartment to answer the phone on the possibility a mobster might call who did not know about her death but might have knowledge that would provide hard-core leads.

The photo taken at the Forum, with the hand-printing on the back, had been forwarded to the FBI. Its files, containing thousands of hand-printed specimens, would be checked to determine if any matched.

Inquiries at the mortuary brought a denial that anyone had phoned Cathy Doyle from there. "We never use phone solicitation," the owner said indignantly.

At the downtown library, in the periodical section, an investigator found a bright young librarian who took one look at the clipping headed GIRL STRANGLED IN NORTH WOODS and identified the newspaper from which it had been cut as the Denver *Post*. The Denver police were requested to advise if there had been any arrest or conviction, and if any suspect or convicted party had an alias of the Gorilla.

Miami reported that the Carney mob, operating under the name of the Hong Kong Finance Company, was a conglomerate with many divisions. Some were criminal, some legal. They included: Hotels and Resorts; Computers (thefts on a vast scale by manipulating computers); Off Shore Operations (a cover for the smuggling of drugs from Central and South American countries); General (extortion, blackmail, and similar projects); Gold and Silver (the theft, resale, and smuggling of bullion); Stocks and Bonds (forged and counterfeit); Off Shore Financial (the laundering and hiding of money in Caribbean banks). The list went on and on.

A Miami authority estimated that the Hong Kong Finance Company was engaged in a billion-dollar operation, masterminded so cleverly that it was difficult to find the kind of evidence needed for successful prosecution. Occasionally there would be arrests and convictions, and a division would be closed temporarily. Within a few months, the division would resume operations with a new face and invariably new methods that were more impregnable than the previous ones.

The Arizona authorities had little to report about Samuel Porter alias Soft Shoe. Tucson had no record on him. He lived quietly with his wife Vivian and their two teen-age sons in a long, low adobe brick home of Territorial architecture that sat on an acre of desert growth in the Catalina foothills. Unlike other big-time mobsters who had migrated to Arizona, the Porters had no high chain-link fences topped with barbed wire, or police dogs, or electronic warning devices.

Although they kept to themselves, the neighbors liked them. They contributed generously to community projects and were patrons of the Sunday Evening Forum, the civic theater, and the Tucson Ballet. He told people he was "in investments," and as a cover had taken an office in the La Placita complex in downtown Tucson. Only his name, in small letters, appeared on the door. No one had seen him about the office since he rented it.

There was no evidence he was engaged in drug running across the Mexican border, seventy miles to the south, or prostitution, the two major operations of the mobs. He had no apparent association, either, with the parties responsible for the murder of Don Bolles, the Phoenix newspaperman whose car blew up one hot day when he turned on the ignition. A brilliant investigative reporter, Bolles had succeeded in ferreting out information about the operations of the Mafia and the syndicates.

Along with thousands of other snow birds, as the natives called them, who had fled the Midwest and East for the Sun Belt, had come the mobster big shots from Chicago and New York. They moved their crime with them. Never again would Arizona be the same. Arizona could no more eradicate them than could Chicago or New York or Miami. They would murder any Don Bolles who poked too far into their affairs. As far as could be determined, Sammy Porter was not a part of their setups. He was a loner, a free-lancer for hire to any outfit that wanted his highly specialized technique.

A surveillance team that had begun a "loose" tail job on him at Zuma beach reported they had trailed him to a small residential hotel in Westwood, an area of high-rise buildings, expensive apartments, and beautiful, expansive homes, all sharing space with the University of California at Los Angeles. The two officers thought it odd that he had never once looked back.

It was as if he had no interest in knowing whether he was being followed. This in itself suggested he was confident that even with the authorities watching, he could bring off any plan he proposed to the victim. Another theory put forth was that he wanted the police present as protection. He had said he was quitting Them. Hawk thought this was only so much fiction, concocted to lull the victim into complacency. Still, if he actually had broken with Them, he might want officers present.

Either way Hawk had a gut feeling a trap was about to be sprung. "He'll try a moving operation."

A moving operation was one in which the criminal choreographed, like a ballet, split-second movements that would throw a surveillance team, which was always more or less in a fixed formation, off base. With no way of determining what was coming, the team would be moments behind in reacting to each move. In a crisis, even the most experienced men might lose the criminal or be gunned down.

Next Jenny reported on a conversation she had had with Dr. Clarence Bosworth, a noted historian at UCLA. He was lean, tall, and weathered. His graying hair was cropped short.

Jenny handed him the card sent Cathy by Soft Shoe with the quote from the unknown author. For several minutes he studied it. "I take it you have an erudite criminal."

"We don't know. I should explain that this was sent to a party we believe innocent with the primary motive being to frighten her. Perhaps that's all there is to it. But we thought possibly there might be symbolism or a hidden meaning, and if we could determine what the author was describing, the people and the place, we might have a lead."

He smiled. "I don't think you'll be arresting the writer who did this."

He read the card again. "I wish we had the entire paragraph. These ellipses shorten it to the point it's most difficult to determine the style. If we had the style, we might identify the writer. There does seem to be a certain cadence, as if the author had a poetic bent."

"I knew it would be difficult," Jenny said.

"Very difficult. Most people don't realize the immense volume of ancient writing that has come down to us. They think of the *Iliad*, Aesop, Herodotus, the Bible, the Koran—the well-known names—and don't know we have the output of thousands of authors over the centuries. Sappho, Solon, Simonides of Ceos, Pindar, Hesiod, Lysistratus, Archilochus of Paros, to name a few from the time of the early Greek culture. And all of the hundreds of cultures we don't do justice to, the Sanskrit, the Urdu—"

She had to interrupt. His vast knowledge was sweeping him off course. "I thought it might have been about Tamerlane, the Mongolian hordes. Something from that era. Our party has a Scythian gold pin. The burial custom . . ."

He warmed up again. "A very good guess. I have to point out, though, that many peoples followed similar burial customs. Frankly, it would take an enormous amount of time to run this down. I couldn't do it myself but I have a student who would find it an exciting project. I couldn't promise when . . ."

They discussed other developments, then broke up. Barney and the General left to plot the setup for the 4 A.M. rendezvous.

Hawk called Jenny back. "I want you along when I talk with Doyle."

She looked her surprise.

"You've got a point," he continued. "I'm sure she hates my guts after this morning."

"I had no right to say—"

"You had every right. I want you to speak up. But only at the proper time when I'm in a good mood." He grinned. "As a psychologist you should know when that is."

She shook her head. "You're quite some guy."

He continued brusquely, "The question is, where are we going to see Doyle so that the subject won't tail her and know about it?"

He rolled a pencil around, then called in Angela. "Put a note in Old 410. 'We must talk with you. Do you have a doctor you go to or a dentist where we could meet who might have the office open nights? If so, give name and address and meet us there at nine.'"

He rose and stretched. "Been a long, rough day."

"You love it," she said. "You're never going back to the Pecos, are you?"

"I hope so."

"This is no kind of life here . . ."

He laughed low. "That's what my mother told my father when they got married back in Pittsburgh, and that's how come we lived on the Pecos. I wish you'd known my mother. She was some kind of gal. She had to ford the Pecos horseback every week to a settlement called Dayton to get us food and things, and I remember her telling about once—she was just a young thing then—meeting up out in the wilds with some rough-looking characters. There were lots of drifters then. But they didn't bother her. It was different in that era. Women were respected. Well, enough of that."

He shoved papers into a desk drawer and they drifted toward the door. He said, "You take the lead with Doyle. I'll come in, though, if there's anything I want to get over. But if she brings that Mitch along . . ."

With Jenny alongside him, Hawk located the address on Ventura Boulevard in Encino of Dr. Douglas Watkins, turned left at the next corner, and took an alley to the back door. It was pitch dark and quiet.

Gail opened the door from the inside and they walked into a small private office. "Where's Lefty?" Hawk asked.

"We left him in the car."

In the limited light from a desk lamp, they saw a desk with Cathy sitting behind it, charcoals on the wall, file cabinets, and on the far side, another door. Beyond it they heard voices. "The receptionist," Gail said.

"Marki," Cathy added. "A beautiful gal." She held up a charcoal. "I used this as an excuse in case anyone was following me. Brought it in to ask Doug what he thought about getting another frame."

Los Angeles' dentists, Hawk recalled, included several who had distinguished themselves in other fields. One had become a film star, another a Broadway playright, and now Watkins, an artist of repute.

Cathy's voice was thin, tired. "You came to pressure me into going."

Outside there was the low talk of the receptionist with arriving patients. Cathy continued, "You don't have to. They'll do something awful to Gary if I don't. I get this feeling about things. It's almost psychic. It usually comes out the way I feel. Do you know what I'm trying to say?"

Hawk sagged with relief. He had come prepared for resistance.

"He's so vulnerable. You know he's deaf and they could slip up on him or break into the house, except that George would kill anyone if he thought they were going to harm Gary."

"Don't torture yourself," Gail said. "He knows the setup. He can look out for himself."

Hawk produced photographs of a low warehouse, sectioned off in narrow compartments, all numbered. "This is the layout. A close-up of Number 14. You'll park right here, alongside the building. We'll see that the space is kept clear. Then you'll take these outside steps up to the dock. I doubt if the subject will talk with you in the open since there's so much noise at that hour with the big rigs coming and going. He may take you inside the warehouse.

"Don't let it throw you if at the last minute he switches you to another dock. They're all about the same except most don't have steps. Except for the parking, it doesn't matter whether it's Number 14 or Number 16 or whatever. We'll have men outside and inside the warehouse and following you from your apartment to the market and back again."

He briefed her on more details. She asked questions, and he felt better because she had. She had a quick, logical mind.

"May we have the photos?" Gail asked. "To study." Hawk handed them over.

"One thing more," Jenny said quietly. "Don't let him talk you into going someplace else with him, no matter how much he threatens. Once you're in his car, you're his hostage and there's not much we can safely do. With a gun in your ribs he holds the upper hand."

"But Gary . . ."

Jenny turned to Hawk. "We should have someone on him."

"We'll put a tight tail on him but we're not going to inform him about it. And you mustn't either. Agreed?"

"Why not?"

Jenny said, "You have to take our word that we know what we're doing."

"I'm sure they have a good reason," Gail said.

"I don't know . . ."

Jenny put a hand on her arm. "Please, darling, trust us."

"You? Okay, you."

Hawk caught her meaning. That Jenny. She could charm anyone. She had more than that. Honesty and integrity. It showed in those big eyes, in her resonant voice.

Jenny continued, "I don't want to frighten you but we have to be frank. In this kind of an ongoing crime, this man may use another ploy besides the threat to kill. It happens occasionally. If he got you in his car alone at that hour of the morning, out in an isolated area, he could threaten to rape you, and if that didn't faze you, he might just do it. You would be in such a state of shock then that you would agree to anything. It would be the final act in the terror technique he has been employing."

Cathy's voice hardened. "I've told you I don't have the money."

"That doesn't matter. He thinks you have. Don't forget that."

Hawk asked, "How're you feeling?"

Jenny intervened quickly. "He means, are you up to this? Do you think you can carry it through?"

Cathy stiffened. "I've got to. I'll do my autogenics, calm myself down, get organized. I'll give Them a fight . . ."

In the soft lamplight Hawk studied her. Depending on interpretation, there was either hardness or determination in her eyes. She had guts all right, no matter whether she had fallen innocently into something or was a mysterious part of a crime. Jenny continued to insist on considering her a victim. He tried but, at moments such as this, found it difficult. All and all, however, she was meeting a desperate character in the dark in a setting where protection was very limited.

She had said she had to keep the rendezvous because of Gary. Hawk had welcomed her concern. It gave him an opportunity to run a surveillance on Gary Edison under the pretext of protecting him, with her knowledge and approval. She had agreed not to tell him. The very fact she had agreed set him to thinking. It was only natural for a woman deeply in love to insist on telling her fiancé.

"If I could only get some sleep," Cathy continued.

"Be sure to eat something before you start out," Hawk said.

Jenny smiled. "He thinks courage comes in a malt. The main thing, try to get a little mental rest. Get your mind off this and think of something else."

"I'll see to that," Gail said. "We've got a lot in common to talk about."

From her own ordeals, though, Gail doubted if it were ever possible to pull one's thoughts off the treadmill in times of near disaster. One might talk intelligently about another subject but at the same time, the brain kept the donkey pulling the treadmill. There was no peace for the tortured.

29

11 P.M.

Lefty sat dozing in a corner, occasionally slitting open his little weasel eyes. Never had he looked to Gail more like a predatory animal on the prowl.

She had said earlier, "You can go now. I'm staying all night."

He turned plaintively to Cathy. "If you want I should leave . . ."

She patted him on the cheek. "Please stay. I feel better when you're around."

Outside, the noisy hubbubbing children who had been playing in the pool had been packed off to solitary confinement. An occasional car lumbered and groaned and on the concrete, heels shuffled, clicked, and pattered. Conversations were hurried and low. Abner Blanton tolerated no happy talk after eleven.

Since returning to the apartment, Cathy had been more distraught than terrified. Distraught because she had held back from Gary the information that she had an early morning rendezvous with the stranger. "He knows I'm not telling him everything, and he's hurt and furious, and I don't blame him. But when you start holding back on someone you just keep doing it."

She calmed immediately, found scratch paper, and took a long time writing a note which she gave to Lefty to deliver to Gary.

When Lefty was gone, Gail said, "He'll open it."

"I don't care. I trust Lefty completely." It was now Lefty, no longer Mr. Morgan. "We all have to have someone close to us we can trust."

Without a word, Cathy went to the bedroom. A half-hour later, worried because of the quiet, Gail softly opened the door. In the dark, Cathy sat in a straight chair, her feet planted on the floor, her hands resting palms up on her knees, not touching to avoid a feedback, her eyes closed, and her lips moving silently.

Later Cathy pushed aside garments in the clothes closet. At the back, stacked against the wall, were old shoe boxes. Each bore the date of a year. She picked up one with 1978 penciled in bold figures on the front and, going to the bed, opened it. A spate of letters fell out. She riffled gently through them and chose one at random.

"For years we've been talking about language, and I wondered if you had noticed the use of 'sort of'? The boy asks, "Did you have a good time?' and the girl answers, 'Sort of.' I decry this mental attitude. Very little is damned outright or supported forcefully. It seems that anything is fine as long as it isn't too positive or believed in too strongly. Such avoidance puts one's opinions in the realm of total acceptance."

She smiled to herself. Her father loved to explore the way language revealed character. Putting the letter back in the envelope, she noticed the postmark, Rabat, Morocco. That was the year he had written several times from Beirut and Rabat.

Suddenly she wanted so badly the little ecstacies that were a precious part of life although you never thought anything about them until one day they were not there. The birds singing, the purr of a cat, the soft touch of Gary's hand on her arm, the peaceful shade of the great old trees on the campus, the quiet of the study period, even the familiar all's-right-with-the-world of the garbage truck and the slamming parts. It was as if she were dying and these were memories never to be known again.

Midnight.

Hawk replaced the phone and looked up at Jenny. Even in the air-cooled office, he felt the sweat and grime of the day. His bones ached from weariness. "Lefty Morgan took off at eleven-twenty-three."

She tried straightening but the effort was too much. "We should have a tail on him."

A young officer hustled in—one could tell from his walk he had just come on duty—and dropped a teletype on Hawk's desk. It was from Denver, in answer to the query about the Denver *Post* story headlined GIRL STRANGLED IN NORTH WOODS. It had not been much of a lead, one of a hundred routine ones that would be checked out.

Hawk glanced at it idly, then his spine straightened like that of a surprised cat. ARCHIBALD WILLIAM WHITE, ALIAS ARCHIE WHITE, ALIAS MUTTY, ALIAS CUDDLY, ALIAS THE GORILLA, REPORTED HIT MAN FOR THE CARNEY ORGANIZATION, MIAMI, WANTED FOR STRANGULATION MURDER JULY 10 OF ISABEL JAMISON, NINETEEN, FRESHMAN, COLORADO STATE. . . . SUBJECT FORTY, SIX-NINE, TWO-TWENTY, LUMBERING GAIT, BROWN EYES, BLACK HAIR BELIEVED DYED, RECEDING FOREHEAD, BROKEN NOSE, RIGHT FRONT TOOTH MISSING. SEVERAL FACIAL AND NECK SCARS, EX-WRESTLER, CHAUFFEUR, TRUCK DRIVER. HOBBIES INCLUDE X-RATED MOVIES, BASEBALL, FOOTBALL, BASKETBALL, PINBALL MACHINES. . . . NO KNOWN CRIMINAL RECORD, NO MOTIVE DEVELOPED TO DATE. . . . TRAVELS WITH OLDER WOMAN WHO POSES AS MOTHER BUT IS NO RELATION. . . . ONLY KNOWN NAME BILLIE RICHARDS. . . . WE HAVE CONFLICTING DESCRIPTIONS AND NO EVIDENCE SHE PARTICIPATED IN SLAYING. . . . AT TIME OF DEATH JAMISON HAD IN PURSE SMALL GOLD PIN SHOWING ANIMAL IDENTIFIED BY JEWELERS AS REPRODUCTION OF ANCIENT SCYTHIAN PIECE KNOWN AS THE SNOW LEOPARD.

He passed the teletype across to Jenny. "I think we've finally got something."

1 A.M.

Gary still sat on the couch where he had flopped to read the note Mr. Morgan had brought. He had his eyes shut tight to hold back the tears. George lay alongside him, his nose nuzzled under Gary's arm and poking into his ribs. Now and then he whined softly in sympathy.

The note read: "I have held some things from you, Gary, even though I love you, and I don't know why I have except that it's something so frightening to me that it hurts me even to think about it, much less to express it to anyone. I should have told you that I am going to talk early tomorrow morning with this man who has been hounding me about money I do not have. I can't tell you where or when I will meet him because I promised the police I wouldn't. But afterward I'll come by and tell you everything—everything—and I pray you'll understand . . ."

Understand? What was there to understand other than she had kept something from him that if she truly did love him she would have told him about?

This was the end. Tomorrow when she came he would tell her quietly that their friendship had dead-ended.

George whined and thrust his nose harder into his ribs. Gary reached out to stroke him. Between them there was no communication barrier. Each knew when the other hurt.

2 A.M.

Mitch rolled out of his bed as if a shell had burst over him. He spread-eagled on the floor trembling and scared. He listened hard. There would be another shell coming over and another, and maybe one of them marked for him. Where were his buddies? He didn't hear them whispering or calling out in agonizing pain. Thank God, no one had been hit. Yet.

He came fully awake and switched on the light. A little after two. When he had first returned home from Vietnam, the nightmares had been frequent. Now they came many months apart. Only his old and close friends knew he had soldiered in Vietnam. He had gone off at eighteen fired with the thought he was doing something for his country and for a people who would be swept up into the horrors of a communistic regime if the United States failed to rescue them. He had returned to a hurt nation that felt contrite and guilty, and couldn't fathom why it had suffered its first defeat in history and withdrawn in panic and shambles.

He shaved and showered and prepared a breakfast of bacon and eggs. Gail was satisfied with only coffee. She studied every diet published and switched often. He liked the heat at 68 winters, she at 76. She was a rabid baseball fan and never missed the Dodgers on television. He preferred serious dramas.

He used the toast to scrub the plate of the remaining egg. Such trivial differences didn't bother him but he wished she would quit harrying him about his law practice. He loved the challenge of each day, the riding forth to joust with the muggers and prostitutes and all of their dirty, evil ilk. He was excited by it. She saw it as only sordid, which he granted it was, but these people, too, had a right to defense in court. And not all were guilty. There were lots of good people out there who were dirty and unkempt and illiterate and beaten down by life, but still struggling for survival, who had never had the breaks and never would. It took a lot of guts to try each day to earn a few bucks to feed a wife and kids.

Gail called to report Lefty had taken off to deliver a note to Cathy's boy friend and had not returned. Mitch was bothered. Just how much had Cathy told Lefty? Suddenly the two were very close. Had she struck up a deal with him about the money? Had he come along at the right time when she needed a confederate?

3 A.M.

"Tonight for sure?" Archie asked. He was driving an empty, forty-foot, refrigerated truck. No one would know, however, that it was empty. He had rented it in the Imperial Valley, the heart of Southern California's vegetable crops. Across both sides and the rear, in large letters, was emblazoned in red: ROSS FARMS, INC.

Billie Richards nodded.

"For sure?" he asked again.

His constant repetition irritated her. "Dammit, I said tonight, didn't I? What the hell you want me to do, swear on it?"

She had come a long way. Born in Battle Mountain, a speck on the map of Nevada, she had fled to New York, failed as a model, and was down to her last eight dollars when she met Wild Bill Dinsmore, who bought her as he would a Ferrari. He was an outgoing, likeable mobster more at home on a golf course playing with millionaires than shooting pool with bragging idiots. Although he wanted children, she secretly had three abortions. She was damned if she was going to have kids. Not even for Wild Bill, whom she never really loved. She was incapable of love for anyone, and knew it, and took pride in the fact. Yet she was a good actress. She could simulate love and Wild Bill always thought she was crazy about him.

She was an apt pupil and when he died she took over his territory in Chicago, a big hunk of the South Side. By then she was in her forties and the knowledge and hold she had on power were better weapons than the sex ploys she had used in her younger years. Soon she had aspirations to move on the national scene, and for the last ten years had aligned her forces with those of the Carney mob. At present, she was only four places away from taking over the Carney organization. Within a few years she would become the first woman on the American scene to head a national underworld organization.

She liked what her peers said about her. They said she was ruthless and quick to liquidate anyone who got in her way. She was completely amoral, had no sense of right or wrong. She had killed three times on her own, and walked away with no regrets from what she called "the incidents."

Archie both pleased and annoyed her. She liked him because he followed orders on command, a police dog trained to kill. He asked for no explanation. He was, however, too much like a dog. He wanted to be petted and praised. He was deeply hurt by the slightest criticism. He repeated himself like a very old person. He asked the same question over and over. He could never remember the answer. He was, however, loyal. If she asked him to walk into a suicidal battle with the police, he would not hesitate. She paid him well and insisted he dress accordingly. Despite the fact he had a few thousand dollars in his pocket at all times, he patronized streetwalkers, which offended her sensibilities.

Shortly after three he pulled the rig into the City Market area. Since they were early, she suggested he park on San Pedro, a block away from Julian.

It was beyond her comprehension why Soft Shoe hadn't broken the girl. He had had sufficient time. As far as she could recall, no one had ever held up to the torture technique as long as the girl had. There was no denying she was hard and tough.

Still, that was no excuse. He could have raped her. No woman, especially a college kid, could stand up under repeated assaults.

"Now for sure," Archie the Gorilla said.

He was smiling.

3:10 A.M.

As per arrangement, Gail stayed behind. At the door, she said, "God be with you."

"He will," Cathy answered. Gail had never seen anyone in crisis so calm.

As Cathy left, Gail's heart went out to her. Gail wanted to take Cathy into her arms, to assure Cathy that they all cared about her.

Outside Cathy took a quick look about. The complex lay quiet and dark. Not a light burned, not a dog sounded off, or a bird talked in his sleep. A half-moon hung overhead beyond murky, smog-filled clouds that blacked out the stars. The temperature had dropped to the mid-seventies.

As she neared her car, a low, scratchy voice stopped her. In momentary fright, she swung about. From the darkness under a thick olive, Abner Blanton materialized. "I hope nothing is wrong, Miss Doyle."

Her insides clutched. He continued, "Not like you to be about so late."

"I'm meeting a friend at the airport."

He opened her car door. "I don't like to see you out alone, not after what happened. I could come with you . . ."

"No," she said quickly. "I mean, that's awfully good of you but I won't be getting out of the car until the airport."

He helped her extricate the seat belt. "There's a car parked down there on the street." He indicated the direction she was headed. "A police car."

She nodded, turned the ignition, and backed out. He walked alongside. "I'd feel better if I was with you."

She shot the car forward down the alley, leaving him standing puzzled, staring after her. She thought: He's always around. Every time I leave or return. Could he be a spy for Them? She dismissed the idea. He was just a good-hearted, nosy old busybody who wanted to be in on everything his tenants did, from conception to death.

In her side-view mirror she studied the police car. She hoped to see Mr. Carlson. But the car appeared uninhabited.

Barney, flat on the front seat, straightened and took over the wheel. A fellow officer in the back came upright.

She was easy to follow. Barney had asked her to hold her speed down and she was following instructions. Man, what a knockout of a girl. When this was wound up, he would ask her out. He would have to be surreptitious about it. Hawk frowned on fraternization even after the police were no longer involved. Not that it usually mattered. The women were mostly old bags, even the young ones. With rare exceptions, crime seemed to attract females whom you wouldn't want to wash your socks even if you were stranded on an atoll out in the Pacific.

At the produce market Hawk had his men stationed for a tight operation. Two officers were hidden behind packing boxes in the cavernous, poorly lighted warehouse where shadows danced eerily; one pretended to go over manifests in a cubby-hole office off the dock; two with dollies helped in loading and unloading the rigs; one was concealed in a dark area thirty feet from the victim's parking space; and two clean-up men roamed along in front of the docks. They were hooked together by radio with a command center Hawk had set up across the street in an old, three-story building painted a dull green. From here, through binoculars, Hawk could bring several docks into sharp focus.

Hawk had issued instructions that Soft Shoe should not be apprehended unless he were about to harm the victim. Hawk anticipated that Soft Shoe would have a plan that would involve others in the Carney outfit. He hoped to identify Them and pull Them in at the same time he arrested Soft Shoe. Hawk wanted the conversation recorded verbatim and had provided her with a highly sensitive radio that was hidden in a wristwatch.

Jenny stood beside him surveying the scene. Hawk felt a strong need for her. If unforeseen events developed and the victim was imperiled by them, then Jenny might ingratiate herself into a situation where a man might be suspect.

On a personal basis, too, he needed her. He had never told her this, although a time or two he had come close. He could never quite get the consent of an ego that made him a strong, decisive, effective peace officer but one who was self-constituted. As Barney once put it, "He doesn't need either God or Jenny although he thinks well of both."

Spread out below them was a scene of seeming pandemonium, brilliantly lit by floodlights over the docks and the beams of the rigs. The rigs were everywhere, their air brakes whistling, squealing, and howling, and their motors shaking the streets, puffing, throbbing, and wheezing. The drivers maneuvered skillfully for position, backing the long, stuffed truck bodies up to ancient, splintering docks with the ease of parking a Volkswagen.

Above all of this mechanical bedlam, men shouted and roared and waved brawny hands. They were running with sweat. Some were stripped to the waist and others in T-shirts. Despite the heat, an owner hustled about in a tailored suit, white shirt, and expensive tie. A Cadillac painted with Chinese characters crawled between trucks. A woman wandered from driver to driver asking if any had seen her man. Another woman, in a simple dress, scavengered with a boy about ten for oranges that had rolled into the gutter. They would wash them and tomorrow sell them on a street corner.

Hawk alerted his officers to the two women. They might not be what they appeared.

Haste was what counted with the produce dealers. Within a few hours, fortunes were made and lost. Tons of foodstuffs had to be unloaded and then put on trucks bound for the big food chains, Ralph's and Safeway and Lucky and the others, for the independent groceries, for hotels and swank restaurants, and wherever crowds would gather that day for quick breakfasts and martini lunches. Tons would be reshipped to other states and air-freighted to foreign countries. Of those tons, California was the sole grower in the United States of dates, figs, olives, and artichokes. From that state came 90 per cent of walnuts, apricots, and plums, 80 per cent of avocados, and 40 per cent of oranges. The world might think of California for its movies, Douglas and Lockheed planes, Disneyland, and Fisherman's Wharf, but a nation—and in the wintertime, London, Paris, Tokyo, and other far-off places—depended on it for its vegetables and fruits.

At this hour, the market was a basketball game in which minutes counted, every play could mean dollars lost or won, and along about 5 A.M. the buzzer sounded ending the contest. Nowhere else in this spread-out, hustling, mind-staggering metropolis of millions did men work so hard.

Crime was not unknown to them. There were hijackings, pay-offs, and extortions, common thefts, two sets of books, and corrupt practices.

But crime of the kind about to unfold this night was uncommon.

Cathy slowed her speed. She had difficulty making her way to Number 14. The big rigs towered like skyscrapers above her. She crawled down Eleventh Street searching for openings large enough to permit the Pinto to sausage through. A warning honk advised her she was about to be crushed. Another driver stopped and motioned for her to pass.

It was a harrowing experience and she pulled into the parking space exhausted. Switching off the ignition, she took a long, deep breath. She saw a sign in English and Spanish: *Private Property—No Parking. Propiedad Privada—No Estacionarse.* Did that mean her? Would someone come shouting at her?

Leaving the car, she stumbled over the rough, cracked asphalt with its small pothole traps. She made her way around empty wooden crates stacked high. Then she was at the outside concrete steps leading to dock Number 14. There were only eight or nine steps. As she started up, a hand reached out from behind and gently restrained her. She whirled in panic. She had programmed herself to meet him calmly, to take a businesslike stance. But the unexpected touch coming from her rear shocked her.

Amused, he stared at her. "Let's get out of all this noise. I've got a rented car over here."

She had to raise her voice to be heard. "No!"

He turned hostile. "Why not?"

"Mister," a truck driver said. "You're blocking the way. Give a working stiff a break."

They moved aside. "I had a horrible time getting in here," she said. "Why'd you say the produce market if you wanted to go somewhere else?"

Jenny shot Hawk a concerned look. Despite the bedlam, both voices were coming over fairly distinctly.

"Unit Ten, Unit Ten. Come in."

"Ten in."

"Subject trying to get victim into his car. If he does, ram him hard. Okay?"

"Roger."

Archie held the rifle as if it were an old friend. His finger was gentle about the trigger. "Damn the damn rigs."

Like elephants trailing each other tail to trunk, they blocked Archie's view. There were only intermittent openings, too brief for a good shot.

Billie Richards was experiencing the same problem with the sound cone.

"I'm moving in closer," Archie said.

"Don't. It'll clear up. We'll get our chance."

One rig held back in the procession. "Now," Archie said. He raised the rifle.

"No!" she screamed. "Not now."

He obeyed.

"A few more minutes," she said. "We've got to be sure."

Directly behind Cathy and Soft Shoe, and partly concealed by a Capri, Lefty leaned against a wall munching a hot dog. He ate slowly. He didn't know how long he would have to make the hot dog last.

If this creep tried anything with his Cathy . . . well, he wasn't a man of violence . . . he couldn't knife or gun him down . . . but he would yell thief, and get a crowd rounded up, and would slip a jeweler's box containing a diamond into the creep's pocket before he knew what was happening. That was using the old brain matter.

From nearby, too, Mitch spotted Lefty, and was as interested in what Lefty was doing as he was in the obvious argument between Cathy and Soft Shoe.

"I don't like it, Cathy. I don't like it at all. You're afraid to come with me—and I'm about to offer you a chance for a half-million bucks. I told you I had a new deal but I can't talk with all this racket going on."

"I can hear you. I *am* hearing you."

He said quietly, "You've got the police here. I can feel them, and that shyster attorney, and that cheap little hood who follows you around like a puppy. You got them all, haven't you, Cathy?"

She screamed, "Would I do that and spoil a big deal?"

"You're giving me a snow job. The Gorilla's just waiting for you. I've a notion to walk away and let him have you."

He took her by the arm. He was pushing her toward his car. The pressure on her elbow mounted. His hips shoved against hers.

"All right," Billie Richards said.

Archie brought the rifle up. He could have got off a quick shot but dared not miss. Even with a silencer, he might not have a second chance. If he missed, the bullet might hit another, or plow into a wall and ricochet and start an outcry.

He put it down.

"What's wrong?" she asked petulantly.

When he failed to answer, she turned about. He was staring dead ahead, encased in his own capsule. When he was on the kill, he heard no one.

Cathy leaned hard against Soft Shoe. "If you push me one more step, I'm going to scream."

Surprised, he eased up. She sagged harder against him. She said, "We either make a deal here or we don't make it."

He was furious. "You little bitch!"

She was calm, forceful. It was not Cathy Doyle who was here. It was an actress playing a scene and Cathy Doyle was watching. "You've tried to break me. You've done everything you could to make me a nervous wreck. But you're not going to make a basket case out of me. Not now or ever. If you've got a deal, let's hear it. Let's get on with it. Right now. Who cares if the police are out there? We're the ones making the deal. Just the two of us."

He let her straighten up. She turned to face him. One second they were brilliantly spotlighted, as a truck swung toward them, then the next in murky light. "You're one hell of a woman."

"Don't tell me your wife is, too. I've heard that one."

He stared at her. He was sizing her up. He doubted if he could trust her. At this point, though, he had nothing to lose. However, if she accepted the offer, he must watch her. She had guts. She might just have the guts to try to outwit him.

"I told you I've quit Them. They want it all. I've done Their work for years and got little out of it compared to what They are hauling in. So I figure we might get together and split the loot ourselves. Leave Them out of it. I know how to get out of the country fast. I've done it many times. I know where we can get the money laundered cheap. There'll be a half million in it for each of us. You get a half million washed clean, without any taxes. You couldn't do it on your own. You don't have the know-how or the contacts. I've got both. What do you say?"

"They'll kill us. They'll hunt us down and murder us."

"A hit, a contract? That's propaganda They put out to keep the troops in line."

Billie Richards sat tense, her face devoid of expression. She heard them talking but could scarcely see them.

Archie breathed easily, waiting. Once he raised the rifle when a rig's spots lighted them up but it was only for a second.

He waited and waited. Then another rig's lights caught them dead on, and held on them as the rig found itself blocked.

Archie squinted, sighted, and squeezed the trigger slowly. That was the secret of a good marksman. Don't hurry the squeeze.

He put the rifle back in his lap, glanced at Billie, and smiled.

Soft Shoe dropped silently at her feet. There was no outcry, nothing. He sagged and doubled up and rolled gently. His shoulder touched her left foot.

It was a long moment before she grasped what had happened.

30

Mitch was the first to reach Cathy. He swept her up into his arms, and half-staggering got her to her car. He dumped her into the seat alongside the driver's. She was whimpering. He kept saying, "You're all right. Don't worry." As ordered, she had left the keys in the switch. The car started on the first turn and he blasted his way with hand on the horn through the milling trucks and people.

He yelled to her, "Keep down! Keep down!" He failed to get through to her and with one hand shoved her roughly to the floor board.

Once away from the market, he kept a careful watch in the rearview mirror. Even at this hour, only a little after four, traffic was fairly heavy. He couldn't be certain they were not being followed. He leaned over to roll up her window, then did the same with his. The glass might deflect a bullet, perhaps no more than a fraction of an inch, but that slight a margin might mean survival.

"Is he dead?" she whispered.

"He looked it."

"They missed me . . . missed me." She let out a scream. "Oh, my God!"

Calmly, clearly, Hawk said into the mike, "All units barricade Julian at Eleventh and Twelfth and Eleventh from Julian to San Pedro—and sit tight until you receive further orders. Stop all traffic, foot and vehicular. Repeat. All units . . ."

It was only a two-block area, and the gunman could have escaped it by now, but Hawk had neither the men nor cars to shut off the ten acres the City Market covered. He knew, too, his officers would meet with strong, even violent resistance from the truckers. A delay in reaching the docks at this hour could mean a loss running into the thousands.

He continued into the mike: "Unit Ten. Move in on subject and determine if he is alive and report immediately. Keep the crowd back. Don't let anyone touch him. Unit Twelve. Assist Unit Ten with crowd control."

The crowd was slow in materializing. No one had heard the shot and only a few had seen the subject fall. Gradually, though, the few who swarmed about him attracted others. By the time Unit Ten moved in, a score had encircled the body, which was curled up slightly, as if napping. In the murkiness there was no bloodstain, no bullet wound, although the bullet had penetrated the right temple.

Gently the officers rolled him over. They felt for his pulse, pulled up an eyelid, and listened for a faint heartbeat. One said into the radio, "Operations. Subject dead."

By the time Mitch reached Cathy, Billie and Archie had dropped down from the produce truck and lost themselves in the crowd. They left the rifle behind. Archie had rasped off the serial number. Still it might be traced if the FBI had on file a bullet with the same markings as the one that had killed Soft Shoe or if by acid etching the FBI Lab could "raise" the serial number from deep down in the metal where it might lie invisible.

"You got to wait," Archie said. "You wait and see your chance and get off a good shot."

They crossed a street to the rented car they had parked. They had left the keys in it.

Archie started to get behind the wheel but Billie shoved him aside. Archie had a tendency to drive too fast after a killing and to buckle if a traffic officer stopped him. She could hold the speed to thirty-five. She had no nerves and never had had.

Mitch drove straight to his and Gail's apartment. Faint light was beginning to permeate the sky. The automatic spots about the pool and courtyard had shut themselves off. A few early workers were moving about. Already the mockingbirds were in full song. They were plagiarists. Whatever they had heard the night before, they sang. He swore that once when Beverly Sills was on television, he heard snatches the next morning from the "Jewel Song" from *Faust*.

He helped Cathy in and led her to the bedroom. "You're going to stay here until this is over. We'll get your things later today."

He put in a call for Gail, in Cathy's apartment, and reported. She would return home at once.

"What to drink? Coffee, tea?"

"A Coke. I'm dying for a Coke."

"At this hour? You're nuts."

He brought two Cokes and sat by her. "I don't care what Hawk says. From now on you're not talking with Them. I'm your attorney. I'll do any negotiating that has to be done."

"They won't know where I am."

"They'll know."

"You needn't stay if you've got something to do. I'm okay now."

"I'd better shave. I'll be in the bathroom."

He was halfway through when the knock came. Sandy, the redhead, stood there. Mitch said, "Don't tell me what you came over for. You know I've got a girl in the bedroom. But I've got Gail's permission. If you want to sleep with me, you've got to get a note from Gail."

Sandy giggled. "I thought maybe there was trouble and I could help."

"Sure you can. Sit down over there and if a guy comes through the front door with a gun, scream."

Cathy was sleeping when Gail returned. Mitch had given her a Valium. After getting rid of Sandy, Gail put Mitch to bed on the front room couch.

A few minutes afterward she took a phone call. Hawk said, "Will you put Doyle on?"

"She's sleeping."

"How is she?"

"The same as you would be if someone took a shot at you."

"No one took a shot at her. They would have hit her if They had. He was an excellent marksman. Dead on target."

"You mean . . . ?"

"They waited until the subject made his offer and once They knew for a certainty he was selling Them out, They executed him. The same as They will Doyle unless we're careful how we play it. I don't want anyone talking to her. Don't let her take any phone calls or leave the house. Where's Lefty Morgan?"

"He hasn't been around."

Barney had talked by phone with Denver. "The victim, Isabel Jamison, had a summer job working as a receptionist for the Gold and Silver Bullion Corporation, dealer in coins, including Krugerrands as well as bullion. The night of June 14, an unknown party or parties broke in and burglarized the property of $347,000 in gold. All of the employees, including the victim, were interrogated and cleared. When the victim was strangled the night of July 10, the investigators pursued a theory that her slaying might be connected with the burglary but they failed to unearth evidence to support it. That's about it, Hawk. They said they'd call if they had any developments. They asked that we reciprocate from this end."

Hawk nodded. "Get some rest."

"I don't need any. Once the sun comes up, it's another day. I'm going to shake down some informants, see if we can get a lead on Billie Richards and Archie. I've got men out checking hotels."

Hawk pulled a desk drawer open and took out an electric shaver. "What do you make of it? The Denver victim had a Scythian gold pin in her purse with something called a snow leopard on it, and our victim had one on when we talked."

He thought out loud. "It couldn't be a coincidence. Not a piece of jewelry that rare, even if they made up several thousand copies. But how does it fit in? Could there be any relationship with the theft of the bullion? Or the million plus our victim is supposed to have? I'm too bushed even to think."

"I'll think about it some."

"Yeah—when you're not thinking about the victim."

"What d'ya mean?"

"Even at my ancient age I've noted she's a very attractive young woman. But she is a woman in a case under heavy investigation."

"You don't think, Hawk—?"

"I do—and good night or good day or whatever it is."

Automatically the shaver found its way over Hawk's stubble. In thought, he scarcely knew he had shaved. Afterward he rough-drafted five teletypes, queries to other police departments seeking information.

Reports drifted in from the team working the produce market. They had found the slug that had killed Soft Shoe. They had gone through his clothes. He had exactly $2.10 in change on him but not a scrap of paper, and the identification markers on his clothing had been removed, even to his silk shorts. This was typical. A man of his caliber would leave as little identification behind as possible.

The team located the rented rig and the .30-.30 rifle. The rifle would be fired before the day was over by ballistics experts into a long cylinder for a comparison of the test bullet with the death slug. The officers had no doubt the striations would match, proving the .30-.30 had been used to kill Soft Shoe. The striations were the microscopic scratches that resulted when a slug passed through a gun barrel.

As for the rented produce truck, investigators would trace it to Brawley in the heart of the truck farm country. They knew in advance, however, they would fail to get a description of the gunman and accomplices, if any. In an operation of this size, with the brains of a complex, highly skillful organization behind it, a front man would have rented the truck. If picked up, he would admit as much. He would state it had been stolen. He might even have filed a police report to that effect.

Gail was finishing the breakfast dishes and Mitch was drying. Both were hung over. "Far into the future," Gail said.

They would have slept later except Mitch had a shoplifting case coming up in Juvenile Court. The girl, sixteen, had stolen a $5.95 dress. She had no record and came from a good but poor family. She had been seized by one of those overwhelming compulsions that ride even the best of youngsters. The hearing would be routine. The judge would deliver a stern lecture, then remand the girl into the custody of her parents.

"We should be getting out to see your mother," Mitch said. The doctor had reported her heartbeat was much stronger.

"She'll understand if we don't."

"I'll run by after the hearing for a few minutes."

"She'd love that. But don't stay too long."

Wearily, Gail picked up the phone on the first ring, then stiffened. The caller, a woman, had a raspy, punch-drunk voice. "Miss Doyle, please."

Mitch put a plate down and stood by Gail listening. "May I ask who's calling?"

"A friend."

"Your name, please."

"Why?"

"She's sleeping. I can have her call you back."

Mitch whispered, "Let me have it," and took over. "Frank Mitchell speaking. I'm Miss Doyle's attorney and empowered by her to enter into negotiations if this pertains to a sum of money Miss Doyle reputedly has."

The woman was wary. "What kind of negotiations?"

"How to make the delivery and where and when. How much she retains."

"You bastard! I've heard about you. You're nothing but a cheap shyster."

She was trying to anger him, an old ploy. He kept his tone impersonal. "I could talk with you anywhere you say and any time you set."

There was no answer. He continued, "Why not now, over the phone?"

"I don't trust you son-of-a-bitch."

"She's knocked out. We had to give her Valium after the murder of your friend. If he was a friend."

"She'll get the same if she doesn't talk with me."

"You must understand—Miss—Mrs.—"

She left him stranded. She was not about to offer a name. He continued, "With so much money involved anyone would want legal advice. To begin with, they would want to assure themselves they were dealing with the rightful party."

"You think you can keep me from getting to her—or your wife?"

"My wife?"

She hung up. Mitch was jolted.

One of the officers running the tail job on Gary Edison radioed in, and a few minutes later a transcript was dropped on Hawk's desk. The message read: "At eight-twenty-five a messenger from Red Dart delivered an envelope that looked like an eight-by-ten Jiffy bag to Gary Edison. The dog barked as usual, then got Edison and brought him to the door. We checked Red Dart by phone and was advised Red Dart had made no delivery to the Gary Edison address. The supervisor reported furthermore that one of their small trucks had been missing for an hour and was found a block away, undamaged. They assumed it had been taken by a teen-ager . . ."

31

Cathy was doing her autogenics when she heard George barking. She went screaming to the door, and opening it, threw herself into Gary's arms. She was sobbing and trying to talk and holding him as if never to let go. George was going wild, jumping up, licking her, deliriously happy.

Lefty, stretched out on the living room couch, barely opened his eyes, then closed them. He had drifted in shortly after breakfast with no explanation of his whereabouts following the killing of Soft Shoe. Gail hurried in from the kitchen. She had remained behind when Mitch went off to the office.

She pulled at Cathy. "Come in," she said to Gary. It was an order. "Don't stand out there."

"I've got to talk to you—alone," he said to Cathy.

Gail took him by the arm but he resisted. "In our bedroom. You can talk by yourselves in the bedroom."

"By the pool," Cathy insisted. "It's beautiful out there."

"No," Gail repeated. "Absolutely not."

Cathy turned on her. "I'm not your prisoner!" Immediately she was contrite. "I didn't mean it that way. I don't know what I'm saying. I'm so shook up . . ."

Lefty sat up. "I'll go to the pool with them, ma'am."

"Okay," Cathy said, as if that ended it.

Gail said, "They could be hiding in some apartment, behind the oleanders over there."

"Say, what goes on?" Gary asked.

"Please, not the pool," Gail said, "You'll be putting Cathy in danger."

Gary backed up a step. "I've got to talk with you right away, Cathy. Something's happened and you've got to know about it."

"Come on, Lefty." Cathy started for the pool area.

"You're asking for it," Gail said.

Cathy hesitated. "I believe in fate. If it's going to happen, it will."

Gail stared in anger, then turned abruptly and went to phone Mitch.

Cathy and Gary sat Indian-fashion by the water. George settled down by her, his wet nose in her lap. Lefty slumped in a folding chair. He appeared indifferent but his gaze roamed over the complex.

Gary spilled the words out so fast they were incoherent. "What?" Cathy asked. "What are you saying?"

"The KNX news this morning. I heard it. Somebody killed at the produce market. A girl was with him but they didn't give her name. You were the girl, weren't you?" He repeated, accusingly, "Weren't you?"

"Yes." She was quiet now. She had to calm Gary. Somehow she had to explain the situation.

"Just 'yes'? Aren't you going to tell me about it?"

"If you'll calm down."

"I can't. I haven't time. We'd better play this first."

Only then did she see the grocery sack. He took out a small Sony recorder. "Somebody sent this to me this morning. A delivery service. Red Dart. I saw the name. A note was taped to it. I've got it somewhere."

He rummaged around in the sack. "Doesn't matter. Said I was to get this to you at once and play it and I was to listen along with you. Said it was a matter of life and death for both of us."

He switched it on too high and a woman's voice screeched. Only one word came out, "Doyle," before Cathy turned it low, so low no one could possibly hear except perhaps Lefty.

As the tape turned she repeated the words in a whisper. He read her lips with disbelief and sheer horror. "Doyle: Because of the death of your friend, I have been assigned the job of collecting the money belonging to us that you have come into possession of.

"Listen carefully since this tape will wipe itself out. You cannot play it over. I have been instructed to permit you to retain $200,000 provided that you turn over at once the even million.

"You will immediately hand over this amount to Gary Edison. I will get in touch with him and instruct him where and when to deliver it. If he should fail . . ."

She halted the tape. "I can't go on, Gary . . . I think we should . . . we should . . ."

"Should what?" His tone was sharp.

"Mr. Mitchell. The woman said it was erasing itself. We'd better—"

"Go on. Now." His anger was subdued but clearly evident. "You won't tell me what it's all about if you give it to your attorney." His voice rose slightly. "I've got a right to know . . ."

She started the tape again. ". . . it would be necessary for us to kill him. I could use the words *terminate* or *liquidate* but I detest euphemisms. *Kill* is the right word."

She hesitated, fighting back the tears. Lefty was walking

about, watching for any sign of a sniper. In circling and turning he had moved closer to them.

In the background Gail approached. Cathy moved to conceal the Sony. "I've got to see you, Cathy. I talked with Mitch—"

"Not now."

"He said—"

"Give me some room! I've got to breathe. You're all closing in on me. Please, just a few minutes."

Gail was taken back. "All right," she said in resignation. She stayed where she was, at one end of the pool, with Lefty at the other, and Cathy, Gary, and George in almost dead center. It was as if a stage director had positioned them.

At Cathy's touch the playback resumed. "We would then seize you and you would be subjected to whatever treatment necessary to force you to confess the whereabouts of the money."

Now the voice paused. The tape spun silently for a moment, then: "The treatment would include, if necessary, rape and torture. If we failed to get this information from you, we would kill you and pursue other means."

"Oh, God," Gary whispered. "What have you got yourself into?"

"I have finished. I will not contact you again in any fashion. My next contact will be with Gary Edison . . ."

The tape spun itself out.

Gary exploded. "You've got to tell me. I want to know what this is about. I demand some frank answers."

She tried to go into his arms. He pushed her away. "Where it came from and whose money it is and why somebody's threatening to kill us and—"

Gail drifted up to them. "Let's go back in the apartment. We can't have a scene out here. We've got to get hold of ourselves. I'll make some coffee or lemonade."

"No!" Gary shouted. "I'm always being put off. Someone's trying to kill us and I'm treated like a little kid. Lemonade!"

Gail put a hand on his arm. "Give Cathy a chance to recover."

They headed for the apartment. "We should've taken it all
down," Lefty said.

32

Mitch scooped up the last of the spaghetti and meatballs and
downed the coffee. He was fuming. Hawk had said twelve and
it was twelve-fifteen.

The waitress, a slender, black-haired, plastic-faced doll, said
sharply, "What happened to your friend?" She indicated the
empty stool alongside Mitch. He had placed his attaché case
on it. Eddie's was jammed and she was losing tips. Mitch slid a
dollar bill under the saucer with the bill showing and she was
mollified.

In ten minutes one could be in and out of Eddie's, which
was a rickety, one-room realty shack left over from the land-
boom days of the twenties. Eddie's lived on its image, dirty
windows, scaling paint, stained menus (if one could be found),
and Eddie himself, a stereotyped comedic character, always on
stage. Lawyers in a rush between court sessions, harried police
officers and deputy sheriffs, bail bondsmen, law clerks, court re-
porters, and secretaries studying the manpower situation found
Eddie's a happy merry-go-round ride.

Hawk dropped the attaché case to the floor. "You're late,"
Mitch said.

"A hot dog with everything," Hawk ordered.

The waitress called out, "One intestine, shoot it."

"I haven't much time," Hawk said.

"Who invited you?" Mitch countered.

"You heard, of course?"

Mitch had but asked, "Heard what?"

"Coffee. Where's the coffee?"

"Sorry, handsome," the waitress said, pouring.

Hawk dumped in sugar and stirred vigorously. "I've been patient with you, Mitch. Kept you posted. I don't know why I did—but I did. So now, as of twelve-twenty-six, you're out. You keep out of my department and I'll keep out of your courtroom. You understand? I've got full jurisdiction."

"Maybe I should have some more coffee," Mitch told the waitress. He looked out the window at the heavy traffic. He counted the cars. He counted eighteen before he had his anger under control. "Funny for you to bring that up—because I made a decision, too. She's not going to talk with anyone on the phone or meet anyone at circuses or produce markets. I'm taking over. I'm going to handle this entirely by negotiation. If They want anything, They come and talk with me. And you do, too. We've handled this all wrong—"

"The hell you say." Hawk burned his mouth on the coffee. He spooned an ice cube from his water glass. "You do that and I'll throw you in the slammer so fast for interfering with justice . . . I've had enough of you, Mitch—"

"Hey, handsome," the waitress called. "Phone."

Hawk looked around for it. "Over here—in the private phone booth."

He squeezed in between two characters talking loudly by the cash register. Oblivious to him, they continued their conversation.

"Yeah, Barney." Barney talked for several minutes. Hawk's features grew sober, then tense, his eyes dark.

"Damn!" he commented once, then later, "Meet me there. I'm leaving now."

Returning, he asked Mitch, "Doyle still at your place?"

Mitch nodded warily. Hawk pushed the half-finished hot dog away. Mitch had never seen him nervous. "I've got to talk to her."

"How're you going to get in? It's my apartment."

"You prefer I bring her in, maybe?"

"You haven't anything on her."

"Haven't I?"

Hawk strode out, brushing several customers without knowing it. Mitch paid hurriedly but the waitress called him back. "Hey, what about your friend?" Cursing softly, Mitch put down two dollar bills.

"Dear Dr. Barton," the memo from Dr. Clarence Bosworth of UCLA began. "I have tried repeatedly to call you to inform you that the student I told you about readily identified the specimen in question as having been written by Herodotus, born about 484 B.C. at Halicarnassus in Asia Minor, died 425 B.C. at Thurii. A Greek, he remains one of the most famous historians of all time as well as a remarkably fine and interesting writer.

"I assume you have read him at some time and will recall he traveled widely from his twentieth to thirty-seventh year and stayed long periods in each place to acquire information for his great work. While that work centered around the Persian invasion of Greece, he covered on the periphery, so to speak, most of the nations of the world considered important by the ancient Greeks. We know he journeyed to the Persian capital of Susa, Palestine, Egypt, Tyre, Thrace, and Scythia."

The phone interrupted. Barney Carlson was calling. Hawk wanted Jenny to report as quickly as possible to Frank Mitchell's apartment for one more interrogation of the Doyle girl. "We've had a break in the case. I'll tell you about it when I see you."

Jenny read faster. "My student located the specimen in question in Herodotus' account about Scythia. Very probably he personally witnessed this burial scene. I hope this answers your questions. If there is anything further I can do, please do not hesitate to call."

33

Gail was serving cold cuts, potato salad, and iced tea on TV tables in the living room when Hawk rapped sharply. When she opened the door, he barged in, followed by Barney and Jenny.

"You, Miss Doyle, sit where you are. The rest of you, out."

"Wait a minute," Gail said, "what're you doing? Did Mitch give you permission . . . ?"

Hawk raised his voice. "Out, all of you. Barney, get them out of here." Lefty and Gary got up to go.

Cathy screamed, "I want Gary!"

"You can't do this!" Gail shouted.

"All right! All *right!*" Hawk turned to Cathy. "I can take you to headquarters and question you there. So which is it? You want to stay here or come with me? Either way I'm not going to have kibitzers sitting around."

"Here," Cathy said weakly.

Jenny whispered to Hawk and as Gail was leaving, he called to her. "You stay, Gail, if you want to."

She came back. "For a witness, Hawk?" She dared him with her eyes. "Okay, as a witness." She added, "She has a right to counsel."

"I told Mitch. He's coming." He continued standing, looking down at Cathy. "I must advise you that anything you say may be used against you in a court of law. Do you understand?"

She sat with her eyes closed, her lips moving silently. Her feet were firmly planted on the floor, each hand resting upright on each knee. The hot sun streaming through the picture window cast a long shaft that caught and illuminated her as if she were a painting. Except for the slightly moving lips, she was ever so still. In the fierce light her blond hair was brilliant, dancing with the facets of many diamonds.

Hawk was grim. He was unaccustomed to silence during an interrogation. Usually the party was whimpering or screaming denials. He started to accuse her of stalling when Jenny caught his eye and shook her head.

Finally Cathy looked up. She raised her hands above her head, stretched, and took a deep breath. She asked quietly, "What did you want to talk to me about, Lieutenant?"

He could have killed her. She had taken over the initiative, one of an interrogator's most valuable tools.

"Did you hear what I said about anything you say may be used against you in a court of law?"

"Nothing will be used against me because I haven't done anything."

Jenny said, "We're not accusing you of anything—but we need your help in clearing up some questions that have come out of our investigations."

"I'll be glad to, if I can."

"Why don't you sit over here?" Gail said to Hawk. "I think it would be better if we were all comfortable."

Reluctantly, Hawk took the chair she offered. Barney sat a little to Cathy's right. "I'm glad to see you again, Mr. Carlson," Cathy said. He tried assuring her with his eyes that he was on her side. Jenny sat on the couch with Gail.

Hawk got back on his feet. Damn these females. They were shoving him around. He mumbled he was restless, then took over with authority. "How many times have you been in Miami?"

"I told you before, Lieutenant, that I have never been in Miami."

"Has anyone written you, telephoned you, or visited you from Miami?"

"No."

"Do you know anyone in Miami?"

"No."

"You never have?"

"Well, there were some girls at Pitzer from Florida but I don't remember whether they said where they were from."

Mitch slipped in quietly and took a straight chair near the door. If Hawk knew of his presence he gave no indication.

"When we talked at the brokerage house, you were wearing a gold pin. You said it was a reproduction of a Scythian piece. You said it was—it was—"

"A snow leopard."

"Where'd you get it?"

"I told you, Lieutenant, my father gave it to me."

Hawk rearranged a picture on the wall, then turned. "A girl was strangled in Denver, a girl fronting for a gold theft operation. She had the identical piece in her purse . . ."

The Denver authorities, who had phoned only an hour ago, had learned from a reputable informant that the girl, Isabel Jamison, who had no record and an excellent reputation, had been paid by the Carney mob five thousand dollars to furnish information. She had advised them about shipments of gold and silver bullion and procured for them a blueprint of the company's electronic alarm system. The night of the burglary she had left doors open and closed them later. For some reason not yet established, the Carney people thought she was about to "blow" and had considered her such a high risk they had ordered her silenced. She had been given the snow leopard by them early in their negotiations with her to establish a good rapport.

Cathy closed her eyes tightly and balled her hands into fists.

Gail spoke up. "I'm sure there are hundreds around. It was a reproduction."

Mitch cleared his throat. "I object to this line of questioning. It is not relevant to anything that concerns my client. You have not shown that my client has been engaged in any facet of the gold business, legal or illegal."

Hawk massaged his neck. "I'm getting to that."

They all stiffened. The tension was a live, ugly presence.

Hawk continued, "Dr. Barton has learned that the quotation on the card comes from the old Greek historian Herodotus, who is describing here a Scythian burial. A Scythian one, Miss Doyle. Your snow leopard might have been buried with the concubine. You have noted, I'm sure, that the word *concubine* is underlined. We have reason to believe that it refers to you."

For a moment Cathy sat quite still. "I'm trying to be calm. I'm telling my nerves to quiet down. I'm telling my emotions to subside. I'm telling the trembling in my legs to quit. I'm telling myself that you have no reason to believe the reference is to me."

"The king you were buried with—who is the king?"

She could no longer contain her anger. "Didn't Herodotus say?"

He let it pass and asked softly, "Tell me when you talked last with Charlie Dickens? Big Charlie? Wasn't that about four weeks ago?"

She glared at him. She had trouble keeping her voice from rising. "I don't know any Charlie Dickens. So how could I have talked with him?"

"You've never heard of Charlie Dickens? Big Charlie?"

"No."

"Never even seen his name in the newspapers?"

Mitch cut in. "I object to your trying to trap my client. The way you put the original question, she naturally thought you were referring to someone she knew personally, not to a mobster who's been in the papers."

Hawk shook a fist at him. "One more interruption out of you, Mitch, and out you go. This isn't a court of law. I'm a police officer conducting a routine interview and I don't have to abide by any rules of court interrogation. She's not on the witness stand."

He turned back to Cathy. "I'll repeat the question. Have you ever read about Charlie Dickens, known in the media as Big Charlie?"

She thought her answer out carefully. "I suppose I've seen the name. I don't know in what connection. I don't usually read crime stories. They scare me."

"Let me put the question another way. When was the last

time you talked with Joe Doyle? Big Joe? Didn't he drop by your apartment about four weeks ago?"

Her lips twisted with anger. "You know he did. I told you he did. He's my father."

"But you don't know anything about Charlie Dickens? He never came by to see you?"

She was fighting back the tears. "How many times do I have to tell you?"

"Joe Doyle." Hawk paced about. "Joe Doyle. A beautiful home in North Carolina, a beautiful second wife, a Cadillac, a church man. He was thought highly of in Clinton. Could do no wrong. You're sure he was your father and not Charlie Dickens?"

She was sobbing. "Joe Doyle's my father. He's my father. I told you, I don't know this Charlie Dickens."

"Joe Doyle. When you were a kid he used to read you Dickens stories, didn't he? He was such a great Dickens buff he collected early editions."

She didn't answer. She had her face covered with hands that trembled.

"Even the Carney mob didn't know Charlie Dickens had a beautiful home in Clinton and a second wife and a Cadillac. Not until he held out a million two on them."

"Joe Doyle's my father."

"He came by and left the million two with you, and you didn't know what to do with it, and you hid it—"

"No! Why would my father—?"

Hawk interrupted. "You won't admit it because he convinced you it was his hard-earned money, so now you've got to guard it with your life."

Her voice grew edgy. "He came by and we talked. He asked if I needed money and I told him no, I was getting along okay. He always asks but he knows I've never taken anything from him except what he put in trust years ago for my education. Not a cent."

Jenny said, "Was that because you thought the money was tainted?"

Cathy flared. "Tainted! I didn't take it because when you're grown you ought to make your own way. Tainted! You're trying to get me to say something against my father . . ."

Her voice dropped to a whisper. "He's all I've had to hold on to through the years. Until I met Gary."

"Where's the money?" Hawk asked.

"I told you . . . I can't help it if you think I'm lying. Go on and say it, You're lying!"

"If you know it's stolen money and you're hiding it, for any reason whatsoever, you're guilty of being an accessory after the fact. A felony."

She cringed.

He continued, "It's your life we're talking about. Either we get the money or They get it and you're dead."

Jenny said gently, "I know it sounds brutal, but he's right. I know you wouldn't want to hold on to money that isn't yours just to be keeping it. You're not a thief and we don't think you are. You've got some reason. If you want to talk it over with me, we could go into the next room. I'd promise to keep it off the record and never repeat it. Maybe I could help."

Cathy seemed to crumple up, to dwindle to half her size. "How can you help me when you don't believe me? Nobody can help me. It's like one of Euripides' tragedies. There's no way out."

Hawk sat on the sofa beside Jenny. He talked softly. "You had to know about him. You had to know that your father was Charlie Dickens. Big Charlie."

She said defiantly, "My father is Joe Doyle." Then she let out a little scream. "What's this all about? What've you done with him? Where is he?"

Hawk sighed heavily. "Cathy," he began and hesitated. He was not good at this sort of thing. "Cathy," he repeated, "the state troopers found his body in an old quarry in Nevada a few days ago. It took a little time to make an ident."

She stared in disbelief, then seemed to slip into a shocked stupor. Tightening her arms about herself, she strove to still the convulsions.

Gail dropped to her side. "I want Gary," Cathy whispered. "I want Gary."

Gail glanced at Hawk, who nodded. Barney left to get Gary.

Hawk stared into space. Damn, it was a rough business. It hurt to watch people suffer. It hurt to turn the screw when there might be nothing there to get out of them. It hurt to see innocent people trapped by a maelstrom of events that were not of their doing, pawns to be murdered and raped and mugged because they happened to be standing in one certain spot at one particular time.

He indicated to Jenny they should leave and, once they were in the car, asked, "What d'ya think about the money?"

"She doesn't have it."

"Not on her, maybe, but she knows something about it. I'm going to put two men on it, to find it—before the Carney mob does."

He drove slowly. He did some of his best thinking while driving. "God, how could anybody ever love a man like Big Charlie?"

She shook her head. "We all build illusions over the years, block by block. I suppose the happiest homes and the happiest marriages are those where the illusions never come tumbling down."

"We've wasted a lot of time. If she'd only told us . . ."

"Told us what? For her Charles Dickens didn't exist. She'd locked him up in a chamber of her mind and tossed the key away."

"I don't get it. Fasten your seat belt."

She took a deep breath. "She's an emotional cripple, torn and lonesome, wanting love that a cold, unaffectionate mother never gave her—and finding it in a fantasy world of her own making, built around a father who never really existed."

"She could have told us."

She fastened the seat belt. "Would you? If you were a mobster's son? You would've lost your job, some of your friends, had a hard time getting credit for a car or home, applied for a lot of jobs before finding one. Worst of all, you'd know people were talking about you every place you went."

Hawk shrugged. "Everyone's got a skeleton in his closet."

"You know that and I do, too, because of the work we're in. But most people think they're the only ones. I know, Hawk. I had this uncle I loved dearly—a businessman, in furniture—and when I was sixteen he was caught in a confidence racket and went to prison. For months I ran to school and ran home, and at school hid my head in a book. I didn't want to talk to anyone. Mother couldn't even get to me to come to the phone . . ."

She moistened her lips. "I talked to Mother today. She'd like to meet you. I know you'd love her. I was thinking, maybe Thanksgiving, if we could get away for a few days we could fly back to see her."

"Why not?"

"I wouldn't want to mention it to her unless it was fairly definite."

He braked to an abrupt stop for a red light. "Let's wait until it's closer to Thanksgiving."

She caught herself staring into space. "To get back to what we were talking about, I was going to say that when you're young and sensitive, skeletons are not easy to live with. Even when you're older, you still hide them if you can."

"In this day and age?"

They were on Sunset Boulevard in Beverly Hills passing deep expanses of dark green, manicured lawns, tall palms, carefully tended flower gardens, and homes bespeaking planned graciousness and costly charm.

"See that for-sale sign?" She pointed to one in English, Arabic, and Japanese. "The world changes but not human needs and hurts."

No, Hawk. Not needs and hurts. Not at any age.

34

The curator at the County Art Museum on Wilshire Boulevard resembled Cary Grant. He was tall, graying, in his sixties, with bright, inquisitive eyes that still found life a challenge.

Jenny had called ahead. He had expected a more masculine type and was pleased to find a very desirable-looking woman.

"We don't get many from the police department in here," he said. "Which speaks well for us even if we do deal mostly in dead subjects."

"We're not usually interested in your dead subjects, either," she said. "Such as the Scythians."

"Ah, the Scythians. A mysterious people. Lost in history. About all we know about them is what Herodotus wrote and what has been found in their tombs. Coffee?"

She nodded and he poured a cup from a much-used carafe. "The bread of life. Sugar? We haven't any cream, only Coffee-Mate.

"Well, old Herodotus—you may have heard of him. . . . A Greek historian, lived in the fifth century B.C.—he described the Scythians as tough barbarians addicted to drugs and hard drinking and violence. But then we're always calling people barbarians whose culture isn't the same as ours. So you have to discount the old man some. We do know that in the sixth, fifth, and fourth centuries—B.C., that is—they controlled more territory than that of all the so-called civilized world combined."

"Excellent coffee," Jenny said, and added, "I was primarily interested in their jewelry."

He laughed. "I do get carried away. Just imagine, a people we know little about who were so powerful . . . they had no written language and no coins. That's why we can't reach back into history and decipher them, perhaps come up with a Rosetta stone . . ."

"The jewelry. I've heard it was exquisite—but how could it be if they were nomads and had no cities?"

"More coffee?" She shook her head.

"The Greeks made much of it for them. We know that in the latter part of the seventh century B.C. the Greeks established colonies on the shores of the Black Sea, and soon the Scythians were packing in grain and cattle and bartering them for jewelry. Gold jewelry. Some of the most beautiful pieces ever created. But a strange combination. Some of them, well, take a gold bottle found in the Kul Oba kurgan near Kerch— the old name of the city was Panticapaeum, a mouthful—the principal art work shows the Scythians and the pendants show the head of Athena, the Greek goddess. And so it goes, Scythian scenes and Greek art."

"When the Scythian collection was being shown around the country—"

"We had lines blocks long. It was from the Hermitage in Leningrad. Magnificent."

"Were reproductions made for sale—like at the time of the King Tut exhibition?"

"Yes, yes. I've got a folder in the file here—"

"Were they good?"

He shrugged. "I never saw one. Why bother when we have the real ones in the cases?"

He handed her the folder. She skimmed it, then stopped suddenly and retraced a few sentences. The type seemed in boldface. The paragraph Soft Shoe had sent Cathy, about the burial of the king and his concubine, stood out.

"May I keep this and return it in a few days?"

He nodded and she went on. "I saw a snow leopard. At least I was told it was a snow leopard."

"Yes, yes. Animal motifs were most common. Reindeer, panthers, felines, birds. They're often in strange positions. Now, the snow leopard, he's coiled up oddly and we don't know whether he is dead, in a fetal position, or what. Very unnatural but the pose is common in Scythian art. Did I tell you that the jewelry all came out of the tombs of kings and noblemen and such? Enormous tombs with walls of wood and stone floors. Filled with gold weapons, drinking vessels, bowls, mirrors, bottles, helmets, and even gold combs. Why, one young woman—fourth century B.C.—had buried with her two hundred and fifty gold plaques, rings, and bracelets along with a crown."

Jenny said, "I love your enthusiasm. In my work I don't come across much of it. I mentioned the snow leopard. Would it be possible for a clever gold artisan to copy an original so exactly that it could be sold to a museum or collector as an authentic piece? The way some of the old masters have been forged?"

He rose, drummed on the desk, and walked about. "Hmmm, a most interesting question. I've never been asked it before."

"Gold is gold, isn't it?"

"Not exactly. The alloy used makes a difference, and I should think the way it is worked. The tools, for example. Take the snow leopard. Was a clay stamp used when the gold was soft or did an artisan work in the design by hand? This is out of my field but if I were to guess I would say that only a craftsman who had studied the Scythian work very carefully could even approach a copy that might deceive the experts. He would have to have the same tools, the identical alloy, and the same thinking. The same thinking. That would be most important."

He hesitated. "Would I be presumptuous if I asked you if there is such an artisan?"

"It was just a theoretical question."

"If you find him, would you let me know? It would be most interesting, most interesting . . ."

Jenny nodded and rose. She offered her hand. "I have friends who can't get excited over a trip to Europe, much less something that happened twenty-five hundred years ago."

35

Barney sat alone in Gail's living room, looking into the forecourt. Somewhere out there about the complex were twelve officers. Two were directly across the way, on the second floor, behind the drapes fluttering at a big picture window. The tenants, once assured they would not be caught in cross fire, had readily given permission. Two were across a patio to the right, in a ground floor apartment adjacent to the manager's office. One was on call in the redhead's place next door. Four were posted at advantageous points about the rear. One, in shorts, who looked in his teens, slumped in a nearby chair reading *Newsweek*. The only other officers visible were two policewomen. They were in shorts and halters playing shuffleboard. After a half-hour of that, they would pretend to doze by the pool. Their tote bags holding revolvers would be within quick reach.

Under Hawk's scalpel-like thrusts, Barney had seen a new side to Cathy. She had a touch of wildcat in her and he liked that. Hawk had broken her but for a time she had clawed him scratch for scratch. What a body she had, too, all the right curves and accents, and she knew how to use it. She had poise, posture and an exciting walk that grabbed him. He could scarcely wait to wind up the case and date her.

Lefty Morgan materialized out of nowhere, like a trick shot in a movie. Coming through the door, he pulled himself to a slow stop. "Wanted to see Cathy before I took off."

Barney nodded. Hawk had said to let Lefty come and go as he pleased. Hawk had bet Barney five dollars that They would use Lefty as a go-between. "Give him plenty of room to move around in," Hawk said.

Inside Lefty proceeded to stretch out, shoes and all, on the couch. He finished half a submarine he took from his pocket, a crumbling piece of apple pie, and iced tea from a flask. He brushed the crumbs on the carpet, then dozed.

In the kitchen, Gail finished the dishes. Mitch leaned against a drainboard, talking mostly to himself. Cathy had finally told them where she had got Mitch's name. From her father. On his last visit he had said if she ever needed an honest attorney, she should look up one Frank Mitchell. Her father said he had a friend whom Mitch had represented. Mitch now was sorting through memorabilia in an effort to identify the friend. Mitch was fascinated that a mobster as famous as Big Charlie would know about him. "Some fame!" Gail said.

She added, "And some honeymoon. The place is so cluttered up with bodies that I scarcely get to see you."

"When it's all over," Mitch said, "we'll barricade the front door, pull the phone out, and hibernate for a week."

"Hibernate?" Her eyes sparkled. "I've never heard it called that before."

They were digging hard for the laughter that was such a part of them.

Cathy had cried until there were no more tears. Gary had consoled her though he was bewildered, shocked, and hurt. He hadn't yet put the pieces together. Someone had thrown him a puzzle and he was picking up the parts.

"You've got to believe me," she said, "I don't know anything about any money."

He didn't "hear." He held her in a grasp that hurt but there was no longing, no hand exploring. In the melding and warmth of their bodies they sought comfort.

"I must talk with you." Barney took Cathy into the bathroom and closed the door. He turned the water on hard in the washbasin. If they talked low, a bug—if there was one around —would pick up more gurgling than conversation.

"We need to know," he said, "what you and Gary plan to do when you receive the instructions."

She had a vacant look. "I don't know."

"Did you talk about it?"

She shook her head. "If Gary doesn't go—but he won't have the money—I don't know." She was fighting back the tears. "What do you think, Mr. Carlson?"

"Barney. It's Barney."

She came up with a wisp of a smile. "Barney."

"I'm not permitted, in case of life and death . . . I mean, I can't recommend. I wish I could."

She tossed her hair back in understanding. She was recovering. "I don't think too good, now."

"We could give him stage money. We've done that. But if They open the package before he gets away . . . or when They find out later, we're back where we started from . . ."

On impulse she kissed him softly on the cheek. "Thank you for believing me. You're the only one. The rest think I've got the money hidden. I'd give it to Gary if I had it. I wouldn't endanger his life. You know that, don't you—Barney?"

"I know it." He wanted to take her into his arms.

"The lieutenant—" he began.

"I detest that man. I'll never talk to him again, ever, not even if he arrests me."

36

Angel brought in one coffee, two teas, and a Pepsi. Jenny kicked off her shoes and massaged her feet. The General tightened his tie and sat ramrod straight. Barney unbuttoned his shirt. Hawk gobbled down a Lifesaver, rearranged the papers on his desk, muttered about Angel disturbing everything, and placed the phone in the spot he had assigned it.

All smiles, Baker hurried in with the evening paper. "How," Hawk said. "Baker, you're coming in here twice a day now. The *Times* in the morning and the *Herald-Examiner* afternoons."

"Yes, sir." He spoke it with enthusiasm.

"But I didn't order the *Herald-Examiner*."

"No, sir. I'm paying for it, Lieutenant. I want you to have the latest news."

"Baker, you're nothing but a con man. You know I wouldn't let you pay for it."

Baker's grin was wide as his face.

"Get out of here," Hawk said, "before I run you in for grand larceny."

He turned to the others. "Let's go over the Doyle matter, see what we've got and what we've got to get. To bring you up to date, Charlie Dickens was shot three times in the chest area with a .45 Magnum. He had been dead several days and the Nevada authorities believe he had been tossed from a car after being killed elsewhere. Someone had used a small branch to obliterate tire tread marks and footprints. They dropped the branch at the scene.

"His face had been worked over so he would be unrecognizable. The morgue technicians failed to get a good set of fingerprints. He had no identification or money on him except his very expensive suit had a number sewn into the inside coat pocket. The manufacturer kept a sales record of the numbers and advised that the suit had been shipped to an exclusive men's shop in Miami.

"The shop produced the names of twelve customers who had bought that particular model but only one would have fitted the size suit in question, and that one was Charles Dickens. Not that he gave his full name. He gave them C. Dickens but the salesman identified C. Dickens from a photo shown him. That's about it. Nothing on why he defected or about the money. We'll be working with Miami on that."

He turned to Barney. "Did you get anything out of Soft Shoe's widow?"

Barney leaned back until the chair tilted on its two hind legs.

"I wasn't expecting much but I did get one surprise that'll knock you over."

He referred to notes. "She goes by his true name, Mrs. Samuel J. Porter. She knows he had an alias, Samuel J. Oscar, and was called Soft Shoe. She hates the nickname Soft Shoe. She's about forty, slender, well kept . . . very well kept for her age, not like the broads most of these guys go for."

"Let's get on with the facts," Hawk said irritably.

"I thought the kind of woman she was was relevant. She was very frank, talked about when they first met, how he never told her anything because she didn't want to hear it, how she begged him to get out of the racket, how she'll never get over loving him, that they have two teen-agers in high school and this will ruin their lives if it hits the papers—"

"Barney!"

"Okay, okay. I asked her what he told her about coming to Los Angeles. She denied she knew anything—except he told her he was coming over here to talk with somebody's girl friend."

"Girl friend?" Hawk came awake.

Barney nodded. "The Carney gang never got the relationship straight between Charles Dickens and Cathy Doyle. It might have been bad information they got from one of their hangers-on here in Los Angeles or they may have jumped to conclusions."

"Girl friend!" Hawk repeated in disbelief.

Barney nodded. "They never knew his true name, Joseph Doyle, or that he was living a respectable front in North Carolina. So the name, Cathy Doyle, meant nothing to them."

Hawk shuffled through a stack of papers and pulled one out. He read, "'. . . around the body of the king . . .'" He interpolated, "That would be Charles Dickens." He continued reading, "'. . . they bury one of his concubines . . .'"

He looked up. "That would be Cathy Doyle."

The General reported he had discussed Hawk's instructions thoroughly with each team command: They were to permit easy access to the front and back doors of Gail and Mitch's apartment and Gary's house. They were to stop no one entering or leaving. Any party, however, visiting either the apartment or house would be placed under immediate surveillance. Hawk figured "the woman," this mysterious Billie Richards, would give someone twenty dollars or so to walk up to one of the front doors and ring the bell. The party would deliver no message. It would be a test to determine if the police had the place under surveillance. If convinced they did not, she might follow up by sending an intermediary who would pass along payment instructions to either Cathy or Gary Edison.

Barney said, "We're covering every hotel and mobile home site as well as all the places they might go. We don't have a mug shot of her but a good one of Archie the Gorilla. Even if we didn't, his face is so cut up we should find him."

"No arrests," Hawk said firmly, "and only a loose surveillance."

"Right."

Hawk ran a handkerchief about his face and neck. "What's giving with the air conditioner?"

Jenny smiled. "Same as always. It can't take hot weather."

Barney opened the door to the squad room. "Okay?"

Hawk nodded. "Let's get back to the Miami end. We informed the Miami police that the victim possessed a Scythian gold pin, believed a reproduction, that was termed a 'snow leopard.' We got this back."

He indicated a teletype. Miami reported that a contact of its informants had failed to turn up any knowledge of the reproduction of the so-called 'snow leopard.' Miami advised, however, that the Hong Kong Finance Company had a division dealing in ancient gold works, believed mostly spurious, and that division sold Scythian jewelry. Miami said that it had requested an informant with "inside sources" to develop additional information. Miami added that Charles Dickens headed the division.

Hawk rose and sat on the desk. He took care not to disturb the papers. "When we learned this, Jenny talked by phone with a curator at the Metropolitan Museum of Art in New York City. Jenny."

Coffee had revived her. "Actually he wasn't a curator. The county museum here suggested I talk with this gentleman, whose name I promised to hold in confidence. He buys for the Metropolitan and knows the world market on about every subject, whether it's painting or sculpture—or Scythian art."

She swung one foot a little faster. "He said that only a very few pieces had ever been on the market in any one year prior to the last one. That was because, he said, the Soviets—the same as with many governments—claimed ownership of all valuable historical and archaeological works. He stated that since the Scythians spread out over such a vast territory, there were many burial sites, called kurgans, and while most have been recorded for years and the precious objects removed, still occasionally a peasant dug into a new one.

"About sixteen months ago, he reported, scores of Scythian pieces were offered on the market by a Miami-based firm, Rare Gold Art Treasures. The firm advised that they were from a new kurgan and had been smuggled out of Russia before the Soviets knew about them.

"The Metropolitan gentleman said he had no idea whether this account was accurate or whether these were clever art works done in the Scythian manner. In other words, forgeries. He had not examined any.

"He said he knew of a number of museums and galleries that had purchased pieces from Rare Gold Art Treasures. He was quite frank. Some museums and galleries asked few questions in the case of stolen or smuggled works. They were willing to accept any reasonable authentication. He said that this was not a new practice, and he pointed out that the British Museum during the last century had acquired many ancient Greek and Egyptian works of art by questionable means. Sometimes outright theft or confiscation with the connivance of Whitehall.

"I think that covers all of the salient points of our phone talk."

"Do I get it right?" Hawk asked. "They may have copied the

old Scythian pieces the same as an artist copies an old master and passes it off as the original?"

Jenny nodded. "It's easier to do, I'm told, with gold than paintings since there usually isn't the detail and there aren't as many experts around to detect a fake. In the entire world, barring the Hermitage, there might be a dozen."

Hawk walked about. "I keep wondering about the two snow leopards. Did Dickens have a lot of them made up for gifts—or something like that?"

The General spoke up. "Sir, I may be able to cast light on that."

Hawk groaned inwardly. That "sir" irritated him. This was a free-wheeling conference and the General acted like they were at the White House with the President presiding.

Hawk said, "The General has been handling the North Carolina leads."

"Yes. The lieutenant asked me to pose certain questions to the Clinton police chief: Was Joseph Doyle interested in collecting Scythian gold? Had he ever expressed an interest to anyone in Clinton in the Scythians?"

He was having difficulty talking. His throat sounded as if it had a broken con rod.

"The chief called me back an hour ago." He held his notes close to his eyes. "No, it was two-thirty-three. Yes, two-thirty-three. He had met considerable resistance in questioning friends of Joseph Doyle. They liked him and suspected he might be in trouble if the chief was asking about him. Be that as it may, the chief learned that Doyle had given to the University of North Carolina, a golden stag measuring fourteen inches in length.

"The university had been informed by Doyle that the stag, a motif found on numerous Scythian pieces, dated from the seventh century B.C. and was worth $300,000. A university professor had confirmed the value later when he visited a famous museum in Munich and found a similar stag for which the Munich institution had paid $325,000. Doyle had insisted that the donation be listed as anonymous and he be given no publicity. He had confided that at some time in the future he would like to be considered for an honorary degree as doctor of humanities."

The General got his throat working smoothly. "I asked the chief specifically if Mr. Doyle had given any Scythian pieces to friends—and your hunch, Lieutenant, was correct. He said Mr. Doyle two Christmases ago had given small gold pins to two or three close friends.

"One more fact. In talking with Doyle's friends, the chief learned that Doyle collected old and rare editions of Charles Dickens. He carried $100,000 insurance on his library."

All the pieces were falling into place, Hawk thought. Most criminals, in choosing an alias, select one that has come out of an association they have had with it in the past. It may be the name of a street, town, a product they use, a girl friend, a cat or dog. Few escape the bonds of personal experience.

Joseph Doyle collected the works of Charles Dickens. What better alias than that? Probably he felt at home with it, more so than if he had chosen a name at random. Probably, too, it conveyed a certain sense of status. Later Hawk was to learn that while he had a fondness for the name of Charles Dickens, he detested being called Charlie.

The General had asked the Clinton chief one more question. Why had no one in Clinton recognized Charlie Dickens—his picture in the newspapers, on television—as Joe Doyle?

"They talked about it in the beginning, years ago," the chief said. "But Joe laughed it off. Said it looked like he had a twin brother, which he didn't. Said, by criminy, he was getting a reputation and he needed one.

"Well, people would see him on the streets and say, 'Hey, Joe, saw you on TV last night,' and he'd say, 'How'd I come over?' and they'd say, 'Fine, how about a hundred thousand? I'm a little short today.'

"You see, it got to be a big joke. No one had any doubts. He was well liked, did a lot of good for the town.

"One thing more, this Dickens fellow didn't look quite like Joe Doyle. He had a tic in his right eye, he was stooped, his lip hung down in one corner. Not like Joe, really. He looked older.

Much older. In doing a little hindsight thinking, I can see that it was easy for Joe to fake a tic and appear stooped and drop one lip."

Hawk nodded. Joe Doyle was not the first to bluff his way through. Several Nazi war criminals had lived twenty and thirty years without discovery. Each had a cover story meticulously worked out to account for similarity in looks with widely circulated photographs. A most notable case in recent years had centered around Patricia Hearst, who moved about unrecognized for more than a year while her picture was plastered all over the newspapers. Some of the FBI's Most Wanted Ten, too, had escaped detection for years, even though mug shots were in every post office.

In running the name Charles Dickens through the indices, Hawk discovered that Interpol, the international police organization based in Paris, had reported that Milan authorities wanted a party by that name in a case involving a fraudulent sale to a Milan museum of a gold bowl, offered as of Scythian origin. Interpol provided a summary background on Charles Dickens which set forth that he was an American citizen living in Miami and was an executive in a corporation known as Rare Gold Art Treasures. The summary stated that the Milan museum had learned that the bowl had been fashioned by a Beirut gold craftsman who had fled Beirut at the height of the civil war and was living at present in Rabat, Morocco. He was described as one of the foremost artisans in reproducing ancient gold works of art.

Angel dropped a teletype on Hawk's desk. Miami was the place of origin. Hawk read the teletype aloud. It recounted briefly the operations of the Carney organization's gold division. Under Charles Dickens, aka Charlie Dickens, aka Big Charlie, the business originally had engaged solely in the sale of stolen gold bullion. With gold soaring in price during recent years, the profit had been enormous.

About two years ago, however, Dickens had persuaded the

Carney heads that considerably more money could be earned by taking part of the stolen bullion and smuggling it into Beirut (and later Rabat) to the gold craftsman. Dickens had seen the Scythian exhibit when it was presented in the United States by Leningrad's Hermitage, which owned it, in co-operation with New York's Metropolitan Museum of Art. If Dickens could obtain copies that could be sold as originals, then the return on the gold would be many times that of the world market price of the metal by itself. He had succeeded fantastically. A few ounces of gold, worth one to two thousand dollars, could be marketed in the form of a twenty-five-hundred-year-old Scythian work for thirty thousand dollars to a half million.

Part of his success was due to the fact he had a good cover story. A new kurgan had been found and the peasants had smuggled the gold in the tomb out of Russia. The Soviets would be expected to deny the account since such a smuggling operation would prove an embarrassment to the government. The proof of its authenticity, he told prospective buyers, was in the work itself. They had only to compare the pieces offered with the large collection in the Hermitage. He was safe in doing this. Few of his customers had access to the Hermitage, and too, his goldsmith's reproductions had deceived even some experts.

His goldsmith was a master forger. He worked up an *investment* (a mold body) similar to the ones the ancient Greeks used. He kept it free of the synthetics found in modern *investments*. He matched the ancient casting marks, which were different from those left by the centrifugal force employed in the creation of today's jewelry. He hand polished with pumice, ash, and oxides. Again, the faint markings were in contrast to those left by contemporary polishing. He fashioned what he believed were likely replicas of the tools used by the Greeks, who had made a considerable part of the gold pieces for the Scythians.

As a goldsmith, he knew, of course, that gold comes in many colors and shades. Depending on where it is mined, gold may be deep yellow, white yellow, orange, and red—and also, if certain alloys are added, pink, green, and even purple. There is even a natural white gold called electrum, which is very rare.

Living in Beirut, he had access to gold mined in the Black Sea area and smuggled into Lebanon. He gambled that the ancient Scythians and Greeks had gotten their gold from the same source. He had to reckon with the fact that a certain patina would develop with gold worked twenty-five hundred years ago if the carat content was twenty-two or under. He guessed and experimented with the amount of alloy used.

Still his works could have been proven forgeries if they had been subjected to certain technological techniques, the same as a "Rembrandt" may be shown to be a counterfeit. Breakthroughs have been achieved by the use of X-ray, carbon dating, radiography, and other techniques. Scientists have employed them not only to detect frauds but also to learn ancient methods. They turned to radiography to discover how Egyptian goldsmiths had assembled King Tut's mask. The experts had used gamma rays to penetrate the mask, and presto, as if by magic, they had a blueprint on Kodak X-ray film that revealed secrets hidden for thirty-three centuries.

For most institutions, however, the use of such techniques was expensive. Moreover, the "detectives" were comparatively few who knew the technologies and had access to the equipment. And too, as in any confidence game, the buyer so often *wanted to believe.*

Dickens committed one error. He flooded the world market. The buyers grew suspicious. They doubted if so much could have been found in a newly discovered tomb.

"What I want to know," Hawk said, "is what happened between Charlie Dickens and the Carney organization? What happened to cause him to defect with better than a million dollars? Where he got it and how did they know he visited the victim here in Los Angeles? And does she have it and if not, why are They positive she has."

He jotted down these leads for Miami to follow up.

After the others were gone, Hawk sat in thought. A simple routine lead, a newspaper clipping with the heading GIRL

STRANGLED IN NORTH WOODS, had led to far places. As happened so often, the criminals had given themselves away.

Shortly after six, Barney charged in. "We've got a development. A woman phoned Lefty Morgan at Mitchell's apartment. She was tough and brief. Lefty's to tell Gary Edison to pick up a note—at midnight—stuck into the brick wall of a building near Santa Monica and La Brea in Hollywood. Cathy put the news on the 410 telecopier to us and Lefty's on his way to Edison's."

"Lefty," Hawk said. "If They're using him as a runner . . ."

Both had the same thought. Lefty had sold out.

"What'll we do?" Barney asked.

Hawk tried rubbing the weariness out of his eyes. "Put it on 410 to Gary Edison that Lefty's on his way. Spell the instructions out. Lefty mumbles so much that Edison may not read him right. And tell Edison we've got to have his decision immediately. Whether he goes or stays put."

Midnight. The usual hour set by criminals in this type of case. The hour when innocent people reach a "scare state." Even returning home to a dark, familiar house, they experience misgivings. They are as cautious as cats until they reach a light switch.

Hawk said, "Either way we'll give him and Doyle what protection we can and hope to God nothing happens."

37

Abner Blanton was most disturbed. He had been to Cathy's apartment repeatedly. She was not there and the police had pulled out of the complex. He knew because he had thoroughly checked the grounds.

Time was running out. He had to reach her before the day ended and it was now six-twenty-three. He could not understand what had happened. Had the police arrested her?

He phoned the West Valley Police Division. He knew the sergeant who answered. The sergeant said cautiously, "I don't know, Mr. Blanton."

Abner Blanton was furious. They lied and covered up. They never gave a decent, law-abiding citizen a straight answer. "You could find out."

"You know I can't give information like that out, Mr. Blanton. It's confidential."

"Don't give me that bull. I've worked with you fellows for three years. I caught seven burglars last year, and what about that rapist, what was his name. Browne, wasn't it? who attacked seventeen women and I cornered him and you got him. So I ask one little favor. Where is Miss Catherine Doyle?"

The sergeant got the frog out of his throat. "Someone will call you in five minutes. A stranger. Don't ask questions." He cut the connection.

Five minutes later to the second the phone rang. "The party you inquired about was moved to the apartment of her attorney, Frank Mitchell." The caller gave the name and address.

Abner Blanton took a deep, happy breath. He believed devoutly in love thy neighbor but there were times when thy neighbor had to be swatted one to impress upon him how much love he was getting.

He got his wallet, loose change, and car keys from under a blanket in the clothes closet. He decided then to change his shoes. He suspected his tan ones were irritating a bunion. Still there was a lot of mileage left in them and he would suffer guilt feelings if he discarded them.

At the door he turned back to get the .38 which he also kept under the blanket.

In his bedroom, Gary jogged without going anywhere. He had to exercise to think. George, asleep on the bed, had all four legs twitching. He was running after or away from something.

Wasn't that the story of one's life? You were chasing or being chased.

At the first fall of a footstep on the front porch, George half fell out of bed and streaked off. He had an instant wakening mechanism. No turning the knob and letting the tubes warm up.

Lefty was puffing as he reeled off the instructions. He had memorized them to the word. He had a good mind if he did say so himself. He also brought a message from Cathy. "I'm terribly afraid for you, Gary, and I don't want you to go. Please stay where you are. I'll get through to Them somehow and insist They negotiate with Mr. Mitchell."

George backed off from Lefty to take up a command post. He needed a few feet for a running start if he decided to spring. He growled incessantly.

"Let me think for a few minutes," Gary said. "Can I get you coffee?"

Lefty said no, he would sit in the living room and read a magazine. When Gary disappeared into the kitchen, Lefty tried to make up with George. "Come here, old boy." Old Boy approached displaying a fine pair of uppers and lowers showing to the gum line. Lefty retreated.

The kitchen was long and narrow with walking room for only one. Gary paced it several times, then sat at the breakfast nook table, and poured himself a Pepsi. He drummed his fingers on the table, pounded with a fist, and repeatedly ran a hand through his hair.

He had believed Cathy. Why hadn't he said so? Why had he tortured her with his innuendoes and hypocrisy? Pretending he had forgiven her, then letting her think that really he hadn't.

He had understood perfectly. She had lived for years under the threat of exposure, a threat too horrible even to think about in a rational way. She loved him, he knew that, and she feared she might lose him if he knew about her father.

His ego had been bruised. Deeply bruised. Didn't he have an intelligence, though, that would stabilize an emotion that was out of balance?

God, am I really like this? I've thought of myself as consid-

erate and compassionate, a reasoning individual. I've thought that because of my handicap, I was more sensitive to the needs of others. That is what I have thought.

Did anybody ever see himself for what he really was? Are we all at a masquerade party and wear the mask no matter how much we hurt one another?

He took from a kitchen drawer a little sign Cathy had handprinted. "*God, grant me the serenity to accept the things I cannot change, the courage to change the things I can, and the wisdom to know the difference.*"

Returning to the living room, he found Lefty sound asleep in a straight chair. He looked like a propped-up dead body.

"Mr. Morgan." He raised his voice. George growled loudly and Lefty woke with a start. "The heat, it gets to my eyes."

"Do you want to write down what I want you to tell Cathy?"

Yawning, Lefty brought himself up out of the chair. "No need. Got a memory like a hippopatamus." He crossed himself.

"Elephant."

"I don't know about them."

"Well, anyway tell her," Gary began and hesitated. He had not thought his decision out. It was a gut reaction. "Tell her I'm going. I've never hidden from anyone or anything."

He stopped abruptly. That was not true and she would know it. He had hidden most of his life because of deafness.

"Skip that. Tell her I'm going to have it out with Them. They'll understand when They find out I don't know anything about the money or the situation in general. If I can see Them and talk with Them, I can get us both out of this. I've got to persuade Them that it's a mistake on Their part, and They're wasting Their time, and the million is getting away from Them somewhere else."

He dropped to a whisper. "Tell her I love her—and if anything happens I want her to know I wanted us to be married, more than anything, if it had been possible."

Lefty nodded. "I felt like you once, something like you, and there was this girl . . . God, what happens? The years go by and . . ."

George damned him all the way to the car.

Two hours later, Lefty answered a sharp knock on Mitch's apartment door to find Abner Blanton standing there.

"Good evening, Mr. Morgan," Abner Blanton said.

Lefty mumbled and called to Cathy in the kitchen. "Mr. Blanton's here."

"Happy birthday!" Abner Blanton said on seeing her. "A most happy birthday." He had brought her a potted white chrysanthemum in full bloom, $4.95 at Ralph's supermarket.

"How thoughtful of you. I'd almost forgotten."

"I've missed you," Blanton said.

She asked quickly, "Everything's all right at the apartment?"

He smiled indulgently. "I've been keeping it under close watch, Miss Doyle. I always do. You know that. My tenants never need worry about anyone rummaging through their things when they're gone. I came over to give you this."

He handed her an envelope. "Your father, when he was here, he said to me, 'Mr. Blanton, I've got a birthday gift for my daughter but I can't be here to give it to her in person. Would you?' And I said, 'Mr. Doyle, I would be honored.' A fine gentleman he is, Miss Doyle. You seldom find the likes of him."

Her hands trembled under the lurch of her heart. She ripped open the long, white envelope with an inscription scrawled across the front in the familiar handwriting, "For my darling daughter on her birthday."

It contained a birthday card with two thin white sheets inside folded three ways. The lines of writing started out straight across, then wavered until they were slanting upward. Seemingly, she absorbed it all in one glance. She let out a little muted scream and dropped to the sofa. She sat in a stupor, her eyes blank, staring dead ahead, her arms and legs rigid. She breathed with difficulty.

Far out on the perimeter of her understanding, there was a frightened voice saying, "Miss Doyle, Miss Doyle."

38

Quite some time before, Gail and Mitch had left the apartment for the office. "We've got to get some money in," Gail said. "We got a second overdue notice from Water and Power."

Mitch had objected. He had a feeling they might be needed. How could they, Gail insisted, with an "army" of police officers out there to protect Cathy.

He had yielded. Both were too tired to drive in the heavy, dinner-hour traffic although each insisted he/she would. Mitch pushed her aside to get behind the wheel.

They drove in silence. They had talked themselves out. Cathy had put it aptly. It was a Greek tragedy with the force of events (the gods) moving the people on stage inexorably toward an unseen and frightening fate.

On the steps leading to their second-floor office sat a dirty four-year-old urchin crying. Gail bent down to comfort him. He was the son of a streetwalker who sometimes parked him here while plying her trade. Gail left saying she would be only a minute. When she returned she had two small cartons of milk. She handed the boy one, and he smiled and was content.

The other carton she kept. "Since when did you start drinking milk at the office?" Mitch asked. She only shrugged.

As Mitch put the key to the office door, he heard movement inside. He tensed. "Someone's in there."

"It's all right," Gail said.

"I distinctly heard someone."

She surprised him by taking the key and opening the door. A bag of bones staggered out in the shape of a cat.

"How the thunder did he get in?" Mitch asked, then swung around to Gail.

"He didn't have any place to go," she said defensively.

He was adamant. "We're not keeping him."

"I wouldn't dream of it." She kissed him.

He recognized the technique. "Get away from me."

"He's awfully cute."

"Looks like every other cat. Stupid."

"He only went to the third grade."

"Quit that. Get away from me. I'm not adopting a stinking cat. If that can be called a cat."

"Yes, my lord and master."

He disappeared into his office, and was looking over the calendar when the phone rang. Someone in Sacramento at the Franchise Tax Board was on the line. "Been trying to get you."

"You're working late," Mitch said.

"Yeah. About those Chicano youngsters, technically they are liable for sales tax but in view of their ages we have decided against pressing charges."

"How about the future?" Mitch asked.

"I can't go on record but they won't be bothered. Just don't quote me. And say, you didn't think we had a heart, did you? Riding us like you did."

"I stand corrected," Mitch said.

Hanging up, he called to Gail. "The kids are off the hook as far as the great state of California goes. But if we hadn't called them on it . . ."

The little people, they needed a defender, a voice, someone to stand up for them. He would take on the city next, about the license to do business, and he knew the city would no more press charges than the state. It was a good feeling, one that didn't come along too often, and he sat a moment savoring it.

Gail fed the cat milk, watered the philodendron, then opened the mail. She let out a yell. "Moose! Two hundred dollars in twenties. Cash on the barrel head. He's held up a bank, I bet."

There was no note. Moose had never learned to write. Someone else had addressed the envelope. "Oh, Mitch," she said, "why can't we have clients who pay by check? I feel I'm part of a holdup, an accomplice, an accessory after the fact . . ."

He kissed her. She pulled away. "Mitch, we've just got to make a change. I can't take it."

She heard Cathy's hurrying footsteps hitting the corridor floor hard. She burst into the office with hair disheveled and the frightened eyes of a trapped wildcat. A few steps behind, Lefty followed, his features impassive. He was panting like an old dog.

"Something awful's happened." Cathy tossed her head to get the hair out of her eyes. "I've got to talk with you and Mr. Mitchell right away. It isn't awful actually. It just seems . . . I shouldn't come barging in like this . . ."

Mitch said from his office door, "Slow down there."

"I got to talk—"

"Come on in."

"Please, Gail, I want you, too."

Gail followed her into Mitch's domain with Lefty trailing. Cathy was too wrought up to sit. "Mr. Blanton, he's the manager at my apartment house . . ."

"I know Mr. Blanton," Mitch said. "Sit down—and let's start from the beginning."

Cathy sat, then got up. "It is the beginning. He came over a few minutes ago . . . I've told you all along I didn't have the money and now you're going to think me a liar. He brought this over." She indicated the long, white envelope she was clutching in a fist.

Mitch said to Lefty, "What're you doing around here?"

"He stays," Cathy said firmly. She was not about to brook any argument. "He'll tell you I'm not a liar. He was there when Mr. Blanton brought the letter. I said I didn't have the money and you'll think I was lying. Well, here, read the letter."

She handed it over but held the birthday card back. Gail looked over Mitch's shoulder to read:

My darling daughter:
I wanted to tell you when we were together that I am

very ill. You suspected as much but I wished our last visit to be a happy one. It was—but how could it be otherwise around you?

You will never know the happiness you have brought me through your letters. What a joy you have been all these years. No father could ever have asked for a more beautiful daughter. Some of the years have been rough for me and then a letter would come from you and the sun would shine again.

In this, my last letter, I don't like bringing you the news that I have only another month or so to live. The doctor says the disease has advanced rapidly and nothing more can be done.

I know you want to make it on your own and I love you for it. You are proud and independent and I admire you. Having said all of that I will get to the point. I have a considerable sum of money that I have saved and I want you to have it. It will mean a great deal to me to leave it to you as well as my home in Clinton, all of the furnishings, the car, etc.

For legal and other reasons too complicated to explain in a letter, I am leaving the money to you in cash. I would have given you this money when I was there but again for reasons that are of no concern to you—these matters can become so very complicated—I am placing the money, so to speak, "on deposit."

I am fearful that this letter might fall into the wrong hands and so I am using the old code that brought us much pleasure a long time ago. So this is how you locate "the deposit." There is only one string attached to this gift. I must ask that you wait one year before collecting it. I know I can count on you to do this which is most important to me. It is perfectly safe where it is.

When you pick it up, please make certain you are not followed. I would suggest that you go alone. Do not take a friend since friends so often are not friends where money is concerned.

You can pick up the money only at night but it must be before midnight. The directions are from your location.

SD 5S/and March 21+6/T Sunset/R/
Till the cows come home+You bet+
Shoot off one's mouth–The cat's meow/
Stop and enter/To chisel/Mac

You must not grieve, Cathy, my darling. You must remember the happy times, the happy letters, and glory in the joy that you brought me. The time comes, as it does for all of us, when we must go, and that time is here for me. Live life to the fullest and give of yourself to others, and never let there be a dark day that you don't light it up a little for yourself and others. I must go now.

All of my love,
Father

Mitch looked up. "Does this tell you where it is?"

Cathy was lost in grief. She straightened and took a deep breath. Her voice was far away. "I'll have to work it out."

"But you know the code?"

"It's been a long time."

He shot a sideways glance at Lefty, who was slumped, his eyes closed. But his ears wide open, Mitch bet.

He scanned the letter. "They couldn't wait for him to die in peace."

Cathy buried her face in her hands. Gail said, "It's a beautiful letter. Something to treasure."

Mitch asked, "Getting back to the code, what kind is it?"

"Something we dreamed up. A long time ago."

"Like what?"

"It's something between my father and me, and no one else will ever know. It's our secret."

The phone ring startled them. Mitch waved Gail aside. The caller was Hawk. He was blunt. "Are you negotiating a deal?"

Mitch leaned back in the swivel and got set to do battle. "I'm in conference with my client and what we discuss is strictly confidential. A client-attorney relationship."

Hawk's voice filled the office. "Not if you are conspiring with party or parties wanted for murder to evade the law and engage in a criminal act with them."

"Hawk, you're a pain in the derrière."

"I'm going to nail you one of these days, Frank Mitchell."

"I'm busy. Anything else?"

"Put Doyle on."

"She's busy, too."

Hawk shouted, "Put her on!"

Mitch said to Cathy, "You heard him."

Cathy raised her voice. "He's a horrible man."

Mitch said into the phone, "She says can you call back?"

Hawk subsided, grew confidential. "Look, Mitch, I'll level with you."

"Thanks."

"One Abner Blanton delivered a letter to Doyle from her father. She falls apart and goes running to you. I have one question: What's in the letter?"

"That's a confidential matter between—"

"I heard you the first time. If you're negotiating a deal—"

"I have every right to. The courts have held that in cases of kidnapping, extortion, and the like, where a life hangs in jeopardy, the party or parties who might save that life may enter into arrangements to free the person in jeopardy, provided they co-operate with the authorities fully after the *fait accompli*."

Hawk slammed down the receiver.

Mitch took a few seconds to recover. "I always feel like I've just come in from jousting on the fields of Groton." He sneaked a glance at Lefty. He hadn't moved.

Mitch said to Cathy, "You'll have to talk with the lieutenant. This concerns money that may or may not be the end product of a criminal act."

The old fire brought her upright. "It isn't! My father—"

"Okay, okay, I'm sorry."

"I'll never talk with that man again."

Gail broke in. "Let's put it this way, this is too important to be kept a secret between us. You might be charged with something if you did."

"I'll talk with Mr. Carlson. You tell the lieutenant—"

"It'll give me great pleasure," Mitch said, smiling. "How soon can you decode this?"

"Why?"

"They'll want to move fast."

"My father said a year."

"You mean . . . ?"

"One year from today."

Mitch sagged back. "Here we go again." He looked at his watch. "Look, in about three hours, your boy friend—"

"He won't have to now, will he?"

"They don't know what's in the letter any more than the police do."

"I'll talk with Gary."

"I'm calling Barney Carlson. Okay?"

She nodded. "But I'm not even going to decode the message for a year. My father . . . I'd never do anything he didn't want me to."

In a dusty, vacant office across the deserted street from Mitch's, also on the second floor, Billie Richards squatted on a hard cushion, her head barely above the dirty window sill. She tried to make herself as inconspicuous as possible, which was difficult since she had arthritis and kept shifting position.

With her was a creature who looked like part sheep dog. He was barely nineteen with golden hair to his shoulders, a full but well-trimmed mustache, and a beard sufficiently copious for a robin's nest. In the faint glow from a street light directly below them, his tight, squinty eyes took shape as rivets.

She and her motley crew had lived out of expensive rental cars for the last two nights and days. They had catnapped in back seats, taking turns driving. They bought take-out meals at fast-food places, and showed their faces only long enough to obtain gas. Even that was done in outlying cities where the search for them would be less well organized than in Los Angeles proper.

She was strict with them. They had to dress like conservative young attorneys and drive like old men, slowly and cautiously. Too many friends had been caught because of reckless driving or other traffic law violations. She had severely lectured them. If they were stopped by officers, they were to appear courteous and contrite. If they were arrested, they were to call a bail bondsman whose name she had given them. He was a referral from the Carney bondsman in Miami.

She realized she had her force spread too thin. She had assigned two expert surveillance men to the girl, Cathy Doyle; two on the boy, Gary Edison; one to watch the Mitchell apartment; and one to man this outpost. She had Archie the Gorilla standing by.

At this moment she was bewildered, a state of mind she never tolerated for long. The sound cone brought in only snatches of talk that fell like pieces of two mixed-up jigsaw puzzles. Although she had Mitch's office on a straight line, with nothing intervening, she suspected there might be a ham operator close by whose set was interfering. This was the only post where she could use a sound cone. Since the police had circled the Doyle and Mitchell apartments, she had to operate far out on the periphery. There were too many structures intervening and the distance too great to pick up conversations.

She heard clearly, "I said I didn't have the money." That had been the Doyle woman's line all along. So that was nothing new, except that she was making the denial to her own attorney.

Then the lawyer read what appeared from this distance a letter. He took his time. He looked up at Doyle. "You know the code?"

That was the first Billie Richards had heard about a code.

The lawyer's wife said: "It's a beautiful letter." From the conversation that followed, it became apparent that the letter was from Doyle's father. Then: ". . . the code, what kind is it? . . . Something . . . dreamed . . . long time . . . between my father and me . . . it's our secret."

At that point, the telephone rang and the ensuing conversation was between the attorney and someone called Hawk. The lawyer was highly antagonistic, and so was the Doyle girl.

Billie Richards duly recorded the fact. Doyle said distinctly, "I'll never talk with that man again."

The lawyer asked, "How soon can you decode this?" The answer was garbled at first but later Doyle said definitely she would not decode the message for a year.

A year? That was baffling. "My father . . . I'd never do anything he didn't want me to."

"What was that all about?" the Sheep Dog asked. He was only mildly curious. He had a boring, tedious job sitting here monitoring that office across the street.

Billie Richards shushed him. While the conversation was fresh in her mind, she wanted to think about it. Not a word had been said about a million two, the delivery, or the fiancé's trip to pick up the note. The talk by all parties had centered around a coded message that Doyle had no intention of deciphering soon—and she apparently was the only one who could.

Billie Richards had a gut feeling that the coded message related to the million two and the Doyle girl intended to stall.

39

Thousands clustered in the darkened Hollywood Bowl on tiers of bench seats that rose high into the hills. They listened with the sacred obeisance that the true believer accords opera as Carmen rejected the advances of the famous toreador Escamillo. The sweet, musky smell of grass sneaked in fitfully on puffs of wind, chased by the acrid odor of smog. Then a big gust would return the air to the virginal innocence of the time before man arrived. No one heard the low roar of a plane in the distance, but those sitting close to the towering eucalyptus trees along one side caught the wind in the leaves gossiping of other nights, other arias.

Cathy slipped quickly into the dressing room area, and past the guard, who had been alerted to her coming. Behind her trod a middle-aged, bushy-haired, bearded man, thrusting his stomach forward to aid his foot-pedal locomotion. His head was down, a mastiff following a scent. The guard stopped him. The man said he was the New York *Times* music critic. The guard planted himself firmly in the way.

Lefty had trailed the man but now he drifted away. He would wait in the shadows until she emerged. He fumbled for change and found a few coins. Not too far back, he had spotted a phone booth. It was lighted and that bothered him. He tarried, thinking, then decided to make the call.

Barney waited in the first dressing room which was the traditional barren cubicle. It had a brightly lighted mirror above a dressing table cluttered with make-up bottles, powder boxes, and sundry other items used in one form or another since the days of the ancient Greeks.

He was conscious of her labored breathing. "You okay?"

"Someone followed me." The man had shadowed her since she left Mitch's office. He had done so openly. They wanted her to know that They could reach out any time and take her. Lefty had slipped behind the man to trail him. If the man knew, he paid no attention. She was more concerned that Lefty might come to harm than she was about herself. She had grown immensely fond of him. He was attentive and truly concerned, and believed her implicitly. Once she had crawled out of this ugly, terrifying trap—and she would somehow—she wanted to continue seeing him. He needed a woman's attention. She would shop for clothes for him, and pay him back in some small measure for his faith in her.

Barney said, "I couldn't think of any other place where we wouldn't be seen together."

She half sat on the dresser, facing him. He was very sober, his eyes kindly but lips firm. "I shouldn't have gone running off to Mitch but I was stunned. I wasn't thinking. Of course, They followed me."

He wanted to reach out and touch her, to dilute the shock. "They'll think it had something to do with the delivery."

She fought back the tears and clenched her right hand. She would not permit herself to fall apart. "It's my father's last letter to me and it tears me up."

"I know."

"Does the lieutenant believe me—that I didn't know about the money until tonight?"

"I do. What about services for your father?"

She brightened. "Would you, could you? In Clinton. And I'll go back."

"I'll see to it tomorrow."

"Nobody but you thought of that. I've got to wait a year to get the money. You understand, don't you. He asked me to . . ."

He had to meet her head on. "But he didn't know. He couldn't possibly have foreseen . . ."

"I thought you'd understand." She was deeply hurt.

He talked along matter-of-factly. "They won't wait a year, not even a couple of days. It's a lot of money and They're going to get it."

She pleaded, "You've got to understand that this is the last thing I can ever do for my father."

A door opened somewhere and from far away Carmen pleaded with Don José to escape with her to the hideout of the smugglers. Then the door closed.

Barney said, "It's not just you and Gary. It's a lot of other people. People who will die in the months and years ahead if They get by with it. If we can get only three or four of Them we'll hurt the Carney organization. It'll take Them time to regroup. We hit Them here, and Chicago hits Them, and New York, and the Justice Department's Strike Force, and one of these days we will have taken the profit out . . ."

He paused, thinking, then said quietly, "They killed your father's best friend, Charlie Dickens."

She downed a sob, straightened. "His best friend. I love you for putting it that way."

"They dumped him in a quarry—as They will Gary. Maybe not a quarry but something like it. Gary's going out there soon

—and They're waiting. If you went for the money tonight . . ."

"But then I'd have it. I would actually have it. And They—"

"You wouldn't have it, Cathy. The IRS or the inheritance tax people or some law enforcement agency would impound it until—until, well, there are several angles. The Carney people would know then that it was beyond Their reach and in the meantime we would have caught some of Them. If all went well. It might not. You never know."

"They'd still come for Gary and me."

"Not if you didn't have the money. They don't kill wantonly, although that's the popular conception. Only if there's a profit to be made, or someone to be punished like your father's best friend. He defected and he had to be made an example of. They have to have law and order. Sounds crazy, doesn't it? But if he had got by with it, others would have tried and the organization would have disintegrated."

She stared at the floor for a long moment, then raised her eyes to his. "If my father was here—and he knew . . ."

His heart picked up a beat. He sensed a breakthrough. "You wouldn't have to go. You give me the deciphered code and we'll send a policewoman who resembles you. At least in build. Give her your clothes. It's hard to do successfully. There's the difference in the way we walk and move about."

She shook her head forcefully. "My father wants me to pick it up. Me. Not someone else. And if I can, I don't know how to say it, but if I can . . . I've got to go through with it for my father, for all of the others if you don't get Them first."

"It'd be a risk. We'd do everything we could to cover you. I can't ask you—it'd be hard to live with if—"

"You're not asking."

"If you and Gary left about the same time, it would split Them."

"You mean now? Tonight?"

"Could you make it? Get it decoded and go?"

She thought it over. "I'd have to get the code book out of my apartment. Lefty could go with me."

He glanced at his watch. "You've got one hour and forty minutes."

She nodded, and after a few seconds said, "I want a marker on my father's grave like some I've seen in old churchyards: JOSEPH Y. DOYLE, BELOVED FATHER OF CATHY.

She had known about her father since she was seventeen. She remembered the day vividly. A cold, gray, rainy winter day, dark by the time she returned home from school. She had been rehearsing a play, *Our Town*, which was so sad.

She switched on the television. Her favorite group, the Jackson Five, would be coming on shortly. She had all of their records. Now the Walter Cronkite newscast was ending. She paid little attention. She wandered around and in the course of doing so, picked up a green plastic sprinkling container and watered the Boston fern. It looked puny, to quote her mother. It required entirely too much attention. She preferred the jade plant, which took care of itself.

Then, glancing around, she saw her father on the screen. Of course, it wasn't her father. It was someone with the name of Charles Dickens who resembled him. He had been indicted for grand larceny. The newscast, out of Miami, described him as the reputed financial brains of the Carney mob.

She proceeded to water the fern. Her hands shook, though, and every muscle in her body. She went outside to walk it off. Since a child she had been walking out her problems. The rain had intensified and she was soon drenched.

He wasn't her father. He couldn't be. Her father was Joseph Y. Doyle and he lived in Clinton, North Carolina.

40

Gary squatted on the closet floor watching 410 as a typed message in capitals appeared. George looked on quizzically, puzzled by his boy's strange position and this alien equipment.

The message read: INSTEAD OF 11:30 LEAVE HOUSE AT 11. DOYLE WILL LEAVE APARTMENT AT SAME TIME TO PICK UP MONEY. IF YOU BOTH BEGIN YOUR OPERATIONS AT SAME HOUR, IT WILL SPLIT SUBJECTS WHO WILL BE RUNNING SURVEILLANCES. WE WILL COVER YOU FROM TIME YOU LEAVE HOUSE UNTIL YOU RETURN. AS PER INSTRUCTIONS EXPLAIN TO ANY PARTY YOU MEET, THERE HAS BEEN SLIP-UP AND YOU CANNOT MAKE DELIVERY UNTIL TOMORROW NIGHT. IF AT ALL POSSIBLE, WE WILL KEEP YOU POSTED ON DEVELOPMENTS CONCERNING DOYLE. HAWKINS.

Gary sagged against the wall. He took a breath that reached to his pelvic region, then rubbed his eyes hard. Never before had he been so torn. All of his life he had suffered crises, people who were unknowingly cruel about his deafness, who made him feel like an outcast of society. He could handle that. He had learned to live with it. But that was personal. This concerned Cathy.

He pushed a pair of pants hanging in his face aside and scratched out a note on a small pad: I'M SPLITTING THE SCENE TO GO WITH CATHY. I'M LEAVING THE HOUSE NOW. EDISON.

He pulled George over to him. George welcomed the attention. He hadn't been sure where he stood with this new contraption that absorbed his boy so completely.

Gary leaned over when the answer popped up: YOU'LL AROUSE SUSPICION IF YOU GO WITH DOYLE. THEY WILL THINK IT'S A TRICK. YOU WILL BE ENDANGERING HER LIFE. YOU'VE EACH GOT TO GO BY YOURSELF AND THEN YOU WLL SPLIT THEM UP AND THROW THEM OFF BALANCE. THEY DON'T KNOW YET ABOUT DOYLE. WE KNOW HOW YOU MUST FEEL BUT DON'T LET YOUR EMOTIONS WRECK EVERYTHING. HAWKINS.

Hawkins and his fellow officers didn't have any idea about how he felt. For that matter, they didn't care. They had it all analyzed. They weren't dealing in human beings but objects, pawns to be moved about a chessboard. Perhaps, like the military experts, they would sacrifice Cathy or himself to gain a goal.

He wrote slowly, angrily: I'D NEVER FEEL RIGHT IF ANYTHING HAPPENED TO HER. I WOULD ALWAYS FEEL I SHOULD HAVE BEEN THERE. I HAVE EVERY RIGHT TO MAKE MY OWN DECISION WITHOUT BEING ORDERED AROUND. EDISON.

There, that would be final. He imagined that most people caved in before the arrogant authority the police were displaying. He waited a long time. The message was slow in coming: DON'T PLAY JOHN WAYNE. IF YOU DON'T GO, YOU WILL PERMIT THEM TO CONCENTRATE EVERYONE THEY HAVE ON DOYLE. YOU WILL REDUCE HER CHANCES OF GETTING THROUGH THIS ALIVE AND YOUR OWN, TOO. YOU MAY UNINTENTIONALLY GET IN THE WAY. BELIEVE US, IT HAS HAPPENED. WE HAVE LOST VICTIMS WHO THOUGHT THEY KNEW MORE THAN WE DID ABOUT THIS KIND OF AN OPERATION. HAWKINS.

They were trying to frighten him. He ran his hand around George's collar. He didn't know what he would do without George. He recognized he had an inordinate love for the dog. He was not a dog, he was not a person, he was love. He wrote with difficulty: I CAN'T DO IT. I LOVE HER. YOU DON'T SEEM TO REALIZE MY PLACE IS WITH HER. EDISON.

The next message came from Jenny. He liked her. She was quiet, unassuming, sympathetic, yet perceptive. It read: YOUR PLACE, GARY, IS WHEREVER IT'S BEST FOR HER. FRANKLY, YOU MIGHT POSSIBLY GET IN THE WAY AND BE THE CAUSE OF HER DYING. WE HAVE BEEN THROUGH THIS BEFORE AND KNOW FROM EXPERIENCE HOW TO HANDLE IT. YOU SURELY MUST REALIZE THAT ONE OF THE KEY FACTORS IS TO KEEP THE LOVED ONES—FATHERS, MOTHERS, MATES—AWAY. IN A TIME OF CRISIS THEY NATURALLY REACT OUT OF LOVE—NOT OUT OF EXPERIENCE, WHICH THEY DON'T HAVE, OR BASIC REASONING. GIVE US AND CATHY A BREAK, WILL YOU? THINK IT OVER HARD AND LONG AND SERIOUSLY. JENNY BARTON.

This time he waited minutes before scribbling a note: OKAY, I'LL THINK ABOUT IT, DR. BARTON. BUT I KNOW WHAT I'VE GOT TO DO. EDISON.

Hawk said angrily, "We almost never get a chance to split the enemy—and now that we've got it—"

"If I were in Cathy's shoes and you in Gary's . . ." Jenny let the thought drop.

"Okay, I get the point. Love is beautiful, love is heroic—but

I'm no poet. I've got a job to get done, with a minimal loss of life, if any. Angel! Get Barney in here."

He turned back to Jenny. "At least we got one break. Barney did a hell of a job on the girl."

Barney hustled in. "The Edison guy's backing out," Hawk told him. "We've got to be prepared to go with Doyle alone. And we don't know where she's headed. What's holding her up? Put a query on Old 410 and put the pressure on."

"She said as soon as she decoded the message."

"Might take her all night, a code."

"She's got a code book."

Hawk shrugged, unconvinced that would help. "I don't remember a case when we've been so unprepared. We don't know the geography, whether the scene's in the city, out of the city, in a business district, residential, or what. We don't know whether we'll have traffic problems, helicopter support, be able to move cars in and out."

Angel appeared. "Frank Mitchell's on the line."

"You take it, Jenny."

Hawk discussed the logistics with Barney. "We don't want Them to know we're around, so that means a loose tail job—and a gamble we might lose her. No, we can't have that. Make it a tight tail and if They discover us we'll have to live with it. But at least we've got her protected."

Jenny put a hand over the mouthpiece. "Mitch says he's got a client or two who might help us if the rendezvous is here in the city. Something about their being 'street smart' and that they 'talk street.' Says they can go places we can't. That they know the people."

Hawk exploded. "Know the people! What does he think this is? An election campaign?"

He took the phone. "Mitch, Hawk here. What're you talking about?" He listened, all the time shaking his head. "That's the wildest, damndest idea I've ever heard."

41

Gail was waiting in Cathy's apartment when Cathy returned. Lefty remained in the car. "What time is it?" Cathy asked breathlessly. From a high-up shelf in the clothes closet, she pulled out an old cardboard notebook, the kind school children used years ago. It was scuffed up and the corners broken.

"Ten-five," Gail said anxiously. "Time enough?"

"I don't know." She pulled up a little chair to the phone stand. "I've had it since I was twelve." She referred to the notebook. "Father and I kept adding to it through the years and when there was something in our letters we didn't want anyone to read we'd use it. Did Barney call about Gary?"

Gail brought a glass of iced tea. "No one's called. Mitch was going to. I'm worried. He promised when I left the office . . ."

Cathy bent her long frame low to reach the table. She tried concentrating on the first line. She was conscious of a score of little things: the chair squeaking when she shifted her weight, the scratching of a dull pencil, Gail moving about in the kitchen, muffled voices rising and falling out by the pool, the eerie, far-off squeal of a car being gunned around a corner.

SD 5S/and March 21+6/T Sunset/R/

SD stood for street directions and 5S for Fifth Street. March 21 baffled her. She talked low to herself, then checked a Savings and Loan calendar hanging in the kitchen.

The box for March 21 had the words imprinted, "Spring Begins." Spring.

Fifth Street and Spring. Now for the +6. Cathy went running to her car to get a map. Returning, she found that San Pedro Street was six blocks beyond Spring. So it was Fifth and San Pedro.

T was simply for *turn*. Sunset was the direction. She and her father read a map clockwise. Translated, Sunset was west. If the code had read Sunset Up, then she would have advanced clockwise to north. Sunrise would be east and Sunrise Down would be south.

The R. What did the R stand for? She was struck briefly by panic. She could find nothing in the code book to help her. It was so simple. The R was for right. The right side.

So now she had it: Go to Fifth and San Pedro streets, turn west, and walk down the right side. She had never been in that area but knew it by reputation as a street of lost men, lost hopes, winos and drunks, flophouses and rescue missions, bars and pawnshops.

The rest of the code centered around the date when scholars believed a slang word or phrase had first become popular. She had pages of such expressions with the date in parentheses after each and she quickly checked out the ones her father had set forth. Slang was a subject which had fascinated her father and her. He had been an amateur word detective, an etymologist. In his search to date a slang term, he would consult all of the current books about the subject and then delve into musty, yellowing ones on the library shelves. While most slang was ephemeral, such as *twenty-three skiddoo,* other terms had become a part of modern language: *Count me out* from the early 1880s and *I don't get it,* about 1910.

Finished, she sat motionless, unable to move. Her heart had picked up tempo. She was hot and harried, her hair a mess, her clothing sweaty. She needed a shower, a chance to rejuvenate herself, to do her autogenics, but there was no time. Gail said, "It's ten-fifty."

Midnight. She had to be there before midnight. Why? she wondered. Was someone going off duty at that hour or a place closing? What a strange part of Los Angeles for hiding all of that money. She had thought her father might have buried it on the desert or the ocean front.

Gail asked, "Did they tell you what you're to do after you pick it up?"

"Play it by ear."

Gail thought that over. "I don't like it. You should have a definite plan. These ad libs seldom work out."

For the transcopier Cathy printed: I'M LEAVING IN FEW MINUTES FOR FIFTH AND SAN PEDRO STREETS AND WILL TURN WEST OFF SAN PEDRO AND ON TO FIFTH. I WILL DECODE AS I GO ALONG AND KEEP YOU POSTED. I WILL LEAVE CAR AT CORNER FIFTH AND SAN PEDRO. MAY I PARK ILLEGALLY IF NECESSARY SINCE TIME IS RUNNING OUT AND I CAN'T DELAY? WHAT IS LATEST WITH GARY? PLEASE TELL HIM WHERE I WILL BE. CATHY.

She brushed her teeth. Why she did at this particular time she never could explain afterward. However, she always brushed her teeth before going out. She put a clip in her hair to hold it back and took from a jewelry case under her lingerie a small silver cross that her father had given her on her fifteenth birthday.

Hurrying into the kitchen, she picked up a paring knife and dropped it in her purse. She had never owned or fired a weapon, and Barney had asked her not to carry one. On second thought, she located an ice pick. She was being ridiculous; she never could bring herself to stab or knife man or woman. Still, if she were about to be raped she didn't know. Nevertheless, having them in her purse gave her a certain psychological assurance.

Ready to go, she checked the transceiver. In bold strokes, Barney had printed: PARK ANYWHERE. WE WILL WATCH CAR. WE WILL GIVE YOU FULL PROTECTION FROM TIME YOU LEAVE APARTMENT AND RUN TIGHT SURVEILLANCE ON YOU FROM TIME YOU LEAVE CAR. EDISON HAS ADVISED US HE WILL NOT UNDERTAKE MISSION TONIGHT. WE DO NOT BELIEVE IT ADVISABLE TO INFORM HIM OF YOUR EXACT WHEREABOUTS UNTIL YOU COMPLETE YOUR TRIP. BARNEY CARLSON.

She was stunned by the news Gary would not follow through on the instructions given him by "the woman." All kinds of reasons swirled through her mind. He was ill or George was. He was frightened for her and planned to join or follow her. His car had broken down.

Her palms were sweating as she hurried for the door. It was eleven-eight. Gail accompanied her. "This is probably no time to be telling you," Gail said, "but I had a call just before you came in from a presiding judge who's an old friend of Mitch's. He said if Gary qualified, the superior courts might use him as an interpreter when cases come along that have witnesses who are deaf or with hearing impairments."

Cathy felt a good feeling surge up. "You did this for me? For Gary? I can't wait to tell him."

As she went out the door, Gail said, "God be with you."

Hawk worked with haste and precision. He had handled so many stakeouts and run so many surveillances that he moved almost by rote. Yet he was cautious. He double-checked each step, conscious that his experience and expertise in themselves might cause him to overlook a vital point or commit a fatal error.

Barney brought him a section map of the Fifth and San Pedro area. All of the sprawling conglomerate of towns and cities that had fused through the years into this fantastic metropolis called Los Angeles had been broken down into small areas.

Hawk informed the Cathy Doyle surveillance team of her destination. He dispatched four unmarked cars manned by eight officers to cruise the nearby streets around Fifth and San Pedro. Previously he had requested a helicopter to stand by, and now he activated it to follow her from home to the intersection. He gave the pilot strict orders to avoid detection, which mean that the pilot was to run the same crazy-quilt routine as the cruise cars: follow her, pass her, proceed a good distance ahead, then circle, drop back, and repeat the pattern.

He hand-picked four of his ablest officers to walk the first block on Fifth Street. "Dig up some old clothes. Look and act like winos. Remember your shoes. Don't forget some beaten-up, worn-out shoes." Once in the past, in a critical situation, one of his men had been trapped. He had looked the part except for a pair of good, polished shoes. "Get rid of rings, watches, all jewelry. Muss up your hair and dig your hands into some dirt. Get it into your fingernails and smear a little on your face and neck. But don't overdo it."

"The next thing you know, that guy," an officer had said once of Hawk, "will come up with a cologne that smells like the characters down there."

Hawk heard and considered it.

Hawk said to Barney, "That's the last place I ever would have figured Doyle-Dickens would hide the money. What d'ya make of it? Where down there, Barney? Where? What could you put it in? A battered-up old case, a blanket, a box, anything is worth a lot. They'd steal it not knowing the money was in it."

Hawk rose to leave. He would set up a command post from a car parked on an adjoining street. "Get me Jenny. Maybe she can come up with something. This isn't like Doyle-Dickens. A brilliant financier, a guy with some erudition. What's he doing down there? He's out of place. If we knew, if Jenny can come up with an educated guess . . ."

A young officer hurried in. A message from Gary Edison had just come in on Old 410.

George had had his dinner at the usual time, around six o'clock, but now Gary put down another helping and filled George's water bowl. George was puzzled but ate voraciously. He looked up at Gary a time or two, seeking to figure out what this change in routine might mean.

Afterward Gary brushed George thoroughly, talking to him all the while. He then got himself a hunk of watermelon from the refrigerator. For a chaser he had a glass of milk.

In the bedroom he dug around in a cluttered drawer for the pair of blue shorts he especially liked. He had to disentangle them from a shirt and a sock. In doing so, he located a white T-shirt he thought he had lost. After donning the blue shorts and the T shirt, he hunted up a pair of running shoes.

He thought about telephoning Cathy at the Mitchell apartment but doubted if she would answer. Probably Mitchell or his wife would. He wanted to tell Cathy that no matter what happened he would love her until their time ran out. He had been jarred by the last few hours. With death walking so near, he realized how much life means, and how petty are the little quarrels that a day ago loomed big. One had to live life as if it were to end tomorrow.

All of this he wanted to tell Cathy with an urgency and intensity he had seldom if ever known. Later tonight he would, if she were alive, if he were. He pushed the latter doubts out of mind. He was being melodramatic to the point of absurdity.

He scratched out a note which he placed on the transceiver: HAVE CHANGED MY MIND. I WILL LEAVE SHORTLY TO PICK UP NOTE. WILL JOG AND TAKE GEORGE WITH ME. YOU SAID YOU WOULD KEEP ME POSTED ABOUT CATHY AND I EXPECT YOU TO DO THIS. EDISON.

"He's going to do what?" Barney asked. "Jog? How're we going to run a surveillance on him? A car creeping behind him, one of our own men jogging behind him? We might as well put up a sign."

Hawk said, "Get me Baker."

"Who?"

"The newspaper boy."

Baker lived two blocks away. He came in sleepy-eyed.

"Hey, Baker," Hawk said, "did you ever get that skateboard you were talking about?"

Baker brightened. "You want to borrow it?"

"How about you running a surveillance for us? It goes like this. We got a guy—a good guy—who will be jogging. Some bad people may try something. You're on your skateboard and if you see anyone approaching him you let us know. We'll give you a radio."

Baker's eyes bulged. "You mean it?"

Barney said, "I don't know, Hawk."

"Who'd ever suspect a boy on a skateboard of running a tail job?"

"A black boy," Baker put in.

"I hadn't noticed," Hawk said.

Barney shook his head. "You'd be putting him in danger."

"Nonsense. We'll pull him off a block before Edison picks up the note. I'll get you some dough for this, Baker."

"I don't want any money, Lieutenant." He hesitated.

"Yeah, what d'ya want?"

"Could I come to your wedding?"

"Wedding? Whose wedding? How do these stories get started?"

His eyes nailed Barney, who shrugged.

"I tell you what," Hawk continued, "if there is a wedding—which isn't likely very soon, if ever—you get the front row. You, your parents, any friends you want to bring. Okay?"

"Okay!"

"Look, Baker, if you sell tickets to it, you gotta charge ten bucks. I don't want any cut-rate seats sold at my wedding. Got it?"

Baker grinned.

42

Cathy kept the speedometer at a steady fifty. She glanced frequently in the rearview and side mirrors. No one appeared, neither the police nor Them.

Traffic was running heavy, a steady swarm of large bees humming. Day and night the traffic ebbed little on the Hollywood Freeway into downtown Los Angeles. Where all the people came from and where they were going, no one knew. With the car lights on, the freeway looked as if it had been choreographed for a film musical.

The pavement rose and dipped through undulating hills. Right now it rose slightly above the city that was Hollywood. Capitol Records, which looked like one gigantic stack of records, rose to her right, lighted brilliantly.

"You all right?" She asked the question quite loudly.

"Don't fret none about me, ma'am." Lefty was scrounged up in a fetal position on the floor back of the front seat. Like a necklace of pearls tossed about, his vertebrae had repeatedly shifted position. He was happy, though; he could watch over her on a journey he considered only a little less terrorizing than *Star Wars*.

"We're passing the Sunset off-ramp."

"Should you be talking, ma'am? Someone might see you and wonder."

"You're so right. I'm going off the air."

She should have thought of that. She knew from being around Gary that there were more lip readers than most people imagined. One could scarcely walk anywhere without there being one. Not all were deaf, either. Many hearing persons read "speech without sound" because of friends or members of their families whose hearing was impaired.

Suddenly she remembered that ages ago, as far back as yesterday, she had needed gas. The needle was not yet on "positive" but on "almost positive." She would have sufficient to reach Fifth and San Pedro but not for the return trip home.

A leg muscle cramped and got worse. She had a problem with muscle spasms. They were exceedingly painful and she often doubled up. A terrifying feeling welled up. What if she experienced one tonight? What would she do or could she do, other than stand in pain and wait for the spasm to pass?

Her thoughts went to Gary. She wished her father could have met him. She knew her father would have liked him. Wasn't it sad that so often a parent you loved deeply missed out on some of the happiest experiences you would ever have?

If Gary could qualify for that job in the courts, he might have an entirely different outlook. It might motivate him to enroll at California State at Northridge, to learn that as a deaf person he had a handicap that could be overcome to a great extent by the development of talents he might not even know he possessed.

Downtown, in a freeway complex that looked from the air like bunched worms, she took the Sixth Street off-ramp. She passed Pershing Square, a plaza with vast underground parking. Traffic slowed her and she was glad. She bisected Broadway with its odd collection of big stores, small shops, and theaters showing mostly exploitation films.

She turned left on San Pedro and as she neared Fifth, looked as far ahead as she could, to locate a parking space. She was in luck. She pulled into a space near the intersection. She locked the doors and sliding into the adjoining seat, planted her feet firmly, put her hands palms up on her knees, took a slow, deep breath. "I am relaxed. I *am* relaxed. My legs will not cramp. My legs will not cramp. I will breathe quietly and steadily. I will breathe quietly and steadily. My heart will slow down. My heart will slow down. My body feels at peace with the world. My body feels at peace with the world."

Men passed her by, one after one. Some stared curiously at her but others were in too much of a rosy wine stupor even to notice the car.

Leaving the Pinto, she walked with eyes straight ahead to the dead center of the intersection. Lefty remained behind.

Gary's heart beat with piston precision. Cars crawled along Ventura Boulevard, their speed slowed by stop signs, but the sidewalks were virtually deserted, the shops dark except for an all-night supermarket. His legs, powered by hardened muscles, moved him along in a slow, rhythmic gait. The night had cooled but sweat rolled down his face and body. He felt no weight and no fatigue. He was an astronaut, earthbound, it was true, but moving through space and he loved every step, every mile.

Following him, six paces behind, came George, who had set his speed to that of Gary's. He never varied the distance between the two. As much so as any trail rider of pioneer days, he was protecting his master's rear. Not much escaped his quick eyes.

A crazy black youngster on a skateboard came up from the rear like a shot and veered wildly around the two. He sped on down the street, his one foot working furiously, and vanished around a corner. At the next intersection, he appeared genie-like, shot ahead of them, stopped, and sat down to examine his skateboard.

Passing him, Gary did a quick inspection. Odd, he thought, that a youngster would be out this time of night by himself.

Several times he glanced back to assure himself that George was still following. He did it by rote. He knew that only death could stop George. God, how he loved that dog, a love that was reciprocated so often every day.

Cathy was in his thoughts. During these last hours of tension, conflict, and outright terror, he realized his love for her was an emotion deeper than any he had ever known, one that when threatened tore him apart. She had become a part of him, a part that if severed would leave him without hope, only an inanimate body moving through a silent world.

He held a hand over his lips to conceal them and said for the benefit of the sensitive microphone hidden under the T-shirt, "I'm passing the turnoff for Universal Studios. Everything okay."

A mile passed and then another. He looked ahead to the next stop sign and set his speed accordingly. Not once did he have to stop. There went that wild kid again, shooting around him at a dangerous speed. He remembered from before he went deaf that speed was as much sound as visual. He tried to imagine the noise the skate was making.

In Hollywood he encountered more foot traffic. Sometimes he had to slow his pace. Once he thought he would have to stop. A bevy of youngsters, returning home from a movie, blocked the sidewalk. They saw him coming, parted and shouted, "Faster, faster!" He glanced back. He feared they might have bothered George. They had not. They even made way for the boy on his skateboard, cheering him on as they had Gary and George. Youngsters, he thought, were wonderful. Most could find happiness anywhere they landed. After the age of ten, he had never been a youngster. He wished he had but his world had been limited to reading, taking walks alone, going to basketball and other games. In reflecting, though, they had not been bad years, not after the first one was past and he had adjusted to the fact he would never hear again.

He easily found the brick wall and spotted the note, about seven feet up, high enough so that no one could reach it without stretching. The wall, solid and badly weathered, proved to be the side of a two-story building that probably dated from the 1920s. It had several long cracks and some bricks missing. In places the mortar had been eroded by time, wind, and rain, leaving gaping holes. Around the corner were entrances to three small shops and there were living quarters upstairs.

He stood on a cracked, partially uprooted sidewalk across the street, waiting until he had a chance to get the note unseen. Even at this hour, quite a few people were passing by. There were no street lights and it was fairly dark. He kept turning, peering about, seeking to determine if he were under observation. George sat by him on his haunches, patiently waiting. A woman hobbled along carrying a sack of groceries. She had a thin, worn scarf tied tightly about her head and wore a long, full, black skirt. She looked as if she were a European peasant, and probably was, a mother whose son or daughter had brought her over. In passing him, she stepped into the street to put distance between the two. There were muggings in this neighborhood, a good neighborhood, and in the daytime as well as night. A couple of chattering girls approached. At sight of him, their chatter stilled. Walking rapidly, they crossed to the other side.

Then no one was in sight and Gary struck off quickly for the wall. In a matter of seconds, he removed a slip of white scratch paper from a crack.

George grabbed him by the leg and pulled. Gary turned quickly to come face to face with a big, brawny guy who had the imprint of middle age on his face, belly, and hip breadth. "What the hell are you up to?" the man bellowed. It was too dark. Gary couldn't read him. The man seized him by an arm. George immediately fastened his jaws about the man's right leg. The man screamed in pain and bent to hit George. Gary tore loose and fled up the street a short distance, then turned, fearful George might be in trouble. George came streaking toward him. A half-block beyond, they slipped into an alley. By the light from a back shop window, Gary read the typed note: WE CANNOT MEET YOU TONIGHT BUT WILL CONTACT YOU TOMOR-ROW AND TAKE DELIVERY TOMORROW NIGHT.

There was no signature. Gary read the message in a whisper into the concealed mike. George was moving about nervously. The brawny guy might track them down or some other party could emerge from a rear door.

Cathy walked slowly with eyes straight ahead. From the dead center of the intersection she counted her steps. "Till the cows come home" was a slang expression that had originated in the 1890s. She struck off the eighteen. The ninety stood for ninety steps. She veered to the right sidewalk.

Overhead an aging pawnshop sign hanging precariously screeched in the wind. Tag ends of papers swirled about. The air was cloying with the stench of cheap wine and sweat-soaked bodies and clothes.

A wino, bundled in an army coat despite the heat, slept dead to the world in a grubby store front. He had a knotty bedroll for a pillow. Cars crawled along slowly, with preying eyes on her, a lone female, an attractive female, and one alien to this refuge for the displaced.

"You bet." From the 1860s. Add sixty steps more.

She put behind her the Skid Row and Prince of Peace missions. Ahead was the Panama Hotel and Singapore Bar. Alongside was a fenced-in vacant lot. A heavy metal gate groaned at someone's touch. Startled, she moved to the curb and almost collided with a grocery cart. An old man pushed it along, stopping now and then to pick up empty cans, milk cartons, and other refuse.

A young guy in greasy coveralls, sucking a candy bar, sized up her frontal structure, and as she passed, her buttocks. She felt her clothes being ripped off. A horribly emaciated man, not more than forty, sat on the curb loving a starved little dog that was as sad-looking as he was. The fact that he was giving the dog affection and taking affection from him seemed to say he had not yet given up on tomorrow. A man in his sixties with neither teeth nor dentures shuffled along. He wore a threadbare gray suit that had not been pressed or cleaned in years, and yet he had a once white handkerchief in the breast pocket.

She was getting deep into the area. An old man, mostly bones, shuffled toward her. He hadn't shaved in days, his hair was shaggy and matted; he had no outer shirt, only a rumpled, graying undershirt that exposed a sunken, wrinkled belly; trousers ripped at one knee were held up by rope.

"Pardon, miss." Even with an alcoholic accent, it was obvious he once had cared about his speech. "I'm hungry. Could you help me with a sandwich? A dollar, miss?"

She held her pace, counting steps. She must not err or she would have to start over again. She had no money or she would have given him a dollar. A dollar for more cheap wine, most likely, but maybe not. She believed that one must never turn away a fellow human. For every nine who take advantage of you, one might be in honest need.

He tottered alongside. "A quarter, miss. Please, miss a quarter." In his rheumy eyes was terrible anguish. There would be few tomorrows.

"Sorry, I don't have it." He believed her and dropped behind.

Her heart ached. For many this was the end of the line. The next step, the coroner and burial at county expense. Most were terminal, by their own choice. They had given up. They had been husbands and fathers but then their world had caved in. It's the competitive system, she thought. Many cannot make it. The lucky ones have an offspring's doorstep to sit on in their last years; the unlucky slip into stinking holes such as this, forgotten and usually wanting to be forgotten.

"Shoot off one's mouth." The 1880s. And eighty more steps.

Pretending she was half blind, Billie Richards tottered along on the opposite side of the street. Occasionally she stopped and peered out of half-closed eyes, as if straining to see. Her hair was matted, her skirt wrong side out, and her blouse reversed.

It was the best she could do, this attempt to look slovenly, in the few minutes she had had.

She had sent her men scurrying down the street after she had given them curt orders about their attire. Get off those ties, turn your shirt collars in, rip off a few buttons, let some stomach show or a navel, pull off the belts, let your trousers ride low, tousle up your hair, buy a bottle of cheap liquor but don't put on a drunk act and get picked up.

For Archie the Gorilla, she had specific instructions. He was to keep fairly abreast of Doyle and if she entered a building, he was to scout around quickly for a second-story spot on the opposite side of the street, from which point he might fell Doyle or a confederate with a quick bullet—if and when Billie Richards gave the order.

Billie Richards could never remember a time when she had been so confused. She had no specific reason to believe Doyle was headed for a rendezvous at which she would collect the money. The Carney people had assured her that Doyle already had it. Yet Billie Richards had a strong visceral feeling that Doyle was taking delivery from an unknown party.

43

Cathy approached two police officers who were picking up a drunk to take to the detoxification center. The youngest stopped her. She had counted off twenty-one steps. She fixed the number in her mind.

"You alone, miss?"

She realized he had no idea she was a part of an undercover operation. She went rigid. If They saw him, as They must, They would think she had called in the police.

She started on. "I'm meeting a friend."

He walked with her. "You shouldn't be down here. We had a fatal stabbing up ahead a couple of hours ago."

"Thank you." She walked a little faster and he dropped back.

A smashed-up car that looked as if only a miracle was keeping it running pulled up close to the curb. A face that had been cleavered on one side leaned out. "Want a ride?"

She counted seventy-eight, seventy-nine, eighty. "The cat's meow." The 1920s. It was a minus. Twenty steps back. She turned sharply about.

The car reversed itself. "Twenty bucks. All night."

She counted four, five, six, seven.

"Twenty-five bucks. Last offer."

Eight, nine, ten, eleven, twelve.

As he screamed an oath at her, the car shot forward with a squeal of rubber.

Eighteen, nineteen, twenty steps. She looked up over the door. The Mission of Jesus Christ Saves. From inside floated the faint strains of a hymn. She hesitated. The code read: Stop and enter. There must be a mistake. She had miscounted. She took a step back and looked up and down the dark street. Lights burned at the Singapore Bar, and on the corner of Fifth and Wall, and at the Hard Rock Café, "the workingman's friend." They were likely spots. She had deciphered the code wrongly.

Her body shook. She could scarcely read the notes on the scratch sheet she held up to the weak light under the mission sign. "Till the cows come home." Ninety steps. "You bet." Sixty. "Shoot off one's mouth." Eighty. "The cat's meow." Minus twenty.

That was correct. She hadn't skipped any.

She was bumped hard from behind and was within seconds of hitting the pavement when she righted herself. A drunk went careening by. The shock of being struck by another body exploded through her. In desperation she pushed through the screeching, weathered door into a big, dark, divided room.

She stopped to adjust her eyes. On her right, men were clearing tables, and on her left was a small churchlike area. A young man with a rugged, outdoor look was leading the singing of an old hymn. He had a robust, earnest voice that rocked off the paint-scaling walls. The congregation, on straight-backed chairs, numbered about twenty, all men, all down and out. They sang without spirit. Some mumbled. They had no heart for the song.

No one stared at her, as men had on the street. She was accepted, as were all who entered.

"To chisel." The 1820s. Twenty steps dead ahead.

Walking, she spotted the door. Nearing it, she saw a name written in chalk in a big, bold hand: MAC.

She was conscious she was being followed. Lefty, perhaps, or Barney Carlson, or one of Them. She couldn't bring herself to look back.

She knocked but there was no answer. She eased the door open on pitch blackness.

From across the street, Barney had trailed her. He wore his old yard clothes. They were stained, ripped, and dirty. "I'm going to get me another gardener," his mother had threatened. "You're a disgrace to the neighborhood." He had on sneakers that dated to his high school days. A toe stuck out of one and the other had lost a tongue.

In every operation, the unexpected invariably happened. He was horrified when the young officer stepped up to Cathy. And Barney would have blown the whole operation if the driver with the cleavered face had tried to pull Cathy into his car.

Barney was in command of the minute-to-minute strategy on the street. The over-all belonged to Hawk, who sat in a command car on Wall Street. Hawk would give the order to "blow it," if the danger to Cathy Doyle was too great, to open fire under certain circumstances, or pull out.

Hawk had laid out the general plan. One officer ahead of her; one far behind; another who trailed Barney by a few steps; two who paid no attention to her but scanned buildings for a possible sniper; and two more who watched for something tell-tale about a passer-by that indicated he was not native to this street.

When the report came over that Gary Edison's trip had been aborted, Hawk accepted it without surprise. Obviously, the Carney people had pulled everyone off Gary, save possibly for a lone man. Hawk reasoned that They had to suspect a major development was taking place about Doyle. They had been tipped off by her frantic, hurried trip to Mitch's office and her subsequent journey to the Hollywood Bowl.

Now Barney was whispering: Victim is stopping before Mission of Jesus Christ Saves. Almost knocked down by drunk. She's standing looking at notes. Something seems to be wrong. She is entering mission. Lefty is entering. He's too close to her. He may tip off subjects if They are watching. Hold on a second . . ."

Cathy stood stock still. She sensed that someone was nearby. She thought she heard breathing. As she started to back out, a voice whispered, "What do you want, sister?"

There was a hand scratching along the wall. It found an electric switch and a fairly bright light jumped on. The bulb dangled over a small, badly battered table in the center of a large room that had no windows and no door other than the one she had come through. Shelves lined the four walls. They were stacked with a motley collection of boxes, blankets, beaten-up suitcases, and the like.

"Is there something I can do for you, sister?"

He was the singer but the hymn continued without him. He had the mauled face of a prize fighter who had lost too often, a shock of intensely black hair, ears that protruded, and eyes as deep blue as Hawaiian waters. He was in an old pair of Levis, immaculately clean, and a faded blue shirt that clung in the heat to his big chest.

She stammered. She had no idea what to say. "You have a beautiful voice."

He relaxed, closed the door behind them, and locked it. He explained, "Those guys out there haven't seen a pretty girl in a long time. They'll be in here if I don't lock it."

She stood very still, paralyzed. Lefty could not get in or Barney.

He walked around the table. "Sit down, won't you, please?" He indicated the only other chair. "You're Catherine Doyle aren't you? I hadn't expected you so soon."

She took the chair. She became aware then of the stench, that very particular odor of unwashed clothing. The room lay heavy with it, from the bundles on the shelves.

He tumbled through correspondence tossed willy-nilly in the top drawer and took out a picture of her. Her college graduation photograph. "I got it in the mail a short time ago. Your father sent it. For identification."

"My father?" She was nonplused.

"I assume he died or you wouldn't be here—and I'm sorry about that. I knew him only for a few minutes, when he walked in. But there was something about him . . . I can't quite peg it. . . . He hadn't given up. . . . So many do. We talked for a little while. He had such tremendous love for you, and I found myself wondering what you would be like."

"My father came here?" She struggled to put the pieces together.

He took the photograph back. "I'll keep this if I may. To remind me that there is still love in the world. There is so little here. I work hard, I do my best . . ."

"You say my father came and talked with you?"

He leaned back. "Perhaps I should explain this room, I call it my room of lost dreams and hopes. The men come in with a bundle or box of keepsakes, some letters, a few photos, trinkets that hold meaning only for them, all they have left from their lives. . . . For many reasons they can't carry them around with them any longer . . . mostly they're afraid they will be stolen in the flophouses where they sleep. I take them and put them up on the shelves and tell them I'll keep them for five years and any time they want them, or their loved ones do, they can come and get them."

"My father left—left something—for me?"

He nodded, rose and walked along the shelves. "We got to talking and he told me he worked at this mission thirty years ago when he was a student at USC, and when he got to wondering where he might leave some keepsakes for you he remembered. But I didn't expect you so soon. It was very strange, I didn't understand it, but he said you wouldn't come for a year. I'm glad that you did, though. He said something about it being your birthday and he wanted to surprise you after he was gone."

She fought to stop the sobbing.

"Here it is." He took down a small beaten-up suitcase, tied with rope. He handed it to her. "Happy birthday, Miss Doyle."

"Thank you. Thank you for keeping it and thank you for telling me about my father. You see, we were very close."

He took a deep breath. "This has been a special night for me. I'm the minister here, in charge of the mission. You heard them singing out there. Not really singing. They've forgotten how. It doesn't mean anything to most of them. Just a place to rest their bodies for an hour. But if a song like you heard or something I say renews life for only one man a week, then I think I've done something for the Lord. But I don't get many happy moments such as this one."

He opened the door and said, "God bless you, Miss Doyle. God be with you always."

She hesitated. Out there lay the unknown. If she could only tell him. . . . "Thank you again. You've been very kind. If I ever get any money . . ."

"Yes, remember us. We can use it. Good night."

She walked unsteadily. She feared she was going to lose her balance. They were singing "Amazing Grace." She remembered being in church a long time ago—she was only ten—and her father was beside her singing "Amazing Grace" in his deep bass . . . a long time ago.

She glanced frantically about for Barney, Lefty, or a face she might know. But the light was dim, and she was walking a little too rapidly, all was a blur.

Holding the case tightly, a fist clenched about it, she pushed through the heavy door out into the dark street.

44

In a barren hotel room across the street, on the second floor, Billie Richards sat tense and straight-backed watching the scene below. With her was Archie the Gorilla, squatting Indian-fashion on the floor by a window, his rifle resting across his lap. Four other men, ranging from the nineteen-year-old Sheep Dog to one in his fifties, were gathered about at the other window. By muscle power, they had broken in only twenty minutes before. They dared not register and pay. Most likely, a wanted notice was out on them.

"She's hitting the street," Archie shouted. Billie Richards strained her eyes. The figure was murky but when Cathy Doyle stepped directly under the mission light, They saw she carried a small suitcase.

Billie Richards went into action. She ordered the four men down to get the case. "Any way you can. Kill her if she resists. But get it." Her voice was a man's, harsh, tough, determined.

Archie said petulantly, "You told me I could kill her."

"Shut up!"

And then she could not make out what was happening. A crowd was enveloping Doyle. Billie Richards had trouble finding her. "What's happening? Who are all those people? Fire a shot down there and scatter them. Go on, go on."

Archie had them in his sights. He mumbled something.

"What? What?" Billie cried.

He looked up. "I can't. I might hit the kids."

"What kids?"

He looked into the sights again. "I'm not going to kill a kid. I've never killed a kid."

"Give it to me." Billie yelled. She tried to grab the rifle but Archie resisted. "Okay, I've got the girl lined up. No—no . . . she's stooping down talking to a boy."

"Go on, kill him. Kill Doyle. Kill anyone. We've got to spread them out." She had lost her poise. For the first time in her life, Billie Richards panicked. A million two in the suitcase. It had to be. That was what the code was about. The Doyle girl had taken delivery for herself from an unknown. And now she was about to get away with it because for some mystifying reason there were people crowding about her. On a street where at this time of night there weren't a half dozen.

She heard the beat of a drum. Pound, pound, pound. And someone singing "Swanee River" in a loud, strident voice. "Swanee River"? It couldn't be. She was losing her mind.

"Kill them. Kill them all."

Archie took a tight grip on the rifle. "I never killed no kid, Miss Richards, and I ain't going to now."

Stunned, Cathy stared in bewilderment. A woman loomed up pounding a big bass drum and shouting, "Jesus saves." The drum and her screaming voice deafened Cathy, who staggered backward. All the time her hand was welded to the case.

A little Chicano boy with a girl clinging to him was in her way. He held out a bouquet of roses. "A dozen for a dollar, lady. We just picked them. *Por favor*, beautiful señorita, one dollar, no more."

She bent down. "I haven't any money."

"Here I give them to you." He turned to the girl. "Give the flowers to the nice lady."

The boom, boom, boom of the drum thundered again in her ears "Jesus saves," the woman screamed. "Jesus saves."

A redhead—Cathy recognized her as the Mitchells' next-door neighbor—was strumming a guitar on Cathy's other side. She raised her voice above the constant beat of the drum, singing Stephen Foster's "Swanee River."

In the midst of the pandemonium Barney materialized. He tried to take the case but she hung on. She had programmed her hand to hold the case come what may. "Hey," he said, shouting in her ear, "it's me, Barney."

She let go and he disappeared. Gradually, slowly, she realized the people about her were moving her toward her car.

From some distance away, she heard a familiar voice shouting. "Look at their shoes! Look at their shoes!" That was Mr. Mitchell. What was he saying about shoes? Why look at shoes?

Mitch was everywhere. His "people," the little people, had turned out, every one he had asked. And two he hadn't. The little Mexican-American boy and his sister. They had heard and shown up to help out. Mitch had ordered them home. He feared for their safety. But they had laughed, and ducked away from him, and stayed.

Like he had told Hawk, his people knew this street. They knew who belonged and who didn't. They were all here. The Bible woman beating her drum and shouting, "Jesus saves." And Lefty. He was picking pockets as fast as he could. After looking into the wallets, he tossed them aside until he came to one. He held up a hand and yelled, "Florida driver's license." Two officers grabbed the man and hustled him away.

And Marilyn. She stopped a handsome guy, seized him by one arm, and said, "You want some fun? I've got a nice room." He screamed at her, "Get away. Let me go." She hung on and blew a whistle, and two disreputable characters apprehended the guy. "We're police officers," one said. "You're under arrest."

Billie Richards had worked herself into a state of fury. Archie continued to refuse to shoot into the crowd. "You crazy fool! I'll have a contract put out on you for this."

Archie was shaken. He lined up the sights again. "A little time. I'll get Doyle. The damn, blasted kids!"

She saw a man grab the case from Doyle. Looked like a wino. "Get him," she cried.

"Who?"

"That guy running by himself—with the suitcase. See?"

Archie squeezed the trigger. It was a neat shot, one of his best. The guy fell and lay sprawled on the pavement in dead center of the street. There was no need for a second shot. Archie prided himself on saving ammunition.

As Barney fell, the case hit the ground with considerable impact and split open. Thousand-dollar bills floated here and there. Barney watched them. The bulk lay in a heap. Only on the fringe did the breeze puff them about.

Barney waited, not moving a muscle, scarcely breathing, feeling the heat of the asphalt. He was conscious of every pebble, every crack. A searing pain shot up one arm where he had skinned it in the fall.

He heard a shot. He thought then it was safe to get up. But he waited until a fellow officer said, "Okay, Barney, we got him."

Billie Richards had always been the administrator, the organizer, but in this moment she had no one to organize. Archie was dead, fallen at her feet, and she had no idea where her men had disappeared.

She would get the case herself. There it was right out in plain sight. A million two hundred thousand dollars.

She hurried as fast as she dared down the stairs. She cautioned herself to take it easy. Her arthritic joints could not be trusted.

Once out on the street, she broke into a half run. Lefty saw her coming and for a few steps he ran alongside her, bending low to check her shoes. He then stuck one foot out and tripped her. She fell flat on her face and the blow stunned her.

Lefty bent solicitously over her. "Ma'am, ma'am, are you all right? I didn't mean to hurt you."

Barney was scooping up the bills and putting them back in the case when a wino passed several feet away. He stopped and returned to look at the money. He picked up a bill and examined it, then tossed it back in the heap. "Counterfeit." He shook a finger at Barney. "You can't get away with it, mister."

Suddenly the street was quiet. The Bible woman and the redhead and Marilyn and the Chicano boy and girl and Lefty were gone, and Mitch and Cathy had taken off for home.

The old man sleeping in his army overcoat in the doorway, who had turned his back to the street when the pandemonium was at its peak, reversed positions. A huge black who stood straight and tall passed without a glance at the mortuary ambulance that was picking up Archie's body. The ambulance came every few nights. It was no big deal. One died, one went to a better world. It had to be a better world than this hell.

Mac locked up the mission. He was humming "Amazing Grace." If he could reach only one derelict a week . . .

45

City Councilman Hugh Z. Lara, lounging in his self-bought, hundred-dollar scarlet dressing robe, scanned the *Times* carefully. Finally he turned back to page three (the *Times* seldom fed its customers crime on page one) and again read the story. The Carney organization had been dealt a serious blow. Billie Richards, whom the Justice Department's Strike Force described as the foremost woman mobster in the nation, had been captured. Archie White, whose peers dubbed him the Gorilla, had been killed. Three mobsters had been apprehended, three had escaped.

Hugh Lara was fascinated by two facets of the story, which was brief since it had broken very close to the *Times*'s deadline. First, the episode had taken place in the district of that little fop, Randy McGill, who liked to boast that no crime worthy of mention ever occurred in his bailiwick. Second, the report carried the name of Lefty Morgan, who singlehandedly had captured Billie Richards. It was not the name, Lefty Morgan, that stopped Lara in his reading but Mr. Morgan's address, which was in Lara's district.

"Lucy," he yelled, "get me the phone book. And some hot coffee. Bring me another bear claw, too. Hurry it up. I've got to get going."

With much scurrying about, his wife of twenty-seven years obliged. He located Mr. Morgan's name and phone number. Lefty Morgan. He seemed to recall having seen that name somewhere. However, he was certain he had never met Mr. Morgan. He remembered the name of everyone he ever talked with. His memory had paid off. At election time no one could even come close to defeating him. The little old ladies voted for him en masse. Imagine, he called them by name. Sometimes years after he met them. And for the same reason, quite a few bankers, professors, and executives voted for him, too.

Lefty Morgan. No, he had never talked with him. For what Hugh Lara had in mind, that was good. A total stranger.

At straight up 8 A.M. Hawk started the day at his desk. He was beaten. The cause was more smog and heat than the operation of a few hours ago. He could remember when Los Angeles was paradise, with clear, invigorating air, and brilliant sunshine. That was before the millions trooped in. Now it was people-infested, which in some ways, to his thinking, was worse than rat-infested.

Angel briefed him quickly and efficiently. The Doyle case

was almost a thing of the past. Reports to dictate, a few court appearances. The ball had now passed to the local and federal prosecutors. A high bail would be set for Billie Richards and conviction was almost a certainty. The authorities would wrangle and file numerous briefs about who would get control of the money and Joe Doyle's property in North Carolina. Hawk doubted if Cathy Doyle would ever see a penny.

Barney hurried in to report that the nineteen-year-old whom they called Sheep Dog before his identity was established had talked. He had the same loyalty most mobsters display when trapped. Zilch.

"He says when the Carney people discovered Big Joe Doyle was ill they decided to dump him fast, without giving him any advance notice."

Barney referred to notes. "They called him in and told him he was through. He handed over the checkbooks but got out of town before the Carney outfit discovered he had cleaned out the bank accounts. He knew what was coming. He had it all figured.

"They got busy and learned he had taken a National Airlines plane out of Miami for Los Angeles. They sent one of their best trackers out here, a guy by the name of Horse McNamara. It took him only a few hours to locate Doyle. At the Biltmore Hotel.

"By this time twenty-four hours had elapsed. Apparently soon after arriving Doyle went to the mission. Sheep Dog figures Horse McNamara missed out on that visit although it's possible McNamara didn't figure it worth reporting. Who would hide a million two at a mission on Skid Row?

"Anyway, Sheep Dog does know that McNamara followed him to Cathy's apartment. Horse knew him, of course, only as Big Charlie Dickens and Horse jumped to the conclusion that Cathy Doyle was his girl friend. Doyle went into her apartment carrying a largish box and when he left he didn't have the box."

(Subsequent investigation disclosed that the box was a gift for Cathy Doyle, an ornate brass tray from Morocco.)

Barney continued, "Horse tracked him from Los Angeles to Las Vegas and somewhere between Las Vegas and Boulder City, near Boulder Dam, the Carney execution squad ran him off the road and demanded the money. When he said he didn't have it and wouldn't disclose what he had done with it, they killed him. Sheep Dog says he doesn't know who did the job. I think he's covering. He wants to plea bargain. He's told us this much to prove that he does have information. But the name of the actual hit man is his ace."

Hawk plugged in the shaver. "Good work, Barney. Let him rest awhile, do some heavy thinking, and then go after him again. I don't like plea bargaining. I think it's a cop-out. It's an easy way out for the prosecutors. Instead of doing some digging and using a little gray matter, they let the guilty parties get out of serving the time they should. So keep pounding at him and maybe we can get a confession before his attorney gets an opportunity to plea bargain."

Hawk pulled down his upper lip to let the shaver glide easier. He mumbled, "Thank Doyle for us. She's got guts. You going to marry the girl?"

Barney faked surprise. "I only know her professionally."

"Don't hand me crap. It's in your eyes. Every time you look at her. I'll volunteer. I'll give the bride away."

"You mean—"

"After the creeps you've dated, yes. She's a fine girl. A little mixed up—but aren't all females? I've never met one yet . . . oh, morning, Jenny."

Jenny looked radiant despite little sleep. "Am I interrupting anything?"

Hawk put the razor away. "I want to talk to you. I got to thinking last night . . ."

"I've got to go," Barney said.

"Don't. I want to see you."

"You got to thinking . . ." Jenny repeated.

"Yeah. What would you think about waiting until Valentine's Day? Christmas is such a busy time."

"What year?"

Hawk looked at her sharply, surprised. "Oh, come now, Jenny."

Barney cleared his throat. "I'm going if there's nothing else."

"There is," Hawk said. "Sit down."

Jenny took a deep breath. "I love you, Hawk. I don't suppose there'll ever be another. But I'm thirty."

"You've got a thing about that."

"Every woman has. I can't wait until I'm forty."

Barney headed for the door. "Cathy's waiting for me."

"Hold it, Barney." He turned to Jenny. "Who said anything about forty? I said—"

"You're a sweet, wonderful guy—but I'm returning the engagement ring you never got around to giving me."

Barney asked, "What about Baker?"

"Baker?" Jenny was nonplused.

"Yeah," Barney continued, "the newspaper boy. Hawk promised him the first row at the wedding."

Hawk managed a weak laugh. "A pay-off. He ran a surveillance for us last night."

Jenny gasped.

Barney was in the doorway. "Honest to goodness, I've got to go."

"Sit down and shut up and keep your big mouth closed!"

Barney stared in amazement. He dutifully took the nearest straight chair.

Hawk said to Jenny, "Now hold it, Jenny. You're upset."

"Shouldn't I be?" she answered angrily, then calmed. "I know you love me—in our present relationship. But you're afraid of me, too—about what might happen if we married. You're so busy. You can't take on more responsibilities. You haven't time for a wife and home . . ."

Hawk started around the desk. "I don't know what you're talking about."

She backed toward the door. "All females are a little mixed up, aren't they? You've never met one yet . . ."

"Jenny, please."

"I'll be seeing you around." She disappeared on two quick feet.

Barney broke the silence. "What'd you want to see me about?"

Hawk stared at him. "Who wants to see you? Get out of here."

Angel came in with a batch of reports. "You blew that one." Carefully, she put the papers down. "Well, are you just going to sit there?"

He came awake with a start. "Hell, no!"

He kicked the swivel back. It screeched. He disappeared, a projectile thrust into space.

Cathy pulled the Pinto up before Gary's place, and getting out, patted it. For her a car was a person and the Pinto had taken her through a lot these last few days. She glanced up and down the street, not in fear this time but once more seeing and hearing all the little familiar sights and sounds of a sleepy neighborhood on a hot, late afternoon: a dog panting along, children hop-skipping to miss the cracks in the sidewalk, an older woman carting groceries, a young guy trimming a hedge with electric shearers that had a homey click-click.

Before she was halfway up the walk, George heard her and let out a welcome woof. By the time she reached the door, he had brought Gary. They went into each other's arms.

"You okay?" she asked Gary. He had lines under his eyes.

"Like Mohammed Ali hit me."

"Same here. I'm all wrung out."

In the last twenty-four hours she had experienced almost every emotion known. Shock and grief, terror, and a great exultation when it was all over, gratitude for the caring of those about her, surprise and ultimate contentment, and love.

Gary held her at arm's length. "I'm sorry, awfully sorry about the way I acted."

She ruffled up George. "Don't be. You didn't know."

He smiled. "My feelings got hurt. It was childish."

"Mine do, too, when people don't tell me things."

His lips encompassed hers and held until George came between them, like a referee breaking a hold at a prize fight.

She walked about to catch her breath, then turned back to

Gary. "I've been evicted. Kicked out. Mr. Blanton says the owners say I've given the complex a bad name."

"What're you going to do?"

"I thought I'd move in here with you and George after we get married."

He took a deep breath. "Oh, God . . ."

"He's for it?"

"Who?"

"God."

He asked in exasperation, "Is he going to feed us?"

She pointed out the window. "He does the birds."

He shook his head. "You know something, Cathy, you're nuts."

"I'll get a job and you go to Cal State and one of these days you'll have an important position. Maybe as prof at some university or with the government."

His eyes lighted but only momentarily. "Maybe."

"No maybe about it. Oh, Gary, don't you see? How can you be so blind? We've got so much going for us if we're together. You have—I have."

"The wallop of death."

"What?"

"That's what I call it—when death's breathing down your neck, like it was for us. You get an awful wallop. You see things differently."

"You mean you accept my offer of marriage?"

He pushed George away. "I'll propose when any proposing's done."

"Well, are you going to kick me out? Where am I going to sleep tonight?"

He grinned. "You're crazy."

"You said that."

"You have to wait three days in California . . ."

"We'll go to Nevada. I just filled the tank."

"What about that police officer? What's his name? I thought . . ."

"You came along first."

He took a moment to run that through again. "You mean it's like Maury's delicatessen? You take a number . . ."

"Something like that. Gary, we'll go to the nearest place we can get married without waiting—and I'll think of my father and how happy he would be—but I won't cry, because what is, is—and we'll celebrate my birthday—and you'll get me a cake at 3 A.M. . . ."

She put her arms gently about him and her head on his chest, and held him for a time. Then she backed away so he could read her. "You've got tremendous potential, Gary. All you have to do is believe. And you need me to tell you that every day of the world for the rest of your life."

George was at their feet whining. "You know it, too, don't you, George?"

Gary straightened. "You say you've got your car all gassed up?"

"Yes."

"Well, what're we waiting for? Come on, George."

The Los Angeles City Council chamber was packed. The subject of rent control would be debated this day, and tenants and landlords would clash before the microphone as the council conducted a hearing prior to taking a vote.

The council president hit the gavel hard and the uproar simmered to a hubbub. He said, "Before taking up today's business, we have a very happy chore to perform. Councilman Lara."

Beaming, Hugh Lara rose. He held a large document that he brandished like a sword. "Mr. Lefty Morgan," he called out in a stentorian voice.

Sitting in the first row, Lefty looked around, as if someone else by that name had been summoned. Then he got his bones and joints working and walked with eyes rotating suspiciously to a microphone before which Hugh Lara had positioned himself. The news photographers and television cameramen moved in.

Hugh Lara grabbed Lefty's fishlike hand and pumped it vigorously. "My very dear friend, Mr. Lefty Morgan," he announced to the chamber. "One of my most valued constituents." Again, Lefty looked as if he were not the recipient of this praise. He fidgeted with his hands, not knowing what to do with them. He wished he could detach them and put them safely away for the duration of what Hugh Lara was now calling "a most propitious occasion."

"With the greatest of pleasure, the council has voted unanimously to bestow upon you this considerable honor as becomes the heroic acts of one of our finest citizens."

Occasionally the council presented an "outstanding citizenship" award to an Angeleno who had performed a remarkable service to the community. For the councilmen, it was good publicity and flattered their constituents. Still, the council did attempt to maintain certain standards and it had been a long time since Hugh Lara had had one of his nominees approved.

While Lefty glanced nervously about, as if in a tiger cage, Hugh Lara proceeded to read: ". . . for his heroism, at risk to his life, in capturing one of the most dangerous criminals in modern crime annals, at the top of the FBI's most-wanted list, sought by the Justice Department's Strike Force, and the object of a long search by Interpol, be it known to all men that the Los Angeles City Council does commend Lefty Morgan and grant its outstanding citizenship award to Lefty Morgan, who singlehandedly, without regard to his own safety, did apprehend the notorious and armed mobster Billie Richards."

Lefty swallowed and swallowed. For him this was a sad day. It was the end of a career that dated to his thirteenth year, the passing of an era. Never again could he take from the wealthy. Now that he had this award—and Miss Cathy Doyle thought so highly of him—he must find another way of making a living.

He was a man of principles. He would never betray the City Council.

The guy on the phone said, "I opened up the dude and smoked out at eighty-five and burned rubber to ninety-five—"

"Just a minute," Gail said, "my English isn't too good."

"That's okay. You old folks talk funny. This dude was smoking at ninety-five when a fuzz on new wheels leans on me."

"Could I have Mr. Mitchell call you?"

"Don't have a phone. Too much pollution."

"From a phone?"

"The people. Obscene. Like all that yak-yak. Like bugging you. Obscene. Really obscene."

He agreed to call back. At least, she thought he did. Afterward she fed the cat and weighed him. He had gained four ounces. She watered the philodendron and straightened Justice Oliver Wendell Holmes.

When Mitch came in for a few minutes between hearings, he brought news. Lefty had found employment as an assistant to a diamond cutter in the wholesale district.

"He'll wipe out the entire wholesale market," she said.

"He's serious. Cathy's done for him what the law couldn't do."

"It won't last."

"Who knows? The influence of a good person . . ."

She went into his arms. "Mitch, you're a dreamer—and I love you for it."

"Thanks." He kissed her tenderly.

"You're welcome."

As he was going out, she called after him, "Don't forget to get a hair cut."

In her teens she had dreamed of the one great love but never had any dream matched this one with Mitch. Passion in the bedroom. Caring, gentle love outside. All neatly categorized.

She looked about her. This was Mitch's world. He was happy here and his happiness would be hers. In a big Beverly Hills law firm he might go far. Why, in time they might be able to afford a home, a decent car, even take a honeymoon to Hawaii. But would Mitch be content inside the Establishment? She doubted it, and his regrets and resentments would be hers. With the passing of the years, the erosion of the spirit would devastate him. And her.

This was her world.

The phone rang and a rough voice barked, "Put Mitch on."

"He just left. I'll have him call you—"

Slam bang went the receiver at the other end.

Damn, she thought.

The day had started normally.